BETRAYAL

BETRAYAL

Clare Francis

First published in England by William Heinemann Limited in 1995

Copyright © by Clare Francis, 1995, 2002

First published in the United States in 2002
by Soho Press, Inc.
853 Broadway
New York, NY 10003

Library of Congress Cataloging-in-Publication Data

Francis, Clare.
Betrayal / Clare Francis.
p. cm.
ISBN 1-56947-290-4 (alk. paper)
1. Married people—Fiction. 2. Mistresses—Fiction.
3. Adultery—Fiction. 4. England—Fiction. I. Title.

PR6056.R268 B47 2002
823'.914—dc21
2002017564

10   9   8   7   6   5   4   3   2   1

For Andrew,
with love and gratitude

ONE

I woke with a terrible start, my heart crashing against my ribs, and fumbled for the burbling alarm. Sinking back on the pillow, I waited for my heart to quieten down and my brain to stop racketing. Dream fragments jostled disturbingly in my mind. Most were nightmarish, riddled with scenes where I was caught red-handed in some misdemeanour. Only one held any comfort, and for a moment I clung to the warm echo of a time long ago, a faded image of a remote bay and firelight, and, at the water's edge, the slim elusive figure of Sylvie.

Then, in the harsh dawn light, this, too, plunged into nightmare as it came to me with a fresh lurch of disbelief that Sylvie was dead, and that I would have to wake to this stark knowledge for the rest of my life.

My violent awakening hadn't disturbed Ginny. She lay on the far side of the bed, her thin arm reaching out across the pillows towards me, the eye-mask reducing her face to a ghostly triangle of mouth and chin. At some point in the night she had turned on the light and taken a pill. She had glanced towards me but I had feigned sleep. In the dark of the night I had felt too raw for conversation, too unsure of where it might lead. Ginny hadn't been fooled, she'd known I was awake, but we'd both kept up the pretence.

I slid out of bed, sending a shower of papers to the floor: the amended buyout terms I had tried to read at one-thirty or whenever it was I had got to bed. Soundlessly, I put the pages into some sort of order and noticed that my hands were trembling. I showered and shaved, nicking the scar on my upper lip as I always did when I was tense or more than usually

1

overtired. Some beads of watery blood dropped into the basin and I wiped them away with a tissue. I didn't have to look too closely into the mirror to know that the worries of the last few months were stamped all over my face.

I reached for a cord jacket, the sort of thing I generally wore for a day at Hartford, but, remembering the message I would be delivering to the people there, I changed it for a suit of sober grey worsted. I must have lost some weight because the waistband was slack and I had to search out a pair of braces.

I went down to make some three-spoon coffee to keep me awake on the journey. It was barely six-thirty but someone had already been into the house. The girl we contracted to do the flowers must have been to market early because through the open door to the laundry room I could see several large buckets crammed with fresh blooms standing amid spatterings of water. That meant we were having a party tonight. It also meant that, not for the first time, it had slipped my mind. The prospect of a houseful of chattering people filled me with dismay. I dimly hoped it wasn't going to be a charity event, then at least I might know a few of them.

A soft conspiratorial knock sounded from the hall. I unbolted the door to find Julia, my assistant, poised tensely on the step.

In my jittery state I assumed bad news. 'What's happened?'

'Nothing's happened,' she said hastily.

'Then what are you doing here?' I asked, more in curiosity than annoyance.

She handed me a file. 'I thought you might want this.' She made a doubtful face that admitted to the thinness of the excuse.

I waved her in. 'A bit early for you, isn't it?'

She gave a short laugh, glad that I could still tease her. 'I *have* been up at dawn before, you know. Well – once.'

The file was one we both knew I didn't really need. I raised a questioning eyebrow.

'Today's *Times*,' she announced. Pulling the business section out of her bag, she found the page for me.

It was in the snippets column, the place where they put the news that isn't going to influence share prices. The source, whoever it was, had been meticulous with the facts. 'Buoyant'

2

china and lighting manufacturer A. L. Cumberland, fresh from its takeover of – and it stung me to read it – 'debt-ridden' HartWell Glass, the family-owned crystal and tableware company, was putting HartWell's loss-making Hartford Crystal division up for grabs. Cumberland's chairman was quoted as saying that slow-moving crystal did not mesh well with Cumberland's dynamic mass-market product profile.

But it was the final paragraph that really needled. *After years of lacklustre sales and low investment, Hartford Crystal would seem ripe for absorption by brand leaders in the highly competitive export-dependent crystal market. An attempted management buyout led by HartWell's erstwhile joint managing director and major shareholder, Hugh Wellesley, is thought to be facing an uphill struggle.*

Julia remarked, 'A bitch, eh?'

'Yup,' I said bitterly.

'I thought you'd better see it.' Julia fought a losing battle against her indignation. 'You can't help noticing the timing!' she hissed. 'I had an idea something like this was coming, that's why I went and got the papers on the way over.'

If she meant to surprise me, she succeeded. 'You knew?'

'Well, I guessed. Don't ask how. You wouldn't approve.'

Not yet thirty, Julia was the best assistant I'd ever had, exceptionally shrewd and efficient, yet when she'd first arrived her attitude, openly cynical and opportunistic, had rather disturbed me. Now I took a more ambivalent view.

'You think it came from inside Cumberland?'

She gave me a heavy look. 'I *know* it did.'

She meant it had come from Howard who, until the takeover, had shared the managing directorship of HartWell with me. In the process of courting Cumberland and negotiating the takeover, Howard had managed to secure himself a seat on the Cumberland board and a lucrative share option deal. For Howard there was no such thing as an old loyalty, and the moment he'd stepped over the Cumberland threshold six weeks ago he'd belonged to them, heart and soul.

'It could have come from a City guru,' I suggested.

'Sometimes, Hugh, I think you're too trusting for this world.'

I shook suddenly, the tensions welled up, I heard myself snap, 'And sometimes I think you're too damn sure of yourself!'

Her eyes rounded, she stared at me, eventually she stammered, 'Sorry. You're right. That was out of order.'

'It's just . . . ' I pressed a hand to my head, I couldn't explain.

Julia was still looking astonished. I think she had been under the illusion that I never lost my temper.

Regaining some control, I gestured apology. 'It's just that I don't want to think about who might have done it. Not when it's too late to do anything about it.'

'No, of course . . . '

There was a short silence while we both recovered from our second angry words in the two years we had worked together. The first, I realised with dismay, had been only yesterday.

Finally Julia said in a muted voice, 'I know you said you wanted to drive yourself down to Hartford, but I've got a driver on standby just in case. I thought you'd be exhausted.'

'I'll drive myself.'

She gave it one more try. 'It's such a long way and he's just outside.'

But I wouldn't have been comfortable arriving at Hartford in a chauffeur-driven car, not when there was an axe hanging over the factory's future.

'No, but thanks anyway.' I took *The Times* and *Telegraph* from her and opened the door.

'Sorry I was out of line,' she repeated unhappily. 'I think you're right, it's altogether too early for me.'

'For all of us,' I smiled.

She hesitated. 'You're looking terribly tired.'

'I'll catch up on the weekend.'

'If there's any more I can do. To take some of the load . . .

'I don't think so, but thanks anyway.'

She paused on the point of saying more, then, thinking better of it, declared, 'Good luck for today. I hope it goes well. You really deserve it!' In a gesture that was uncharacteristically demonstrative she reached out and grasped my hand in both of hers before striding off down the street.

In the kitchen I quickly leafed through the papers. I turned each

4

page with an odd mixture of dread and hope, but there was nothing more about Sylvie. The initial report two days ago had been sparse: a woman's body had been recovered from the River Dart; it had been identified as that of Sylvie Mathieson. I wasn't sure what I expected now. Some details of how she had died perhaps; some idea of what the police were doing. But maybe there was simply nothing to report. Maybe the police had imposed a news blackout. The uncertainty did nothing for the anxiety that coiled and twisted in my belly.

I gulped the rest of my coffee and thrust the *Times* article into my briefcase. Crossing the kitchen, I glimpsed the flowers again. I picked out a white fluffy bloom – it might have been a dahlia – and, not really sure what I meant by the gesture, carried it upstairs and propped it on the pillow next to Ginny. I took a sheet from the pad and scribbled 'Sorry'. I didn't know what I meant by that either. All I knew was that flowers and notes were thin substitutes for all the time we never had together.

Looking down at Ginny, I felt the familiar blend of bewilderment and guilt, mainly guilt. Things hadn't been right between us for such a long time, and I didn't really know why. But then my whole life seemed to have gone adrift, and I wasn't absolutely sure why that had happened either.

I changed my mind about the flower – too crass – and thrust it into the bin.

I was halfway down the stairs when Ginny's voice cried out, 'Hugh. *Hugh?*'

She was sitting up in bed, her mask pushed back over her head. 'What's the time?'

She looked so fragile that I felt a pull in my chest somewhere, a tug of emotion and regret.

'Sorry, I didn't mean to wake you— '

She focused on me. 'Where are you going?'

'Hartford.'

'Must you?'

'I've got a meeting.'

She seemed momentarily confused by this and I guessed she was still groggy from the sleeping pill or whatever it was she had taken in the night.

'You won't be late back?' she asked.

'I'll do my best.'

'You haven't forgotten tonight?'

'No.' But I couldn't maintain the pretence. 'What's the party for exactly?'

Usually Ginny would cast me a flicker of resentment at such lapses, as though I made a point of forgetting these things simply to belittle the importance of her work, but nothing showed on her face. Instead she said dully, 'It's for the premature baby unit, the fund-raising committee. I promised ages ago.'

'Am I essential?' Seeing her eyes widen in reproach, I added hurriedly, 'I'll try not to be too late. I'll do my best.' For all her shoulder-rubbing with the great and the good, for all her grace and poise, Ginny had never found it easy to face the world on her own. Even as I made my promise I knew with sinking heart that I'd be unlikely to keep it, and that by letting her down I would yet again be fulfilling her gloomy expectations of me.

Aware of the time, I moved towards the door.

'It's the last party,' Ginny said abruptly. 'No more after this.'

I turned back. I wasn't sure what to make of this statement, except that it was meant to be momentous in some way. 'No more?'

She gave a slow shake of the head and pressed her fingertips to the corners of her eyes. I tried to read the signs. Was I expected to question her, to listen to whatever social disappointments or imagined slights had led to this decision? If so, Ginny's timing was as unerring as ever; she always managed to choose a moment when I was rushing off to some meeting or so tired that I could barely think. Yet she could never understand how this, more than anything, doomed our conversations to failure before they had even started.

'I'm desperately late,' I ventured. 'Otherwise— '

I waited for the soft glance of injury she produced on these occasions, but her face was bare of emotion. She gave the faintest of nods, and my heart lifted as it always did when we avoided a tiff.

'I'll see you later,' she said, reaching up to pull the mask back over her eyes. 'Oh, and Hugh?'

Trying not to show the slightest impatience, I put my head back round the door.

'Take care, won't you?'

She said it with strange solemnity, and it struck me again how very thin she looked.

'Of course.'

'You're overdoing it at the moment.'

'Just until the buyout's over . . . '

Her eyes were unfocused, she was hardly listening. 'Well, take care anyway.'

Winding my way through the Chelsea streets, driving out through the suburbs, I did take care. The coffee and lack of sleep had made me light-headed and I didn't entirely trust my reactions. But as the well-worn road to Totnes unwound before me and my mind skittered over the myriad problems that lay ahead, my concentration began to waver. To keep alert, I turned on the radio and aimed the air vents at my face.

The *Times* article kept returning to haunt me. The more I tried to persuade myself that it wouldn't diminish our chances of funding the buyout, the more damaging it seemed to become. And, when I really wanted to torture myself, which was quite often, I imagined Zircon, the venture capitalists who were backing our bid, having second thoughts and pulling out altogether.

Needing to take some action, however unproductive, I called Julia on the car phone and asked her to find a corporate PR adviser for us. Then I spent a fruitless twenty minutes trying to locate Pollinger, our contact at Zircon, but, despite mobiles, pagers and home numbers, he seemed to lead an elusive life.

In search of distraction, I switched on the radio again and, finding a discussion programme, raised the volume until the voices filled the car.

I was on the M5, somewhere past Taunton, when a blaring horn brought me to my senses with a jolt of adrenalin. A car was looming up in front of me. In the instant that I realised it was stationary I also knew that I couldn't possibly stop in time. I jerked the wheel to the left and braked hard and felt the car kick round as the rear wheels lost their grip. I must have twisted the wheel the other way because the car performed a snake-like manoeuvre and skidded again as it shot across the middle lane, narrowly missing the front of a large coach. The inside lane came at me in slow motion, any approaching traffic hidden by the bulk of the coach, but the lane must have been empty because the next moment the car was shuddering sideways across the hard shoulder and hitting the kerb with an almighty bang that almost lifted me off my seat.

The car rocked to a standstill, the engine stalled. All I could hear was the radio newscaster droning on. I sat motionless with my hands clutched to the wheel, the sweat cold against my ribs, until someone opened the door and asked me if I was all right.

I heard myself say I was okay. I must have sounded convincing because, after the man told me several times to stop driving like a bloody maniac, he slammed the door and walked back to the coach, which was parked some way ahead on the hard shoulder.

It was a long time before I could think about setting off again. I kept reliving the near-miss and the seconds preceding it, when the newscaster had spoken Sylvie's name. His cool detached voice kept running through my mind, like a tape being played over and over again, yet only two words really registered, and both felt like something driven against my heart. *Stabbed and bound.*

I got shakily out of the car and heaved the sparse contents of my stomach onto the grass verge. When I felt a bit better I walked round the car to look for signs of damage, but the wheels seemed all right, the tyres still had air. Not knowing what else I should check, I got back into the driver's seat and, after a last five minutes with my head back and my eyes closed, I started the engine.

I drove gingerly, half expecting knocking sounds or wobbles from the steering, but after a time I forgot to worry about the car and slowly accelerated to mid-lane speed, my mind miles away again, in a dark and distant place.

I arrived at Hartford half an hour late. Driving in through the gates, I tried to picture the factory through the eyes of potential investors. With its twenties architecture, drab brickwork and

8

mean windows, the place had the air of old glories long faded, while its clusters of ventilation pipes and aluminium chimneys suggested spasmodic and piece-meal modernisation. Only the recently completed warehouse, a spare metal structure in cobalt blue, emitted anything approaching an up-to-date image. *Lacklustre sales ... Low investment ...* The newspaper's comments were ill-founded but they still pricked at me.

George Banes came out to meet me. The production director was a burly man, his large belly testing the fastenings on his shirt, with a thick head of hair that had been silvery grey for as long as I had known him, which was almost twenty years.

'Thought the traffic might delay you,' he commented as we shook hands and made for the entrance, 'so I told the staff we'd meet at ten minutes to noon.'

'You explained that it was just an update?'

'I did. I said you wanted to keep them abreast of developments but that there was nothing definite at the moment.'

Even now, in my state of preoccupation, I couldn't walk through the doors of the factory without feeling a proprietorial thrill. I was too much my father's son, too deeply instilled with his old-style paternalistic pride not to feel an attachment to the place that was decidedly emotional.

George took me into the office that had been my father's and would have been mine if Howard hadn't pressed for what he liked to call an integrated management structure, and insisted we put the management and sales of all three divisions under one roof at Slough.

The room was virtually unchanged since my father's retirement ten years ago. His wide oak desk stood in the same spot by the window, the ancient wooden in- and out-trays squatting on a worn leather surface that still bore the pattern of a hundred ink marks. When I was a small boy this room had seemed cavernous, and my father, behind the mass of his desk, an oddly distant figure. It was only when he finished his business and took me down to the factory floor and chatted in his easy soft-voiced manner that I had felt I knew him again.

George brought coffee and we sat down at the conference table.

'So it's all signed up with Zircon?' he demanded eagerly.

'It's signed.'

'No quibbles with the business plan?'

George and I had worked so hard on the business plan that we knew every word and financial projection by heart. 'No quibbles with the business plan,' I reassured him, and saw his eyes spark with satisfaction. 'But I tell you, George, whatever happened to them on the playing fields of Eton, it turned their hearts to stone.' I was thinking of the additional leverage the venture capitalists had demanded, and the personal guarantees covering the fifty per cent of my personal worth that was not already committed to the buyout. 'They've made financial pain into an art form.' I managed an ironic laugh.

'But they're behind us now, that's the important thing.'

'They still have their doubts about me, I think. Or rather the idea of me.'

'What? *Why?*'

'According to the City, family firms are breeding grounds for inefficiency and nepotism. And a family buyout – well!' I rolled my eyes. 'That's even more unhealthy. Incest.'

'But that's ridiculous! It's not like that here. Don't they realise that? We've always been a team, for God's sake! And, this buyout – well, we're all in it together, aren't we?'

We certainly were. George was putting fifty thousand cash into the buyout, and another fifty thousand against his house. So were Alan and John, the other Hartford directors. But that was how the venture capitalists liked it, to have the whole lot of us over a financial barrel.

I passed George the page from *The Times*. 'This may not help.'

George read the article and spluttered, 'What's this? Years of low investment? What are they damn well talking about! We've upgraded the batching plant, for God's sake. We've installed the stem-pulling machines— '

'It's nonsense, of course— '

'And lacklustre sales! They've stood up bloody well, considering. Apart from Packenhams.'

This was one of our worst blows, being de-listed by London's second largest department store.

George thrashed a hand against the paper. 'Who gives them this rubbish?'

But I didn't try to answer that.

George hadn't cooled down yet. 'It makes Hartford sound like some cottage industry filled with Luddites! As if we'd fought change tooth and nail!'

The irony wasn't lost on either of us. While Howard and I had been running the company it had hardly stopped changing. That was the whole trouble. We had moved too far, too fast, expanding rapidly into mass-market glass and chinaware just as trading conditions began to worsen. While my father was alive he hadn't liked much of what we had been doing but had never tried to interfere. I was glad he had died in February. It had saved him the anguish of seeing quite what a mess I had made of everything.

'At the end of the day it's only a newspaper story,' I said.

George, forcing himself back to his natural state of optimism, declared, 'Right! Right!' He laughed loudly and abruptly. 'We never thought it was going to be easy, did we?'

I laughed too, awkwardly. This deal was the hardest thing I had ever attempted. In the six weeks since the Cumberland takeover, I had been cut loose from the new parent company to run Hartford Crystal on a nil-salary basis, while simultaneously planning to buy it out. Raising the three million pounds of leverage from the banks, keeping all the financial and legal balls in the air, pulling together all the strands of what was an amazingly complex deal, was a Herculean task which, even on an eighteen-hour day, was stretching me to my limits. Much of the time I was suffused with a wild conviction that we would pull it off, and then I flew on adrenalin. At other times, faced by endless setbacks, I settled into something more mechanical, a mindless persistence fuelled by the determination to save what I had so foolishly jeopardised.

There was no mystery about my motives. For me this buyout was about restitution. My father had worked hard for twenty years to build up the company and pass it on to me in good shape, while I had worked hard for ten to achieve nothing more, it seemed, than to let it slip away and threaten the livelihoods of all the people who worked for us. I wanted it back, I wanted to show what I could do with it now that I was free of Howard and his remorseless drive for diversification. I wanted to make a success of it for my own sake, certainly, but more than that I wanted to feel I could look the employees in the eye again.

George and I talked our way through the monthly sales figures and were just starting on the cash flow analysis when a woman's voice sounded in the outer office. There was something about it, the suggestion of a lazy laugh, of dark overtones, that caught at my memory and chilled my heart.

'You all right?' George asked.

'Fine.' Reaching for my coffee, I promptly knocked it over. Trying to retrieve the cup, I got that wrong too and sent it flying across the table.

I muttered 'Jesus!' Then as I picked the cup off the floor: 'What an idiot!' I gave a disbelieving laugh. But as soon as George had gone in search of a cloth I sat in silence, wondering what on earth was happening to me and whether this was just frayed nerves or a form of delayed shock. Whatever, the loss of control frightened me, and I was unnerved by the thought that it might happen again.

By the time George returned with a roll of kitchen paper, I was staring bleakly at the pool of coffee, trying to suppress visions of dark water and Sylvie's flesh, mutilated and cold.

'Do you want something to eat?' George asked when he had finished clearing up. 'A sandwich? Biscuits?'

'Thanks, no.'

He peered at me. 'You look as though you need something. If you don't mind my saying so.'

I shook my head and jumped to my feet. 'We'd better go.'

As we made our way towards the factory floor George's secretary hailed me from her office. 'Mr Hugh, a message from Dr Wellesley. He'll be free from twelve-thirty.'

'Hugh or Mr Wellesley,' I corrected her half-heartedly, having largely abandoned the hope that the long-serving staff would drop their archaic terms of address. 'My brother will be at home, will he?'

'Yes. And there was an enquiry from a Detective Inspector Henderson. No details. Just could you call him?'

She gave me a slip of paper with a number. The area code was Exeter. 'Thank you.'

I glanced at the number again, then, stuffing it into my pocket, walked quickly away. George caught up and started singing the praises of some training scheme, but I was hardly listening. I was wondering what questions the police would ask me. I had no doubt it was Sylvie they wanted to talk to me about, it could hardly be anything else. We must have been seen together, on the pontoon perhaps, or the boat. Such things did not go unnoticed in a small community like Dittisham. Ever since Sylvie's death I had been telling myself that this summons would come, yet now it had materialised I felt oddly shaken.

We reached the batching plant and I managed to ask the warehousemen some sensible questions about the new forklift and the revised storage bay layout. The route George and I took through the factory had been laid down since the beginning of time. After a circuit of the storage bay which took us past pallets of silica, lead oxide, litharge and potassium, we inspected the computerised batch mixer, then, after a few minutes with the batch quality control staff, we went through to the heat of the blowing room.

The dull roar of the furnaces still stirred me in some atavistic way. The transmutation of the dry amalgam into clear lava still seemed like some mysterious alchemy. The groups of schoolchildren and visitors who toured the factory on the overhead walkways lingered longest over the blowers as they ballooned and moulded the cooling lava into shape, or beside the cutters as they chased the designs into the glass, waiting in nervous delight for them to make an error and abandon the goblet, tumbler or bowl to the reprocessing bin with a crash of splintering glass. But for me the fascination had always lain here, in the unimaginable heat, in the impenetrable trembling magma that seemed incapable of any transformation, let alone the miraculous metamorphosis into a material both dense and transparent, both complex and flawless.

Bill, our senior master blower, raised his eyebrows in greeting. Many years ago when I had worked here in my university vacations, sweeping floors and wheeling bins, Bill had tried to teach me to blow the simplest shape. My best effort sat at home somewhere, a far-from-round object of uneven thickness with a trail of bubbles up one side.

The factory buzzer cut our tour short at the grinding and polishing area. Following George towards the canteen, the ideas for my speech, such as they were, seemed to scatter, and I wished I'd made more time to prepare.

As the staff gathered I greeted as many as I could by name. A few had been at Hartford for thirty years or more; some twenty; a good number for more than ten. There were two entire families – father, sons, daughters-in-law. We even had a grandmother and granddaughter on the payroll. A hundred and fifty employees in all, people whose lives were dependent on this factory, and – never had I needed less reminding – on my ability to restore its fortunes.

The moment came. George called for silence and I stepped forward, beset by strange emotions.

'As soon as the takeover was agreed I promised to keep you in touch with developments,' I began. 'I also promised you that we were going to do everything in our power to get this management buyout off the ground.' Voicing it, I felt a new weight of responsibility. 'Well, the good news is that we've reached agreement with some venture capital people called Zircon. They're going to put up about a quarter of the money. That still leaves a full half to be raised from the banks, and I won't pretend that it's proving to be easy, because it isn't. We're in the second round of talks with two banks, the Chartered and the West Country Mutual. We haven't been turned down yet. That's all I can tell you so far.'

I caught the eye of Madge, grader and glass washer, sitting solidly on a chair directly in front of me. She was glaring at me: a combative expression, an anxious one, or a combination of both.

'Now, when Cumberland took us over I warned you that sentiment would play no part in their calculations. And though they've given us first call on buying Hartford, we still have to match the best price on offer. I have to tell you that according to our latest information they're talking to Donington and maybe some other companies too.'

14

The feeling of disconnection hit me again. Without warning my brain did an abrupt shift, a sort of sideways jump, and I completely lost track. When I finally managed to speak, I stumbled, not sure if I was making sense. I heard myself say, 'Now we're very attractive . . . ' A lone titter rose up, and, glancing uncertainly towards the sound, I grappled for the thread of my argument. 'Our name and reputation are the attractions,' I said at last. 'And of course our designs. But valuing a name and reputation is not the same as valuing a workforce.'

That had sounded all right, but my brain was functioning with agonising slowness. 'People like Donington have the capacity to produce the Hartford range at their own plants so, if they outbid us, well – you can imagine. This factory will almost certainly close.'

I was back on track at last, my mind free of whatever had constrained it. I thrust some optimism back into my voice. 'But we can make damned sure that doesn't happen! We can make sure that our bid is bigger and better than any one else's!' I paused, trying unsuccessfully to gauge their mood, before plunging on. 'Now, we've already asked a lot from you, I know that. And you've responded one hundred per cent and that's the entire reason we've managed to keep going as long as we have. But the venture capital people want one more undertaking, and that's what I've come to ask you today. They want a formal undertaking that you'll agree to a two-year period of wage restraint.'

I explained how this would work, how their share options and profit-sharing schemes would remain unaffected. I told them that if it had been left to me I wouldn't have asked them for anything in writing, but venture capitalists were altogether more cautious animals.

I said a lot more of what I hoped were the right things before halting with a sense of relief. My brain was clear, but my momentary disorientation had shaken me and I didn't want to risk it happening again. I had no intention of going on, I certainly didn't mean to get onto emotional ground, but my judgment was all over the place and, without any idea of where it might lead, I found myself saying forcibly, 'You know, some people believe tradition's a bad thing, that it's the enemy of change – the great modern god Change. But I believe that the traditions we've built up here really matter, that they actually *help* us to change in a productive way. We've been together so long that we think like a family, we take each other into account, we're not just out for ourselves and to hell with the next man . . . ' I broke off, aware of how pretentious this must sound to people who, at the end of the day, just wanted a regular job like everyone else. 'What I mean is – I believe that this company is worth fighting for. And not just for what comes off the end of the production line. But for the way we do things here.'

A voice piped up, 'We certainly do it our way!' and there was a ripple of laughter followed by a call of 'You can say that again!' and a smattering of applause.

Buoyed by their irreverence, I laughed with them before delivering a few last words.

When I stepped down my shirt was damp with sweat and I pulled at my collar to loosen it. Madge brought me a glass of water. 'No need to worry about us, Hugh.' After twenty-five years at Hartford she used my name with a disarming familiarity. 'We're the least of your troubles.'

'Madge . . . That's good to know.'

'We don't mind the wages, we don't mind being asked to do the overtime, what we *don't* like is being second best to cheap glass and tableware.'

'I never meant Hartford to be second best.'

'Got your head turned, didn't you?' Madge prided herself on her blunt speaking. 'Big ideas.'

I couldn't deny it and I didn't try.

Madge, who was a grandmother ten times over, gave me the sort of admonitory nod she probably reserved for her own middle-aged sons.

George and I lingered for a few minutes answering questions before walking back to the office.

'Good speech,' he exclaimed delightedly. 'Just what we needed.' He caught my expression. 'You weren't happy with it?'

I gestured inarticulately. 'Take no notice of me. Too much on my mind.'

'You really don't look well. I noticed the moment you arrived. Are you sure you won't have something to eat?'

'I'm all right.' I made a feeble attempt at humour. 'Just a nervous breakdown. Well – if I could ever find the time.' I looked at my watch and made for the door.

Before leaving, I found an empty office and phoned the Exeter number. Detective Inspector Henderson wasn't available but I spoke to a Detective Sergeant Jones who asked if I could call in during the afternoon.

'Will it take long?'

'Can't say, sir.'

'I have to be back in London by seven. I could give you half an hour at two-thirty. If you wanted longer we'd have to make it another day.'

'Very well, sir. We'll see you at two-thirty then.'

'Who should I ask for?'

'Anyone on Detective Inspector Henderson's team.'

I thought I knew where the police station was, but asked for directions just in case. It was only after I'd put the phone down that I realised that Sergeant Jones hadn't offered to tell me what the matter was about and I hadn't asked him.

George walked me to the car. 'They're right behind the buyout, you know,' he said. 'Everyone here, they'll back us all the way.'

Behind my smile, I was beset by doubts. Having worked so single-mindedly towards the buyout, having pursued it to the point of obsession, it had suddenly lost focus and significance, like some all-consuming passion that inexplicably falls flat. I told myself that my loss of momentum was due to exhaustion, to the punishing pace I had forced on myself in recent weeks. I kept telling myself this because I didn't want to think about my other problems and how they were eating into my confidence.

The road was clogged with the last of the summer caravans, there were roadworks in the town, and I didn't turn onto the Dartmouth road until almost a quarter to one. I drove as fast as I dared and probably faster than I should have. I had the idea that if I was forced to concentrate on my driving then I wouldn't have time to think.

It didn't work, of course. My thoughts simply became less controllable, popping up like muggers in the night. I kept thinking of the last time I had travelled this road, heading not for my brother's place, but for Dittisham and my old family home, standing empty on the dark river. It seemed incredible that I had driven along this road just five days ago, that I had travelled with longing still dragging at my heart, and that when I had arrived at the house and opened it up and drawn back the curtains and put on all the lights I had still half hoped that Sylvie would see my childish signal and come.

I turned off the road into David's drive with relief. I couldn't have faced Dittisham today.

Furze Lodge was an early-nineteenth-century rectory in the grand style, with eight bedrooms, a staff flat and stable block in grounds of five acres. Seeing the immaculate garden, the freshly painted doors and windows, I wondered how much the place cost David and Mary to run. It couldn't be less than fifty thousand a year, not with a live-in couple and at least two horses. When you added the school fees – they had a boy and a girl, both teenagers, both at expensive boarding schools – the charity events Mary hosted and the rest of their community commitments, their expenditure must have exceeded David's income as a GP by a very wide margin indeed. Like me, he had relied heavily on his HartWell dividends. Like me, I imagined he had been feeling the pinch.

I found David in the rather gloomy study which doubled as a consulting room for his private patients. He sat behind his ancient kneehole desk in a charcoal pinstripe suit complete with waistcoat and watch chain, and when he looked up he eyed me over gold-rimmed half-moon spectacles, so completely the doctor that he had taken the image almost to the point of parody.

'You look terrible,' he remarked immediately.

'Thanks,' I said. 'I'm glad I'm not one of your patients or I might get depressed.'

'Have you seen anyone?'

'What? No. I'm fine.'

He was shuffling paper as he talked. 'You should see someone.'

'I'll be all right once this business is over. It's just frantic at the moment, that's all.'

'Are you sleeping?'

'Don't find the time.'

'What about those tablets I gave you? Have you been taking them?'

I vaguely remembered the tablets he was talking about, but couldn't think where I'd put them. 'Probably not.'

'They don't work unless you take them regularly.'

'What are they meant to do anyway?'

David pulled open a drawer, took out a bottle of pills and chucked them across to me. 'Don't forget this time.'

It was easier to put them into my pocket than to argue. Until this summer David had rarely showed much interest in my health, and I had never expected him to. David was two years older than me, we had been close as children, but since growing up we had never been too involved in each other's lives. If I'd ever stopped to consider our relationship, I suppose I would have described it as practical.

'How are things with you?' I asked automatically.

'Me?' he said in a tone of self-mockery. I noticed that his hair, once so dark, was greying rapidly at the temples and that his cheeks were criss-crossed with deepening lines, though these signs of age did little to detract from his patrician looks, which women found impressive enough to remark on. Like me, he seemed to have gone against the trend and kept his waistline. Unlike me, he had lost none of his hair. 'Oh, I survive,' he said with irony.

'The old loves playing up?' South Devon was retirement country, with a population that David had once described as ninety and skyrocketing.

'They get ill and fed up,' he said heavily. 'They want magic potions.'

Watching him tidy his desk it occurred to me that he, too, was a tired man, and that he was tired because he didn't enjoy his work. With his sharp brain and wide skills, he would have made a good consultant, but though he'd completed two years as a senior houseman he had failed the big surgical exams and

19

never given them another shot. This had caused my father much grief, not because of the failure itself, but because David hadn't had the backbone to persevere. For my father, lack of effort was almost the greatest sin of all, and doubly so when you were blessed with inherited money. He believed that financial security gave you a duty not to depend on it, that it was almost immoral to rely on the sweat and tears of previous generations. It seemed to Pa that David had succumbed to the easy option, and he never quite got over it.

I looked nervously at my watch.

David stood up. 'I'll fetch Mary.'

But he made no move towards the door. Instead he glanced back at me and said in his cool professional voice, 'You heard about Sylvie Mathieson?'

'I did, yes. Awful.'

'She was stabbed apparently.'

'God,' I breathed.

'Dumped in the river.'

'They have no idea who—?'

'No.'

I wasn't sure I wanted more details, but I couldn't stop myself asking, 'Where did they find her?'

'On the first bend there, near the Anchor Stone. The body was caught against a rock. Dead less than a day, they think. Wrapped in plastic, tied up with rope.'

'God.'

David picked up a pen and examined the nib, then put it down again as if it had been guilty of distracting him. When he spoke again his tone was hedged with reservations, as though he were still debating the wisdom of mentioning the subject. 'She was all over the place, you know.'

I stared at him, my mouth suddenly dry. 'What do you mean?'

'Oh, the full bit,' he said airily. 'Lovers. Drugs.'

My stomach tightened, I felt an unreasonable anger. 'How do you know?'

'Oh . . .' His shrug implied contacts in the right places. 'One hears.'

I wanted to ask him why he was so quick to believe such

rumours, but I pushed myself to my feet instead so that he couldn't read my face. 'She was always a free spirit,' I proclaimed. 'She always went her own way.'

I didn't have to look at him to know he was wearing a sceptical expression.

'Thought you'd better know, that's all.'

I turned. 'Me? Why?'

'Well, you were in love with her once, weren't you?' He spoke in the curt voice he used to distance himself from anything that bordered on the emotional.

'Yes . . . ' Why had I thought he meant anything else? 'Yes, I was. Yes.' And saying it, I had a fleeting memory of those distant feelings, so intense and innocent and full of hope. 'A long time ago.'

'Look—' David began irritably. But he broke off at the sound of footsteps in the hall.

Mary came in and her face lit up. 'Hugh!' she sang.

I went to kiss her cheek but, with the reproving tut of a mother hen, she pulled me into a generous hug. Standing back to inspect me, she cried, 'How *are* you?'

'I'm fine.'

She shook her head and rolled her eyes in mock exasperation. 'I don't know . . . Is it worth it? Just look at you!'

'Don't *you* start,' I protested. 'David's bad enough, giving me pills.'

'It's not pills you want, it's a rest! Isn't it, darling?' she flung at David. Turning back to me: 'You'll stay for lunch at least?'

'I've got to leave at two.'

'Hopeless!' she declared. 'Hopeless!' And her eyes flashed with their habitual amusement.

I said, 'I can always come back again if we don't get through it—'

'I meant, you have to eat! I'll go and fetch something now.' She threw a questioning glance at David. 'Shall I?'

'Well, perhaps we can just get started . . . '

'Fine!' she said immediately. 'In a minute then!' She perched on the chair David had pulled up for her and fixed me with a bright stare. I had always liked Mary. She was a determined

21

extrovert who believed that the secret of life was to laugh at whatever came your way. If her high spirits were sometimes a little relentless they hid a compassionate and generous personality, quick to leap to the aid of those in trouble. A solicitor who had given up her practice on marrying David, she did good works on the boards of hospices and children's homes, and was a prison visitor at Dartmoor.

She had a sturdy body with an angular face, ruddy cheeks, and eyebrows that seemed too dark and bold for her colouring, and her appearance wasn't enhanced by her practical tweed skirt, shapeless jumper and cropped hair. But if her looks were plain, they were thoroughly redeemed by her unwavering good nature.

She could not have been more different from Howard, either in appearance or personality, and sometimes I had to remind myself that they were brother and sister. Mary was so much a part of our family, both in spirit and fact, that I tended to forget she might sometimes have divided loyalties. When our two families had jointly and harmoniously controlled HartWell this had not been an issue. But if Mary had felt torn over the acrimonious falling out between Howard and me, she had been very discreet about it.

'We've looked through this buyout proposal thing,' David began, leaning back in his chair and pulling his spectacles off his nose in a practised gesture. 'I can't say we're a hundred per cent clear on *everything* . . . '

So I took them through it, item by item. The investment opportunity, the risks, the potential for significant capital gains. I told them what the new team had already achieved, what was left to get right. When I talked about the future, how we believed we could turn the company round in a few months, some of my old fire returned, I began to sound evangelical again.

Mary listened with partial attention, her sharp eyes on mine, a smile hovering at the corners of her mouth. When I had finished she looked meaningfully at David, and I guessed she was prompting him to ask some pre-arranged question.

'Yes . . . ' murmured David, catching her eye. 'Suppose we put in, say, fifty thousand now, could we put in more later?'

I tried not to show my disappointment. Only last week David had been talking about a minimum of a hundred and fifty thousand. 'It would be difficult,' I said carefully. 'You see, there's only going to be so much equity and once the buyout's gone through, that's it, there won't be any more for sale.' I glanced from one to the other and wondered if they had actually decided on this reduced figure but didn't like to tell me.

Mary recognised my anxiety and gave me a sympathetic little grin.

David roused himself to murmur, 'After the last two years, the losses . . .'

'I know. And that's why I want you to come in with us, David. To make good your losses. The potential is there, we believe that very strongly.'

Engrossed in some inner deliberations, David narrowed his eyes and tapped his fingertips together.

Mary tried to catch his attention again but, failing, shrugged at me and said in a theatrical whisper, 'We wanted to ask – what about income? What income could we expect?'

'There would be no dividends until we got into profit.'

David picked up on that. 'And that could be years?'

'Hopefully a lot less.'

'*Hopefully*,' he repeated with a censorious look, as though he had succeeded in catching me out.

I started on our strategy then, how we intended to go out and sell ourselves hard on the Hartford name and quality. But catching the expression of boredom on David's face, an expression I knew so well – lids hooded, his dark winged eyebrows lifted outwards in a satanic arch – I cut it short.

'Listen—' I said forcefully, 'I'm putting everything I have into this. I wouldn't be doing it unless I believed *absolutely* that we could pull it off.'

Mary exclaimed in mock horror, 'Everything?'

'Certainly all the cash I have. And' – I gave a weak chuckle – 'quite a lot I don't. I'm borrowing as much as I can.' And far more than was safe or wise, though I didn't say that.

I tried not to think of how much I stood to lose if the buyout failed, and how much I had at risk if it succeeded. I tried to forget how very overextended I already was. Ginny and I had a lifestyle that didn't come cheap. We had second homes in Provence and

Wiltshire, we had staff and cars, until last year we had bought good modern pictures, and we entertained on what could only be described as a grand scale. Even allowing for all this, the outpouring of cash was so relentless that I could never quite grasp where it went. Since last year when the HartWell dividends had plummeted and I had taken a voluntary reduction in salary, we had tried to cut back. Ginny had been in charge of the economies, but for some reason I could never understand her cuts seemed to make little impact on our bank balance, and whenever I thought of the future I felt an upsurge of panic.

Mary screwed up her face in an extravagant imitation of alarm. 'I hope you're not expecting us to do the same!'

'Of course not. I wouldn't want you to. You must only invest what you can afford.'

David drawled, 'And if the company goes down the plughole?'

'It won't.'

'But if it does?' he insisted with a tinge of impatience.

'Then the banks would get first call.'

'And we'd get—?'

'Nothing.'

He grimaced, '*Exactly!*'

I was aware of Mary watching me closely again. She gave a sudden chuckle. 'A bit of a gamble then!' She made it sound like a flutter on the horses.

David sat forward. 'We'll need time to think about it.'

'Of course.' I looked from one to the other. 'Though it would help enormously if you could give me some idea of how long you'll need.'

David pursed his lips. 'I don't know— ' He shot a look at Mary. 'The weekend? Say, Tuesday?'

She shrugged her agreement.

'Tuesday then.'

It could have been worse. Suppressing the urge to press my case further, I mustered a grin.

In the short silence that followed, Mary jumped to her feet. 'I'll go and do that lunch!'

'I'm not sure I've got time, Mary.'

She wagged her finger at me. 'It's only a sandwich. Won't take a

24

moment.' There was something brittle, almost peremptory, in her tone. She paused at the door. 'Have you told Hugh about Dittisham, David?'

'Ah . . . no.'

Mary caught my eye and, reverting to her more familiar role, made a face of jokey forbearance as she disappeared into the hall.

'The thing is, we might have a buyer,' David told me when she had gone. 'Someone who wants it pretty quick. We heard this morning. Prepared to pay the asking price.'

I felt a pinch of loss. Dittisham had been the home of our childhood, the place in which I had spent many untroubled years, the house in which our parents had lived all their married lives. Until our mother's death twenty years ago, it had stood at the very core of the family. Yet while the child in me hated to think of other people living there, the realist knew that, with Pa dead too, it had to go.

'When do these people want it?' I asked.

'In a month.'

'You'll let me know, will you? I'll need to clear some stuff out.'

'You can't clear it out now?'

'No chance.' Reminded as always of the time, I reached for my briefcase and jumped to my feet.

'Hugh— '

There was something about his tone, a warning note, which made me pause. He came round the desk and, half sitting on it, folded his arms. 'The thing is . . . ' he said with a sigh of annoyance, 'the police have been asking about Sylvie.'

A small pull in my chest somewhere. 'Asking?'

'They came to see me yesterday.'

'You? Why you?'

David frowned as if I were being particularly dense. 'Because she was my patient.'

I must have let some of the surprise show in my face because he said, 'Didn't you realise?'

I gave a shrug. 'No . . . Well, I simply never thought about it. You didn't say . . .'

'Anyway, the point is' – and he hesitated as if he would rather have avoided the whole subject – 'they seem to think that Sylvie was on the boat a few weeks ago.'

I didn't need to ask which boat he meant. During the summer David and I had been keeping an eye on Pa's cruiser *Ellie Miller* while we decided what to do with her.

I made a show of puzzlement. I asked evenly, 'Why do they think that?'

'They didn't say. Listen, it's none of my business, but . . . Well, be careful of those cretins, won't you?'

'Careful?' But we both knew what he meant.

'If Sylvie was seen on the boat with you, they might make too much out of it. Assume you were, you know – ' he flapped an impatient hand – 'together.'

'Did they say that?' I blurted.

'No, *no*. But you know how their minds work. One track. In *my* experience, anyway.'

I had been so desperate to talk to someone about Sylvie for such a long time that I almost told him then. I wanted to explain the extraordinary hold she had always exercised over my imagination, and in telling him perhaps to explain it better to myself. I think I wanted to hear him say that he understood, that it could have been the same for him. Yet something held me back: an instinct for secrecy, a fear of being misunderstood, a doubt as to how he would receive such confidences. David had never been one for letting his feelings get the better of him; as far as I knew he had never lost his head over anything, far less a woman.

I said abruptly, 'They've already been in touch, actually.'

'The police? You've seen them?'

'Soon. In half an hour, in fact.'

'Oh!' He looked at his watch, reached back over his desk for his diary and flicked a page over. 'If you want me to come along, I *might* be able to swing it.'

'I don't think that'll be necessary.' But the fact that he'd suggested it planted a small seed of anxiety in my heart.

'Sure?'

'Sure.'

'All right,' he conceded immediately. 'But don't forget, Hugh – they have small brains. Strictly one-track.'

Two

The detective settled himself in his seat. 'Sorry to have kept you, sir.'

'I am rather pressed for time,' I remarked. 'Is this likely to take long?'

His look suggested that police business did not hurry for anyone, especially people who liked to think they had more important things to do.

Taking the cap off his pen, he began to write laboriously on a pro forma pad.

'E . . . S . . .' I said, reading my name upside down. 'After Well, it's E . . . S . . .'

'Ah . . .' He amended it to Wellesley. 'And your address?'

I gave it to him, complete with post code.

'That's central London, is it, sir?'

'Yes. Chelsea.'

'Now . . .' He fixed me with a bland stare. 'You were acquainted with Sylvie Mathieson, were you, Mr Wellesley?'

'Yes.'

'And did you know Sylvie well?' His use of her first name threw me a little, it made our conversation sound like some casual discussion about an old friend. But then the whole interview had an unexpectedly informal air, with the comfortable chairs, the open door, the chatter floating in from the passage and the way the interview had been allocated to neither Henderson nor Jones, but to this Detective Constable Reith, who, with his smooth unshadowed chin and clear complexion, looked far too young to be doing this or any other job.

'At one time I knew her well,' I said. 'We met – oh, fifteen or sixteen years ago. But I didn't see her for a long time after that, not until this summer in fact.'

'This summer. And did you see her often?'

I inhaled abruptly. 'No. She came to the boat once. No – twice.'

'The boat?'

'My father's cruising yacht. My father died recently. I was keeping an eye on the boat. Pumping it out, that sort of thing. She swam by one day.'

He blinked. 'Swam by?'

'Yes, swam up to the boat. We started talking. She came aboard for tea.' Tea: how quaint that sounded, redolent of afternoon and sunlight and respectability.

'Where did this happen?'

'At Dittisham. The boat's moored in front of my father's house.'

'And when was this?'

'It must have been—' I frowned with the effort of memory. 'June? Some time then.'

'And the other time Sylvie came to the boat, did she swim over on that occasion as well?' He was intrigued by the swimming, as if this marked Sylvie out as some kind of oddity.

'No, she was rowing a small dinghy. She was on her way to another boat.'

'And which boat was that?'

'Oh, I don't know its name. But it's an old-fashioned boat, thirty-five feet or so, a white cutter with a bowsprit. Moored a little further down river, past the ferry.'

'You saw her go to it, did you?'

'Well – I knew she was on her way to a boat. I assumed it was that one. I'd seen her on it before.'

'You'd seen Sylvie on it before?' he repeated stolidly.

'Yes.'

'And when was that?'

'She was with a group of people, they were going off somewhere. It must have been around . . . the beginning of July? Yes – the beginning of July.'

'Did you recognise the people she was with?'

'No.'

'You could point the boat out to us, though?'

28

'I *could* . . .' I made no effort to conceal my reluctance. 'But I'd rather not. I don't come down here very often. I'm just on my way back to London now. It would be rather inconvenient. I'm extremely busy at the moment.'

'I mean – if necessary.'

'If necessary,' I conceded, trying not to sound openly unco-operative. 'But I'm sure the harbour master will be able to tell you straight away. There can't be many cutters with bow-sprits moored the other side of the ferry.'

Reith nodded in an unfocused way. 'So, er . . . apart from these two visits, did you see Sylvie on any other occasions?'

'I saw her by the river once. We chatted for a minute.'

'And that was all? You saw her just the three times?'

'To talk to, yes.' And saying this I felt a sudden heat, a prickle of sweat against my shirt, and thought what a poor liar I would make if I had to do it on a grand scale.

'Did you know who she mixed with? Who her friends were?'

'No,' I said a little too hastily. Then, more matter-of-factly: 'The only time I saw her with anyone was when she was on the boat with that group. And once I saw her walking with someone. Well, I *think* it was Sylvie. She was a long way off.' How these tiny untruths seemed to slip effortlessly off my tongue. Yet I could hardly admit that I had watched her covertly through binoculars, like some pathetic Peeping Tom.

'It was a man she was with?'

'It looked like it, yes. Though he had long hair. Noticeably long, onto his shoulders or even longer.'

'And she didn't mention the names of any friends when she was in conversation with you?'

'No.'

Reith shuffled a piece of paper. 'Now, Mr Wellesley, where were you between noon on Saturday last, the thirtieth of September, and noon on Sunday, the following day?'

I thought I had maintained my expression but perhaps he caught a hint of alarm in my eyes because he added coolly, 'A standard question, Mr Wellesley.'

As I met his unwavering gaze he suddenly didn't seem so young any more. 'Of course . . .' I cleared my throat. 'On Saturday

I worked in my office in Hammersmith until mid-afternoon. I left at . . . it must have been about three. Then I drove straight down to Dittisham. I arrived at dusk – so, about seven-thirty, I suppose. I opened up the house— '

'What house are we talking about, sir?' He was making detailed notes now.

'My late father's house – Dittisham House. And then . . . I drove into Dartmouth to buy some food— '

A pause while he got it down. 'So, what time would that have been?'

I really had to get this right. 'Oh . . . eight-fifteen? Maybe a little after. Yes, about eight-thirty.'

'And where did you shop, sir?'

'Well, I went to the Co-op first, but it was closed, so I went to the Spar shop by the church. It was the only place I could find. That was open, I mean.'

'Which church is that, sir?'

'Which church?' I repeated, momentarily confounded by the pedantry of the question. 'I've no idea what it's called, if that's what you mean. But the one right down in the town, near the quay.'

I wondered if he was writing so slowly out of an overdeveloped sense of clerical diligence, or a perverse wish to delay me even longer. 'Then?' he asked at last.

'I went back to the house. My wife arrived shortly afterwards.'

'Your wife? And her name is—?'

'Virginia Wellesley.'

'Mrs Virginia Wellesley.' I watched him record it in block capitals. 'And she is of the same address?'

'I'm sorry?'

'London. She lives with you at— ' He peered at his notes. 'Glebe Place?'

'Yes.'

The conversation had taken on a fantastic quality, both predictable and bizarre. The leisurely nature of the proceedings, the meandering questions, seemed grotesquely inappropriate to the terrible event that had brought us here.

'So at what time did you get back to the house and see your wife?'

I went through the motions of dredging my memory again. 'Well – nine or so.'

'And then?'

'We had some supper and went to bed.'

'And the next day?'

'Oh, wait a minute, I forgot . . . That evening my brother called in briefly, at about ten.'

'Your brother being?'

'David Wellesley. Dr Wellesley. He practises in Dartmouth.'

Reith held his pen awkwardly, knuckles bent like a child, and the nib laboured ever more slowly across the page. 'And the next day?'

'Help . . .' I rubbed my forehead. 'We must have got up at about eight and then we worked on the house and the boat. Clearing out cupboards and attics, that sort of thing.' Yet again I waited for his pen to catch up. 'Then in the evening we went back to London.'

'What time would that be, sir?'

'When we left? Oh – nine. Just after.'

He read laboriously through what he had written, then looked up and smiled his bleak professional smile. 'Thank you, sir.'

Even then I wasn't sure he had finished until he closed his notebook and got to his feet. I rose and shook his hand. 'I hope you find whoever did it,' I said. 'She was . . .' What was I trying to say? Why had I even started? '. . . a lovely person.'

'Was she, sir?' And his eyes slid away knowingly.

I drove fast again, often touching a hundred, sometimes exceeding it, stopping only to buy petrol and a mineral water. Julia called me on the car phone and gave me the messages in her cool staccato. The Chartered Bank had brought forward our next meeting to the following day at eleven-thirty, which I took as a wholly encouraging sign, but my satisfaction evaporated with the next message. Graham Moncrieff, the leader of our legal team, had called to say that he'd hit a problem with the Cumberland lawyers. It seemed Cumberland were backing out of their agreement to lease us the Hartford properties, and were suddenly insisting we buy the factory and warehousing outright.

31

For the second time that day I almost had an accident, straying out of my lane to earn a prolonged blast from a Range Rover.

Containing my anger and disbelief only with difficulty, slowing down to a sedate sixty, I told Julia to fix a meeting with Howard for some time the next day.

'You don't have any slots left.'

'Breakfast. Evening. Midnight, if necessary. But some time tomorrow, Julia.'

I asked her to save the rest of the messages and rang off. I needed time to calm down; I needed time to absorb the full implications of Cumberland's about-turn. If they forced this issue, if they made us purchase the factory, we would have to raise more money, another million at the very least. Just when we'd presented our final figures to the banks; just when we had the last of the money almost within our grasp. Cumberland weren't just moving the goalposts, they were taking them away altogether. Finding another million would be hard: we had tapped every source, we had called in every debt, we had milked every contact.

If this manoeuvre was designed to defeat us then it registered high on the scale of dirty tricks. But was it a manoeuvre? Did Cumberland want us to lose, or did they simply want to squeeze more cash out of us? Howard would know. Though whether he would be prepared to tell me was another matter.

This was the aspect of business I had always disliked and tried my best to avoid, the backbiting and chicanery, the breaking of trust, the pressing of every last advantage until your opponent bled. Howard regarded my scruples as a quaint but fatal flaw. He thought I was soft, and he was probably right. But I quite liked the idea of leaving the dignity of my opponents intact; if it was a flaw to dislike making enemies, then I possessed it in good measure.

I was going to be late. I almost called Julia to ask her to let Ginny know, but in recent weeks such second-hand messages had resulted in ruffled feelings. Ginny had accused me of finding excuses to avoid calling her. Realising that there was a small but undeniable grain of truth in this, feeling ashamed of it, I determined to call her myself.

'I've been held up,' I said as soon as she answered. I could hear voices in the background.

'Will you be very late?'

'Seven, I hope. Seven-thirty at the latest. If you don't mind me unwashed.'

'I don't mind if you don't.'

She sounded so subdued that I asked, 'Are you all right?'

'Feeling a bit rough. A touch of flu, I think.'

One of the voices in the background was male, a caterer or maintenance man. In the old days we would have joked about Ginny having a secret lover, but we didn't joke about that sort of thing any more.

I said, 'I'm sorry not to be there to help.'

'I'll manage.'

'You're sure you don't need a doctor?'

'No, no. I'll just go to bed as soon as everyone's gone.'

It was a quarter to eight by the time I finally turned into Glebe Place. The party was larger than I'd imagined. After a long hunt for a parking place – the garage was blocked, the adjacent streets tightly packed – I followed some guests into the house to find a wall of backs in every doorway and people spilling out of the drawing room into the conservatory.

A woman loomed up. 'Hello, Hugh! What a super party! You always give such super parties!'

Mouthing greetings, wearing my best smile, I moved through the room in search of Ginny. I finally spotted her by the fireplace, her back to me. She had done her hair a new way, or perhaps it was an old way that I'd forgotten, pulled severely back and held at her neck in a thick band, though this did nothing to diminish the brilliance of her hair, which was auburn and exceptionally glossy. She was wearing a plain black dress and when she turned I noticed that, apart from pearl earrings, she wore no jewellery. This didn't prevent her from looking exquisite; nothing could ever do that. She had a heart-shaped face with high cheekbones, a fine nose, and winged eyebrows that gave her an elfin quality.

She was smiling at someone. It was a smile I recognised, brittle and nervous.

'I'm here,' I announced unnecessarily. 'Everything okay?'

'The caterers got the food wrong.'

'Is it serious?'

'It's all doughy stuff. And spiced chicken. They forgot the smoked salmon parcels and the roulades!' She exhaled with a tiny shudder. 'Well, it's too late now, I suppose.' Her eyes, bright with illness or anxiety or both, darted constantly around the room. For a moment we stood silently amid the cacophonous swell, two castaways in a storm of our own making, then Ginny drifted away and I found myself talking to a City man about interest rates.

Slowly I succumbed to the rhythm of the party: enquiring after health and business, deflecting questions, spinning thin jokes, talking but not listening too well. The champagne made me tired and slow-witted, and I soon abandoned it for mineral water. Later someone made a speech about the premature baby unit and the need for funds and we all applauded.

A voice sighed at my elbow, 'Hello, you.' It was Caroline Adam, a friend of Ginny's and something high-powered in PR. She had wide red lips and tousled silvery blonde hair and was tall enough to look me straight in the eye. 'The man of the moment,' she declared.

'I am?'

'I call you two the golden couple. So beautiful, so clever, so – *everything*.'

I couldn't begin to respond to that, and didn't try.

'How are you in fact?' There was a slyness in her manner.

'Fine,' I said.

'And Ginny? She's looking a bit pale. I noticed straight away.'

'She thinks she might have flu.'

'Ah,' Caroline breathed, her heavy-lashed eyes fixed on mine. 'But you guys are okay?' Her smile did nothing to take the edge off the question.

A sickening thought struck me: that Ginny had confided in this woman, had spilled out the most painful details of our unhappiness. And fast on this thought came the idea that Ginny had talked about my visits to Dittisham, had even – a sinking thought – read something suspicious into them.

'Couldn't be better,' I said with terrible joviality.

Caroline searched my face, and I had the feeling that little escaped her voracious eyes. 'Glad to hear it,' she said at last. 'So many people falling by the wayside. Owing their last bootlace to Lloyd's. Jobless at fifty. Reduced to selling herbal remedies from their dining rooms. No wonder marriages creak under the strain. And we're all meant to be more caring!'

Had Ginny suspected something all this time? Had she thought I was having an affair? As the idea took hold, my spirits shrank at the prospect of the confrontations ahead.

'Though when it comes to caring,' Caroline was saying with a provocative smile, 'I think you poor beleaguered men have had a raw deal. I think us beastly women have pushed you too far, and you all need spoiling and cosseting again, just like in the bad old days.' She gave me a look that even I, in my state of abstraction, recognised as an invitation that wasn't entirely frivolous.

The noise seemed to rise up around me, the drink sang in my brain, I had reached some limit that I barely recognised. With an indeterminate salute, I moved rapidly away and escaped into the garden. I knew I shouldn't let the Carolines of this world get to me. Mischief-making was a compulsion with her and if it hadn't been such a very long day I would have remembered that sooner. I would also have remembered that, whatever else Ginny had reproached me for, she had never hinted at infidelity. Besides, our unhappiness had set in long before the summer, at some point in the long years since love had given way to bewilderment.

Standing there in the sulphurous darkness of the London night, the party a distant murmur, I tried to picture a time when things might be different, when the business would be back on its feet, when Ginny and I would be happy again, when in some miraculous way I would be free of worry and guilt. But the idea wouldn't form, it seemed too remote, and, taking a last breath of damp leafy air, I trudged back towards the house.

A few guests lingered remorselessly until nine-thirty, and we didn't close the door on the caterers until after ten.

'You go to bed,' I told Ginny. 'I'll finish down here.'

'I'm all right.' She sat on the edge of a chair by the fireplace. 'I don't think it's flu after all.'

'Are you sure?'

35

She gave a faint nod, her eyes doggedly on mine, and I realised she wanted to talk.

I poured myself a brandy, almost certainly the last thing I needed, and sat in the chair opposite. 'Well, that seemed to go all right, didn't it?' I said with forced brightness. 'I don't think anyone noticed the food.'

She sat like a governess, her arms held into her sides, her shoulders braced, austere and unyielding. 'How was your day?' she asked.

'Oh, you know . . .'

'No, I don't. Tell me.' And she fixed me with a look of strange intensity.

'Well . . . I told the Hartford staff what was happening. I saw David and Mary for lunch.'

'And what was it you told the staff?' she persisted solemnly.

'Oh, I gave them the latest news in all its glory!'

'Please, Hugh – I'd like to know.'

If I looked surprised it was because Ginny had never shown much interest in the details of the business. 'Sorry,' I said penitently. 'What did I tell them? Well . . . I made Cumberland sound pretty ogre-ish. I said they'd sell Hartford to the highest bidder, and, if it didn't happen to be us, then the staff faced almost certain redundancy. I said the future under a buyout would be pretty tough. But I think I made the bad times with us sound marginally more attractive than being out of work.'

She was listening intently, a small frown on her forehead, so I went on, explaining some of the risks involved in making our bid, and the hard work that lay ahead.

'But you believe in the buyout?' she said. 'It's what you want?'

'What I want?' I gave a shaky laugh. 'I think so! When I last did any rational thinking anyway.'

'There you go again,' she said, her voice rising.

'Where again?'

'Not answering me properly.'

'I'm sorry.' I heard the note of injury in my voice and suppressed it. 'Yes, it's what I want.' Articulating this gave my feelings new force. 'Yes. *Yes.* I can't just let it be written off. Not when it's got so much going for it. Oh, I know what you all think,' I said as if she represented the rest of my family. 'You think it's just the *tradition* or something, that I'm incapable of letting go. But it's not just that. It's the people at Hartford, and the place . . . I love it! I love everything to do with it!'

Ginny said gravely, 'So long as it's what you want.'

'Okay, and I want to be the person running it!' I conceded, as if this had been in dispute. 'I want to run it because I think I can do a better job than anyone else. With the right team beside me – and without crazy delusions of grandeur!' Just thinking about Howard stirred me to anger once more, and it was a moment before I took in what Ginny was saying.

'. . . I phoned the estate agent, threatened to take the house elsewhere unless they drummed up more interest in Melton. The man suggested some ads in the glossy magazines – which *we* pay for, of course. I agreed, but I told him he was on trial, that we'd give him six weeks at the most. Then . . .' Some thought distracted her, she blinked rapidly. 'Then . . . I asked the Murrays which agent they used for their place in France. Those local people are sharks, you know.'

Her calm acceptance caused me a flutter of remorse. 'I'm sorry it's come to this.'

She dismissed this with a slight lift of her shoulders. 'Too many houses anyway.'

'But you loved Melton.' And she had loved the house in Provence too. Her great passion was for decorating, her great talent for putting furniture and objects and colours together in fabulous combinations. She had made the houses into showcases, and their loss would be far more painful for her than for me. But at least we were talking about it. There had been a time when Ginny seemed to think that I wanted to sell the houses for some capricious reasons of my own, out of perversity, or even, in her blacker moments, because I wanted to undermine her in some way. For a while I had hardly dared to ask how the agents were getting on.

I ventured another risky subject, the matter of the costly couple who ran Melton. 'The Kemps, have we managed to . . . ?'

'Yes, yes. They left a week ago. I told you.'

'You did? Sorry.' Another apology, another small descent.

'Mrs Hoskins has agreed to go in three times a week.'

'Well done.'

'Will we have to sell this place as well?' she asked in a voice that was deliberately calm.

'No, of course not!' I made a poor stab at humour. 'No, I thought we'd go mad and keep at least one roof over our heads! The doorways along the Strand are a bit draughty. And you don't meet the same class of dosser, so they tell me . . . Old Etonians, Lloyd's bankrupts—'

'Please don't!' she exclaimed suddenly, and the tension stretched out between us. 'I do wish you'd just – *tell* me things! Sometimes you treat me like an idiot!'

'I *am* telling you,' I responded mildly. 'And I've never treated you like—'

'But if you're going to be at Hartford all the time, we can't live up here, can we?'

'In time we could certainly think about moving nearer, yes.'

She exhaled sharply with exasperation. 'Of course we'll have to. It's the only thing to do.'

I wasn't sure what to make of this Ginny, vibrating with the usual tensions, yet unexpectedly and miraculously focused.

'But we don't have to live at Dittisham, do we?' she demanded.

'No.'

'But you *were* thinking about it.'

It had been the briefest of suggestions, made soon after my father died, when I was still in a state of disbelief. The thought of losing both my father and the house where I had grown up had seemed too much to bear, and for a few weeks I'd nursed emotional ideas of restoring the place and using it for summer weekends. My imagination had cast a golden wash of nostalgia over the prospect; I had seen children in the garden again, and barbecues on the terrace, and Easter treasure hunts, and expeditions on the river. 'It was just a thought. But no, it's being sold. There was an offer today.'

'Ah.' And the relief showed in her face.

We both looked away into the unlit fire. The fake logs were so cleverly finished with ash and scorch marks that they were indistinguishable from the real thing; Ginny had seen them in

America and ordered them specially. I felt her glance back at me, gathering herself to speak again.

'That girl – the one they found in the river – did you hear anything?'

I kept myself steady, I showed nothing in my face. I brought my eyes back to hers. 'Oh, David mentioned something. She was stabbed, apparently. Then dumped in the water.'

'They haven't got any idea who did it?'

'I don't think so.'

A pause. 'You might have told me, you know.'

'Told you what?'

'That it was *her*.' And Ginny's voice was charged with an emotion I couldn't read.

I didn't say anything.

'That she was the one you were in love with.'

I took a slow breath. 'It was a long time ago, Ginny.'

'But it *was* her?' And her voice trembled slightly.

'Yes.'

'The one you wanted to marry, but couldn't.'

'Who said that?'

She dropped her eyes briefly, as if caught in some subterfuge. 'Mary.'

'Well, I wouldn't believe everything Mary tells you,' I retorted, wondering what else Mary had said. Then, to soften my words: 'Honestly, darling . . .'

'I don't mind, it's not that,' she said, her voice high. 'I just wish you'd told me.'

'Really, it wasn't anything . . .'

'You did want to marry her though?'

There was a relentlessness in Ginny, an inability to let go, that reverberated through our arguments like the beat of a discordant drum. Hearing it now in her voice, knowing what was to come, I said hotly, 'It never got to that stage. There was never any question . . .' She was waiting for me to elaborate. 'Sylvie was very young,' I explained unhappily. 'Only sixteen.'

Something in the way Ginny took this, the suggestion of a nod, made me think that she already knew, that Mary must have told

39

her, and, fired by the drink and the endless day, I felt a surge of resentment against this exchange of notes.

Ginny took a moment to frame her next question. 'You saw her this summer?' And the coolness of her voice did nothing to disguise its tautness.

'Once or twice.'

'And she was' – the hesitation again, the careful choice of words – 'living in Dittisham?'

'I don't know. I didn't ask.'

'Mary said she was running a shop. Pottery or handicrafts . . . '

'Well, Mary would be the one to know.' I threw the last of the brandy down my throat and got up.

'Mary thought— '

I twisted away to hide my exasperation and despair. I was so exhausted, I had survived so much today, that I longed to shout out, to beg her to leave it alone and give me some peace.

'She thought the police would want to question everyone who was near the river on the weekend.'

Constrained by habit, or possibly futility, I made myself turn back and say, 'Yes, I expect she's right.'

'So they might want to question us?'

I gestured the possibility.

'And you? Because you used to know her?'

'Yes. Well, in fact— ' I would have given anything not to talk about it just then, but one bad moment was probably as good as another. 'They already have. Today.' And I thought: now we start the argument in earnest. Because I have failed to tell her immediately. Because she'll think I have something to hide.

But she was very still, her eyes fastened on my face. 'And?'

'Oh, it was just what you'd expect. They asked if I knew Sylvie. If I'd seen her this summer. It didn't take long. Mainly because I didn't have much to tell them.'

A progression of thoughts flickered over Ginny's face like shadows across a screen. 'There we are, then,' she exhaled finally.

It was a moment before I realised that there was to be no row after all, that she was going to leave the subject alone. With the relief came an extraordinary fatigue, like a coat of lead.

'I must get to bed.'

'Yes,' she declared. 'You've had it! So've I!' She swung away and walked towards the stairs without looking back.

Yet I didn't sleep immediately. And nor did Ginny. We lay on either side of the bed, facing away from each other, and I thought that this must be the loneliest feeling in the world, to lie beside each other yet find ourselves unable to reach out, to have things to say yet find it impossible to speak. Also – and the thought travelled painfully out of the past – to remember how different it had been at the beginning, the closeness – and yes, the love – that we had once felt for each other, and to realise that, for some reason that neither of us understood, those times seemed to have slipped for ever beyond our grasp.

Later something made me wake. The wind, the distant pattering of rain. And close by, the sound of Ginny's breathing, coming in uneven jerks. A tiny gasp, then another. I rolled over and put my hand on her shoulder. She stiffened and held her breath. I moved to touch her cheek beneath the mask, to feel the tears I knew I would find there, but she pushed my hand away and said in a harsh voice, 'What is it? What's the matter?'

I had no answer, and in the end it was easier to say 'Nothing' and turn away.

*

It was just before seven-thirty as I pressed the security code into the keypad at the entrance of the HartWell offices in Slough. The panel shrieked at me and for a moment I thought Cumberland must have had the code changed, but I must have had the code wrong first time because at my second attempt the door buzzed its acceptance. I noticed that the heavy inner doors of solid glass emblazoned with the HartWell logo had not yet been replaced. That logo. Howard and I had argued about every detail of it – the style, the size, the colour, you name it. In those days we had thrived on argument, it had been the lifeblood of our partnership, a stimulus for problem solving and fresh ideas, a constant source of hilarity, and the only way we knew to keep our minds sharp in the face of our terrifying success. Well, success that had been terrifying for me anyway; Howard took it as his due.

41

In the early days of our expansion into mass-market glass and china we had measured success in terms of turnover and profit margins. But profit margins don't protect you from recession or cut-throat tactics by your competitors. And for Hartford, heavily dependent on exports, margins don't defend you against the dollar taking a nosedive from which it never recovers.

I looked into my old office. The large Hartford crystal vase dating from the fifties stood in its usual place on the side table, now bereft of flowers. The aerial photograph of the Hartford factory still hung on the wall next to the dusty outlines of the two pictures I had removed to my temporary office in Hammersmith: a photograph of my father greeting a young Prince of Wales at Hartford during a visit in the seventies; and a picture of me as a self-conscious eighteen-year-old, trying to blow crystal.

No amount of framed pictures or crystal vases could ever have made me feel comfortable in this hermetically sealed glass-house. Slough may have been equidistant from Hartford and our factories to the north, and convenient for Heathrow, but for me, imbued with the hands-on philosophy of my father, the place was a bureaucratic no-man's land that had left me feeling dangerously out of touch.

I waited in Howard's outer office. One thing I had learnt to rely on in my years with Howard was that he would always be late for our meetings, and, knowing full well that today would be no exception, I determined to remain calm.

It was ten to eight when Howard made one of the silent entrances at which he was so proficient. I looked up and there he was, filling the doorway. He was wearing a dark suit, expensively cut to disguise the weight which had settled evenly, and, despite his much-vaunted gym expeditions, it seemed permanently, over his broad frame. Crossing the room, he slid a hand elegantly down one lapel and unbuttoned his jacket with a flick of his thumb.

'Is it just us?' he asked in feigned surprise.

'Who else was there meant to be?'

'I thought – lawyers, accountants. No?' He affected this ironic air when he wanted to intimidate me.

'Don't talk rubbish.'

42

He attempted an ingenuous look, something he had never quite managed to master, and I noticed that his grey eyes were looking puffy, and his hair, normally immaculate, was unkempt around the collar, while his cheeks were beginning to develop an unhealthy mottled look. But then if my social life was full, Howard's was frenetic. Since his divorce four years before, he frequently featured in the glossy magazines that Ginny liked to read, pictured with a string of society women. When I had last chosen to listen, someone had told me that he was keen to marry the twice-divorced daughter of a landed duke.

He unlocked his office and led the way to his desk.

'This isn't to do with the buyout then?' he drawled, sinking into his high-backed leather chair.

'Of course it is!' I said tightly, avoiding the strategically low-seated guest chair opposite his desk and fetching a higher one from the conference area.

'And you really don't feel you want anyone else here?'

Recognising this as a no-win question, I ignored it and demanded, 'What's this problem about the leasing agreement for the Hartford properties?'

But he was still playing games. 'I need coffee,' he announced languidly, casting around as if this might cause a cup to appear out of nowhere.

I growled, 'Forget the coffee. I've only got fifteen minutes.'

Suddenly he laughed, a rich chuckle that rumbled on after he had stopped smiling. 'Hugh,' he scolded. 'Always in such a rush.'

'Too damned right!'

He regarded me with something approaching affection, though it could just as easily have been pity, and then, this show of indulgence having served its purpose, which was to wind me up, he got down to business.

'Is there a problem?' he murmured.

'You know damn well there is. It was agreed that we could *lease* all the properties from Cumberland. There was never any talk of buying!'

'Oh?' He affected puzzlement. 'Wasn't there? Are you sure you aren't thinking of the earlier discussions? At the first merger talks perhaps?'

43

I was never sure why Howard liked to call the takeover a merger. Because he had instigated the deal perhaps. Or because it boosted his view of his own standing on the main board. 'You know perfectly well which discussions I'm talking about, Howard,' I said, determined not to give him the satisfaction of seeing me lose my temper. 'When the outline buyout terms were agreed. In August.'

Howard grimaced elegantly. 'I don't think anything was actually *decided*, Hugh.' He made a show of testing this recollection against his memory. 'No,' he murmured, 'I'm sure I'm right in saying Cumberland didn't commit itself to a leasing arrangement.'

'It was agreed in principle, Howard!'

'It was just one *option*, Hugh.'

'More than an option, Howard! A commitment!'

His face took on an expression of forbearance wearing thin. 'Whatever your recollection, Hugh, the situation is that Cumberland cannot possibly agree to a leasing agreement. In a buyout you expect the customer to *buy*. Cumberland doesn't want the Hartford properties left on its books. It wants to dispose of them. *Not* unreasonable in the circumstances.'

'Unreasonable if you've made a commitment.'

'Hugh – a commitment is something in writing, something agreed by one's lawyers.'

'For Cumberland, maybe.'

'Come – for anyone, surely.'

'So do I take it the matter's no longer open to negotiation?' I said stiffly.

'On the price?' he asked, deliberately choosing to misunderstand.

'On the option to lease!'

He sighed with a sort of paternal irritation. 'I thought I'd made it clear, Hugh. Didn't I make it clear?' He spread his hands questioningly. 'Leasing is not an option.'

Despite my intention to remain calm, I heard my resentment break through. 'Cumberland are reneging, then? I just want to be quite clear.'

'Hugh, I strongly object to that. There's no question of reneging. How can there be when we never agreed anything?'

'You realise this could sabotage the entire buyout?'

'Oh?' He was suddenly a picture of imitation concern. 'Well, I'm very sorry to hear that, I really am. I know how hard you've been working on it.'

'Come on, don't tell me you didn't realise!' I said bitterly.

'Realise?' The shrug was hopelessly exaggerated. Such a bloody bad actor. But then overplaying the scene was all part of the satisfaction for him. 'How could I realise, Hugh?'

I shook my head, not trusting myself to speak.

'Surely the additional cash won't be that hard to find?'

He was fishing, he wanted to know just how far we had got with the banks, but I was damned if I was going to give him that sort of information. 'It's not the money, Howard, it's the timing, as you well know! The Cumberland board have had the outline agreement for six weeks – *six weeks* – and they suddenly decide on this *now*. That's as close to sabotage as you can get!'

'Well, I'm sorry but Cumberland can hardly be blamed if you've rushed things at *your* end, Hugh. The proposal had to be evaluated very carefully. You couldn't expect us to do it overnight. I'm sorry if you're going to have to go back and renegotiate with the banks, but that's hardly our problem, is it?'

Looking at him, a suspicion formed in my mind. It came to me that Howard himself had engineered this whole situation, that, for some reasons of his own, he wanted my bid to fail.

I stood up. I fully intended to leave with my pride intact, but my anger got the better of me. 'Sleeping all right, are you, Howard?'

'Oh, come on, Hugh,' he said with the injured air of someone fending off an unprovoked attack. 'That's always been your trouble, you know – taking things personally.'

'With you, I don't know any other way to take them.'

'Business is business, Hugh. You've never been able to grasp that, have you?'

*

The morning tailback began just beyond Heathrow. As I joined the haze of shuffling traffic, I thought back over the years of my partnership with Howard. Though I'd never harboured too many illusions about him, while I'd seen him instigate some pretty ruthless manoeuvres in his time, I'd always liked to think there were certain limits beyond which he wouldn't go, that the sixty years during which our two families had jointly owned and run HartWell counted for something – a remnant of loyalty, perhaps; a fragment of sympathy – and that he would draw the line at actively plotting against me.

I liked to think such fine noble thoughts because if I didn't I began to contemplate walking away from the whole miserable business and going to live a hermit's life in France. I'd had such thoughts before, in early summer when the full extent of the crisis at HartWell was becoming clear, when I realised that Howard had engineered the takeover behind my back, when I began to appreciate just how completely I had let the real control slip from my grasp. Then I was dogged by a sense of worthlessness and futility: my mid-life crisis. An absurdly frivolous term for the doubt that had taken to descending on me without warning, turning my thinking inside out, making me question things that at my age did not bear questioning. Despairing of the present, clutching at the past; harbouring visions of what might have been. Hungry for escape and solace; ripe for the idea of Sylvie.

Fumbling with the radio, I turned on the eight-thirty headlines, knowing that there would be nothing about Sylvie, yet needing to hear it for myself. An exercise in reassurance. Or paranoia.

The traffic did not ease and I reached the three-room office suite in Hammersmith five minutes before Julia and I were due to leave for the meeting with the Chartered Bank. I had rented this place as a temporary London base while we negotiated the buyout. It wasn't so much an office as a space from which I made calls and sent letters. All the meetings – and there were up to three a day – took place at the City offices of the various bankers, lawyers and accountants acting for us or for Cumberland. Very occasionally meetings were held at Hartford itself, four hours' drive to the south-west.

Before Julia could collar me, I phoned Moncrieff to check what I already knew, that we had no legal remedy against Cumberland for reneging on the leasing agreement. I followed this with a swift call to Pollinger at Zircon to alert him to the fact that we would be asking for more money. He warned me that unless I was prepared to give Zircon a bigger slice of the equity then the most I could expect from them would be a quarter of the extra million.

Julia put her head round the door. 'I know I shouldn't, but I couldn't help overhearing. That bastard!' I didn't need to ask who she was referring to. So far as Julia was concerned, Howard had rat status.

'It would have been a board decision, Julia.'

'Yes, but who proposed the idea?'

'No point in worrying about that now.'

'That's what you always say.' Instantly she made a disclaiming wave of the hand. 'Sorry. *Sorry*. What I meant was, *I* wouldn't be half as forgiving. You're too nice, that's your trouble.'

'It's nothing to do with being *nice*,' I grimaced, smarting at the compliment. 'It's a question of being realistic.'

Julia conceded this with a dubious face, and looked at her watch. 'We've got to go.'

'One more call,' I bargained.

My bank manager was a bland insubstantial character named Elliott. With the various personal loans I had been forced to negotiate, I had got to see quite a lot of him over the last two years. He did not sound surprised that I was asking for money again.

'This mortgage would be additional to your existing building society mortgage?'

'That's right.'

'Five hundred thousand is rather a large sum for a mortgage, Mr Wellesley. That sort of sum would usually come into the range of a business loan, subject to business rates.'

'But you'll consider it?'

'This would be in addition to the loan on the country property?'

'That's right.'

A pause. 'So on the Chelsea house, the new mortgage would take the loan up to ninety per cent of its value?'

'That would be on a conservative valuation. But – yes.'

'Well – I'll look into it,' he said cautiously. 'But, Mr Wellesley, are you quite sure you want to put your home at stake?'

'Yes.'

'You have considered what would happen if your business were to fail?'

'Yes,' I said testily.

'And your wife – she's happy with the arrangement?'

'I realise she'll have to agree to it,' I said. 'I'm aware of the law.'

'Very well. I'll come back to you as soon as I can.'

Julia appeared in the doorway wearing her we-really-have-to-leave face, but I held up a delaying hand and, when she had frowned her disapproval and disappeared, I called Ginny, only to get the answering machine. I told the tape I should be home by eight. It was only after I'd rung off that it occurred to me that Ginny might have flu after all and be lying ill in bed. She was prone to catch all the nastier bugs and to suffer them badly. Convalescence, with its inactivity, always depressed her, and it was then that I became acutely aware of how isolated she was without children. During the five or so years when we had actively discussed our childlessness and gone through various fertility investigations I had once or twice mentioned adoption, but she had brimmed with dark resentment at the idea, as though it were an admission of defeat or an allotment of blame, and I hadn't brought up the subject again. Now we never talked about children at all.

Julia came in briskly. 'We really have to go.' She tipped her head to one side and cast me a sharp glance. 'Are you okay?'

'Don't you start.'

'You look awful again.'

'What do you mean *again*?' I grabbed my briefcase and sprang to my feet. 'You're as bad as my old nanny. I'm fine.'

But I can't have sounded too convincing because as we headed for the door she demanded, 'When did you last eat?' Interpreting my silence correctly, she announced that she would get some sandwiches on the way.

Hurrying down the stairs I tried to concentrate on the crucial meeting ahead. I dreaded pitching to bankers, it was like reasoning with wet dough. They were malleable enough, you felt things were shaping up, but at the end of the day you were never quite sure what you had ended up with.

We emerged fast into the lobby. Through the doors I could see Tony, the driver Julia regularly hired to take us into the City, standing at the bottom of the steps beside his Rover. Two men crossed in front of the Rover and came up the steps towards the entrance. I swung the door back for Julia just as the first of the visitors pushed through the opposite door. I registered a crumpled raincoat, sparse greying hair, a thin mouth in a fleshy face. The second man was younger, taller and fitter. I wasn't sure what it was about them – the white shirts, the well-worn clothes, their air of purpose – but, coloured by the events of the previous day, my imagination momentarily cast them as policemen.

I hurried on towards the car.

Tony had the rear door open and I was just about to duck in when a voice called, 'Mr Wellesley?'

I straightened up and looked round. Julia said sharply, 'Can I help you?' and turned to intercept the approaching men.

The one with grey hair ignored her and continued towards me with the rolling gait of someone with a hip problem. Digging into his breast pocket, he produced a card mounted in a leather case and, holding it up at eye level so there was no possibility of my missing it, announced himself as Detective Inspector Henderson.

'You are Mr Hugh William Wellesley?'

'Yes.'

'I'd like to ask you to accompany us to Exeter, sir, to help us with our inquiries into the death of Sylvie Mathieson.'

I felt a draining in my stomach. 'But yesterday – I saw your man Reith. I told him everything.'

'We'd be grateful for more details, sir,' he said in a flat voice. 'And a statement, if you don't mind.'

I spread my hands helplessly, I opened my mouth a couple of times to speak, I felt a sudden heat. 'I'll be glad to help in any way I can – of course,' I said at last. 'But I'm on my way to a vital meeting and I'm already late.' I glanced towards Julia as if for support and met her startled gaze.

'The matter is rather important, sir.'

Disbelief and mounting alarm made me exclaim, 'So is *this!* You don't understand, Inspector – I *have* to get to this meeting!'

Henderson pondered this with the air of someone who has heard a lot of excuses in his time, but my incredulity and panic must have made some sort of impression because, after a show of consideration, he agreed to wait. I told him my meeting would take one and a half hours. We settled on two.

In accepting this, I realised with dismay that I had agreed to go all the way back to Exeter.

THREE

Were arrived in darkness and monsoon rain. The approaches to the police station were blocked by manoeuvring cars, and we were forced to scurry head down through the deluge to the shimmering entrance. Inside, Henderson shook the water from his collar and pressed his thin hair down to his scalp. Wiping my forehead, I glanced up and saw David.

I grinned weakly. I'd guessed he might be here, I knew Julia had called ahead, but the sight of his sardonic face still gave my spirits a lift. The long journey from London had done nothing for my peace of mind.

David had someone with him, a young thin-faced man with floppy blond hair and a cast in one eye. 'This is Charles Tingwall of Ruthven & Forbes,' David announced. 'He's here to look after your interests.'

I wasn't sure how I felt about this. To my impressionable mind, programmed by a hundred television dramas, hiring yourself a solicitor suggested you had something to hide. But in the next more considered moment, I realised that, irrespective of appearances, it was a sensible precaution that I would be foolish not to take.

Tingwall gave me a dry handshake and turned to Henderson.

'On what basis is Mr Wellesley here, Inspector?' The two men moved to one side, as if for negotiations. I could just hear the policeman recite, 'We are hoping Mr Wellesley can help us with our inquiries into the death of Sylvie Mathieson.'

Tingwall then asked: 'Is Mr Wellesley here as a witness, then, or a suspect?'

'As a witness.'

51

'In which case—'

I didn't hear any more as David said to me in a robust voice that seemed to carry across the reception area to the duty officer at the enquiry window, 'What did I tell you? Small brains.'

I frowned a protest at him.

Deliberately misreading my look, he added, 'Don't worry, Tingwall will get it sorted. He came highly recommended.' He added in a tone that was almost offhand, 'Have they said why you're here?'

'No.'

'Well . . . it has to be the lover scenario, doesn't it?'

'Oh thanks. *Thanks.*'

'What else could it be?' he said with a flicker of impatience. 'I told you – they've got one-track minds. Just remember, they're guessing. Don't let them rattle you. Just tell them where to get off.'

I wasn't so sure it would be that easy. I wasn't so sure I would feel quite so confident on this alien territory.

Tingwall and Henderson turned back.

'I'd like some time with Mr Wellesley,' Tingwall announced.

Henderson offered, 'Five minutes?'

'I'm sure Mr Wellesley could do with a sandwich and a wash and brush up.'

'Fifteen, then.'

'Twenty?' Tingwall raised an eyebrow at me. 'Mr Wellesley's come a very long way.'

Henderson yielded with a cursory nod before limping away.

For some reason this well-practised professional exchange did nothing to reassure me.

I said I wasn't hungry but Tingwall sent David off to buy sandwiches anyway and led me to a bench in a corner of the reception area, away from the lugubrious gaze of the duty officer.

'Now, Mr Wellesley,' Tingwall began in a hushed tone, 'I just want to be sure – they didn't arrest you?'

'Arrest me? *No.*'

'They didn't caution you?'

'No.'

'There was no mention of anything you may say being given in evidence?'

'No.'

'Fine.' He gave me a brief smile which was undermined by the cast in his left eye. 'And you haven't said anything to them already?'

'I gave them a statement yesterday.'

This was obviously the first he'd heard of it. 'And what did you tell them exactly?'

I gave him a rough summary, and found myself wondering for the hundredth time where I might have slipped up.

'And you didn't say anything in the car on the way down?'

'What? No.' Apart from a couple of offers to stop at service areas, Henderson and his cohort Phipps had maintained a steadfast silence during the entire journey. If their intention had been to unnerve me, then they had partially succeeded.

'Have you anything to add to yesterday's statement?'

'No.'

'They haven't given you any idea of why they've asked you back?' Tingwall enquired cautiously.

I shrugged, 'No.'

'And you yourself can't think of any reason?'

'No.'

Tingwall tapped his fingers together pensively. 'Well, if they've got their wires crossed, I mean if they're completely on the wrong track, then you must say so.' He waited for a sign that I had understood this. Getting nothing back, he spelled it out again. 'If they have some notion that's completely wrong, then you must put them right.'

The thought of what they could have got wrong made me feel ill, but I managed a faint nod.

'Now, you should be aware of your rights—'

'My rights?' I protested. 'God – you make it sound as though I'm about to be charged or something.'

'I apologise. I didn't make myself clear. I meant your rights at interview.'

'I'm not sure that makes me feel a whole lot better. The way everyone's going on I'm beginning to feel like a suspect.'

'The police do that to everyone, I'm afraid. It's their way.' He gave the unconvincing smile again. 'Now, you are here in an entirely voluntary capacity, to help them with their inquiries. As a result, nothing you say can be held against you. If, however, they suddenly decide to caution you, mid-interview or whatever, then I must warn you that everything will change.'

Far from bolstering my confidence, this conversation was eroding it fast. 'So you think I *am* a suspect?'

'Er – no, Mr Wellesley.' Tingwall chose his words with the care of someone picking his way over barbed wire. 'Not at all. At the same time . . .' He was struggling to get it right. '. . . they don't usually bring someone all this way unless they think, rightly or wrongly, that he or she has information of some kind.'

Even in my more optimistic moments I'd realised that the police wouldn't have sent their big guns to bring me all the way down here unless they believed I had something to tell them. But it was one thing to think it, and quite another to hear it from a professional.

'In that case,' I said, 'you'd better spell it out for me.'

Now that he was on firmer ground, Tingwall moved confidently into his stride. 'The important thing to remember is that you don't have to answer any questions you don't want to.'

My anxieties shot back to the surface. 'Won't that look bad?'

'It doesn't matter how it looks. If there are any areas that you feel are best left unanswered – for whatever reason – then you shouldn't answer them.'

'But it's not like that,' I murmured. 'I told them everything yesterday.'

'Fine. But bear it in mind, all the same,' Tingwall said.

I felt bound to ask, 'And if I don't want to answer? What do I say?'

'I leave that up to you,' he said with curious emphasis, as if there was an obvious conclusion to be drawn from this.

I didn't understand and said so.

'Well, let's put it this way . . .' His disconcerting squinty eyes seemed to focus somewhere on my left cheek. 'It's better to say you can't remember than to be vague or to change your mind. And if you're simply not sure of something, again, don't just take a stab at it, don't give a vague answer. Just say you can't remember. Keep it simple.'

54

I took a long breath. 'Okay.'

David came back with the sandwiches, but I still wasn't hungry and, leaving David with Tingwall, I asked the duty officer the way to the gents. The basins were smeared with dirt, one was missing its plug, and the taps were the type that switch themselves off after yielding a niggardly trickle. I splashed some water over my face and washed my hands. Drying my face with a paper towel, I told myself I felt refreshed.

When I got back to the reception area David was pulling on his coat. 'I'm going over to the hospital. I'll come back later.'

'Don't feel you have to.'

'Well, it's hardly out of my way, is it?' he replied in the brusque tone he used to discourage further discussion.

I followed him outside and we stood under the dripping porch. 'I was thinking,' I said, 'if this gets out, if the press get hold of it . . . *Christ*.' The idea was enough to shake me.

'I've talked to Tingwall about that. He's dealing with it.'

'He is?'

'No guarantees, though. The press are always sniffing around. He can only try.'

I clamped my eyes shut in an attempt to close out images of the newspaper headlines. 'What a time to choose!'

David couldn't think what I was talking about.

'The buyout!'

'Oh.'

'The Chartered Bank is on the brink of committing itself. The thing's practically off the ground.'

'Well, that's good.' But his tone conveyed a lack of interest.

'Off the ground, subject to raising the rest of the money, I mean.'

I said this so that he wouldn't think I was taking his support for granted, but he interpreted it as an untimely attempt to push my case.

'Yes, well,' he said with visible irritation, 'Give us time, eh?'

'I didn't mean that.' But it was too complicated to put the matter right and reluctantly I let it pass.

David looked at his watch. He frequently gave this impression of needing to be somewhere else; it was one of his stratagems for keeping people, particularly difficult patients, at arm's length.

'Listen,' I said, 'Ginny doesn't know where I am. I thought it best, in case she worried – you know. But now . . . well, I'm not so sure. I'd hate her to hear about this from someone else.'

'Ah, she knows, in fact. I called and told her.'

'You did?' I should have been annoyed at such peremptory action, and part of me was, yet Ginny would have had to know sooner or later, and I was quite relieved that David had been the one to tell her. He could always be relied on to down-play a crisis, and his uncompromising brand of logic would have checked Ginny's tendency to overreaction.

As if to confirm this, he said, 'I told her not to come down. I said there was absolutely no point, that it was just a routine thing and she was best at home.'

'And she was happy about that?'

'Oh yes,' he said emphatically.

I said with a tremor of emotion, 'Thanks.'

With an offhand wave and a sharp twitch of the mouth in what might have been intended as a smile, he went out into the rain.

Tingwall announced our readiness and a uniformed officer let us through a security door and along a passage to a door marked Interview Room 2. This was a different room from the one where I'd talked to Reith. The floor was uncarpeted, the chairs hard and upright, and there was a tape recorder at one end of the table. The fluorescent lighting gave off a ghostly flicker, and there was a stale tang of cigarettes and heavily scented floor polish.

Tingwall and I sat on one side of the table, Henderson on the other, with Reith to his left. Phipps stood against the wall, by the door.

Henderson intoned some preliminaries in an expressionless voice, thanking me for my willingness to help them with their inquiries – as if he had offered me much option – explaining that he simply wished to establish one or two facts. His thin, lipless mouth was like a slit set at random amid the broad heavy features. He had the skin of a heavy smoker, porous and etched with webs of deep lines, and his eyes were hooded and droopy as a spaniel's. It was a spent and punished face, but not, I felt, a stupid one.

He repeated most of the questions that Reith had asked me the

56

day before. How did I know Sylvie, when and where had I seen her in the last few months, what had happened when we met.

I took my answers slowly, matching them to the ones I had given Reith the day before, conscious of Henderson's washed-out eyes and his air of quiet watchfulness. As we progressed, part of me stood outside myself wondering what sort of an impression I was making, yet the more self-aware I became the more unnatural I sounded to my own ears and the more I felt I was exhibiting the body language of someone with something to hide.

'To summarise then,' Henderson said, 'the first time you saw Sylvie Mathieson this summer was when she swam to the boat and you had tea together for perhaps forty-five minutes?'

'Yes.'

'The second time she also came to the boat and you—'

'She didn't come on board,' I corrected him mildly. 'She just tapped on the hull.'

'So she remained in this other boat she came in, and you talked for ten minutes?'

'Yes.'

'And the third time you met on the quay?'

'We bumped into each other, yes.'

'And you talked for—?'

'Oh . . . two, three minutes. At the most.'

'So, it was just the three times then?'

I hated the way that repetition etched these details deeper and deeper into the stone of fact. 'I think so, yes.'

'You *think* so?'

'Well, as far as I remember.'

His eyes flickered to life. 'Your memory could be faulty then? Might it have been four times that you met, or five, or even more?'

'No. *No.* If it was more than three, then it wasn't much more. Four at the outside.' This was sounding terrible. I was beginning to appreciate Tingwall's warning about vague answers.

'Well, if it was four, on what other occasion did you meet her?'

'Look, I'm not sure I did meet her again. But if I did it was probably on the water. But really, I can't remember.'

I felt sure Henderson would pursue this, but for some reason he took on a distant look, and asked, 'You spent a lot of time on the water this summer, did you?'

'A few weekends, that's all.'

'Out sailing?'

'Only once. Mainly I was just doing the maintenance.'

Appearing distracted, Henderson dropped his eyes and gave a slight nod. When he looked up again his gaze had regained its watchfulness. 'How would you describe your relationship with Sylvie Mathieson?' he asked, and suddenly there was a charge in the air.

'Well – old friends, I suppose. Though we hadn't seen each other for many years.'

'Nothing more than that?'

So David was right: I was to be cast as Sylvie's secret lover. 'No,' I said.

'You weren't involved in a sexual relationship?'

I took a moment to answer. I wanted to strike the right note, somewhere between indignation and candour. 'No.'

'Just . . . er, *friends*?'

'That's right.'

His old man's eyes appraised me coldly. 'You had known each other in the past?'

I had already told him this. 'Yes.'

'When was it that you met exactly?'

'It must be . . .' I frowned with the effort of the mental arithmetic. 'Sixteen years ago.'

'And what was your relationship then?'

I didn't want to answer that, not with anything that approached the truth anyway. The very thought of telling this leery grey-faced man with his pasted-down hair and tight collar what I had once felt for Sylvie made me bristle. Eventually I said, 'We used to go out together.'

'She was your girlfriend?'

'For a time, yes.'

'Was it a sexual relationship?'

My resentment rose in a hot wave. I threw a glance at Tingwall, who was already protesting, 'That can hardly be relevant to your present inquiries, Inspector.'

'We're talking about sixteen years ago,' Henderson said reasonably. 'Surely that's not a problem, Mr Wellesley?'

Before Tingwall could interject again, I said hotly, 'Well, it is, actually, because it's really none of your business.'

'You prefer not to answer the question then, Mr Wellesley?'

'That's right,' I said shakily.

There was a shift in the atmosphere then, a palpable hardening in their attitude towards me. I felt as though I had the word *suspect* tattooed across my forehead.

'May I ask how long this non-specific relationship lasted?' Henderson asked drily.

I thought about not answering that as well, but murmured grudgingly, 'A year and a half.'

'You were how old at the time, Mr Wellesley?'

I had no doubt he knew the answer to that, he just wanted to hear me say it. 'I was twenty-six.'

'And when you met Sylvie Mathieson she was fifteen years old?'

'Sixteen.'

'Er . . . Not if it was sixteen years ago, Mr Wellesley.'

'I remembered her as sixteen – but you may be right.'

'I ask because I'm wondering if that's why there appears to be a difficulty over the question.' When I made no response he explained, 'If she was fifteen, a sexual relationship would of course have been illegal. If it would help, I can ask about your relationship after Miss Mathieson had turned sixteen. What was the nature of it then?'

Tingwall broke in angrily, 'I think we've established that this question can have no relevance to the present inquiry, and that my client is perfectly entitled not to answer it. He is here to help with your inquiries, Inspector, not to be grilled on his personal life.'

Henderson accepted this with a splaying of his thick fingers, a slight shrug of the shoulders, as if the approach, though doomed to failure, had been worth one last try.

'Well, let's move on then,' he said, sticking out his fleshy chin with something like relish. 'Perhaps we could go over your movements last weekend? In some detail.'

59

He wanted everything. What time I had left for work on the Saturday morning, what I had done in the office, who could vouch for the fact that I had left Hammersmith at about three.

'There was no one else there,' I explained. 'I was alone in the office.'

'No security staff?'

'At the main door, yes. But I don't know the weekend staff, and they don't know me. There are dozens of companies in the building. I just rent rooms there.'

'So no one saw you leave?'

'No.'

'And nothing to confirm the time you started your journey?'

I thought for a moment. 'No.'

'And you say it took you four and a half hours to reach Dittisham?'

'Well – a little less. I arrived between seven-fifteen and seven-thirty. But longer than usual, certainly. The traffic was terrible. There was a crash on the M4 near Swindon, a big tailback.'

'No one saw you arrive at Dittisham?'

'Not that I'm aware of, no. Someone in the village, maybe.'

'You came through the village?'

'It's the only way to the house.'

'What car were you driving?'

'My BMW.' A memory stirred. 'But I did stop for petrol.'

'Where was this?'

'I can never remember the name of the place. It's on the motorway somewhere this side of Bristol. But I'll have the receipt somewhere.'

A glimmer of something like disappointment showed in Henderson's face. 'So what time would this have been?'

'I don't know. About five-thirty, I suppose. Maybe even later. Six, possibly. The jam was terrible.'

Henderson leant back in his chair and eyed me thoughtfully before saying to Tingwall, 'Perhaps this receipt could be found?'

Tingwall played hard to get. 'I'll look into it,' he said.

Henderson brought his attention back to me. 'So you didn't see anyone when you arrived at Dittisham?'

I was finding this a strain and made no effort to hide it. 'No,' I sighed heavily.

'You went straight to your late father's house?'

'Yes.'

We established that on arriving I had done some fairly normal things like putting on lights, having a drink, taking a look around.

'And then?'

'I went into Dartmouth to buy some food.' Anticipating the next question, I added, 'It must have been about eight-thirty when I got to the Co-op and found it shut.'

'If I may interrupt,' Tingwall cut in smoothly. 'It couldn't have been any later than eight when Mr Wellesley arrived in town.'

There was a silence while we stared expectantly at Tingwall.

'My client's brother, Dr David Wellesley, left a meeting in the town just before eight and saw Mr Wellesley driving along Duke Street shortly afterwards.'

'Dr Wellesley is sure about that?' Henderson asked.

'Quite certain.'

'Was he alone?'

'Was who alone?' Tingwall asked, deliberately choosing to be obtuse.

'Doctor Wellesley.'

Tingwall pulled an expression of exaggerated surprise, as if he couldn't imagine the relevance of the question. 'I *believe* so, yes. I could check, of course. But, er, there's no doubt about the time and place.'

'And he can make a statement to that effect?'

'If *necessary*, of course.'

Henderson turned back to me with a fusion of disappointment and irritation written on his face. He had thought I was his man, and he didn't like the idea of getting it wrong.

'And your wife arrived at about nine?' he asked mechanically.

'Yes.'

'And you were together for the rest of the weekend?'

'Yes.'

'Very well, Mr Wellesley, that'll be all for the moment,' he said crisply, pushing his chair back. 'But I'd be grateful if this petrol receipt could be found,' he said to Tingwall. 'And I'd like Mr

61

Wellesley to return in the morning to make a formal statement, if he would be agreeable. And I'd be grateful if Mrs Wellesley could make a short statement too.'

Catching my glance, Tingwall launched into negotiations over Ginny, asking if a statement was really necessary, and if so, whether she couldn't make it in London. Then they moved on to David's statement and whether that was really necessary either, but by that time I was hardly listening. I was adjusting to the idea that I seemed to be off the hook.

*

David slowed as we approached the entrance to Furze Lodge. 'Sure you won't change your mind?'

'No,' I said. 'Thanks anyway.'

'The children'll be doing their own thing. They won't bother you. I'm lucky if they talk to *me*.'

'It's not that. Really.'

David shrugged as he accelerated past the gates. 'There mightn't be any bedding at Dittisham, you know. Mary's been clearing things out.'

'I'll find something. Don't worry. I just need to crash out . . .' I explained lamely.

'Fine.'

For several minutes we continued in silence towards Dittisham, with only the hiss of the wipers and the swish of the wet tyres and the blurred beams of the headlights on the shining road ahead.

Since picking me up from the police station David had talked almost continuously, a dry monologue about tying up the last details of Pa's estate, about the children's progress at school; about anything except what had just happened. I was grateful not to have to talk, I needed time to regain my equilibrium, but now there was something I had to say. 'I'm not sure you did the right thing, you know – telling Tingwall that – but thanks anyway.'

He knew perfectly well what I was referring to but affected a lack of interest and understanding.

I said it for both of us: 'Telling Tingwall you saw me in town.' I had already broached this at the beginning of the journey, but he hadn't responded then either. 'But look, David, I don't want you to get yourself into a corner.'

'Don't be ridiculous!'

'You say that, but what happens if they find out? Who knows, I might have been seen somewhere else at eight, driving through Dittisham, something like that.'

'But you *did* go into town about then, didn't you?' And he threw me a look of complete innocence.

'David – it was more like eight-thirty.'

He tossed a hand in the air. 'A few minutes. So what?'

'Half an hour,' I argued unhappily.

He slowed to take the steep hill down through the village. 'I wouldn't worry about it.'

'Wouldn't it be best not to tie yourself to a definite time, though, just in case?'

'Really, Hugh.' He shook his head as if I were a total mystery to him.

A whorl of leaves spun across our path as we turned through the gates of Dittisham House. The security lights blinked on, the shrubs glinted darkly, we rounded the slight bend and the house rose up before us, its tall windows gaping blackly like empty eyes. This was the moment I had been dreading, the moment when the memories would pounce. And for an instant the images did rear up, of Sylvie leaning lazily against the french windows, the sunlight making a halo of her hair, and then, like turning the page of an album, a darker picture took its place, of Sylvie on the boat, shivering in my sweater, hair dripping wet, mouth poised provocatively in that laughing way of hers.

Then we parked, the wind shivered against the car and the images faded. I thought that if this was the worst it would get then I would survive it.

Something was different about the house but in the shadowy beams of the outside lights it took me a moment to work out what it was. The ceanothus that covered much of the stonework, forming a ledge for the upstairs windows and an arch for the porch, had come away from the wall and fallen, broken and shrivelled, onto the gravel in a forlorn heap of rotting leaves. Pa had only been dead a few months, yet already the place seemed to have acquired a long-abandoned air. For a moment I felt so woebegone that I considered going to stay at David's after all.

'Lucky to be getting the price for this place, you know,' David remarked. 'Not many houses fetching the full whack nowadays.'

'It's the water,' I suggested. 'People love the idea of water.'

David, having chosen to live inland, wasn't ready to admit to the drawing power of the river. 'Mmm,' he grunted dubiously. 'It's a good-sized house, remember. Not so many of those around.'

And not so many that were quite so pretty either. An early-nineteenth-century villa with an Edwardian extension, it had floor-length windows and on the river side two bays with a verandah supported by iron trellises. The garden fell in a succession of two terraces and a lawn to the river below.

'Drink?' I asked brightly.

David hesitated, and I realised how much I wanted him to accept.

'But if you can't . . .' I offered immediately. 'If you have to get back . . .'

'Well . . . Unless you're desperate?'

I was desperate to talk, but this wouldn't be what David had in mind. For him a couple of stiff drinks were a palliative against the trials of the day, not an excuse for unburdening the soul, an exercise he had always regarded with the greatest suspicion.

'No, I'm fine,' I said.

'You've got a key?'

'I left one in the porch, thanks.' I pushed open the door and the wind swooped into the car. I couldn't leave without saying, 'You were dead right, by the way.'

'Oh?'

The wind shook the door, threatening to slam it, and I pulled it shut again.

'About what the police had in mind. I was meant to be the jealous lover.'

David gave a derisive grunt. 'I told you, they're cretins.'

He restarted the engine and, still shaking his head, waited for me to get out.

'Look, when you said she had lovers—'

He made a face. 'Did I?'

'Yesterday. You said she was all over the place, that she had several lovers,' I persisted.

He shrugged dismissively. 'It was just gossip.'

'But this gossip – did it mention me?' I was still brooding over what had brought the police to my door.

'No, *no.*'

'Nobody even hinted . . . ?'

'No! There was no mention of any names. It was nothing like that.'

'What about the chap with long hair, the one she went around with? Presumably the police are on to him?'

'God only knows. Really, I have no idea.'

'You'd think the police would be on to him.'

'Perhaps they are,' he said briskly.

But still I couldn't leave it alone. After the events of the last week I had to talk to someone. 'The thing is . . . well, I didn't quite tell them everything. You see, I did see something of Sylvie this summer. More than I said I did, anyway. She . . . I—'

'Look, I'd forget it, if I were you,' he cut in, his eyes alight with impatience or anger. 'I wouldn't discuss it with anyone.'

I felt like saying: Since when were you anyone? With an effort I stayed silent, but the reproach must have shown in my face because he made a grudging gesture of appeasement. 'Best to let things lie.'

'I wasn't actually planning on talking to a whole lot of people about it,' I protested.

'Not with anyone,' he repeated in the tone of a stern parent.

It's amazing how your family can undermine you, how in the space of a few words they can catch you unawares and demolish your confidence. What did David imagine I might be about to admit to? What did he think I knew? When we were young he had had a talent for putting me down, for ridiculing my efforts, and for an instant I felt echoes of old humiliations and childish resentments, the younger brother once more.

We said a stiff goodnight. Watching him drive off, I felt relieved to be alone.

The house was cold but once I had turned on some lights and put a match to the gas fire in Pa's study the gloom soon lifted. The good furniture had gone to the salerooms some weeks ago, but the heavy damask curtains still hung at the windows, the carpets and older rugs remained, Pa's battered kneehole desk still straddled one corner, and there was a comfortable chair to pull up to the fire.

The Scotch wasn't on the mantelpiece where I had last seen it and for an anxious moment I thought Mary or Mrs Perry, the cleaner, had removed it, but after a quick hunt I found it standing in solitary state in the cupboard where the family photo albums had always lived. There were no albums there now, and I assumed the family mementoes were accumulating at Furze Lodge with David and Mary.

I poured myself a hefty measure and took several large gulps before topping the glass up again. Until this summer I'd never been a great drinker – I'd never particularly liked the sensation of losing my wits – but tonight like a few other nights recently I wanted a small measure of oblivion.

The wind was racketing in the chimneys, the windows were humming and rattling to a frenetic rhythm and, outside, the rushing trees sounded as though they were about to storm the house.

The phone made me start. Imbued with the day's paranoia, I considered not answering it.

'There you are,' gasped Ginny when I finally picked up the receiver. 'How did it go?'

'Not an experience I'd like to repeat.'

'But it's over?'

I gave a pale laugh. 'I sincerely hope so.'

'They've finished with you?'

'It looks like it.'

She made a slight sound, an exhalation or a sigh. 'Well, thank God for that.' A pause, then: 'You're staying there?'

'I'll get a train back tomorrow.'

'When will you arrive?'

'In the afternoon some time. Not sure when.' I didn't say I had to go to Exeter first to make the statement.

A hesitation, then she said in a rush, 'Why did they want you back? What was it all about?'

'I've no idea.'

'But there must have been a reason,' she said, and there was an edge to her voice.

'They didn't say, Ginny. But they want you to make a statement, I'm afraid.'

'What do you mean?'

'It's a routine thing,' I said, playing it down. 'Establishing where everyone was. They just want to confirm that we met up at nine that night and left for London on Sunday evening.'

She didn't reply.

'Ginny?'

'When? When do I have to make this statement?'

'There's no hurry, I don't think. There's this lawyer Charles Tingwall who's arranging it for us. He's fixing it so you can do yours in London. It won't be very complicated.'

'And it's a routine thing, you say? They're asking everyone?'

'Well – people who were around,' I lied.

I could hear her breathing, always a sign that she was getting tense. 'I see.'

'I'll tell you more tomorrow. All right?'

Another pause, and I knew she was working up to something. 'But why did they want to see you? Please tell me. They must have given you a reason.'

'They didn't.'

'What did they ask you, then? What sort of questions?'

'Look, I'll tell you all about it tomorrow.'

'Will you?' I caught a note of accusation in her voice.

'Of course.'

'Of course,' she echoed in a tone of open scepticism.

'Sorry?'

'Nothing.'

'Ginny – they had it all wrong.'

'Did they?'

Suddenly I felt beleaguered. Where was the unconditional family support? First David, now Ginny. Suppressing a dart of self-pity, I said, 'Tomorrow, Ginny. Let's talk about it tomorrow.'

Her voice broke slightly as she said a curt 'Fine', and I could picture the uncertainty and reproach in her face. I nearly called her back, I fully intended to, but, unable to face more questions, I poured myself another Scotch instead.

I took my drink to the window and stared out into the darkness. A light on the far side of the river blinked through the flickering branches, the wind whistled in the eaves. Draining my glass, I pulled at the bolts of the french windows and walked out into the blustering gale. Crossing the stone terrace to the steps, I felt my way down to the next level where sodden grass pulled at my shoes. A last flight of steps and I was descending the sloping lawn towards the water. The arches of the pergola rose dimly to one side, the bare branches of the fruit trees swished angrily near by, the deeper blackness of the summerhouse loomed somewhere to the right. Misjudging the distance, I almost walked into the low wall that marked the river boundary.

The wind was barrelling down the deep cut of the river, pulling at my jacket, buffeting my ears, and it was much colder. The darkness was so thick that I couldn't make out the state of the tide, whether the water was high or there was a sea of mud, though I fancied I could hear the rip of the ebb close by. A sprinkling of lights gave height and form to the ridges and creeks of the opposite banks, while away to my right the lights of Dittisham and the ferry landing gave shape to the curve of the river. But the water itself was hidden, a secretive ribbon of ink coursing towards the sea.

Somewhere in front of me was *Ellie Miller*, lying to her mooring, her squat shape lost against the greater blackness of the night. No cabin lights showing now, no laughter echoing across the water, no lazy rippling of the tide in the warm summer air. Maybe it was the drink, maybe it was the tensions of the day, but I felt such a jumble of emotions that my eyelids pricked with fierce heat and I gasped for breath. Visions came: of water pressing into Sylvie's mouth and eyes, of her body bumping against the rocks, of unspeakable wounds in her flesh. The images were vivid yet curiously opaque, like my images of Sylvie as she had been in life. I saw her clearly: I saw her dimly.

She was fearless and exhilarating and proud; she was distant and elusive and cold. She was open and devious; she was sensuous and cruel and base. I realised then that she would baffle me just as thoroughly in death as she had confused me in life.

I turned away and stumbled up the slope. Above the thrashing of the trees I heard a baleful cry. I stopped. It rose again, a chilling sound carried high on the wind. It seemed to come from the river, and in a moment of disorientation and fear my nightmare roared back to life and everything stalled inside me, my heart and breathing seized, and I was overcome by a sensation of imminent disaster.

The next whoop brought me bumping back to reality. It was a very human sound, very much in the present. Looking up the slope I saw a figure outlined against the french windows.

'There you are!' sang Mary as I climbed the last of the steps and entered the pool of light. Drawing me inside the house, she gave a theatrical shiver. 'Wow, it's wild out there!' Railing against the climate, she pulled the windows shut and drew the curtains. 'I've brought some sheets for you!' she declared heartily. 'And some breakfast. Can't have you camping! But how are you? I want to know how you are!'

I couldn't hide my feelings, perhaps I didn't try, because when she took a better look at me her face creased into a picture of concern. 'Oh, Hugh!' she sighed. 'That bad?'

'Just a bit tired and emotional.' I laughed to make it sound like a joke. I went in search of another glass. 'I'm awfully glad to see you.'

'You should have come and stayed with us, you twit. But I know –' she added with a laugh and a flip of the wrist '– the kids are home for the weekend! You're not the only one. They get too much for me sometimes. All those teenage moods. All that ghastly music – rock or rap or whatever it is.'

I fetched a chair from Pa's desk and offered her a whisky which she accepted with a show of conspiratorial glee, as though drinking was always a bit of a lark.

We sat on either side of the fire.

'So,' she grimaced sympathetically. 'What a beastly day for you.'

'Yes, as days go . . .' I sank back into my chair. 'Cumberland put another million quid on the price of the buyout. Just when we'd raised most of the money.'

'I hope that wasn't Howard's doing.'

'Oh . . . I wouldn't have thought so.'

Perhaps it was my hesitation, perhaps it was something in my tone, but Mary rolled her eyes and sighed, 'Oh, you don't have to hide it from me. Nothing surprises me about my brother. You know, I'll be glad when the buyout's over and our two families never work together again.' She tutted, 'But this extra money – will you be able to raise it?'

'I don't honestly know.'

'It's too bad, after all your efforts . . .' She watched me for a moment. 'Now what about the police? Were they horrible?' Her tone was feisty, like a warrior who at the slightest provocation would take up cudgels in my defence.

'It may seem crazy,' I said, 'but for a while back there I really thought they were going to lock me up.'

She wasn't sure how seriously she was meant to take this and her mouth jerked into an uncertain smile. 'Poor Hugh! How awful!'

'They seemed so *fixed* on me. That's what was so bloody terrifying.'

She looked fierce again. 'They gave you a bad time?'

'It felt like it, but then I haven't exactly got a lot of experience to measure it against. But you know the worst thing? It was not knowing why they'd called me in. Was my crime to have been seen with Sylvie? Christ, if that's a crime! Or did they think they had something else on me – you know, something they didn't tell me about? I suppose that's how they get people,' I laughed grimly. 'By making them think they know something damning about them.'

'Skunks!' Mary declared. 'It's just bullying, isn't it?' Taking a gulp of her drink, she eyed me over the rim of her glass. 'They didn't give you any idea then? What it was?'

I shook my head. 'With all these lovers she was meant to have, you'd have thought they'd have had plenty of other candidates to interview.'

Mary looked at me with open interest. 'She had lots of lovers?'

'According to David.'

'Really?' Her eyes flashed, she gave a sudden snort. 'Well, well! We all knew about the youth with the long hair – at least, we *assumed* he was the lover – but as for the rest ... Mmm!' She widened her eyes in anticipation of disclosures to come. 'I must get David to tell me more.'

'He says he doesn't know any more. It was just a rumour.'

'A rumour. Ahh.' She looked away into the fire, then, trying to lift my mood: 'But they're satisfied now, the police?'

I considered this. 'You know something? I'm really not sure. I have this feeling that they'll come back.'

'Come back ... But, Hugh, that's ridiculous – why should they?' Yet the question wasn't entirely rhetorical, there was curiosity behind it, and I realised that Mary, like the rest of my family, didn't seem to have ruled out the possibility that I had something to hide.

'I was going to ask *you* actually,' I said. 'Was I meant to be having an affair with Sylvie? Was the neighbourhood buzzing with it? If so I'd really like someone to tell me because I seem to be the last to know.'

'I've never heard anything.' But her tone was so hedged with reservations, her manner so strained, that I looked up sharply. Taking the opportunity with obvious relief, she said, 'Look, Hugh, I'd better tell you – it's just possible Mrs Perry may have told the police something.'

'Mrs *Perry*? But what?'

'That she saw your car outside Sylvie Mathieson's cottage. In fact ... well' – she made a regretful face – 'we both did. I was driving her, you see. Her car had broken down, she hadn't been here for weeks, and the place was getting so dirty that I drove her here one day and picked her up again when she'd finished. And on the way back we saw your car ...'

Something folded in me then, my defences evaporated, and all the accumulated tensions spilled out in a rush of dread. 'Oh God ...'

Mary asked tentatively, 'You, er . . . didn't tell the police you'd been there?'

'No.' I clasped a hand over my eyes.

I heard her scramble to her feet. Crouching beside my chair, she gave me a rough comradely hug. 'Hugh, they can't make too much out of that.'

'No?' I exclaimed bitterly. 'They'll assume I've lied about everything, won't they?'

She sat back on her sturdy haunches. 'But an assumption? That's nothing, *nothing*.'

I looked into her strong irrepressible face, I saw the concern there, and the fierce loyalty, and I said, 'Mary . . . It wasn't the only thing I didn't tell them about.'

She said in a small voice, 'Oh dear.'

Neither of us spoke for a long moment, then she said almost gruffly, 'Do you want to tell me about it?'

Aware that I was taking a step whose consequences I hadn't begun to consider but not caring too much, I said weakly, 'It's a complete mess, Mary.'

'Hugh . . . don't be silly!' She grasped my shoulder and shook it, as if to imbue me with optimism. 'Wait . . .' Getting up, she replenished our glasses from the bottle on the mantel before pulling her chair closer and sitting down with a look of anxious concentration.

'I don't know where to start . . .'

But I did know. I knew exactly where I should start if I was going to make any sense of it. 'There was this dreadful week,' I began slowly. 'A nightmare week at the end of the most appalling month.' I paused. 'I think I cracked up a bit . . .' I thought about this. 'Yes – that was it, really. At the end of the day, Mary, I think I went off my head.'

FOUR

'D avid called it depression. He even prescribed me anti-depressants. Typical David! If only it'd been that simple. Pop the pills and lose your troubles! But it wasn't depression, you see. Not in the way he meant it anyway. It was sheer disbelief. Everything was going wrong and I couldn't seem to do anything to stop it. The business was in trouble and still sliding, the banks were moving in for their pound of flesh, and it suddenly hit me – I mean, quite suddenly, in the period of a day or so – that we were in real danger of losing the company. And then . . .' It was still mortifying to say it. 'Howard was going behind my back, setting up the takeover. It took me for ever to realise it. God, I was so slow! Good old Hugh – blind to the obvious!' My laugh sounded bitter to my ears.

'And then . . . things were difficult at home. Ginny thought – well, I don't know what she thought, that was half the trouble – but we started to disagree over nothing, everything. There was this awful *wall* between us. We couldn't seem to make contact. We seemed to wear each other down the whole time. And the money . . . She couldn't see how desperately we needed to cut down, she had this blind spot. She just . . .' But my words were stifled by the peculiar mixture of exasperation and guilt that Ginny always seemed to engender in me, and I returned to less confusing ground. 'You know the worst thing, though, about the company? The worst thing was knowing that it was my own stupidity, my own pig-headed bloody idiocy that had got us into trouble.'

'Come on – what about Howard?' Mary protested. 'It must have been his fault too.'

73

'Oh, Howard didn't know any better,' I exclaimed sweep-ingly. 'Howard was the ideas man, always had been, while my talent, such as it was, was for keeping us on the tracks financially. That was the theory anyway. But then I completely lost it! I let myself get seduced by ideas of easy money and limitless expansion. Pure conceit. I thought I knew best, you see! Prudence, restraint, all the things Pa had preached – well, they were just quaint and outdated, weren't they? Leverage was the name of the game. You borrowed up to the hilt, you traded right up to your limits.'

'But the board, the accountants,' Mary argued, 'they should have realised, surely?'

'They were under Howard's spell, just like the rest of us. And everything seemed to go so well at first, you see. Profits booming. Sales rocketing. Except for poor old Hartford, of course, which was left in the dumps.'

'So it all seemed hopeless?' she said, drawing me back to the story.

'Not immediately, no. For a long time I believed the situation could be salvaged. I worked like mad on the restructuring plan, I took a pay cut – half my salary. I really thought I could get it all together.'

'Then?'

'Then . . .' The memory caught me with fresh force. 'Then I realised what Howard was up to.'

I found out purely by chance. One day my driver was off sick and it was Howard's driver, Brian, who chauffeured me to our bankers for yet another fraught meeting on restructuring – a City euphemism for raising more money at heavy cost. I made some remark about the traffic and Brian launched into a stream of good-natured complaint about contraflows and roadworks, and how it was getting increasingly difficult to outmanoeuvre them. Stafford last week had been a particular challenge, he told me, because an accident on the M6 had caused a ten-mile tailback.

I thought of reasons for Howard to go to Stafford, I came up with a few, all perfectly plausible, yet, even as I tried to talk myself into believing them, a single thought chimed insistently in my mind: that Cumberland had its headquarters in Stafford, along with three of its four factories.

Watching Brian in the rear-view mirror, I went through a show of searching my memory. 'Ah yes . . . that was Howard's meeting with – who was it?'

Brian was about to reply when his eyes jumped guiltily and there was an awkward pause before he mumbled something unconvincing about some lunch engagement Howard had had at a hotel whose name he couldn't recall. When he dropped me off he was still looking uneasy, and then I knew all I needed to know.

Over the years I had discovered that there were only two ways of approaching Howard on subjects he wasn't ready to discuss. One was to lift his mood with a joke; the other was to tackle him head-on, with something approaching aggression.

The next morning as soon as he was free I strode into his office and planted myself in front of his desk. I hadn't slept much the night before, my nerves were humming, and I could feel a pulse beating high in my head. Howard glanced up from some report and raised a lazy eyebrow.

'Tell me about Cumberland,' I said.

He sank back in his chair. He took his time. I could almost see his mind working. 'Cumberland?'

'You've had a meeting with them?'

'There's no need to get upset, Hugh,' he said smoothly. 'I was just opening out our options. The beginning of a contingency plan, if you like. Something to consider if the banks get threatening.'

A wild inarticulate anger rose over me, I had to clamp my lips together to stop them trembling. 'How could you?' I knew it was the wrong thing to say to Howard, for whom a moral stance was always a source of irritation, but I was beyond discretion.

'Look, it's no good taking an emotional line on this,' he intoned in his most infuriating way. 'That's been half our trouble, Hugh. No objectivity.'

I couldn't begin to work out what objectivity had to do with betrayal. I said unsteadily, 'Behind my *back*, Howard.'

'Don't be ridiculous!' he declared. 'It was just a preliminary chat to see how the ground lay. Nothing to get excited about. I was going to talk to you about it today. I mean, just *think* about it, Hugh,' he argued archly, 'I could hardly progress anything without you, could I?'

'And how *does* the ground lie, Howard?'

Reverting to old mannerisms, he gave a cat-like smile and dropped a half-wink in an expression that wouldn't have looked amiss on a used-car dealer. 'I tell you – they're rather hot for us! Oh, they're not letting on, of course, but they'd be mad not to progress the idea and they know it.'

'And what exactly is the idea, Howard? A takeover?'

He looked offended. 'God, no! A merger. A *merger*,' he repeated, as if I were incapable of taking it in first time. 'Integration of administration, distribution and sales. Big savings to be made, Hugh, big savings.'

'And where would Hartford fit into this?'

He tightened his lips and slowly shook his head as though I had conjured up this remark just to try him. 'Hartford is a great asset, Hugh. Nobody's going to throw it away, now are they?'

Staring at him then, I wondered which of us had gone mad, whether he had always been like this or I was the one who had changed. It seemed incredible that we had ever worked happily together, or that I had ever trusted him.

But even then I hadn't really grasped the situation. 'No more clandestine meetings,' I warned him. 'No more going behind my back, Howard. No more going behind the board's back!'

The way his eyes slid away, the knowing look that drifted across his face told me the rest of the story.

'I *see*. How silly of me,' I said bitterly. 'You've been setting the scene for the board, have you?'

'Hugh, all this anger really doesn't help, you know. I do wish we could discuss this rationally.' He gave a small sigh and waited, as though a little sensible reflection would cause me to see the childishness of my ways.

'And your family?' I asked as levelly as possible.

'My family are all in favour of finding a happy conclusion.'

A suspicion leapt into my mind. 'And *my* family? Where do they stand?'

He spread his hands, the picture of baffled innocence. 'I wouldn't know. But presumably they're aware of how precarious the situation is? Presumably they've read the financial reports? I mean – I *presume*.'

He wanted me to see through him. He wanted me to think he'd already persuaded my family to vote for a takeover. He wanted me to think it, and, hating myself for being so easily manipulated, I did.

'Thanks for letting me know,' I said tightly.

Howard shook his head again and pulled himself indolently to his feet. He paused, running his hand down his tie as if to test its smoothness. 'Sometimes it's important to remember that there's no disgrace in making money, Hugh. No disgrace in cashing in one's hard-earned assets and reaping the rewards of success.'

'*Success?*' Sometimes Howard simply robbed me of speech.

'Success.' He lifted his head to the sound of it. 'You seem to have a problem with that, Hugh.'

'No, Howard, no. I don't have a problem with that.'

I stopped sleeping then. I spent hours staring into the darkness, burning with disbelief. The shock wasn't so much that Howard was prepared to sell the business out – he had absolutely no sentimentality where money was concerned – but that after all our years together he was prepared to treat me with such contempt.

In the next couple of days I embarked on a frantic damage limitation exercise. I phoned each of the board in turn, I threw together a paper listing the reasons a merger would be a bad idea, but of course Howard had been there ahead of me. He'd laid his ground very carefully. He'd already won them over.

'It was then I began to lose heart, Mary. Or to lose faith in myself, which probably amounted to the same thing. I began to question things I hadn't questioned in a long time. Wondering why on earth I'd been slaving away for most of my working life if it was to get stabbed in the back by my partner.'

Mary nodded ruefully at this. She never took exception to criticism of Howard; sometimes she actively endorsed it.

'I thought of all the years that had just vanished – just *gone*. I thought of the hours I'd worked, all the evenings and weekends I'd never got home, all the time I'd never found for Ginny . . .'

'She never seemed to mind too much.'

'Oh, she never complained. But it mattered. It mattered a lot. We were always in such a rush that in the end I think we simply forgot how to talk.' I grasped at a new realisation and floated it tentatively. 'Or we were frightened to talk. I think there may have been something of that too. We were frightened in case we had to face up to how . . . *wrong* things were. How very differently things had turned out from the way we'd expected.'

Mary leant forward and turned the fire down.

'And then . . . oh, it was everything, really. I began to think a lot about Pa. How much I missed the old devil – you know? And how little time I'd found for him towards the end.'

'Not your fault.'

'Oh, but I should have *made* time, Mary. You can always make time if you really try. I didn't try hard enough. I think I was ashamed. I didn't want to have to tell him how badly the business was doing. I didn't want to admit how everything he'd worked for was slipping away.' Halted by force of memory, I felt a fresh pull of affection and loss. The old man had maddened me sometimes, especially when I was a young man; he had been forceful and opinionated, he had been shamelessly paternalistic, particularly towards women, my mother included, but he had also been a spectacularly successful human being, full of warmth and feeling, and ingrained with a strong sense of duty and loyalty.

'So you were feeling pretty low?'

'Low? Yes – *low*. But you know something?'

Mary shook her head, and her sharp eyes did not leave my face.

'The idea of losing the business was terrible, of course it was, but I would have bounced back all right. I was stunned – yes, and angry, too – but it was more of a *reaction* than a state of mind. I hadn't really given up. I was just exhausted, utterly wiped out. All I needed, really, was some sleep and the chance to work things out. A bit of time, that was all.'

78

Mary read my expression and raised an eyebrow. 'But you didn't get it?'

'It wasn't Ginny's fault,' I insisted, betraying my guilts. 'People, fund-raising, parties . . . It was her whole life. I'd left her alone so much, what else did she have?'

Mary's face was still, deliberately so.

I continued to argue unhappily, 'What else did she have? No, whatever went wrong, Mary, it wasn't Ginny's fault.'

It was on the Friday at breakfast – the first breakfast we'd managed to have together in some time – that I realised what sort of a weekend lay ahead.

Ginny peered at me and exclaimed, 'Oh, such woe!'

I arranged my face into something more cheerful and mumbled about bankers giving us a hard time, and how life would be a lot easier without them.

When I picked up the newspaper she turned away to make the orange juice. The whir of the electric squeezer rose to a sudden shriek. 'This thing's playing up,' she tutted. 'I might buy us one of those shiny steel things. You know, the smart Italian jobs that look like cappuccino machines.'

She poured the juice into a glass and wiped her slender fingers on a cloth. She stood in profile, the glossy fall of her hair tucked behind one ear, her features unreadable, and for an instant she seemed like a stranger, someone I had always known yet hardly knew at all. I looked away abruptly because the idea frightened me so much.

She put the juice on the counter and, sliding onto the stool opposite, flicked her hair back from her forehead with a characteristic sweep of her hand. 'I thought I'd leave about ten, as soon as the fish man delivers,' she announced in the light rapid tones she used to discuss arrangements. 'You did order enough wine, didn't you, darling? It's soup then fish then duck, remember.'

It came back to me then that we were having one of our social weekends in Wiltshire. Ginny always went down to Melton early to make sure everything was ready. 'How many people?' I asked, trying not to think of the expense.

'Twelve. And Cook thinks the pudding could do with some dessert wine. Is that all right, darling? I mean, I would organise it, but . . .' She gave a tiny shrug. She took a strange pride in boasting that she knew absolutely nothing about wine, except whether it was any good or not, which she could establish at the first sip.

Weekends at Melton followed a pattern. We gave a dinner party on the Friday or Saturday with never less than four courses produced by a hired cook we referred to as Cook, and served by the male half of our housekeeping couple masquerading as a butler. On the Saturday we went to some sporting event with our house guests – usually racing or polo – and on whichever evening we were not entertaining we dined at another large house. On Sunday nights, if no guests were staying on, I caught up with some of my paperwork before getting up at five-thirty to drive to London.

'You'll be sitting next to Lady Werner,' Ginny informed me. 'She's on lots of boards and welfare organisations. Limps a bit, injured herself hunting years ago, still very horsy. They've got lots in training, Derby-winners and things . . .'

I tried to speak, but Ginny was at full gallop.

'. . . But she's a trustee of the family charitable trust, you see, along with Sir Frank – they run it together – and they give big donations . . . well, the trust does. We might get as much as fifty thousand for three years running. And they're awfully nice really—'

'Ginny—!' It came out more harshly than I meant it to.

Her eyes widened, her mouth twitched. 'What?'

I was going to bring up the subject of our expenses, but I faltered. I wasn't sure I could face the inevitable upset. I could never work out if Ginny believed against all the evidence that she was cutting back, or whether she was simply incapable of doing so, but whenever I mentioned the subject she grew so prickly and defensive that reasonable discussion became virtually impossible.

'Nothing,' I said hastily. 'Anything else I need to do for the weekend?'

'Absolutely not,' she declared with the touchy pride of a born organiser. Then, eyeing me: 'What on earth's the matter?'

'Just desperately tired, that's all.'

'I can never understand why you have to do it all. Why can't some of these people take the work off your hands?'

But I didn't have the energy to explain. 'They just can't.'

When she realised I wasn't going to elaborate she tightened her mouth and went to fetch fresh coffee. Returning, she rested her small chin on her hands and blinked rapidly, a sure sign that she was nervous of whatever she was about to say. 'By the way,' she began with studied casualness, 'Eddie Maynard's going off to that shooting school for a weekend course. He wanted to know if you were interested in going with him, but I said you were far too busy—'

'Ginny,' I said with more patience than I was feeling, 'it's not a matter of being too busy. I'm simply not interested in shooting, and that's all there is to it.'

'But you used to be.'

'No, Ginny. I may have said once—'

'More than once.'

'Only as a sort of joke,' I protested.

'I see,' she said in a small voice, as if I had altered my story simply to make her look foolish.

She had clung to this ridiculous hope that I would take up shooting for some time; why, I could never fathom. I loathed guns and it saddened me to see wild ducks hanging in people's game larders.

'Having a place in the country doesn't mean we have to do what country people do.' I realised too late how critical this sounded.

'It's not that!' she protested, breathing fast. 'You seem to think I want you to take it up for some ... some ...' She agitated her hand. 'For some *snobbish* reason! I just thought how lovely it'd be for you to have an interest down there, something that'd give you a bit of exercise and fresh air. And you make it sound ...' She was gasping for air now, wheezing from low in her chest. I fetched her inhaler from the basket in the corner of the kitchen. Grabbing it, she pulled two squirts into her lungs.

I dropped an arm lightly round her shoulders. 'Darling, I didn't mean it like that.'

'Oh yes you did,' she cried between gulps.

'I just like to relax at Melton, that's all.'

She fought to speak. Eventually, after an agonising pull on her lungs, she managed to gasp, 'You really think other people's opinions are important to me! It's so insulting!'

I dropped wearily onto the stool next to her.

'That's what you think, isn't it?' she demanded.

What I really thought came to me with the clarity that only unhappiness can bring: that it was in Ginny's nature to strive for perfection, that she couldn't bear any area of our lives to fall short of some far-reaching ideal, and that, by setting herself such high standards, she doomed both of us to constant struggle. With this insight came another, equally clear: that I was deeply weary of this self-imposed burden, that I would gladly leave it all behind.

'I think it'd be nice to slow down a bit,' I said.

She cast me a guarded look. 'Slow down . . .? In what way?'

'Try not to do quite so much.'

'You mean – my charity work?'

'Of course not, no! I meant, see friends less often. Have more evenings to ourselves.'

She was fighting for breath again. 'But we don't see people *that* often! And you've always said you loved seeing them! And now suddenly . . . ! You're being very confusing, Hugh. And very unfair!'

'It's partly the expense,' I said, grasping the nettle. 'We have to cut back.'

She cast me a look of quiet injury, as if I had broken all the rules of fair argument. 'I know that,' she said stiffly.

'Any joy with the accounts?' I tried to hit a light note, absolutely free of reproach.

She gave a long rasping cough and reached for her inhaler again. 'I've had a look through the bills, if that's what you mean.'

'You can see, then, that we're way over budget.'

'But we never had a budget, darling! You talk about this budget as if it was something passed at a board meeting.' Her eyes were exceptionally bright, close to anger or tears. 'I never knew anything about this budget until you invented it! You seem to think I've been spending money like water! D'you think I don't check the bills? D'you think I don't get the best prices? And I can't just cancel dinners arranged *months* ago. It's taken me a *year* to get the Werners to dinner, a whole year!'

'All I'm saying is that we really must cut back.'

'You make it sound as though it's my fault—'

'No, no,' I said hastily. 'Of course it's not your fault . . .'

'Provence was your idea!'

This was old ground. 'Yes.'

'And Melton.'

I let that one pass; it simply wasn't worth arguing about. 'Melton *has* to go as quickly as possible,' I said.

'D'you think I don't know that?' she cried. 'I've been on to the estate agent every day! *Every* day!'

I remembered other things, the redecorating of the drawing room here at Glebe Place that appeared to be going ahead though I thought we'd agreed to cancel it, and the housekeeper in Provence who was meant to have left last month but still seemed to be in place, and I got that sick clammy feeling I always got when I realised that our spending was still way out of control.

'I'm doing all I can!' Ginny declared, sparking with reproach. 'You make it sound as though I'm trying to make things worse or something!'

'Of course I don't think that. I just—' But a futility blocked my words.

Ginny's mouth was buttoned down in that expression of hurt and abandonment I knew so well, and, with a swoop of defeat, I reached for her hand. 'Sorry, sorry . . .' I wondered how many times we said sorry to each other in the course of an average tiff, and how little this immense weight of apology seemed to achieve.

'It's all right,' she said, with a glint of the uncertain humour she used to signal the end of our arguments. 'I'll cut down on the cat food and serve up leftovers and fire Consuela. And if all else fails I can always go on the streets.' She gave a brave little smile. 'Not past it yet.'

I took my cue. 'You can say that again. You'd make a fortune.'

As I put my arms round her I had the sensation of falling off the edge of my life and not being able to stop.

*

'Do you shoot?' asked Lady Werner.

'No, I'm afraid not.'

'Ride?'

'The last horse spotted my beginner's label at fifty yards and rubbed me off against a tree.'

Lady Werner had the generosity to laugh before turning to respond to the man on her right. It was a relief not to talk for a moment. I was finding conversation hard, partly because I'd drunk too much wine – I was making the most of the last of the good claret I'd laid down ten years ago – partly because my troubles kept blundering into the forefront of my mind, obstructing my words.

I stared dimly at the brilliant scene before me, at the banks of candles and flowers extending down the table, at the rich ruby glow of the wall hangings, at the blood-red and gold of the wine reflected off the crystal; I saw Ginny at the far end of the table, her marble complexion and fine-etched beauty perfectly framed by the vibrant colours around her. I watched her tilt her head towards Werner and listen with rapt attention, and I felt disconnected from the scene, like an imposter in some exotic spectacle.

When the party moved to the drawing room for coffee, I slipped away upstairs and sat in the quiet of the bathroom, gripping my head in my hands, staring unseeing at the carpet. When a return could be avoided no longer, I splashed cold water over my face and made my way back downstairs.

Fortunately Werner wasn't a demanding conversationalist. I only had to slip in the occasional nod or comment to keep him going for half an hour on the subject of art sponsorship. Harder to stomach was a lawyer called Hodgworth-Hill, whose smooth overbearing manner and open contempt for what he called the common herd began to grate on my overstretched nerves. I wondered why Ginny had asked him; I couldn't imagine he was involved in charity work. Listening to his gabble I felt a sudden upsurge of resentment. I had the suspicion he would be the last of the dinner guests to leave and I was right.

'But he's staying,' Ginny declared when I caught her in the hall.

'I told you! Come and play backgammon!' she urged with feverish gaiety. 'Come on! We'll set up two boards!'

She pulled at my hand but I mumbled an excuse about needing to go upstairs for a minute.

Her return to the drawing room was greeted with a cheer. I heard the bombastic tones of the lawyer, followed by shouts of raucous laughter and the clink of glasses, and something over-turned inside me. I stood there in the hall, trying to make sense of my raging thoughts, aware that I had reached some terrifying crisis but not absolutely sure what it was about, let alone how to contain it. I only knew that I couldn't face another moment among these people, that I had to get away.

Once the urge to flee overtook me, it became a desperate compulsion. I didn't stop to think where I would go or how long I would stay away, I didn't pause to consider Ginny, I only knew I had to escape. I raced upstairs and, throwing my evening clothes on the floor, pulled on some old jeans and a sweater. Pausing only to scribble a note to Ginny, I blundered out to my car and careered off.

It was madness to drive. I was way over the drink-driving limit, but the stupidity of what I was doing was lost in my greater panic and the need to feel that I was, in some muddled way, regaining a degree of control over my life.

I set out blindly, yet there was never any question of where I would go. Dittisham was the one place I could be alone, the one place where I would have a chance to think.

There was little traffic, the motorway was like a wide black tunnel, I had the sensation of flying. Somehow I stayed awake, miraculously I didn't kill anyone. Arriving at Dittisham in the dead of night, I wandered from room to room. I couldn't get over how quiet it was. The hush was miraculous, an all-enveloping cocoon of calm. It seemed to me that I had never really noticed it before, that my mind had been closed to such things for a long time.

Exhaustion made me maudlin. I felt a sudden longing for the past, for the simplicity and focus of my early life. I thought of my father and how much he had meant to me. I grasped at the

85

more elusive memories of my mother, dead for more than twenty years, and thought how little I had really known her.

Eventually I climbed the stairs and, hesitating outside the guest room Ginny and I had always used when we came to stay, passed on down the passage to the small room that had been mine as a boy. It was a storage room now, stacked with trunks and tea chests, but an old metal bed still stood in one corner, and, perched on a rickety table next to it, a lamp from my Indian travels, crowned by a parchment shade. Beneath the bed were my watercolours, hundreds of them, bundled into cardboard folders, relics of the years when I'd had the ambition to paint. It was many years since I had attempted any sort of picture.

Opening the window, I lay down on the hard mattress under an ancient blanket. There was hardly any wind, just a faint movement in the air, but it must have been wafting from the river because I could hear the faint lapping of water. Stupefied by the memories of a thousand untroubled nights, I slept like a child.

'Nothing gentle about the way David woke me, of course. Rattled the bed head. He wasn't too pleased with me.'

'Well, we hadn't had the best of nights,' Mary commented drily. 'Ginny called at something like two, then again half an hour later, not to mention the calls the next morning. We told her you probably weren't answering the phone, but she wanted David to go and find you there and then, in the middle of the night.'

'I didn't hear the phone, I'm afraid.'

'Why should you?' For the first time it struck me that Mary actively disapproved of Ginny's permanent state of edgy anxiety.

'I didn't mean to worry Ginny.'

'David flatly refused, of course. To go out and look for you. Until the morning anyway.'

'I wasn't leaving her – it was nothing like that,' I said, seeking to justify myself further. 'I never stopped loving her . . .' But in saying this I was no longer sure what I meant by love, and whether it must always contain so much effort and pain. 'She worked so hard at everything, at making our lives . . . *full*.'

Mary studied her drink. 'But you had to get away,' she reminded me.

Defending Ginny was something of a reflex with me, but for once I let it pass. 'Yes, I had to get away.'

'We all need space from time to time.'

'Yes.'

But my response was too half-hearted for Mary. 'Nothing wrong in that,' she argued.

'No. You're right.'

She nodded firmly.

'So . . . There was poor David,' I said, finding my way back into the story. 'He made the mistake of asking me what the matter was – and got the lot. All my angst, yards of it. The business, Howard, Pa's death. And of course, me and Ginny . . . It just poured out, I'm afraid.'

'I hope he was sympathetic.'

'Well, you know how he is. Not his strongest suit. But on the whole – yes. Apart from the one subject that he really should have learnt to leave well alone by now. He kept on about fertility treatment and whether Ginny'd tried the latest method, whatever its name is. He'd sent us some information about it. He was convinced that not having children was at the root of our problems, and however much I told him that it wasn't an issue he just listened with that maddening all-knowing expression on his face. Sometimes I think he sees absolutely everything in medical terms, even relationships.'

Mary raised her eyebrows slightly at this, but made no comment. She never voiced any grumbles about her marriage, although among the family it had long been acknowledged that my brother wasn't the easiest of people to live with.

'Anyway, at the end of it all he declared that I was just depressed, and gave me some tablets. Typical David! Nothing that can't be fixed by getting dosed up! Oh, don't get me wrong – I didn't really expect any more. I mean, David has quite enough on his plate, doesn't he? People's troubles all day long. No, it was enough to have someone to talk to – that was all I needed really.'

I looked into the fire. 'But then, Mary, the strangest thing, the strangest thing . . .' I hunched forward as the memory gripped me. 'We went down to the river – David wanted to look at the river wall or whatever it was that needed repairing – and I was rambling on about the past, about the summers we used to have, the golden times – I was still in a bit of state, I can tell you – and, talking about those years, the best years, I thought of Sylvie. Nothing too surprising about that – we'd spent that long summer together, do you remember? The one when it was really scorching?'

'I remember.'

'But the thing was – just as she came into my mind, at the very instant I thought of her, I looked across the river and there she was! I thought I was dreaming. Well, I thought I was seeing things, actually. Then I thought it must be someone else who looked just like her. She was in a dinghy with a whole lot of other people, going up river. But that hair, the way she sat, her profile ... David couldn't see the likeness, but for me it was blinding. I felt a great bolt of recognition and – well, I'm not sure what. Hope? Something like that. I couldn't get her out of my mind. I was overwhelmed ... bewitched. I had the strangest feeling – this sounds mad – that everything would be all right if I could get to see her again, that she would be able to *save* me in some way. Crazy! *Crazy!* But you have to remember I wasn't thinking straight. I still hadn't had much sleep – what time did David come over that morning? Seven? Eight? So, four hours at the most. I wasn't sure what was real any more. I told myself my mind was playing tricks. But somewhere deep down there was this tiny irrational ray of hope that it *was* her. Part of me was desperate for some sort of escape, I suppose, and Sylvie represented something precious and beautiful. She was my Avalon; or the *idea* of her ... I'd been so happy with her, you see. I'd felt so full of – *possibilities*. It was the only time in my life that I'd felt free.' The wind roared outside, the house creaked like an old ship. I looked up. 'I don't know – is this making any sense?'

She gave a slight nod, though her eyes seemed to have taken on a harsher, more judgmental light.

'By the time I went out to *Ellie Miller* that afternoon, I'd persuaded myself it was a hallucination. I'd slept a bit by

88

then, I'd come down to earth with a bang, I was feeling bloody awful, in fact—'

'What were you doing on *Ellie*?'

'Oh, checking her over, pumping the bilges. David asked me to go out, to save him a trip. I was glad, actually. It gave me a reason to stay down. I couldn't have gone back to Melton. I couldn't have faced anybody just then.'

'No.'

'But Mary, I'd forgotten how utterly glorious the river could be. It was a perfect day, quiet, warm, no one about. It was so peaceful! So I stayed on board for a while, sitting there on the mooring, drinking Pa's whisky, thinking things through. Mentally, it was rather a toss-up between shooting myself and dying of sheer love of life. I was a bit emotional, to say the least.'

Sitting there on the boat I had remembered all the good times I'd had when I was young, the trips with Pa on *Ellie Miller*, the passages up the coast, the expeditions ashore; the excitement of the night watches, the running jokes we'd enjoyed, the long companionable silences.

It was on one of these trips in my late teens that my father had confided in me about his early life, about his strained relationship with his own father, the lack of communication and affection, and how he had strived to succeed because he'd felt it was the only way to win his father's approval. He wanted it to be different for me. He wanted me to succeed for my own sake, and because I loved the business.

There had been a time when I'd resented his blithe assumption that I would follow him into the business. At seventeen I'd made up my mind to become a designer, which was the closest I could get to being an artist and still get paid. My father hadn't tried to talk me out of it exactly, but he'd got various family friends and godparents to point out some of the disadvantages. I hadn't improved my chances by failing to get in to the first two art colleges I'd tried. And when I was offered a place at Oxford to read languages, I began to recognise the inevitability of what lay ahead. My father was characteristically generous, sending me round the world in my gap year, funding all my travel in the vacations. After that I felt it would have been ungrateful not to give the business a try.

I hadn't regretted my choice, only my failure to make a success of it.

I missed my father. No one tells you how to grieve properly, how much pain to expect, how much guilt and anger, and whether it's normal to have long periods when you feel nothing at all. In the months since his death, my grief had seemed both inadequate and incomplete.

Going to the chart table, I lifted the lid and found his job list lying on the top of the charts where he always kept it. I picked it up with gentle hands and laid it on the table. Seeing the elegant handwriting made shaky by age, the neat columns of jobs with all but three systematically crossed off, I wept for him at last.

'And then . . .' The picture burned brightly in my mind. 'Sylvie appeared. I heard this knocking on the hull and I went up on deck but I couldn't see anything. No boat, nothing. Then the knocking came again and I went to the stern and there she was in the water. Well, I couldn't believe my eyes. I just stared at her. Then she laughed at me, and, Mary, it was like a dream only *more* so. You see, she hadn't changed. She was just the same. It was as though . . . as though *nothing* had changed.'

My throat was dry, I coughed, and Mary passed me the last of her whisky.

Gulping it, I echoed, 'She was just the same.' I saw her standing in the cabin, with that dramatic colouring she had inherited from her French mother, the long black hair sticking wetly to her shoulders, and the white translucent skin touched with faint freckles; and I could only wonder again at the smoothness of her skin, the way it was completely untouched by time, as if she'd skipped all the intervening years and lived no other life.

'I pulled her out of the water and she scolded me for letting her stand there and shiver. I just laughed because she was talking to me as if we'd last seen each other a few hours ago. That was her gift . . .' I reached for a thought I had never fully identified before. 'Her gift was for *intimacy*. She could make you feel you were the only person in the world, or at least the only person she really cared about. She made you feel that being with her was everything, that there couldn't be anything more important or more exciting. That suddenly everything was possible. And I needed that, Mary! I needed to feel . . . well, that I could have some sort of life away from all the pressure, the endless succession of disasters. That I could forget – for a while anyway – and be . . .' I gave an ironic gasp. 'Be *free.*'

I heard Sylvie's voice again, that extraordinarily rich voice of hers that could communicate so many different, often contradictory, messages. She was sitting in the saloon, wrapped in the only towel I could find and an old waterproof jacket of Pa's, a whisky in her hand, with her head tilted to one side, chin tucked in or suddenly thrown up in that French way of hers. Only her gaze was unwavering, her almond eyes fixed on mine with a glittering absorption, as if no time had intervened and we had never stopped being soul-mates. She told me about her new life, the pottery shop in Dartmouth where she was working, the cottage she was renting just outside Dittisham. She loved it here, she told me. Her return was a spiritual thing, she needed to be in touch with elemental things, with water and wind and creativity. She was going to start sculpting. Near water she felt empowered, she could draw on wells of creativity, she felt supremely in touch with her body and her spiritual energies.

No one I knew talked in this way. Among my contemporaries this would have been dismissed as New Age psycho-babble, yet Sylvie imbued it with a sort of grandeur, and an earthiness too. There was an undercurrent of self-indulgence there, a strong hint of physicality and hedonism. But then even at fifteen Sylvie had exuded a powerful animal sensuality, a breathtaking sexual assurance, which, with her flamboyant defiance for convention, had produced an overwhelming effect on the rather staid young man I had been when we'd met.

The effect she had on me as we sat in the boat drinking whisky sixteen years later wasn't terribly different. I laughed too much and too quickly, I heard myself trying to impress and amuse her, I felt a ridiculous effervescent pleasure. With a sense of the miraculous, I felt myself come alive again.

When she got up to leave she rested the back of her hand against my face, and gave that little cat-grin of hers, all enchantment and promise.

Mary clasped her hands under her chin. 'Then?' She was urging me forward, and I realised how late it must be.

'Then?' I sighed. 'Well, I had to see her again. In fact, I couldn't think of much else. It was a desperate thing – a sort of compulsion. I couldn't get her out of my mind. It was . . .' But the memory caught at me, and stalled my thoughts.

After a while Mary said softly, 'You had an affair?'

Distracted, I stared into the fire, I shook my head in lingering disbelief. 'For a long time nothing happened. I thought she was just wary of involvement, I thought it was her conscience. That she was bothered by me being married. Quite funny, really, in retrospect.' My smile emerged as a bleak grimace. 'By the time I realised she had no conscience whatsoever, it was too late. I was completely hooked. I'd completely lost my judgment. And she used that, she used *me*.' Saying it, I felt a fresh plunge of humiliation. 'She led me a complete dance. That's exactly what it was – a dance!'

Mary said something which I missed, and she had to repeat it. 'Did you see her last weekend?' Her voice had a sudden tension to it.

'No.' Then, as I absorbed the implications of what she had said, I stared at her. '*No*, Mary, I did not.'

Mary said rapidly, as if to get it over and done with, 'You weren't on the boat with her?'

'No.'

She cast me an odd look, as though something about this disturbed her.

'*Mary.* '

'I only meant that it wouldn't have looked too good if you had been,' she explained in a rush. 'That was all.'

'I did not see her last weekend,' I repeated forcefully.

She nodded but her eyes still held a spark of doubt.

'I hadn't seen her for two weeks!'

She held up a defensive hand. 'Hugh, I believe you. Really. *Really.*'

The ringing of the phone cut into the unhappy pause that followed.

It was Tingwall. 'Look,' he said, 'I didn't want to bother you so late, but I thought you'd better know that I've had a call from the press.'

'Christ. What did they want?'

'I think I've quashed any ideas they might have had. Told them you and your wife were just possible witnesses because you lived on the river. That sort of thing.'

'Did they buy it?'

'One can but hope.'

FIVE

Ginny appeared on the landing above, a wraith against the sunlit window. 'You're back,' she declared, sounding agitated. She touched an anxious hand to her uncombed hair, then to the fastening of her wrap. 'What's the time? I fell asleep . . .'

'It's about four. Are you all right?' And asking this, I wasn't sure what sort of response to expect. Even at the best of times I found it difficult to gauge Ginny's mood.

'It was flu after all,' she said matter-of-factly, 'but I think I'm over the worst of it now. And you? No more from the police?'

'No.'

'Well,' she breathed, 'that's something. And me? Do I still have to . . . ?'

'Tingwall's arranged for you to go to Chelsea police station on Monday, if that's all right. They'll only need a brief statement.'

She nodded solemnly.

Turning towards the bedroom, she paused for long enough to catch my eye and issue a silent but unequivocal plea. The moment of account was not to be delayed, I realised, and climbing the stairs I attempted to prepare myself for whatever was to come, wrath or recrimination.

She was smoothing the bed. 'I'm sorry about what I said on the phone,' she announced immediately, and there was a note of rehearsal in her voice. 'I didn't mean to be unhelpful.'

'No . . . I wasn't too helpful myself.'

'I just wanted to know what the police thought they were up to, that was all. I was worried.' She was on the point of saying more but, ducking her eyes, sat down abruptly at her dressing table and began to brush her hair with sharp strokes that made it crackle.

I asked, 'Do you want to talk about it now?'

She twisted round and said, 'Please,' as though we had plucked this subject out of the air.

I sat on the edge of the bed. 'Well . . . They knew Sylvie had dropped in to see me on the boat a couple of times. This was ages ago, June some time. I'd already told them that. And I'd told them I'd bumped into her by the ferry once. But for some reason – and I've no idea what – they came down on me like a ton of bricks. The full treatment.' I gave a shuddering laugh. 'They have this way of making you feel they're not going to believe a word you say. Scary. *Terrifying*. Anyway, they were extremely keen to know where I was when Sylvie was killed. Luckily, I could account for most of that Saturday – David saw me in Dartmouth hunting for food and then you arrived and then David popped in later . . . So, one way and another, there wasn't time for me to have been anywhere else.'

She absorbed this with stern concentration. 'And you've no idea what it was that made them pick on you?'

I shook my head.

'But there was *something*?'

'Possibly – presumably . . .'

'And they didn't tell you what?'

'No.'

She gave a anxious laugh which hid none of her curiosity. 'But what reason could they have had for dragging you all the way down there again?'

'Ginny, I don't know.'

She searched my face for the lie, and I met her gaze as best I could.

She looked away. 'What else did they want to know?'

'Oh, you can imagine. How well I knew Sylvie, that sort of thing.'

'And they were happy with . . . what you said?'

I shrugged. 'They had to be, didn't they?'

She drew a ragged breath. 'How could they do it anyway – drag you off like that? Did they have the right?'

95

'I'm not sure, darling. But it would have looked strange if I'd refused, wouldn't it?'

She considered this. 'Yes, I suppose it would.' She twisted the hairbrush in her lap, her delicate features etched with unease. 'And you don't know what it was that made them want to see you again?'

'No.'

She made an attempt to smile. 'But you must have some idea.'

Here it was again, the inability to let go, the constant chafing. 'I really don't know, Ginny. But they must have thought I was having an affair with Sylvie, mustn't they? If I was meant to have killed her I would hardly have done it without a reason, and that's the obvious one, isn't it?'

I could hear the sound of her breathing, the rasping that preceded an attack, and I wondered how long it would be before she reached for the inhaler.

'And you've no idea what made them think . . . ?'

It wasn't a challenge this time, more a craving for reassurance. So I denied it again, because it was far too late to do anything else.

Conflicting emotions passed across Ginny's face, then with a jerky movement she put the hairbrush back in its place on the dressing table. 'Well, at least they've got it straight at last!' she said, striking a bright nervy note. 'We can begin to forget the whole wretched business.'

She was waiting for me to agree; she wanted to hear me say that I was putting everything to do with Sylvie behind me.

'Let's hope so.'

She shot me a sharp look.

'It's the press,' I explained. 'They seem to have heard about my visit to the police. And we all know what they're like. Given half a chance, they'll blow it up out of all proportion. That'd be all I need, with the buyout coming together.'

She was blinking rapidly, pulling hard on her lungs. 'But how did the press hear about it?'

'Who knows? These things get out, don't they?' And for no apparent reason I thought of Howard.

Her forehead wrinkled into a rare frown, and I noticed how

strained she was looking, and how dark were the shadows around her eyes. 'What happened? Did they phone?'

'They called Tingwall. He seems to think he's palmed them off all right.'

She shook her head. 'It's not so easy to palm them off! They have a way of coming back. We should make a plan.'

Ginny's mother had been a famous beauty who'd led what in charitable terms might be described as an eventful life, with three husbands, numerous lovers, and an unwavering talent for attracting scandal. After a childhood in the spotlight, Ginny had good reason to consider herself something of an expert on the press.

'The thing is . . .' she murmured, thinking her way through it. 'You must be sure to speak to them if they call. Be completely open. Utterly polite and terribly nice. Even jokey. Mummy always said that you could get away with murder if you made the press laugh.' She looked at me with her great fluid eyes, the irony of what she had said completely lost on her, or calmly unacknowledged.

'I'm not sure I'm quite up to cracking jokes, Ginny.'

'Be jolly, then. Carefree. If they catch the slightest hint of panic around you, they'll be back for more, like jackals.'

This was what I always forgot, her astuteness, her talent for reading situations.

'It's terribly important to appear friendly,' she stressed. 'You can be rather cool, you know. I've heard you with journalists. You can sound rather offhand.'

'Can I? I hadn't realised. Well, I'll do my best.' I picked up her inhaler from the bedside table and took it across to her.

'Tone makes all the difference . . .' But she could hardly say it, she was so short of breath.

She took the inhaler from my hand, drew on it greedily and gave two or three harsh coughs. From the gardens below came the sound of children playing and the wail of an electric lawn mower. I kept forgetting it was Saturday.

After a while I asked, 'All right?'

She nodded impatiently. She never liked to talk about her

asthma. 'Oh, Julia came by with a stack of papers for you. I put them in the study.'

'Thanks.'

She twisted round on the stool and examined her face in the mirror. 'Will you have time for dinner?' Above the breathlessness her voice was still taut.

'Of course. I'll make time.'

'I thought we'd have something silly, like eggs and baked beans.' She reached for her face cream and I saw that her hand was trembling.

I felt a surge of remorse. 'Ginny—'

'It's all right!' she declared, smearing the cream fiercely over her cheeks, 'I'm not going to ask if you had an affair! I assure you – I don't want to know!' Abandoning her face abruptly, she clamped her hands together on the surface of the table and stared down at them. She whispered, 'But I would like to know if you loved her.'

I stared at her dumbly in the glass.

'And don't lie, please,' she added, her voice rising sharply. 'I couldn't bear it.'

'I didn't love her,' I said.

She looked up and our eyes met in the mirror. I saw hope in her face, and wretchedness.

'I didn't love her,' I repeated.

She searched my expression, then, gasping, looked down and nodded rapidly.

'It was—'

'No! Don't say any more!' She fumbled for the cream again. 'Don't!'

I felt a familiar gust of helplessness and uncertainty. Did she mean it? Sometimes her most effusive denials turned out to be cries for reassurance which, despite the absence of firm clues, I was meant to decipher and assuage. I was still searching for the right thing to say when she glanced up and said briskly, 'I'll see you later then. You really don't mind eggs and baked beans?'

Relief made me smile stupidly. 'Can't think of anything better.'

She nodded again, and returned to her makeup.

I leant down and kissed the top of her head. When I looked up again she had averted her eyes.

*

With the paperwork was a note from Julia. 'I can't find that petrol receipt,' she wrote. 'I don't think you ever gave it to me. It's no great problem. I can get the details from MasterCard and/or the service station, but I just thought I'd mention it, in case you had it lying around.'

I looked in the compartment of my wallet where I usually put receipts and credit card counterfoils before handing them over to Julia at the end of each week. The petrol receipt wasn't there, nor the credit card voucher. I remembered handing my card to the cashier at the service station, I remembered signing the slip, but the rest of the exchange, like the drive itself, was a blur. I had spent the journey trying not to think about Sylvie but thinking, in the end, of little else. All sorts of fantasies had crowded my brain: I imagined her waiting for me at Dittisham, I heard the phone ringing as I walked in, or if these were too much to hope for, I saw myself finding a note, telling me where to find her. They were desperate impossible fantasies, born of obsession. I knew full well that there would be no sign of her, that as usual she would be doing her best to avoid me, and that if I was to have any chance of seeing her I would have to go and search for her myself.

Nearing Dittisham I persuaded myself that I would be able to exercise some self-control, that I would have the strength of will to maintain some dignity and stay away from her, yet I knew perfectly well that I would go and look for her. I was incapable of stopping myself. The urge to see her was like a craving. I was consumed by the need to know what had gone wrong, why she had so brutally cut me out of her life. I was desperate to retrieve what she had so tantalisingly proffered and so abruptly snatched away; I wanted the euphoria again, the surge of long-forgotten emotions, the sensation of being completely and spectacularly alive. I knew our affair was over, yet I couldn't accept it. I needed to know if she'd intended to humiliate me, if she'd meant to set me up quite so effortlessly: I needed to know just how thoroughly I'd been deceived.

Approaching Dittisham, I went through a pantomime of normality. I avoided Sylvie's cottage and drove straight to the house. I forced myself to go inside and turn on the water heater, to pour myself a drink and sit by the window as if I intended to have a quiet evening. I even convinced myself that I would be satisfied by going upstairs to David's old bedroom and focusing my specially purchased binoculars on the stretch of river just beyond the ferry where the white yacht with the bowsprit lay at her mooring. But the stillness of the scene, the complete absence of life on board were both a torment and a challenge. It was then that I gave up all pretence of self-possession and drove off in search of her.

*

I had spent an hour on some amended cash flow projections when Ginny buzzed through to say that David was on the line.

'We're just on our way out,' he declared, ever swift to establish that his time was limited. 'Wanted to let you know what we've decided for the buyout. It'll be fifty thousand. Can't do more, I'm afraid.'

Overcoming my disappointment, I said, 'David – thank you.'

'The thing is, we've tied up quite a bit in this trust for the children. And the terms of the trust – you know, we're simply not allowed to invest in anything risky.'

'I understand.'

'Well, there we are.'

'You won't regret it.'

'I should hope not!' And his tone wasn't entirely facetious.

'Thanks again for yesterday.'

'Mmm?' he murmured distractedly, and I could hear the sound of turning pages as his attention wandered.

'For coming to the police station.'

'Oh, that reminds me,' he drawled. 'Mary heard something on the lawyers' scandal-vine this morning – you know how she is for having her ear to the ground. She was going to call you. She didn't get a name,' he said, meandering towards the point, 'but she heard that someone got hauled in for questioning late last night.'

'But who? Does she know?'

'I told you, she didn't get the details,' he said in his busy voice, the one he used to presage the end of his conversations. 'But I told you it would be all right, didn't I?' David's confidence had a certain steamroller quality to it, a momentum that did not allow for dissent.

'Yes, I suppose—'

'Got to rush.'

'David, I can't thank you enough for putting your faith in the buyout—'

'Not a bit,' he cut in and, with a grunt that might have been a goodbye, he rang off.

I brooded for a long time, wondering who Henderson might have hauled in for questioning. The unprepossessing long-haired youth perhaps? The owner of the white cutter? Or another of this tribe of lovers that Sylvie was meant to have had?

She was all over the place. David's words still reverberated in my mind. I had always known that Sylvie lived by her own rules, that her addiction to the sensual took her beyond normal limits, but I had pushed the obvious consequences of this thought from my mind. During our affair I had not dared to face the idea that I was sharing her with someone else. I had been too frightened of the emotions that such a suspicion might unleash in me.

The wail of a siren sounded from the direction of the King's Road. Gazing out into the dark gardens, beyond the tracery of branches to the lights of the neighbouring houses, I felt immensely glad that it was all over, that I had recovered most of my sanity and equilibrium. I had not liked myself very much while I was in thrall to Sylvie, I had not enjoyed being in a state of misery and abject longing; most of all, I had disliked being at the mercy of emotions that were so intense, obsessive and ultimately demeaning.

The siren echoed in the distance. Returning to the present with a sense of relief, I pulled out a sheet of paper and set down the figures that were already written large in my head. A shortfall of a hundred thousand from David; one million more to be found on the total price tag of the company. Against this I might be able to raise five hundred thousand on this house and Zircon might come up with two hundred and fifty thousand. I didn't need to be an Einstein to see I was still short by three hundred and fifty thousand.

I didn't blame David for reducing his investment. The takeover had brought him some shares in Cumberland and a little cash, but the total was less than a third of what he could have expected a few years back if we'd sold HartWell at the height of its fortunes. And for all I knew he and Mary might need cash for other things: they might be planning early retirement, they could even be up to their ears in debt. David might have been my brother, but so far as his financial affairs went I hardly knew him at all.

Given enough sweat and tears, I could probably raise the extra money from the Chartered Bank, but I was loathe to go back to them cap in hand unless absolutely necessary. At best it would look as though George and I had failed to do our homework properly, at worst we would simply appear incompetent. Then there was the time element. Renegotiations could take weeks and I suspected that Cumberland would use the time to solicit a better offer from elsewhere and announce a tight cut-off date for final bids. When I really wanted to frighten myself I imagined that the juicy offer was already on the table and that Howard had planted his million-pound bombshell to raise the stakes, and, accidentally or otherwise, jeopardise our chances of success.

Three hundred and fifty thousand. It shouldn't be too hard to find, so long as nothing happened to rock the boat. I tried not to think of the press and the positive storm they could raise without uttering a single word of libel.

I scribbled a line through my calculations and threw them into the bin. I heard Ginny approaching to summon me to supper, and an absurd bubble of contentment rose up in me at the thought of baked beans at the kitchen table with my wife.

*

'Everything went into the wash.' Already Ginny's expression was taking on the defensive look she acquired whenever she thought

102

she might have done the wrong thing. We were in the dressing room, standing in front of the open wardrobe.

'What about the beige cords?'

'They went to the cleaners.'

'And you didn't happen to notice anything in the pockets?'

'No.' She said it a little too quickly, and I guessed she hadn't looked. 'Was it something vital?' she asked.

I shrugged, 'Not really,' and began to get undressed.

'What was it?'

'Just a receipt.'

'What for?'

'Oh – petrol, that's all.'

'But you have to find it?'

She had sensed something. It was ridiculous not to tell her. 'The police want to have a look at it. To establish what time I was on the motorway last Saturday.'

This seemed to confuse her. 'On Saturday?' She half turned towards the wardrobe as though to start undressing, only to turn back with a frown. '*Saturday?* And it's important, the time you got the petrol?'

'The police think so.' I threw my socks into the basket and reached for a robe. 'I told them I arrived at Dittisham shortly after seven, but they weren't inclined to believe me, not without some backup anyway. Not the most trusting of souls.'

'And it's *lost*, this receipt!'

'Oh, it doesn't matter. It's not essential.' I explained how the information could be tracked down through the credit card company.

But something was still disturbing her. 'What will it tell them, the receipt?'

'Tell them? That I was somewhere near Bristol at five-thirty that afternoon. Well, I *think* it was five-thirty, but I'm not so sure now. I wish I hadn't said five-thirty, in fact, in case I was wrong.'

'Could you be wrong?'

'Who knows? It wouldn't be the end of the world anyway.'

'You say that! But supposing it was earlier? Could it have been earlier?'

'Well, maybe half an hour or so – not a lot.'

103

She was looking appalled.

'Ginny!' I laughed, putting an arm round her shoulders. 'It's all right, really.'

But she was wasn't so easily pacified. 'You say that . . .'

'I *know* it.'

She cried, 'You can't *know*.'

'You worry too much.' I drew her into an embrace and rested my cheek against the richness of her hair. Her stiff body seemed to tremble in my arms, like a frail storm-tossed bird.

I began to rock her slightly and to murmur soft reassurances, as I had always done in times of stress or reconciliation. Her body did not yield.

I whispered, 'It's so good to be home, Ginny. You can't imagine.' I meant, good to be home with just the two of us and no hordes to be wined and dined, though I didn't say that.

Eventually I pulled back a little and, cupping a hand under her chin, leant down to kiss her.

She didn't retreat, but she didn't kiss me back either.

I didn't blame her, I didn't expect instant absolution, but I did need to know that forgiveness wasn't a total impossibility either.

'Ginny,' I whispered awkwardly. 'Darling . . . if I caused you any grief then I'm—'

She gave a small cry and wrenched herself free. For a moment she agitated a hand at me, unable to speak. 'Not now,' she gulped, her eyes brimming. 'I can't deal with that *now!*' She turned and hurried into the bedroom.

'Ginny!'

But something prevented me from pursuing her, futility or weariness. Retreating to a hot bath, I stayed in it for a long time. I comforted myself with thoughts of a not-too-distant time when life would be more settled, when memories of this summer would have faded and Ginny and I would be established not too far from Hartford, in a country house that might look something like David's, with land and gardens and an interior with enough potential to stimulate Ginny's designer instincts, a time when we would have adjusted our lives to an altogether gentler pace and in some as yet unidentifiable way moved our relationship forward, into calmer waters.

It was after midnight when I finally went into the bedroom. The lights were off but I knew Ginny wasn't asleep. Going softly round to her side of the bed, I leant down and kissed her head.

Her eyes glittered up at me.

I said, 'Do you want me to sleep in the other room?'

'I'd prefer it if you didn't.'

My heart lifted. 'Then I'll stay.'

'I don't want to be alone.' It was a statement delivered without emotion.

I thought of all the weekends when I had left her to go down to Dittisham. 'No.'

'I don't think I could bear to be alone again.'

Was this the bargain then? A commitment to curtail my freedom?

I steeled myself to say, 'I'll never leave you alone again, I promise.'

'That would mean so much. If you could manage it.' There was no irony in her voice.

A little later, as I was beginning to doze off, she propped herself up on one elbow and, without switching on the light, shook a tablet from a bottle and washed it down with water. When she settled down again her foot touched my leg and she did not move it away.

*

It was a good twenty years since, as a fresh-faced graduate with more confidence than sense, I had undertaken my sales training under Ronald Simms and got my first inkling of what it was like at the sharp end of the business. Ronald Simms was a representative of the old school. He worked his patch to a hallowed schedule, he knew the names of the buyers' children and the ailments of their wives, he wore white shirts with starched collars which did permanent battle with his Adam's apple, and he called me Mr Hugh, just as he called my father Mr Richard.

Sitting in the lounge of the Churchill Hotel with the Packenhams buyer I was reminded of the time Ronald and I had been preparing to pitch a difficult sale. 'You remember what I told

105

you?' he'd remarked. 'That with the Hartford name there's no such thing as a cold sale? Well, that doesn't stop some sales from being a bit chillier than others.'

This sale was definitely on the chilly side. Miss Stevens, who with her doll face and timid posture appeared a disconcerting twenty though she must have been a good eight to ten years older, had been the Packenhams china and glass buyer for two years, and was showing no chinks in her considerable armour. She had de-listed Hartford Crystal five months ago because we had given Harrods a better price, and since walking into the lounge and offering me her limp handshake she had made it plain that she wasn't about to relent.

'Miss Stevens, I can only say I'm horrified by what happened. I can assure you quite categorically that it's never been our policy to discriminate. I can only imagine it was an appalling error on the part of the sales people. The only thing I can do is to offer you my sincere apologies. And my personal guarantee that it will never happen again.'

Her unyielding look said: It's a little too late for that now.

'All I can tell you is that things are going to be very different at Hartford once the buyout goes through. We're putting everything we have into it – financially, I mean, as well as blood, sweat and tears – and we wouldn't be doing that unless we believed one hundred per cent in the product. You see, we feel we have something really special in Hartford crystal. We feel—' I broke off as another of Ronald's maxims came back to rap me over the knuckles: Don't tell them what to think, tell them what's new. 'What's new,' I said, 'is that Hartford will be run by the people on the spot, the people who know the business backwards. And I can honestly say that we're going to make a damned sight better job of it.'

Behind Miss Stevens' spectacles something stirred, though it was hard to tell what sort of emotion it might be. 'It wouldn't be hard to make a better job of it,' she commented in her wispy voice.

'But, Miss Stevens, however successful we are – and we *are* going to be successful – none of it'll be any good if Hartford crystal isn't on sale in Packenhams—'

My mobile phone sent up a warble from my briefcase. 'I'm so

sorry,' I said rapidly. 'Only my secretary has this number and she wouldn't call me unless it was extremely urgent.'

Miss Stevens looked at her watch as she reached for her coffee.

I snatched up the phone and growled, 'Yes?'

'*Sorry*,' Julia hissed, 'but there's a photographer snooping around outside the office and your wife just called to say there're a couple at Glebe Place too. Thought you ought to be warned.'

'Hell.'

Above the coffee cup Miss Stevens' eyes, enlarged by her lenses, watched me speculatively.

'Have they phoned, the press?'

'No.'

'Well, let me know if they do. And don't say a word to anyone about this, will you?'

'Of course not,' she said indignantly. 'Oh, and George called to say he thinks he can raise another forty-five thousand.'

I dropped the phone into my case. 'I'm so sorry about that. It was, umm ... urgent.' For an instant I imagined that the photographers had followed me here, that they were waiting for me to leave the hotel. 'So ... I was saying that ...' I groped for my thread. 'Our plans ... Yes, we're going to advertise in the colour supplements over the three weeks leading up to Christmas, and what we'd really like to do is mount a special spring promotion with Packenhams.' I brought out a folder and passed it across to her. 'It's all in here.'

Miss Stevens slid her cup onto the table and sat forward, preparing to leave.

'Look,' I said hastily, 'I very much want you to change your mind about us, Miss Stevens. I'm not sure how I can achieve that, but – well, I'm going to keep trying!'

'Mr Wellesley, I'll consider your proposals. That's all I can say.' Her little-girl voice reminded me more than ever of a shop girl fresh out of school. Standing up, she smoothed the skirt of her bad suit. She hesitated before announcing, 'My father risked our home for his business.'

I didn't say anything.

'He lost both the house and the business.'

'I'm sorry.'

107

'So were we.'

'Miss Stevens – we're not going to fail.'

She eyed me appraisingly. 'No,' she said, 'I don't suppose you are.' And in the moment before she turned away she gave me a look that wasn't entirely unsympathetic.

*

'They're standing right outside the door,' Ginny told me. Her voice faded and crackled in the earpiece as my cab spun along the Bayswater Road. '. . . Photographers and a reporter.'

'How many?'

'Three of them. I have to go out in a minute. But I know what I'm going to say to them.'

'Ginny . . .' I didn't want her to realise how appalled I was. 'Wouldn't it be better to say nothing?'

'Don't worry – it won't be much.'

I felt powerless. 'Well, be careful, for God's sake.'

'I will.' She sounded listless, or depressed; it was hard to tell with such a bad connection.

'How are you feeling?'

'Me? Umm . . .' She took her time. 'Oh, all right.'

'What about the doctor?'

'That's where I'm going, to see him.'

'Let me know what he says, won't you?'

'Yes.'

'Don't let him give you any old thing.'

'No.'

She had slept most of the day before. When she'd finally got up we had spent the time like two battle-weary warriors home from the fray. After the tensions of the previous night we'd kept a respectful distance, speaking little and with caution. Over an early supper we had discussed the sale of Melton and its contents, and I had drawn some comfort from the prosaicness of our conversation. Later we'd watched television in bed and as we'd fallen asleep Ginny had made no objection when I'd slid an arm loosely round her waist.

I said, 'You haven't been to the police station then?'

'I didn't feel well enough.'

'No, of course not. I left a message for Tingwall, to warn him you might not be up to it. He'll square it with the people at Exeter.'

'While you're on,' she said. 'The petrol receipt, have you . . . ?'

'Julia's still chasing it. But it'll be fine, really.' A roaring came over the ether as though we were entering a tunnel. 'Take care,' I shouted. 'And do watch out for those people.' I had a vision of the photographers pushing their lenses into Ginny's face.

'Don't worry.' Her voice was breaking up badly, but I thought she said, 'I'm used to them, remember.'

*

Nearing the office I peered over the cabbie's shoulder, but there were no photographers outside the building and no one loitering in the entrance. I strode inside with an itchy feeling between my shoulder blades and a powerful urge to look behind me.

Julia told me the photographer had abandoned his vigil twenty minutes before.

'And it was definitely me he was looking for?' I asked, knowing the answer.

She put the messages in front of me and nodded. 'He tried to get information from the security man. Wanted to know if you'd been in today.'

I tried to shrug it off, I tried to tell myself that they would lose interest quickly enough, but all the time a small doom-laden voice wondered why they should come now, when the police had finished with me.

Julia waited for me to read the messages. 'Oh, that petrol receipt?' she said. 'I got the MasterCard details. It was the Gordano service station on the M5. Just past Bristol. And the time – you've no idea what I had to go through to get this, I had to bribe the station manager to sort through all his till rolls! Anyway, it was four-fifteen.'

I felt a pull of apprehension. 'Are you sure?'

'Yes.' But giving me the benefit of the doubt she hurried into her office and came back with her notebook. 'Here we are.' She showed me the entry. 'Four-fifteen.'

I'd been miles out then. I had told Henderson five-thirty to six. What on earth had made me say that? I realised that, far from leaving the office at three, I must have left long before, maybe as early as two. I had been in such a state of confusion that afternoon that anything was possible.

I could see now that it had been a mistake to commit myself to such a firm guess. Being half an hour out might have looked understandable, but a whole hour was going to seem careless. Yet it was the easiest thing in the world to make a mistake about the time. Well, I hoped that was how the police would view it anyway. Suddenly I needed reassurance. I was about to call Tingwall when Julia buzzed through to tell me Mary was on the line.

'Hang on,' called Mary the moment I greeted her. In the background I could hear the squawky voices of cartoon characters on the television, then, rising above the sound, Mary yelling good-naturedly to someone to turn the thing down.

'Henry's home with flu,' she complained cheerfully. 'If it's not one thing it's another. Listen, did you speak to David? Did he call you?'

'Yes. Look, I'm really very grateful for your support.'

'But it's only fifty thousand.'

'Whatever you feel comfortable with is fine with me.'

'Well, it's not fine with me,' she declared in the crisp authoritative tones she'd retained from her legal days. 'I'd like to put in some of my own money.'

'Mary, that's sweet of you, but I couldn't accept it.'

'Why not?'

'Because . . . I wouldn't feel happy.'

'Why wouldn't you feel happy? It's my money. Nothing to do with David. Oh, I'll tell him, if that's what you're worried about – though I very much hope it isn't!'

I knew Mary had money of her own; quite apart from the HartWell shares which she and Howard had inherited from their father, they had also been left antiques and silver and cash, though I'd never been clear on how much was involved, nor the extent to which Mary's capital had been merged with David's or tied up in the children's trusts.

She asked, 'How much do you need?'

I laughed, 'Mary, you don't want to ask!'

'I am asking!'

I laughed again. 'Okay . . . As of today we're still short by three hundred and five thousand. Assuming Cumberland agrees the valuation.'

'Can't manage all of that, but you can count me in for a hundred thousand.'

'*Mary.*'

'Actually on second thoughts I might not tell David. What do you think? No, no . . . I'll have to, won't I?' She sighed, an overblown sound made for effect. 'He won't like it, will he? You know how he is – caution, caution. Never backed a horse in his life.'

'Mary, I don't know what to say.'

'Don't say anything, then. Oh!' she gasped. 'One person who must never find out – Howard!'

'There's no risk of that, Mary. We're not exactly speaking.'

'You'll keep it totally anonymous? Just you, me and David?'

'Of course.'

'Well, there we are then!'

'Mary, you're amazing.'

'Since you mention it . . .' And she gave a gravelly laugh.

'You don't want time to think about it?'

'I've done my thinking. And my thinking says you're going to make me rich.'

'Mary, I'll certainly do my best.'

She gave a hum of amusement and we said goodbye.

I sat in a state of barely controlled elation, knowing that there was still some way to go, that I mustn't on any account think of celebrating, but feeling too optimistic and too starved of good fortune not to do so.

Julia came in and, catching my mood, demanded, 'The good news?'

'Only two hundred and five thousand to go!'

Julia thrust a fist into the air, and performed a curious shimmy with her hips.

Pushing thoughts of the press to the back of my mind, I rang

Hartford to tell George, then spent the rest of the afternoon calculating the revised figures for Zircon, which Julia typed and sent off by special messenger, and arranging the necessary meetings for the rest of the week. There were three sets of documents to be finalised urgently: the company articles for the new firm, Hartford Crystal Ltd; the Shareholders' Agreement with Zircon; and the agreement for the new company to purchase the assets, trading names and working capital of the old Hartford Division. I wanted everything ready for signature before the end of the week, in case Howard pulled a fast one. It was an ambitious schedule, but not an impossible one.

At five, lifted by the satisfactions of the day, I said to Julia, 'You know something? I'm beginning to think we're making some progress.' I was too superstitious to talk about success.

'I keep telling you – the light at the end of the tunnel isn't always an approaching train.'

I had been trying Ginny all afternoon and getting the answering machine. Now the line was engaged. I hoped the doctor had given her some vitamins. It was a long time since I had seen her so low, though I hardly needed reminding that much of the responsibility for that lay at my door. I hated the idea of having made her unhappy, yet it seemed to me that unhappiness had been creeping up on us for a long time, and that without it I would almost certainly have resisted the final slide into betrayal.

There are a dozen ways to block out unhappiness. Ginny and I had chosen work, as much as we could fit into a single day, so that we never had time to question the purpose of it all.

I knew the structure of Ginny's days, where she went, who she saw; I knew about the committee meetings, the working lunches, the hours on the phone, the shopping; but I had never known if these activities were a real source of contentment to her. She had always taken her duties seriously, the duties of keeping house – the food on the table, the flowers and decorations, the supervision of the diary – and the duties of her charity work, which she undertook with immense conscientiousness; but did she feel a sense of achievement at the end of it all? She never expressed any views one way or the other. She seemed to distrust discussions of

112

happiness, as though such scrutiny would tempt fate and undermine whatever joys she did possess.

I was packing my briefcase when Julia buzzed through to say that Tingwall was on the line.

'I was going to call you,' I said immediately, and started to tell him about the petrol receipt.

'Perhaps we can leave that for another time,' he interrupted. 'I have bad news, I'm afraid. The police want you to come in again, and this time it'll be as a suspect. They've served a number of search warrants on us.'

My heart thumped once against my chest. 'What do you mean?'

'They've obtained warrants to search Dittisham House, and the *Ellie Miller*, and to remove your car.'

The room seemed to sway, I felt the blood drain from my head. 'You're joking!' I could hardly get the words out. 'You're bloody joking!'

'They'll arrest you on suspicion as a formality. But please remember it's not the same as being charged.'

'Christ ... *Christ* ...' I found my way onto my chair. 'Why? *Why?*'

'They don't have to tell us, I'm afraid. And we have no way of finding out.'

'But there must be some reason!'

'In so far as the police have to show the magistrate good cause before he'll sign the warrants – yes, there must be. Magistrates do vary, of course, some let things through on a nod, but on the whole ...'

My disbelief was overtaken by the painful realisation that, like it or not, I had to deal with this nightmare which had so suddenly and firmly attached itself to me. 'The boat, you say? And the car?'

'I've arranged for your brother to hand over the keys to Dittisham House and the boat. They've got your car.'

It took me a moment to grasp what he was saying. 'They've got it?'

'They're at your house. I said you'd surrender to them there. I thought you might find it more convenient.'

'They're there *now?*'

'Yes. And Mr Wellesley? I need hardly tell you not to say anything until you get to Exeter. I'll see you there.'

'Charles?'

'Yes?'

It hit me suddenly, the enormity of what lay ahead, and my throat swelled, I felt a surge of panic and self-pity. 'This whole thing is ridiculous!'

'I'm sure.'

'They're quite wrong.'

A slight pause. 'We'll sort it out.'

'They're wrong.' I heard the entreaty in my voice, and the desperation.

'Just remember not to say anything on the way down. All right?'

I blurted something to an astonished Julia before walking blindly down to the street and hailing a cab. The driver set off at a fair lick and as we sped towards Chelsea I had the sensation that everything in my life was moving too fast, like a film run at double speed. I tried to prepare myself for what was to come but my mind was all over the place, caught between despair, reason and a growing panic. Sporadically I tried to reach Ginny on the mobile but the line was always engaged.

I'd forgotten the photographers. As we entered Glebe Place I saw them clustered around the gate. Thrusting money at the cabbie, I walked through their clicking lenses, not looking at them but not hiding my head either.

Ginny must have been watching for me because she opened the door as I approached.

Phipps and Reith were standing behind her in the hall.

Ginny whispered, 'They have a warrant.'

Reith stepped forward and delivered in a dull monotone, 'Hugh William Wellesley, I am arresting you on suspicion of the murder of Sylvie Anne Mathieson—'

I began to shake my head.

'—You do not have to say anything. But it may harm your defence if you do not mention when questioned something which you later rely on in court. Anything you do say may be given in evidence. Do you understand?'

114

My brain responded, but it took a little longer for my lips to obey. 'I understand.'

Ginny said, 'I would like to accompany my husband to Devon. I hope that'll be acceptable.'

Reith exchanged a look with Phipps. 'If you wish, ma'am.'

'And my husband will need a few minutes to wash and collect a change of clothes.'

Reith looked uncertain, but he must have decided I wasn't suicide material because he nodded abruptly and stood back to let me pass.

Ginny followed me upstairs to the bedroom and closed the door rapidly. 'What have they found out?' she breathed.

'Do you think I know? Do you think they called and told me?' Hearing the childishness in my voice, I groaned, 'Sorry. *Sorry.*'

'Hugh – we've got to think this through.'

'There's nothing to think through! There's nothing we can do!' I was choking with frustration. 'This time it'll be all over the papers – you realise that? Over everything. Christ!'

Ginny gripped my forearm. 'Hugh – we must think!' she gasped. 'We must think!' And her voice was trembling. 'Listen – what did you tell the police? No, no,' she corrected herself with an impatient wave of both hands. 'No – what I mean is, was Sylvie ever in the car with you?'

I didn't understand what she was getting at. 'I think ... once.' I went through the exercise of sifting my memory, though I knew perfectly well I wasn't mistaken. 'Yes. Once.'

'Did you tell the police that?'

I looked at Ginny and suddenly I began to understand. 'Oh God.'

'And the house? Did you say she'd been there?'

I shook my head miserably.

'Tell me what you did say, tell me!' And she was alive with a furious energy.

'It's not so much what I did say, it's what I didn't say. When they asked me when and where I'd seen her, I just didn't mention the house. Or the car.'

Ginny closed her eyes for a moment as if to absorb the full

115

impact of what I was saying. 'And she *touched* things at the house?'

'What?'

'Doors. Glasses – I don't know, I don't know. *Things.*'

I saw Sylvie watching me over the rim of her glass, I saw her holding a cup of coffee. 'Yes, she touched things.'

There was a silence like darkness. Ginny took a sudden breath and seemed to speak by sheer force of will. 'They'll know then.'

I sat on the bed and leant forward with my head in my hands. 'Oh, Ginny . . . I'm so sorry. I'm so sorry.'

'No, no!' she cried. 'Listen!' She sat beside me and pulled my hands away from my face and shook my shoulder until I looked at her. 'I'll say that *I* invited her to the house.'

'What?'

She nodded sharply. 'I'll say you introduced us, and I saw her in the village and invited her for coffee. I'll say it was just at the end of August. I'll say you were out on the boat, getting it ready for the weekend—'

'Ginny, *Ginny* . . .' My heart squeezed with gratitude, she meant so well. 'But, darling, they'll want exact dates, times. It simply wouldn't work. If – no, *when* they found out you weren't there – it would only make things worse.'

She clamped her lips together, she intertwined her long nervous fingers, she gave a small ironic laugh. 'But I *was* there that weekend, you see.' She took a breath halfway between a rasp and a sob. 'And I did see her. I saw her at the house.'

I could only stare at her.

'I didn't go to Provence,' she explained. 'I drove down to find you.'

I looked into her face, I saw the slight shame there, and the hurt, and knew it was true. 'Oh, Ginny.'

She was straining to breathe but when I tried to fetch her inhaler she grasped my arm and held me back. 'I saw you go to the boat too. I saw you sailing off. But Hugh, I wasn't the only one. Someone else saw you go – someone at the inn – and they told David, and David asked me if it had been me on board, and I told him it was. I said it was me!' As if to impress this on me, she shook my arm again. 'And then Mary asked me as well, and I told her. I

116

told her it was me. So that's what we've got to stick to, Hugh,' she urged through the labouring of her lungs, 'that's what we must swear to! We must say that it was *me*.'

I felt an inner crumbling, a sudden loss of will. The idea of committing myself to more lies was bad enough, but to try and carry off such fragile deceits seemed utterly futile. 'It's no good, Ginny. It's no good.'

'What do you mean?' And her grasp was very tight.

'They'll find out. Honestly, Ginny, it'll only make things worse.'

'No!' Her vehemence took me by surprise. '*No!* What are you thinking of! *What are you thinking of!*' She was trembling again.

'It'll be better to tell them the truth. They'll find out anyway!' And the thought sent me into a new chasm of despair.

'You can't! You can't!' She knelt in front of me and clasped my face in her hands so that I was forced to look into the fierceness of her eyes. 'Think of *me*, Hugh! Think of *me!*'

The tears sparkled angrily in her eyes, she cried for breath. Hurriedly I fetched her inhaler. As she pulled the drug into her lungs her gaze didn't leave my face.

'Ginny, I'm sorry,' I said wearily. 'I'm so very sorry.'

'Don't be sorry,' she gasped angrily, 'be brave! Be *brave!* For me, Hugh. *Please*. Do it for *me!*'

SIX

I've forgotten what excuse I found for going back to Dittisham that first time. To sort out the attics, to do some work on the boat. It didn't matter, really, because Ginny soon got the message that I wanted to be on my own. Coming on top of my late-night flight from the house party, this did little to ease the tension between us. Ginny wanted explanations and reassurances which I could not give her, while I dreamed of solitude and peace of mind, longings which I dared not voice for fear of making things worse.

We were meant to be having dinner with some friends from New York on the Friday, and Sunday lunch with neighbours, but I said I couldn't face people, which was true, and suggested Ginny go without me, which I knew full well she would never do.

I had a conscience about that, but it got lost in the desperation to get away. That week I had been on a two-day whistle-stop to some of our major customers in France and Belgium, I had been fighting the banks tooth and claw on a daily basis to extend our loan arrangements, and at an acrimonious meeting the HartWell board had outvoted me and passed Howard's motion to open formal merger discussions with Cumberland. By Friday I was drained of small talk, I was incapable of putting on a front for other people and pretending that things were just fine. Things were far from fine, and I knew that the greatest crisis of all was in myself.

Sylvie had been drifting through my mind ever since the swimming incident two weeks before, yet I told myself I wasn't going back to Dittisham to see her. I told myself I was going back to Dittisham to sort myself out, which contained more than enough truth to placate my conscience.

I reached the house after midnight on Friday and slept through until six, which in those insomniac times was something of a record. Then, seized with the fierce energy that exhaustion brings, I drove into town and took the ferry to Kingswear and, parking up on the cliffs, walked the coastal path until my legs ached. On the way back I took a detour into Brixham and, finding a dingy cafe near the harbour, devoured a plate of limp bacon and crusty eggs, washed down with bitter tea.

On returning to the house I made a half-hearted attempt to sort through Pa's books, but restlessness soon had me wandering aimlessly from window to window and back again. Eventually I put the books to one side and walked down the garden to the edge of the water. Down river, beyond the ferry, I could see the old-fashioned cutter with the bowsprit that Sylvie'd told me she and her friends took out most weekends. This Saturday the boat floated at its mooring, devoid of life.

I sat on the bank, watching the tide creeping in and the gulls squabbling in the sky above *Ellie Miller* and the scurrying ferry as it carried the hikers and holiday-makers across to Greenway. I stayed for almost an hour, finally trudging back up the hill when heavy clouds covered the sun. Approaching the house I heard the phone ringing, but something prevented me from hurrying to answer it and by the time I got inside it had stopped.

Still unable to settle, I went into town again and drove the streets until I found the pottery shop where Sylvie worked. It was a small place squeezed into a row of handicraft shops in a narrow street near the harbour. Brightly coloured pots and bowls lined the shelves that straddled the window. Through the open door I could make out a fiftyish woman in an ethnic dress sitting by the till, reading a newspaper. She seemed to be alone. I drove on to the supermarket, roaming desultorily among the shelves, buying whisky, milk and breakfast cereal, before ending up in a pub and passing an unsatisfactory twenty minutes with a beer and a solid meat pie.

As soon as I got back to the house I went upstairs to David's old room and looked down river.

The cutter had gone.

I felt a ridiculous sense of aggrievement, as if I had been

119

unfairly excluded. I searched the house for binoculars and, finding none, strode down to the water's edge to take another look. There was no doubt: the cutter had gone, leaving a squat wooden dinghy at her mooring.

My resentment burned on childishly. When I made sense of this absurd emotion, I realised it was based on envy, a naive and sentimental longing to be part of Sylvie's adventure, to sail off to God knows where, as we had done in the languorous days of that endless summer long ago, to some quiet cove maybe, or France, or nowhere very much at all. I yearned for the simplicity of those days, when we were faced by nothing more challenging than a trick at the tiller or a change of sail. Most of all perhaps, I yearned for the love and laughter we had shared, and which seemed to have faded inexorably from my life.

I had told Ginny I would be back by the following evening but I found reasons to put off my departure. Sorting Pa's books took a lot longer than I'd thought – or I made sure it did – then I persuaded myself that I needed to go out to *Ellie Miller* and pump her bilges. In the soft summer afternoon I collected oars and rowlocks from the garage and walked through the village to the quay.

I found the dinghy underneath two others in a stack of tenders jostling for space on the end of the ferry pontoon. Setting out, I didn't take my usual route to *Ellie*, which was to run parallel to the mud flats until the river widened a little and I could cross where the current was weakest, but rowed straight into the ebbing tide which would carry me close by the cutter's mooring. When I reached the mooring, there was nothing to see, of course, just the buoy and a battered plywood dinghy with badly chipped gunwales and a gash down one side.

Ellie had quite a bit of water in her, so I guessed David hadn't been aboard for a while. Once I had pumped her dry I looked around for other jobs to do: anything to delay my return. I pottered about for an hour or so, running the engine, doing odd bits of maintenance; and all the time I was keeping an eye out for the cutter's return.

Closing the engine compartment, on the point of packing up and going home, I looked out through the main hatch and saw the top of a mast in movement. I climbed up the companionway for a better view, and there was the white cutter, coming up to her mooring. I counted four people on board. Even at that distance Sylvie's slim figure was unmistakable.

It was then that I should have understood the nature of my secret hopes for Sylvie. My agitation should have warned me, and the unwarranted hostility I felt at the sight of the two men in the group, one of whom I immediately cast as Sylvie's lover.

The four were in a hurry to get ashore. If they had a mainsail cover they didn't put it on, and they forgot to tighten the halyards, let alone tie them off to the shrouds. As they pulled the dinghy alongside and started to load it, Sylvie stood in the cockpit, hands on hips, and I had the idea she was arguing with one of the men, a tall figure with bushy fair hair. The second man, a wiry figure with dark shoulder-length hair, got into the dinghy and took the bags handed down by the other woman.

I reached into the companionway for the binoculars. By the time I had focused on Sylvie, she had moved to the side deck. If she wasn't arguing with the fair-haired man then she was putting her message over pretty forcefully, weaving expansive gestures in the air, and I almost laughed to watch her, her body was so expressive. The fair-haired man seemed to make a point of turning his back on her before climbing down into the dinghy. Finally, after another exchange of words, Sylvie chucked a dismissive hand in the air and, with apparent bad grace, joined her companions in the dinghy.

Up until that moment I' might still have held back, I might have persuaded myself to keep my distance, but as the fair-haired man rowed the dinghy towards the quay Sylvie twisted in her seat and, in a pose that would have looked utterly affected if it hadn't been so typical of her, thrust a hand into the water and, turning her head as if to watch the ripples, let her cheek fall against her shoulder.

Quite suddenly I felt sure she was looking at me. It was as though she had known from the beginning that I was there and had expressly engineered this scene for our benefit.

I lifted my hand and waved to her, and though I couldn't be absolutely sure it seemed to me that she returned my smile before turning back to her companions. This small inconsequential smile rapidly took on a mammoth significance in my mind. My pulse quickened, I felt a foolish excitement. It was then that I knew I must see her again.

By the time I reached the quay she and her friends had disappeared. I hurried back to the house and, sitting at Pa's desk, spent half an hour composing a note. I would love to see her again, I wrote; our meeting on the boat had been all too brief, I would be down the next weekend, would she be interested in going for a sail . . .

In my new mood of calculation I realised it would be better to meet on the boat where there was no danger of David or Mary walking in on us, where the exigencies of finding crew members often threw the unlikeliest of people together. Even then I recognised that any relationship I might have with Sylvie, however innocent, would need to be discreet. Sylvie carried her sexuality too blatantly for anyone to believe she was capable of anything so casual as friendship. Even at fifteen, her style, her indifference to opinion, had attracted misunderstanding and gossip.

I found an envelope and, sealing the note, drove into town and posted it through the pottery shop's door before heading back to London.

The week brought a succession of crisis meetings. Galvanised by inflammatory talk of imminent financial disaster from Howard the board voted to rush the takeover proposal straight to the shareholders, which was little more than a formality when half the shareholders sat on the board, and the rest were married or related to them.

Facing almost certain defeat, I functioned in a schizophrenic state of acceptance and despair. I threw myself at problems, as if by sheer force of effort I might find some miraculous solution to HartWell's difficulties. I rarely got home before ten and then it was only to work until late in the night. Conversations with Ginny seemed to be confined to the subjects of meals, transport and laundry.

I tried not to think about the weekend, yet the idea of seeing

Sylvie glittered quietly in the back of my mind like a distant beacon across a dark sea.

By Friday what I had discounted as unshakeable tiredness had turned into the first flutterings of fever. That didn't stop me from driving down to Dittisham, of course. I told Ginny I needed to work away from the telephone.

There was no message from Sylvie at the house, no answering note on the mat.

I had a bad night, sweating heavily and periodically kicking the covers off, only to wake cold and shivering a short time later. I came to at nine the next morning, my mouth parched and my forehead burning. I found some aspirin in a medicine cabinet and took a couple. Then I dragged a duvet and pillow down to Pa's study and, pulling the sofa in front of the open windows, lay propped up against the arm so that I could see down the length of the garden to the water. Armed with a jug of water and a book, I dozed sporadically.

I woke to see a figure standing in the window. It was Sylvie.

You're ill, she said with a small sniff.

You don't sound very sympathetic, I smiled.

No, I'm not, she declared, because it means we won't be able to go sailing and the weather's perfect.

You would have come? It was the foolish question of an anxious lover.

She gave that laughing shrug of hers. Yes, why not?

I offered: I might be well enough by tomorrow.

But that prospect didn't seem to interest her.

I couldn't stop looking at her. I had forgotten the way her hair clouded out from her head and fell softly to her shoulders. I had forgotten the fullness of her lips and the way she pushed them forward whenever she finished speaking, so that every statement, however mundane, seemed to contain an invitation.

Next weekend, I said. Let's make it next weekend.

She lit a cigarette and sniffed again. Leaning back against the window frame, she gave me a sideways look, her almond eyes slanted like a cat's. Can we go to France? she said.

France? I repeated stupidly.

She was serious. She was waiting for my answer.

Well, I said hurriedly, it would be great, of course it would, but the boat's not really in commission. And I'm not sure I am, either. I mean, I haven't been sailing for a long time.

Her fluid lips had taken on a brooding look. It would be so nice, she said. And she gave the 'nice' an enticing quality.

My heart pulled with long-forgotten excitement. I knew I would agree. The thought of leaving my muddled life behind for a couple of days was irresistible.

I don't know, I said, putting up a last pretence of reluctance. I could ask the yard to look at the boat, I suppose. They could probably get her ready in time.

Her smile seemed to say: You see how easy it could be.

I hope you can navigate, I said, only half joking.

Sylvie frowned. Don't you have GPS?

It's installed, yes.

She flashed her eyes at me. Well, then.

I don't know how to work it, I admitted.

But *I* do, she said.

I shook my head and laughed. Can you organise the food? I asked.

She repeated with mock horror: Food? as though she never deigned to touch the stuff.

I laughed again because her ploy was so outrageously transparent and because I was soaring with a feverish elation.

Where would we go? I asked.

She drew on her cigarette and blew out a long plume of smoke. Cherbourg.

Cherbourg? I said. But it's always so crowded.

She looked away. Oh, there's a good restaurant there. And I want to buy some shoes.

Shoes!

She gave another sniff. Yes, shoes. And now it was her turn to laugh.

I tried not to remember how easy it was to get to Cherbourg but how very hard it was to sail back against the prevailing winds.

We could leave on Friday? she asked.

We'd have to, I said, to be sure of getting back by Sunday.

That's good, she said.

We wouldn't have very long in Cherbourg.

Who cares? It'll be wonderful! And she gave a low chuckle, a mischievous smile.

I looked at that smile and suddenly my desire for her expanded into something so intense that it seemed to grip my heart, to rob me of breath. But if in that moment my longing sharpened into something more passionate, it also darkened into something more possessive. Even then, before our affair had begun, I was haunted by the thought that she would leave me.

Tell me what you've been doing all these years, I asked her.

She waved her cigarette dismissively in the air.

I pressed her: No, really – where have you been? What have you been doing?

The past, she shrugged. It's over. There's nothing to tell.

Come on, Sylvie, I remonstrated lightly.

But she wouldn't tell me, not much anyway. All she would say was that there had been good times and bad times. She had travelled a bit – she tilted an upturned hand towards what might have been far-off places – then she had lived in Paris, then the Midi. Then . . . She shrugged. Really, she said, the past is past. The important thing is that I'm here and I'm going to do my sculpture and I feel so happy and free. She repeated: So happy and free! And languidly, in a gesture that contained an element of self-parody, she laughingly raised her arms as if to embrace the sun.

I had no reason to think that this lazy extravagant rapture was anything but an expression of genuine pleasure. I did not glimpse the determination in her eyes, nor the singlemindedness.

She turned back to me. You look bad, she said.

Thanks for your encouragement, I laughed.

Isn't anyone looking after you? she asked in mock surprise.

No one knows I'm here.

She came closer and peered at me. Have you taken anything? she said. I have this herbal stuff that cleanses the bloodstream.

Anything that does things for my bloodstream must be good, I said.

Shall I bring some food, too?

I thought you refused to have anything to do with food.

Ha, ha, she said. But you're sick, aren't you?

And that's different?

That means I'll take pity on you. She poured me a glass of water as if to prove it. Coughing suddenly, she pulled out a handkerchief and blew her nose.

You don't sound so good yourself, I said.

She brushed this thought aside with a flip of one hand.

Will you eat with me? I asked.

Her lips formed an arch of uncertainty, her shoulders rose slightly, not so much a shrug as a granting of possibilities. What would you like to eat? she asked.

I'm not too hungry at the moment.

But you will be later. She was already moving towards the windows.

Will I?

Oh, I think so, she said, and there was a subtle but deliberate duality in her voice that made me laugh again.

Grinning back, she fluttered her fingers in farewell and was gone.

When will you be back? I called after her, suspecting, quite rightly, that I would get no reply.

I dozed again, but fitfully. My sleep was disturbed by a recurring dream in which I was waiting endlessly for Sylvie aboard *Ellie Miller*, only to look up and see her on the white cutter, sailing away with her friends. In the way of such dreams I opened my mouth to yell to her but no sound came.

The telephone woke me and took me unsteadily across to the desk. It was Ginny, wanting to know if I was all right. I told her I had flu and would be heading back at around noon the next day. If I hadn't been feeling so rough I would have remembered that mention of flu was bound to be a mistake. Ginny would fret, she would urge me to hire a driver to take me home, and, though she wouldn't mean to, she would be unable to leave the subject alone and then, despite my best intentions, I would become brusque and impatient until, finally, we both retreated, bruised and hurt.

But you can't drive with flu, she said.

I'll be all right by tomorrow.

But have you still got a temperature?

No, it's gone. I'm sure it's gone.

But Hugh, you mustn't even *think* of driving while you've got a fever.

I really do think it's gone.

But you must be very weak.

Honestly, darling—

A movement caught my eye and I looked round to see Sylvie moving silently into the room with a bag of shopping under one arm.

She put a finger against her lips, making conspirators of us both, and I felt a lurch of guilty excitement.

Really, I'll be fine, I said to Ginny as I watched Sylvie disappear in the direction of the kitchen. If not, I'll catch a train.

Promise?

Feeling a twinge of remorse, I said: I promise. And it didn't make me feel any better to know that remorse alone wouldn't stop me from going to France with Sylvie the next weekend.

Ashamed of my capacity for duplicity but unable, it seemed, to suppress it, I did not interrupt Ginny's repeated expressions of concern, I took time to reassure her. Yet the moment I had put the phone down I pushed thoughts of loyalty and conscience to the back of my mind and hurried towards the kitchen, my heart beating absurdly.

Sylvie was standing by the kettle, waiting for it to boil.

It tastes disgusting, she said.

What does?

What I'm going to give you.

I creased my nose. I'm not very brave, I said.

I think you talk nonsense. And she used that tone of intimacy again, the one that suggested we might still be lovers.

Do I have to? I said.

Things that are good for you are always hard to swallow.

Always? I said, assuming a roguish expression. Oh, I do hope not!

I thought I was so witty, I thought I was so dazzling. But that was the effect she had on me; she made me feel attractive and clever again, and in restoring my self-esteem gave me a new sense of my own possibilities.

127

I inspected the meal she had brought. A tin of soup, a tin of sardines, a few tomatoes, a couple of bread rolls, two apples.

A banquet, I said facetiously.

She lit a cigarette and held it between thumb and forefinger, like a screen gangster. I didn't have any money, she said.

You should have told me!

She smiled her cat-smile. Why? Would you have given me some?

I cast my eyes heavenwards in mock despair.

Are you nice and rich? she asked, and, being Sylvie, it was a direct question.

Rich is a relative word, I said. But I've got enough to take us to France at any rate, and give us a good meal when we get there.

She considered this with the pretence of gravity, and gave a characteristic sniff. Well, it's a start, she said. And she tilted me an expression of mock disdain.

A start? I said, thrilling to this game of words. A start of what? A start to where?

But she turned away as the kettle boiled and, pouring some hot water into a mug, stirred in some grey powder. She lifted the potion to her nose and pulled down her mouth in a show of disgust before handing it to me.

That bad? I said.

Let's see just how brave you are, she said, and her eyes issued all sorts of challenges.

The liquid was far too hot and, putting the mug to one side, I held her gaze for a long moment before stepping into the space that separated us and, reaching slowly up, rested the back of my hand against the softness of her cheek. Her eyes, which seemed at a distance to be almost black, glittered with a fierce amber light, and when I began to move the back of my fingers against her skin her lids drooped in bliss, like a basking cat.

I ran my palm down her hair and onto her neck and she let her head fall back as if to open herself up to me.

It was she who heard the sound first. She straightened her head and her eyes flashed a warning. Then I heard it too, the crunch of a car on the gravel.

I made a face and, leaving Sylvie where she was, crossed to the hall window to see David getting out of his car. I went back to alert Sylvie, but there was no sign of her in the kitchen and it wasn't until I had looked into the study and the garden that I realised she had vanished.

David wasn't too thrilled to see me, especially when I told him I'd been ill, because then he felt duty-bound to do doctorly things like taking my temperature and pulse. If he thought it strange that I should have come down on my own without telling him or Mary, then he didn't comment on it. He had come to check the house and didn't stay long. As soon as he had gone I went out into the garden and called Sylvie's name but, though I waited hopefully, she did not return.

I called the boat yard first thing on Monday morning and they promised to go and inspect *Ellie Miller* within the hour. I should have remembered that for boat yards time is an elastic concept. When I chased them up on Wednesday they'd only just decided that *Ellie*'s fastenings looked a bit dodgy around the stem and she'd need to come out of the water for a week while they fixed them. I questioned the need for such drastic work, but I was only making noises to vent my disappointment. I had learnt enough from my father to know that fastenings were serious, and that you didn't put to sea if they weren't in good shape.

I sat through two interminable meetings that afternoon. Whenever the discussion flagged, my mind strayed to ways of salvaging the weekend. It would be difficult to stay at Dittisham – David dropped in at odd times to check the house and Mary was still clearing the attics – and I had the feeling that Sylvie's cottage wouldn't be suitable either, though I didn't care to think too closely about why that should be. A hotel then? A weekend abroad? There would be a risk of discovery but, overruling my last shreds of judgment, I persuaded myself that it would be too small to worry about.

As soon as I had the chance I found a private phone and, my stomach tight, my palms damp, I called the pottery shop. A strange female answered and, overtaken by some guilty reflex, I put the phone down without speaking. Calming myself, I called again and asked for Sylvie, to be told that she wasn't in and might not be in again until Friday. The woman wouldn't give me

Sylvie's number but offered to take mine and pass it on. I didn't leave my name, I just said it was about the weekend and gave the number of my direct line at the office.

But I couldn't leave it there, it was all too indefinite, so I sent a letter by express delivery to the pottery shop with a note asking the shop to forward it urgently. In the letter I explained to Sylvie about the problems with the boat and suggested, with all the subtlety of a determined man, that a quiet weekend at a guide-recommended hotel on the northern edge of Dartmoor might be quite fun. Or else – trying to pre-empt Sylvie's disdain for the mundane and predictable – a couple of days in Nice or Madrid. I asked her to ring me at the office as soon as possible, or, if all else failed, I would meet her at Dittisham on Friday at six.

She didn't ring. I tried calling the pottery shop but it was always the same woman and I kept putting the phone down. On Friday I skipped a midday meeting and drove down early in a state of jittery anxiety.

I went past the pottery shop but it was closed. I opened up the house and waited until past six but she did not come. I poured myself a whisky and forced myself to wait for another half hour before climbing the stairs to David's old room and going to the window.

I had to brace myself to look down river because part of me dreaded what I might see. The cutter was not at her mooring.

I topped up my whisky and forced myself to wait for another two hours. At ten, despite the evidence of the absent cutter, I went looking for her. I knew the pottery shop would be just as empty as before, but that didn't stop me from driving past and peering into the darkened interior.

On the way back I examined every cottage I passed, as if their lights might provide some clue as to which was Sylvie's. Several had cars outside, but I didn't know if she had a car, let alone what make it might be.

I parked near the bottom of the village and went into the pub overlooking the ferry. As I made my way through the crowd to the bar I recognised some men from the boat yard, and with them an assistant harbour master named Horrocks who had known my father well. They were a jovial loquacious bunch, flushed with beer, and, after I'd bought them a drink, it didn't take long to bring the conversation round to the white cutter. Oh, that lot! they cackled derisively. The hippies and weirdos! The boat was called *Samphire*, they informed me, and her owner was a dropout by the name of Hayden who had once been a professional skipper on a massive private yacht in the Med and now lived up Totnes way with no apparent means of support.

She's a pretty boat, I said to explain my interest.

Pretty on board too! cracked one of the lads. All the boys got long hair!

I asked if they cruised far. The same wag reckoned they went just as far as they needed to get out of sight of the shore and start one their sex and drugs parties. With drunken relish he told me that earlier in the summer they'd been spotted in a quiet bay prancing around the deck naked or as near as dammit.

They went to Alderney a lot, Horrocks the assistant harbour master told me more soberly, but this weekend he happened to know they were headed for Barfleur. That was the destination they'd filed with the customs anyway, though he doubted they'd make it back in a hurry with a westerly gale forecast.

I slept badly, waking regularly through the night. At first light I went to the window in David's room and looked down river. Driving rain blotted out the dawn and it was another half an hour before I could be certain that the cutter hadn't yet returned to her mooring.

I closed up the house and drove back to London. I don't remember what reason I gave Ginny for coming home sooner than I'd planned, something about the weather being so dreadful that I couldn't work on the boat. Having received my decision to spend yet another weekend at Dittisham with a burst of exasperation, she greeted my unexpected return in stony silence.

Haunted though I was by Sylvie, I wasn't yet so obsessed that I could abandon Ginny for a third weekend running, and we spent a quiet two days at Melton, with only a drinks party and a casual supper with neighbours to be survived. I don't know whether Ginny had decided tenderness was her best tactic or had recognised that beneath my moods and preoccupations lay a bedrock of despair, but she treated me with cautious affection and sudden eruptions of bleak humour. When we made love I thought of Sylvie and had the decency to feel ashamed.

I might have kept away from Dittisham for another weekend, maybe a lot longer, if Sylvie hadn't called. She came through on my direct line and, in typical Sylvie fashion, did not give her name or even say hello, but announced herself with a question.

Is the boat ready? she asked.

It was a moment before I could speak. What happened to you? I said at last.

What do you mean? she said with breezy innocence.

You know what I mean, I said sternly. When we were meant to be going to France.

But the boat wasn't ready. You said it wasn't ready.

Yes, but I'd made other plans for us, if you remember. I was expecting you. You could at least have let me know. I heard the peevishness in my voice and tried to suppress it.

Oh, but it wouldn't have been any fun going somewhere else, she said. It's so lovely to sail. I love to sail.

You seem to get plenty of sailing on *Samphire*.

She gave a dreamy murmuring laugh, and I couldn't tell if she had missed the reproof in my remark or had merely chosen to ignore it.

She asked: So is the boat ready? Can we go?

It's not that easy, I said. And saying this I remembered how true this was, how Ginny had arranged something for the weekend and I would have to lie to her if I was to get away.

Ahh, Sylvie said. It was a long lingering sound, a sigh but also a signal of dwindling interest.

I have other plans, I explained. But it was a feeble attempt at resistance; I had been prepared to forgive her the moment I heard her voice.

So we can't go?

I made more doubtful noises to bolster the remnants of my pride, then caved in. It might be possible, I said.

Possible?

Possible.

You don't sound very keen.

It's not that. I *am* keen. But after last time how can I be sure you'll turn up?

Oh, I'll be there, Munchkin.

The nickname caught me unawares and bowled me back to the past, to a time when her promises had contained untold possibilities and our greatest intimacy had sprung from the exchange of our most secret thoughts.

We'd have to leave by six, I said.

Sure, she said. And I had the idea she was wearing her cat-smile.

Give me your address and number, I said, in case there're any problems.

Will there be problems?

No, but I must be able to get hold of you, just in case.

She hummed a little, as though considering the merits of my request, then informed me lazily that she lived at Blackwell Cottage up Farrars Lane. She could never remember the phone number, she said – a statement I tried not to greet with scepticism – and took three shots at it before deciding that she probably had it right.

Where shall we meet? I asked.

I don't know. The end of the pontoon, by the dinghies?

No, I said quickly, thinking of who might see us.

Oh, Hugh, she sang teasingly, you haven't changed, have you? All right, pick me up from *Samphire* then.

Is that all right?

Sure, she said.

I said: If you don't turn up, I'll kill you.

She laughed, as though I had made a really witty joke.

Don't forget the food, I said, but she had already rung off.

A doggedness overtook my thinking then, a sort of tunnel vision that left out the more uncomfortable truths. My life was in danger of going off the rails; I knew in my heart that an affair was the very last thing likely to put it back on track, yet I couldn't let go. I clung to the idea of Sylvie as a drowning man clings to a lifeline. I found justifications. I told myself that Sylvie had been the great unrealised love of my life, that she had belonged to a golden future which had been unfairly denied me, and therefore, by some circuitous logic, that I had the right to reclaim her. I persuaded myself that, after stoically enduring the strains of my marriage, I deserved something more exhilarating and undemanding. And the final timeworn excuse: Sylvie's world in no way impinged on mine, Ginny would never find out, no harm would be done. I told myself all this, and sometimes I even managed to believe it.

I didn't like myself very much when I lied to Ginny again, but that didn't stop me from carrying it off effectively. I managed to look her in the eye when I told her I wanted to go sailing at the weekend. Only when she offered to join me did I feel a touch of conscience. Knowing how much she disliked boats, I realised that this suggestion had cost her some effort. But guilt made me unkind. I told her bluntly that I preferred to go on my own.

Ginny flinched slightly. But why alone? she asked.

I need time to think, I said.

But can't I help?

You help a lot, I said. You really do. I just need time away from everything.

It was that Melton weekend, she declared. Something happened then, didn't it? Why can't you tell me what it was?

It wasn't anything in particular.

But you ran out of the house without a word! You just disappeared!

All those people, I said in a fit of honesty. I had nothing to say to them.

So I shouldn't have invited them?

I'm not saying that, I said wearily. It was probably me.

But you didn't like them?

To lie or risk the truth? I said at last: Not all of them, no.

She began to breathe hard, her face took on a cornered look. She said: So it was my fault, then.

I closed my eyes briefly before saying: Ginny, it's not a question of fault. The how and why isn't important, don't you see?

But she didn't see. She gave me a long wounded gaze before tightening her mouth and leaving the room. I found her crying in the kitchen and, like two actors doomed to repeat our lines in a long-running drama, we began our habitual progression through

134

apprehension and reassurance, doubt and comfort. While Ginny demanded to know where she had gone wrong, I repeated the well-used phrases that would eventually restore us to a rocky equilibrium. It seemed to me that we succeeded in reaching an uneasy reconciliation not because either of us was ever truly consoled by what the other had said, but because the prospect of the alternative was too terrible for either of us to contemplate.

I promised to make more of an effort with her friends, I promised us more time together, but I would not give way on the matter of the weekend, and the next day Ginny announced stiffly that she would go and stay at Melton on her own. I felt remorse, but mainly I felt relief.

I ordered a hamper from Fortnum's and supplemented it with some basics from the Dittisham village shop when I got down on Friday afternoon. I tried not to look at the weather, but it was impossible to miss the flailing of the trees and the angry cat's paws on the water. I persuaded myself that the gusts couldn't be stronger than force five, but when I went to pick up an almanac from the chandlery they told me there was a gale warning out.

The first spatterings of rain freckled the water as I rowed out to *Ellie* and by the time I had unloaded the stores and got the boat ready for sea it was hammering down. When I set out for *Samphire* at ten to six the outlines of the cutter were barely visible through the murk.

I waited in *Samphire*'s cockpit, getting increasingly damp and anxious. Sylvie finally appeared at six-thirty, a crouched figure in yellow waterproofs emerging from curtains of rain. I called a bright greeting but she did not reply. Leaving her dinghy tied to the cutter, we went on in mine.

Fabulous weather! I exclaimed wryly. Would you believe it?

But she did not speak until we stood dripping in *Ellie*'s saloon.

I suppose this means we won't be going, she said.

It doesn't look like it, I said and told her about the gale warning.

Her eyes narrowed, she gave a very French display of displeasure, a hiss, a flash of the eyes, and a clamping of her hands to her upper arms, as though to contain her annoyance.

Think about it this way, I said in my most cheering and, I hoped, beguiling manner, the view here is better than Cherbourg

135

and the chef's willing if not able. We have wine. We have food. Even – I made a triumphant gesture – candles!

She did not begin to relent until we were on our second glass of wine. In my mood of insecurity I tried too hard to amuse her, I spoke too loudly, I rattled around the galley like some television chef, stirring extravagantly, making bad jokes, dispensing wine with wild sweeps of the arm. Against logic I felt I was responsible for her discontent and must lift her out of it. But then I was still running blind; I wouldn't have recognised reality if it had come and knocked me on the head. It was a long time before I understood that it was not me who was the main attraction, but France.

We ate, we opened a second bottle of wine. Sylvie emerged slowly from her preoccupations. For a time she sat motionless in her seat, barely listening to what I was saying, then, thrusting an elbow onto the table, she rested her cheek on her hand and watched me with amused detachment. She went to the loo and when she came back she seemed to have made up her mind to enchant me again.

She began to talk lazily, tantalisingly, leading the conversation off in great meandering loops or changing direction abruptly, delighting in her ability to catch me out in small inconsistencies, scolding me now and again in that teasing manner of hers; and once again I had this exhilarating idea that I was the only person in the world for her, that, deep down, there had never been anyone else.

She sneezed, I thought she had a cold, but when I fussed over her she laughed at me fondly and reached across the table to touch my face.

The energy left her as rapidly as it had come. She fell into a dreamy silence, her glass tilted in her hand. I moved onto the seat beside her, my heart racing high in my chest, my nerves taut with hope. Removing her glass to the safety of the table, I touched her hair and kissed her gently on the lips before pulling back, constrained by uncertainty.

She smiled her animal-smile, her eyes narrowed and she came towards me with her head arched back and her lips open.

I rushed at her then, all finesse cast aside. I pushed my mouth

136

onto hers, I grabbed for her breast, it was all I could do not to rip at her clothes.

She flicked her tongue against mine, she gave a low sensuous moan, and it seemed to me that I had never wanted anyone or anything so much in my life.

At first the change was almost imperceptible. Her mouth slackened a little, she became heavier in my arms. Then, quite suddenly, her responses died away altogether and she sank limply against the back of the seat. I stared at her in disbelief. I called her name. She stirred once and laughed softly, then fell into an impenetrable sleep. I shook her, I shouted, but there was no rousing her.

I railed at her, at the wind, at the whole damn world, at myself; by turns I became philosophical and angry and maudlin. Eventually I grew tired. I stretched her out on the bunk and covered her with a sleeping bag, and lay down on the opposite side of the saloon.

I must have slept that night but it didn't seem like it. The gale racketed until dawn. I lay listening to the whine of the halyards and the thrumming of the mast and the fierce slap of the water against the hull, and I felt the night would never end.

The sun was high when I woke. I saw the empty wine bottles, and beyond them, the empty bunk.

She had taken the dinghy.

It was half an hour before I managed to hitch a lift from a passing boat and get ashore. I drove directly to Farrars Lane. Blackwell Cottage was set back from the road behind an overgrown garden. It was a tiny run-down place with mean windows, peeling grey paint and a rusting transit van standing inside the gates on a patch of weedy gravel.

I beat on the door. The silence reached out derisively, and I hammered again, my fist keeping time with the pounding of my heart.

A sound; a door opening or closing. Unhurried steps approached across an uncarpeted floor, the latch clicked and the door opened an inch or two to reveal a man's eye and dark uncombed hair falling across an unshaven chin. The face pulled

137

back. I pushed the door open and stepped into a tiny hall with dark paint, cramped stairs and the smell of damp.

I shouted at the receding back of the long-haired man: Where's Sylvie?

He kept going up the narrow passageway, and I shouted again.

I'm here, Sylvie said. She appeared from the dark front room. I was just coming to find you, she said.

I didn't trust myself to speak.

She lifted a shoulder, she spread a palm. She said again: I was just coming to find you.

Who the hell's he? I jerked my head up the passage.

Joe? He's an old friend. That's all, she said, reading my mind only too well.

Oh yes? I heard the infantile sarcasm in my voice.

Yes, she insisted laughingly. I've known him for ever. She reached up and passed a comforting hand down my cheek, and I shuddered under her touch.

She seemed completely unaffected by the night's alcohol. Her eyes were clear and bright, her skin had a translucent sheen. Her loveliness stood out in stark contrast to the dinginess of the cottage.

Shall we go? she said, and she led the way down the path.

We got into the car and still I couldn't speak.

I had to come and collect something, she explained. I thought I'd get back to the boat before you woke.

Well, you didn't, I said. And there was a choke in my voice.

She put a hand on my knee. Poor Munchkin, she said. Her lips formed the shape of a kiss, her hand moved on my leg, and there was nothing in either gesture that was not completely deliberate. She said: Let's go to the house.

She could have suggested an alleyway and I would have agreed. From that moment on my anger and my lust became inextricably entangled and I never managed to separate them again.

We drove to the house in silence. Once inside we stood slightly apart, weighing each other up as though for combat, then Sylvie took my hand and pulled me upstairs and into David's old room.

I stood before her, not moving, not speaking. Perhaps she liked that, perhaps that made it into a game for her, because she smiled to herself before reaching forward and sliding her hand under my shirt.

Her eyes were very black as her hands travelled over my chest and up my back and then down, down over my bum to curl inwards around the back of my thighs.

I didn't respond immediately, I didn't want her to see how deeply engulfed I was. When I finally touched her it was to grasp her shoulders, but in my attempt to keep some control I must have gripped her more tightly than I realised because she flinched slightly and shivered.

I held my grip. Her lips opened, she gave a harsh sigh, a challenge or a capitulation. I realised with a blend of fascination and exultation that there were no barriers for her, that in her greed for experience she set no bounds, and the realisation was an incitement to a more terrifying desire. In that moment I was finally lost.

We just made it to the bed. It was over in minutes. Later we made love in the study on the sofa with the lights on.

During the night she disappeared, leaving no word. Her telephone didn't answer. This was the pattern of things to come, the pattern of uncertainty and torment that Sylvie practised on me so effortlessly.

It was not long after this, in late July, that Cumberland agreed in principle to the buyout. Leaving Howard and the lawyers to negotiate the finer points of the takeover, I spent much of the next two weeks at Hartford, drawing up a business plan. George offered to put me up, but I always found excuses to stay at Dittisham.

Sometimes Sylvie would announce that she couldn't see me; she never felt she had to give a reason and she laughed at me when I demanded one. And when she did agree to meet me she would often be late or, worst of all, simply fail to turn up. Then, sick at heart, dismayed at my own weakness, I would look for her at the cottage or the shop, I would train my newly purchased binoculars on *Samphire*, I would walk through the village to the quay. Many times I would swear to finish with her, yet I continued to search for her with the same ghastly masochistic craving.

When I finally tracked her down I would question her pathetically, my humiliation mingled with undiminished longing. Finding me in this mood she would regard me with pity, and when I reached for her would pull away impatiently and leave without explanation. In those moments I began to understand how people could kill each other.

When she did let me make love to her – just twice in those two weeks – it was on the promise of making the long-delayed trip to France. I still didn't get it, of course; I was still too dazzled to understand the significance of France.

I couldn't get away over the following two weekends – a family wedding, then a batch of buyout meetings – but I slipped down midweek a couple of times. By then I had lost all restraint, and all caution too. I took risks, I left cryptic phone messages with long-haired Joe – calling myself M, my token to discretion – and once I took Sylvie out to dinner at a restaurant in the country where we could easily have bumped into people I knew. She laid down her terms at that dinner, she said she didn't want to carry on unless we could get away to France. In my blindness I was flattered, I thought she wanted to relive our old adventures, to escape the madding crowd and be alone with me, and, desperate for my moment of happiness, I heard myself promise faithfully to take her to France the next weekend.

By tradition Ginny and I always left for a ten-day break in Provence on the Friday of the August bank holiday weekend, but at two days' notice I told Ginny I couldn't go. I said I had too much work at Hartford, that she should go on her own for a day or so to prod the estate agents into action and inspect the house. If she had put up a fierce argument, if she had challenged me about an affair, my conscience might have got the better of me, but she didn't, and with an adulterer's logic I took her acceptance as some kind of permission.

I couldn't get down to Dittisham until midnight on the Friday. Sylvie was waiting for me at the house. It was too late to go out to the boat that night, so we picnicked in the study by the french windows. The anticipation was like a drug. My head was light, my pulse racing. We made love on the sofa with the curtains undrawn.

As Sylvie moved over my body I thought I heard a sound outside but, lost to the sensations of the moment, I quickly pushed the idea from my mind.

SEVEN

Henderson prepared unhurriedly, arranging his papers, checking the recorder, ignoring me.

Tingwall poured me a cup of water and murmured, 'Okay?'

I nodded, trying to suppress my nerves. 'We'll get a break at some point?'

'Oh yes, I'll make sure we do.'

'I don't want my wife sitting there for hours.'

'Don't worry, we won't go on all night.'

It was the same interview room as before. Reith was sitting a foot or so back from the table, to Henderson's left. Phipps was propping up the wall by the door. The air was hot and stale as though the room had just been vacated by another team in pursuit of a sweating quarry. For an instant I wondered what the air was like in prison, whether it was like this or worse, whether it stank of sweat and urine and drugs, and fear whispered in my stomach.

The tape recorder was switched on. Henderson intoned some preliminaries, informing me the interview was being recorded and that I could take a copy of the tape away with me if I so wished. He then logged the time, the place, and identified each person in the room.

He slid his heavy forearms onto the table and raised his gloomy eyes to mine. 'Mr Wellesley, could you please take us through your movements on Saturday, the thirtieth of September?'

'I got the time of the petrol wrong,' I announced straight away. 'It was earlier than I thought. Four-fifteen.'

'And where did you buy this petrol?'

'At the Gordano service station.'

'And that's on the M5?'

'Yes, just this side of Bristol.'

'Four-fifteen . . . So what time did you leave London?'

'It must have been nearer two-thirty. Maybe even two.'

'In your previous statement you stated that it was three o'clock.'

'I was working hard that day. I was under a lot of pressure. I didn't notice the time.'

'And what time did you arrive in Dittisham?'

'At about quarter past seven.'

'So it took you three hours to get from just past Bristol to Dittisham?'

'Yes.'

'Though the traffic jam you mentioned in your previous statement was *before* Bristol, *before* you stopped for petrol?'

'The traffic was heavy everywhere. It was a Saturday.'

'But three hours, Mr Wellesley?' He tilted his ponderous head. 'Even if the traffic was heavy it would be extremely unusual to take that long, surely?'

I shrugged. 'Well, that's how long it took.'

'These timings seem rather uncertain in your mind, Mr Wellesley.'

'No. I've got them right now.'

'How can you be sure when you arrived at Dittisham?'

'I noticed the time because I needed to buy some food and I realised the village shop would be closed.'

'Yet you can't account for this unusually long journey time?'

'No. Yes. I mean – I can only tell you what happened.'

'Indeed,' he said, and the scepticism showed in his voice.

He looked down briefly. 'What time did you arrange to meet Sylvie Mathieson that day?'

My mouth dried slightly. 'I had no arrangement to meet her.'

'Come now. You had an arrangement to meet her early that evening, didn't you?'

'No, I did not.'

'You had an arrangement to meet her on your father's boat, the *Ellie Miller*?'

'I had no arrangement to meet her that day.'

143

'Not that day?' He affected a look of curiosity. 'Another day then?'

'No.'

'You met Sylvie on the boat regularly, didn't you, Mr Wellesley?'

I glared at him. I didn't reply.

'I repeat, you met her on the boat regularly?'

'I told you – I met her there twice.'

'You also went to her home, didn't you? To Blackwell Cottage?'

I realised, then, that his information could only have come from Joe. Long-haired spaced-out Joe.

'You went to her home more than once?'

I shook my head.

'Could you speak out, please, Mr Wellesley?'

'I've told you how often I saw her.' I was fighting for time. I was trying to work out if Joe would be able to identify me after a brief glimpse through a crack in a door and a slightly longer look in darkness when he was stoned out of his mind. I was also trying to decide whether drug addicts were likely to be regarded as reliable witnesses.

'The question I'm putting to you, Mr Wellesley, is whether you met her regularly?'

'I had no arrangement to meet her that day,' I repeated doggedly, not answering the question.

'But what about all the other times?' Henderson said, still asking it.

'I told you how often I met her.'

'Three or four times?'

'Yes.'

'But that was all lies, wasn't it, Mr Wellesley? You saw her much more often than that, didn't you?'

'I did not meet her on that Saturday.' It was the only tactic I could think of, to repeat the point like a liturgy.

'You're not answering my question, Mr Wellesley. You met Sylvie Mathieson on a regular basis, didn't you?'

'I did not meet her on a regular basis.'

'You're denying it then?'

144

I thought of Ginny, of what she had asked of me, and he got his direct answer at last. 'Yes.'

Henderson turned down his rat-trap mouth and moved on. 'You went on a trip to France on the boat, didn't you? At the end of August?'

'Yes.'

'You went with Sylvie Mathieson?'

'No. I went with my wife.'

Henderson raised his brows slightly at that. 'You went with your wife?'

'Yes.'

'Are you sure about that?'

'It's hardly something I'd be mistaken about.'

His mouth compressed into a sharp line, he fixed me with his droopy eyes. 'Presumably not.' He addressed himself to Tingwall. 'Would Mrs Wellesley be prepared to make a statement to this effect?'

Tingwall gave me the briefest glance. 'Er, I would have to confer, obviously, but I imagine there will be no difficulty.'

Returning to me, Henderson murmured, 'But you did go on a trip with Sylvie Mathieson at some point, didn't you, Mr Wellesley?'

'No.'

'What – no trip at all?'

'No.'

'Never mind France. Anywhere . . . Up the river?'

I exhaled harshly. 'No.'

Henderson tapped his stubby fingers twice on the table. 'What about there in the harbour then? You spent time with Sylvie Mathieson on the boat there, didn't you?'

'Just the once, as I told you. And the time she rowed over and talked to me from a boat.'

'Perhaps you'd care to reconsider your answer, Mr Wellesley. You see, there are witnesses who will say they saw Sylvie Mathieson on the' – he referred to his notes – '*Ellie Miller* more than once or twice. They'll say they saw her there several times.'

'I've already told you she came to the boat just twice.'

'And you don't want to add to that statement?'

145

'No.'

'But there *were* other times, weren't there, Mr Wellesley?'

'I've told you.'

'And what about these witnesses, the ones who saw Sylvie visiting you on the boat?'

'I have no idea.'

'Come now, Mr Wellesley, we know you saw her regularly. Why not tell us about it?'

This was his method then, a kind of verbal bullying. The technique was transparent enough, yet I could see how it might wear people down, how they might tell him what he wanted to hear just to win some respite. I wondered if he realised that in most respects I was already won over, that I hardly needed any wearing down, that if it hadn't been for my solemn promise to Ginny and the dire interpretation I felt sure he would put on any admissions I might make, I would have told him the truth about the affair half an hour ago. An affair was nothing, after all, compared to murder. This thing had gone on too long and become too frightening for considerations of pride.

'There's nothing more to tell.'

Henderson appraised me with open interest, trying to gauge whether I was mad or simply stupid.

'What about Saturday, the thirtieth of September? You met Sylvie Mathieson there on the boat, didn't you?'

'I've told you – no.'

'You met her because you were having an affair with her, didn't you?'

I made no answer.

'You met her in the same way that you'd met her many times before, but this time you had an argument which got out of hand and you killed her.'

Everything had been leading up to this statement, yet the baldness of it still took me aback.

'That's not true.'

'Perhaps you didn't mean to kill her. Perhaps it was just a moment of anger.'

'Listen—' I tried to maintain a reasonable tone. 'I did not see her that day. I did not arrange to meet her. And I certainly did not

146

kill her. And no matter how many times you ask these questions, no matter how often you suggest these – *things* – nothing's ever going to change that.' I added emotionally: 'Because it simply isn't true.'

Reith exchanged a knowing glance with Phipps. Only Henderson's expression did not alter.

'It isn't true,' I repeated, lifting my hands helplessly.

My words fell unheeded into the silence.

Henderson sighed, 'Let's go back to Saturday, the thirtieth of September, shall we?'

I looked at Tingwall but his absorbed expression gave me no guidance.

We went over it again in minute detail, the unusually long journey, the period that Henderson referred to as unaccounted time, the rest of the weekend. We went back over how well I had known Sylvie, the two visits to the boat, the conversations. We continued in this way for an hour or more. I made no slips, I had learnt my story too well by then, yet the air seemed to grow steadily closer, the lights harsher, and I was glad when Tingwall asked for a break.

Henderson agreed calmly, 'Very well.' He went through the signing off procedure for the benefit of the tape, then switched off the machine. 'Oh, and Mr Tingwall? We would like Mr Wellesley's fingerprints, if that's acceptable.'

Tingwall's squint intensified. 'This would be for elimination purposes, would it?'

Henderson conceded with a faint shrug. 'If you like.'

Tingwall asked for a moment to confer and took me into the corridor. 'Listen,' he whispered, 'if we refuse I have the feeling they'll just slap a charge on you, and then the prints'll be compulsory anyway. So it might be best to agree. It seems to me that the longer we put off a charge, the better.'

I nodded meekly and we went back into the room.

'Mr Wellesley will be happy to comply,' Tingwall announced.

'I believe Mrs Wellesley's downstairs, is that correct?'

Tingwall confirmed it.

'I trust she'll also be agreeable to providing prints?'

'Is this necessary?' I demanded.

Studiously ignoring me, Henderson looked to Tingwall for a reply.

Henderson's attitude suddenly infuriated me. 'I'm asking,' I said, 'if this is really necessary.'

Tingwall began to speak but I hushed him with a splayed hand.

When Henderson finally addressed me it was grudgingly, as though he was granting me an unnecessary indulgence. 'To conduct an elimination process,' he intoned, 'we have to have the prints of everyone who had access.'

'That's an awful lot of people,' I retorted, though I didn't know what access he was talking about. 'My whole family for a start!'

Tingwall cut in smoothly, 'Will an hour be all right, Inspector? Mr Wellesley will need something to eat before everything closes for the night. And I will need time to confer.'

Henderson looked at his watch. 'Fingerprints in fifteen minutes? And we'll continue the interview in the morning at nine.'

Tingwall nodded, and drew me aside. 'It'll be a night in the cells, I'm afraid. But I'll bring in a sandwich, otherwise you'll get nothing till breakfast.'

'How long do I have to stay here?'

'They can hold you twenty-four hours without charge. Thirty-six with the superintendent's say-so.'

'I didn't mean to get angry,' I said.

He raised an eyebrow.

'Will it count against me?'

Tingwall caught my bleak attempt at humour. 'Listen – compared to most of his customers you're a saint.'

I waited in the stuffy interview room with a yawning Phipps until Tingwall reappeared.

'Mrs Wellesley has agreed to the fingerprinting,' he said when Phipps had left. 'She asked for you to be present. And I said I thought that could be arranged.' There was admiration in his voice, and deference; it seemed that Tingwall had been rather taken by Ginny.

'Listen,' I said, 'am I going mad or ... If there were drugs in Sylvie's body then why aren't the police looking into that side of things? Why aren't they chasing those connections?'

Tingwall's eyes took on a wary light. 'Drugs? Were there drugs?'

'That's what my brother said. He'd heard from somewhere – the hospital, some doctors. And if she was into drugs there must have been dealers, drug addicts . . . Perhaps she was in debt to them. Perhaps . . . I don't know – but something.'

Tingwall mulled on this. 'It would certainly seem like an area worth investigating,' he said cautiously.

'So why are they ignoring it?'

'We don't know they are. They could well be looking into it.'

'Oh yes?' I said heavily. 'Well, it doesn't seem that way to me. It seems to me that they've made up their minds.'

'It's not easy to tell the police what to do, Hugh. They don't always like it. But I'll try.' He didn't look too hopeful.

Phipps came to lead us to the fingerprinting room. Ginny was already there, sitting apart from the waiting officers. When she saw me she rose hurriedly and kissed me. Standing in that dreary room with her classy Joseph suit and her long slender legs and her curtain of shining hair, she looked like a vision visited on a wasteland.

'All right?' she whispered and there was no mistaking the question in her eyes.

'All right,' I said, and my look told her what she wanted to know, that I had kept my promise and stuck to our story.

She clutched my arm in a gesture of encouragement and complicity.

We stood at the desk side by side like a couple in a register office. When Ginny offered up her hand to the sergeant I saw that she was trembling. As the sergeant rolled the first of her fingers across the paper she gave a shudder that travelled the length of her body. When the last print was taken she exhaled suddenly and, wiping the ink from her fingers, turned and gave me an anxious lopsided smile. Looking at her then I couldn't imagine why I had ever thought I didn't love her.

*

In the morning they let me out of the cell to wash and shave. I turned down the large fried breakfast and settled for dark tea and dry toast. Tingwall appeared at nine, looking very young with his smooth scrubbed skin and bright expression.

He told me the interview had been postponed and no new time fixed.

'Is that good or bad?'

'Impossible to say.'

'So I could be here all day?'

'Yes.'

I didn't ask about the press, because I knew that if there wasn't anything in the papers today, there would be tomorrow, and I wasn't ready to face up to the consequences of that quite yet.

'They've asked for your wife to make her statement this morning so I've arranged it for eleven. Your sister-in-law is driving her in.'

'Will I be able to see her?'

He made an apologetic face. 'Probably not.'

Ginny had stayed the night at Furze Lodge. David and Mary would have been kind and attentive, but probably rather overwhelming too, and I suspected that she would be feeling the strain.

After Tingwall left I asked for pen and paper, which the duty officers let me have, and, in an attempt at normality, I balanced the paper on my knee and tried to work on some marketing plans. But the gesture was hopeless, I simply couldn't concentrate, and after a while I lay on the bunk staring at the ceiling, wondering how people could survive this for days on end. At noon a plate of fish and chips arrived with a gluey pudding and more strong tea. At one Tingwall came to tell me that Ginny had made her statement without a hitch and the whole thing had been completed in just over an hour.

'She did very well,' Tingwall remarked with an odd embarrassed smile, as though he were especially proud of her. 'They haven't said anything about you,' he added. 'No interview time set.'

'Is that good or bad?'

'Can't say. They may be waiting for something.'

The afternoon was endless. By three I was pacing the cell, by

150

five I was asking for Tingwall. It came to me then that, unnerving though imprisonment may be, it is not the lack of freedom which most undermines you, it is the sudden powerlessness, the sheer inability to communicate.

They finally called me at nine. We took our places in the interview room like seasoned players. At first Henderson did not diverge from his routine. He retrod the same ground, I carefully repeated my answers. The new question was an hour coming. We were going through the weekend of Sylvie's death when Henderson said: 'On the Sunday you were away from your wife for some of the time, is that right?'

I wondered exactly what Ginny had told them. 'There were lots of chores to be done that weekend,' I said. 'We split the tasks between us. Mostly I was in the house, and yes – for some of the time my wife was doing other jobs.'

'She was away on the boat for two hours?'

'I can't remember how long she was there, but yes, she went to the boat.'

'You asked her to go there?'

'No. No, it was . . . There were certain jobs that only I could do – sorting through trunks, papers, that sort of thing. It was simply the way it worked out, that she should go to the boat.'

'What was she doing on the boat exactly?'

'Oh . . . Cleaning it out, taking things off. Preparing the boat to be laid up.'

'Laid up?'

'Hauled out of the water and put ashore for the winter.'

'She always did that job, did she?'

'No, it was my father who did that sort of thing. It was his boat. He always looked after it.'

'So why should your wife go and do the job? How would she know what to do?'

I understood now. I had sent Ginny to the boat as a ploy to get her out of the house and win time to cover up my crime of the previous night. Or perhaps they weren't absolutely sure when Sylvie had been killed. Perhaps they thought I had done it on the Sunday morning and calmly proceeded to carry her body down to the river in full view of the walkers and rowers and weekend sailors, and dumped her in the river.

'My wife knew the boat well. She used to sail on it when we were first married. She knew what had to be done – clearing out the galley, taking off the bedding – that kind of thing.'

'That was what you asked her to do, was it? The galley and the bedding?'

'I told you – we didn't go into detail. I left it up to her. She's very good at all that.'

Henderson pondered this. 'And while she was away you . . . ?'

'I went through a trunkful of old letters.'

'You didn't see anyone?'

'Well – no. I was up in the attic.'

'No one came to the house?'

'Not that I know of. I probably wouldn't have heard the doorbell.'

Henderson watched me tensely. 'And what time did your wife return?'

'About one? No – twelve-thirty.'

'And then what happened?'

'We had lunch. As my wife will have told you.'

He was still for a moment, then in a display of disappointment or resignation he fanned out his fleshy fingers and flexed his shoulders before moving back to old ground.

And that was the turning point, though I didn't realise it immediately. Henderson went through the motions for another half hour or so, but his voice took on a weary tone, he looked at his watch from time to time, and Tingwall, reading the signs, began to push for an end to the proceedings. Like barrow boys, they began to negotiate. Taking me aside, Tingwall asked me if as a concession I might be willing to stay in the area for a couple of days.

'Do I have to?'

'No. But it might persuade them not to apply for a custody extension.'

And so I agreed because by that time I would have done almost anything to get out of there.

It wasn't until I walked into the reception area and saw Ginny that I allowed myself anything approaching relief.

She gasped when she saw me. 'Thank God,' she kept saying, 'Thank God.' And she began to cry, half laughing as she did so.

'It may not be over,' I said.

She searched my face, she absorbed this slowly. 'Well, let's cross that bridge when we come to it.'

*

It was almost midnight when the taxi dropped us at Furze Lodge. David opened the door.

'You shouldn't have waited up,' I said.

'What the hell,' he said airily, and kissed Ginny on both cheeks.

'I'm rather tired,' Ginny announced in a subdued voice. 'I think I'll go straight to bed.'

I offered to bring her up a hot drink. At first she said not to bother, but perhaps she understood that in my inept inarticulate way I was trying to show my gratitude to her, because she changed her mind and said if there was a camomile tea she'd love one, otherwise anything would do.

I followed David into the kitchen and watched him hunt vaguely through a couple of cupboards. 'We're not really into herbal stuff,' he declared unapologetically. Eventually he found a lone sachet of peppermint tea.

'Well?' he demanded as he filled the kettle and plumped it on the Aga.

'Well . . . they've let me out, but they think I did it.'

'Think or know?'

'Actually,' I protested stiffly, 'there's nothing to know.'

'I meant,' he retorted with a flash of impatience, 'what evidence do they have?'

'They're not saying.'

Shaking his head, he disappeared and came back almost immediately with a bottle of Scotch and two glasses.

'David, you said that Sylvie was into drugs—'

He slung the glasses onto the counter between us. 'Did I?'

153

'Yes. You said so the other day. You said she was into all sorts of stuff.'

He slopped some whisky into the glasses and pulled his mouth down into an expression of denial. 'I don't think so.'

'For Christ's sake, David!' He had done this when we were younger, made some bold statement only to disclaim it later and somehow shift the blame for the misunderstanding onto me.

Under my furious gaze he made a grudging concession with a lift of one shoulder, and waved an ambiguous hand. 'It was a rumour, that was all. Hospital gossip. You know – the police pathologist drops a hint. Or it might have been a forensic technician. But it's not too reliable that sort of thing. Believe me.'

'But she was your patient.'

'Ha!' My naivety brought a hint of bitter amusement to his face. 'You think patients tell their doctors everything? You think they tell them about their secret drinking and their forty fags a day and their extra-curricular pills?' He lifted his eyes expressively. 'Sylvie only came to see me a couple of times and the subject of whether she was on drugs didn't *exactly* come up.'

'What about the people she mixed with?'

He took a swig of his drink. 'Haven't a clue.'

'There was that deadbeat with the long hair.'

'Which one?' he exclaimed sardonically, as if his surgery was beset by long-haired deadbeats.

'Joe something.'

'Doesn't ring a bell.'

'And someone called Hayden.'

He shook his head. 'Not one of mine. Well – so far as I know.'

'She used to go sailing on Hayden's boat. That's what they said at the boat yard, anyway.'

'And he's a druggy, is that it?'

'Someone must have been.' I dragged my hands wearily down my face. 'Oh, I don't know, I don't bloody know, David. It's all such a bloody nightmare.'

'Well,' he said laconically, 'it's not worth panicking about, is it? They can't get you for something you didn't do, can they?'

'I hope not,' I said fervently. 'But sometimes . . .'

'For what it's worth,' he continued in the same brisk tone, 'we'll do what we can. You know – support and all that.'

After such a day my emotions were running close to the surface, and when I thanked him my eyes misted over, the words caught in my throat.

Looking alarmed at this display, David said sharply, 'I gather they want our fingerprints.'

'Yes,' I said, pulling myself together. 'For elimination purposes – that's what they call it. Tingwall can explain it better than me. Apparently you don't have to agree, but if you don't they could insist.'

David gave a shrug suggesting it was no skin off his nose, then turned away to deal with the boiling kettle.

'The family contacted me,' he said over his shoulder.

'Family?'

'Sylvie's brother. Jean-something. Jean-Paul.'

A memory flickered, an image of a self-absorbed guitar-playing youth who had appeared once or twice during that distant summer. 'God . . . I'd forgotten.'

'An *academic* of some sort. Bristol.'

'What did he want?'

David poured hot water into a mug. 'Oh, where to go for the burial arrangements, that kind of thing.'

I hadn't thought about her family. I hadn't thought about the funeral. 'When will all that be?'

David dunked the bag of mint tea uncertainly into the mug, then lifted it out and, creasing his brows in faint annoyance, dropped it in again. 'Oh, not for quite a time, I wouldn't think.' He added casually: 'He wanted to know how to get in touch with you.'

'*Me?*' The thought disturbed me profoundly. 'Why?'

'Not sure. Old time's sake maybe.' And I couldn't tell if he meant this ironically. 'Anyway I talked him out of it.'

'He didn't realise that I was the prime suspect, then?' I said with a lurch of self-pity.

'Probably not, no.'

This was the way of the future, I realised. In my new state of social unacceptability I would have to rely on my family to shield

155

me from unsuitable encounters, and my lawyers to protect me from the worst intrusions of the press.

David yawned and rubbed his eyes savagely with his fore-fingers.

'Sorry,' I said immediately, 'I'm keeping you up.'

'No, if you want to talk . . .' He stood there doing his best to look approachable, but it was not something that came easily to him, and it showed in the restlessness of his eyes and the wariness of his manner. As boys we had told each other everything, we had been accomplices in many a misdemeanour and covered for each other steadfastly, yet in our early teens David had abruptly distanced himself from me and the world in general, and in the muddle of adolescence I had never been sure why.

'Thanks for the offer,' I said, 'but I'm exhausted.'

He nodded with what might have been relief and, turning off the lights, led the way upstairs.

I carried the tea in to Ginny as she lay reading a magazine in bed and, placing it on the table beside her, kissed her on the forehead. She smiled a loyal smile, and it came to me that, if I was to be locked away, this would be the worst deprivation of all, the loss of such moments of quiet domesticity.

*

After a restless night I woke early to a clear sky and scents of autumn. I lay in bed and remembered waking to a morning like this not so long ago and thinking how lucky I was to be alive. That must have been before the cash flow crisis, before David told me that Pa had cancer.

Ginny had taken some pills and was still asleep. I got up quietly and, making myself some coffee, carried it out into the freshness of the garden. My shoes darkened as I wandered across the dew-laden grass. Above me the leaves of the oaks were saffron, lemon and gold, and on the far side of the croquet lawn a maple blazed. Somewhere a lone bird was calling. It was best not to consider the beauty of it all; that way lay depression and despair.

A sound made me turn and there, in a reprise of our meeting at Dittisham House, was Mary, waving hard. She closed the door behind her and came striding towards me in her Barbour jacket, knee-length skirt and gumboots, her round face cracked into a smile.

'I meant to stay awake last night,' she declared indignantly as soon as she had kissed me, 'I told David to give me a shout the moment you arrived! Honestly!' With a flick of the hand, she gestured the futility of such expectations. 'But listen – how are you?'

'How am I?' I considered this with a mournful laugh. 'Oh, for public consumption, I'm fine. You know – full of righteous indignation and protesting my innocence from the rooftops. But in reality . . . Quite frankly, Mary, when I'm not feeling choked I'm scared stiff.'

'They've found out, have they, about you and Sylvie?'

I lifted my shoulders. 'God only knows. They're not saying.'

'And what have *you* told *them*?'

'Nothing.'

'Nothing,' she repeated thoughtfully, as though she wasn't entirely convinced of the wisdom of this but didn't like to mention it.

'Well, what am I going to tell them, Mary?' I argued with sudden heat. 'That as it happens they're dead on track, that I've lied through my teeth, that I had a wild affair with Sylvie, that I had every reason to kill her—'

'*Every* reason?' she interrupted with a small embarrassed laugh.

In telling her, I realised that I was testing the story against a time when I might have to deliver it on a larger stage. 'Well, she'd dropped me, hadn't she? Finished the whole thing. Just – without warning. For no reason at all. She wouldn't say why. In fact, she wouldn't communicate at all. She deliberately avoided me. Just . . . cut me out! She was brilliant at that,' I added wryly, 'at shutting people out.'

'*Oh*,' Mary murmured, her face puckered with concern. 'Oh. I hadn't realised.'

'Oh, I knew it was no good!' I declared. 'I knew the whole thing was hopeless! I realised she wasn't the same person. I realised she'd changed out of all recognition. In many ways she was

157

utterly *un*likeable. But still, but *still* . . . I couldn't *stop* myself, you see. I just couldn't.'

Mary absorbed this with the faraway look of someone attempting to imagine a passion completely outside her own experience. 'Poor old thing,' she said at last. 'How awful for you!'

We strolled towards the croquet lawn.

'When was this?' Mary asked.

'Oh—' I muttered vaguely. 'At the end of August.'

A pause. 'You mean – when you sailed to France?'

'Thereabouts.'

'Aha.' And she drew the sound out until it took on a wealth of meaning. 'I realised it must have been Sylvie on the boat with you.'

I halted.

'Ginny's always hated sailing so much.'

'God. Does anyone else . . . David . . . ?'

'I don't think so.'

'The thing is . . . we're saying it was Ginny. We're telling the police we went to France together. Ginny's absolutely determined. She's making a statement about it. You won't . . .' I gestured feebly. 'I mean . . . not to anyone?'

Mary fixed me with her most fiery look. 'If you weren't in such a state, I'd take that as a bloomin' insult!'

'Sorry. *Sorry*, Mary. Sometimes I get paranoid.'

She shook her head fondly and we continued our walk.

'Hate to mention it and all that,' she said after a while, 'but Ginny wasn't anywhere else when she was meant to be sailing with you, was she? I mean, nowhere *obvious*.'

'No.'

Whether she was simply being tactful or had deduced that Ginny had come secretly to Dittisham, she didn't ask me to elaborate on this curious answer.

I hesitated, knowing I was about to test Mary's patience yet further. 'I'm going to be paranoid again,' I announced. 'But I've got to ask – you haven't told David anything at all, have you? About me and Sylvie?'

'Don't be ridiculous!' She threw her head back and gave a

sharp laugh, half amusement, half scorn. 'He wouldn't listen anyway!'

We had reached a bench set on a small rise overlooking the croquet lawn. Pulling a scarf out of her pocket, Mary began to sweep the dew from the seat with broad strokes.

'Oh, it's not that he isn't *concerned!*' she assured me. 'It's just that he doesn't like to hear about anything even faintly disturbing. Never has done. He's the original ostrich when it comes to problems and crises. Just blanks them all out. That's why he should never have been a GP – can't deal with the patients. And that's why I've brought up the children almost single-handed. Oh, don't think I'm bleating!' she added breezily, beating the last drops from the wood with whip-like flicks of the scarf end. 'Because I'm not. It's just the way he is. I don't *mind*. Having stuck with his foibles for all these years, I'm certainly not about to give up on him now!' She gave another bray-like laugh and, sitting down and crossing her muscular legs, patted the seat next to her.

'What happens now?' she asked in the bracing tones of a pragmatist.

'Oh, more questioning, I suppose.' I sank disconsolately onto the seat. 'But I want Tingwall to press them on what *else* they're doing. On why they haven't bothered to look into the rest of Sylvie's life. Like her drug connections for a start.'

Mary threw me a glance. 'She was involved with drugs?'

'One way and another.'

'Blimey!' she exhaled noisily with a kind of baffled admiration, as though other people's lives never failed to amaze her. 'She told you, did she?'

'Me?' I gave an ironic laugh. 'Hardly. But then if I'd been in my right mind she wouldn't have had to. It was staring me in the face. She had a runny nose half the time. And she'd be morose one minute and go off to the loo and, hey presto, when she came back she'd be full of life again.'

'And you're saying the police haven't realised this?'

'No,' I conceded. 'I suppose they must have done. I mean, if David knew . . .'

'David knew?'

'Some rumour on the medical grapevine.'

'Ah.'

'But the police don't seem interested in following it up – finding out about her pals, where she got the stuff from, that sort of thing.'

Mary, picking her way cautiously through alien territory, ventured: 'You mean she might have been mixing with dealers and other dubious specimens?'

I chucked the dregs of my coffee onto the grass. 'That's exactly what I mean.'

In the silence a light aircraft droned overhead and we both looked up at it.

I said in a rush, 'She worked for them.' I got it out quickly before I had second thoughts.

Still following the plane, Mary took her time. 'She worked for the dealers?'

'The trips she took on *Samphire*. They were all about drugs.'

Mary turned to examine my face. 'They had them on board?'

'They picked them up in France. I don't know exactly what sort of stuff it was, but it was hard stuff. Powder of some sort.'

Mary waited silently while I found the words to tell the rest of the miserable tale.

'Sylvie fell out with her chums,' I began. 'Well, I guess she did because suddenly *Samphire* went to sea without her or didn't go to sea at all. *So . . .*' I spread my hands derisively. 'Alternative plan. Set up in business on your own. Find a mug with a boat, preferably someone who's pretty naive and malleable—'

'Oh, Hugh.'

'—Use him to get you to France.'

'Oh no.'

'—Collect your package, allow your dewy-eyed lover to stand you an expensive meal before getting him to sail you back. Then leave him to carry the can.'

Mary looked alarmed. 'You mean you got *caught*?'

The memory gripped me and I shuddered. 'So nearly, Mary. So nearly.'

As *Ellie Miller* crept out from under the lee of the land and caught the first uncertain gusts of wind, I felt the elation of someone who

160

had forgotten the extraordinary illusion of freedom you get at sea, the sense of leaving the world behind.

I went about the boat, trimming sheets, tightening halyards, entering the log, and relived the exhilaration of my boyhood trips, when my father had expected no crew member to stop until all the tasks were done, when no sail was considered trimmed until it had passed his beneficent scrutiny, when, at twenty, I was first entrusted with the job of navigator. The pride I had felt, and the fear of failure, and the satisfaction when the destination was made.

The wind was westerly and fresh. It was *Ellie*'s weather, a steady force five on the quarter, downhill all the way. As the old girl gathered pace she groaned and creaked in grumpy content-ment, like a grandmother exercising her stiffened joints. Water hissed and surged along the hull, the crockery rattled in the galley, somewhere wood moved complainingly against wood. Hearing such long-forgotten sounds, feeling the movement of the boat under my feet, it seemed to me that, in abandoning sailing for all these years, I had left something important behind, a part of my past, a part of myself.

Sylvie sat in the cockpit for an hour or so, chatting desultorily, before going below to sleep. After lunch, I dozed for a couple of hours while she kept watch. When I came back on deck she was in one of her more ebullient moods. She told me a little more about her life in France, though not so much that I could piece many facts together. There had been a house in the Midi, with, it seemed, several people in residence, though she wouldn't be drawn on their relationship to each other. Lovers, husbands, wives; it was all very vague. Had it been a happy time? I asked. Oh, happy enough, she said. Then she turned her almond eyes on mine and said in that low sonorous voice of hers: But not happy like we were happy, Munchkin.

That was all it took, one small remark, and my heart squeezed with foolish joy, and, for a short time at least, the doubts that constantly lurked at the edges of my feelings for Sylvie faded away. In a moment of euphoria all my romantic notions of undying love came rushing back, I thought in ludicrously grandiose terms of the great wheels of fate that had brought

Sylvie and me together again. For a short while, until the unease returned, I was besotted again.

As dusk fell and we sighted the beams of the Casquets and Cap de la Hague, the breeze stiffened and *Ellie* picked up her skirts and rushed headlong for land at a galloping six and a half knots. We tied up in the marina at half past midnight. The strange thing was that, though I had nurtured visions of sleeping beside Sylvie in some quiet harbour ever since our affair had begun, something made me retreat. I still wanted her terribly, but it was an ugly craving that drove me to make love to her that night, an urge to possess her at all costs, almost an act of retribution for the helplessness she engendered in me, and once I had left her body, once she had curved against me ready for sleep, something about the intimacy of the position and its implications of domesticity unsettled me and after a few minutes I crept away to a bunk in the saloon.

I woke to find Sylvie on her way out to buy croissants and bread. There was a tautness about her that morning, a barely concealed impatience, and no sooner had she returned than she announced she wanted to go out again.

The shoe shops open? I grinned.

She shrugged: And other things.

I asked if it could wait half an hour while we had our coffee.

You don't have to come, she said, and behind the empty smile there was a dark cold look in her eye.

But I want to, I said lightly, trying to dispel the tension.

She sat still for a minute or two, then climbed up the companionway. I thought she was waiting for me in the cockpit, I didn't hear her step onto the pontoon but, light-footed as she was, she must have gone immediately, because by the time I had taken a last gulp of scorching coffee and gone up to find her she had vanished. Suppressing a fury, I locked the boat up and walked briskly towards the town.

Approaching the shopping area I saw her distinctive figure a long way ahead, turning a corner into a side street. I accelerated to a jog then a steady run but on reaching the corner she had disappeared. It was a street of small family shops: a brilliantly lit *boucherie*, a musty *librairie*, a *boulangerie* with a queue snaking out onto the pavement, then – I congratulated myself – a shoe shop. The window was plastered with sale signs so it wasn't until I went inside that I realised she wasn't there.

My resentment flared again, I felt a surge of anticipation. For the first time I imagined hurting her, taking her arm and squeezing it until she yelped.

At the end of the street was an open market set in a small square. The place was crowded, the stalls tightly packed, but I saw her almost immediately. At first I thought she was eyeing the baubles on a trinket stall, but then she turned to the young man beside her and spoke to him, and I realised with a jolt that they seemed to know each other.

Stupefied, I watched as they walked purposefully towards a narrow lane radiating off the square to the south. Following at a distance I saw them pause halfway down and turn into a doorway. For ten minutes I waited a few yards away, my imagination ballooning uncontrollably, my temper simmering. I was on the point of beating on the door when she calmly reappeared, alone.

I stepped forward so that she could not fail to see me.

She showed no surprise. Rather she gave a vague sign of recognition, as if she'd half expected to find me there, like someone who, having been kind to a stray dog, can't shake the animal off. She walked past me without breaking her stride so that I was forced to catch up with her. This small act was typical of her insensitivity, one of the many small humiliations that she perpetrated quite thoughtlessly and indiscriminately in pursuit of her own interests.

I grabbed her arm and spun her round. How dare you waltz off like that, I hissed.

I thought you'd be bored. I had this errand to do.

Errand? I crowed sarcastically. What, meeting someone?

She shook her head in exasperation or dismissal, and then I did something I had never done in my life before – I hurt a woman. Living out my violent imagining, I gripped her arm until she went white and winced with pain.

Don't ever treat me like that again! I shouted before walking blindly away.

I had lunch alone, going over and over the affair in my mind, wondering how one person could push me to such terrifying extremes of emotion. I had always considered myself a mild man, someone who kept his reason under pressure, yet when I had gripped her arm I had been shaking with rage. It frightened me to have lost control so completely; it terrified me to think it might happen again.

When I returned to the boat Sylvie was sitting on the foredeck reading a book. Ignoring her I went below. She followed and, coming up behind me, circled her arms round my waist and laid her head against my back.

Don't be cross, she sighed. We were having such a good time.

But you just walked off!

I wasn't going to be long. Please, Munchkin, life is too short.

How do I know you won't do it again?

I won't, I promise.

I cross-examined her about the man at the stall, I demanded to know what they'd been doing together in the flat or whatever the place was. He was just a friend of a friend, she said, someone who worked in the market; she'd simply been collecting something from him, a favour for the mutual friend.

I gave up then, because no answer would ever satisfy me nor quell my darker suspicions.

And I forgave her. I forgave her because I wanted the pain and humiliation to end. And because the dreadful sick longing was still dragging at my heart.

Just don't do it again, I said weakly.

Later we went to an expensive restaurant and had a mediocre seafood dinner which took over an hour to arrive. We had agreed to start the return trip immediately after the meal, though that didn't stop me from drinking far too much, and it was more by luck than judgment that we bumped only one boat as we manoeuvred out of the berth.

The wind was dead on the nose, force four or five. After half an hour bucketing about in a nasty chop I returned my dinner to the ocean and, leaving much of the helming to Sylvie, spent a miserable night between the cockpit and the guardrails, retching on an empty stomach.

164

Dawn brought little improvement. The wind rose to a stiff six or seven and showed no signs of backing. In her day *Ellie* had been a tough old girl, but with all the talk of fastenings and planking I didn't dare drive her too hard. By midday we had made good a paltry thirty-five miles and I was beginning to despair of ever getting home. Seeing my exhaustion, ignoring my half-hearted resistance, Sylvie took a long watch in the morning and again in the afternoon, leaving me to curl up on a sodden bunk and, oblivious to the drip of a persistent deck leak, catch some sleep. I loved Sylvie then, I loved her toughness and her resilience and the fearless face she turned to the wind, a wild child in a wild sea.

At six the wind finally backed, and we began to make up some time, but it was still four in the morning before we turned up the path of the Kingswear light. Motoring past the Blackstone, Sylvie handed me a brandy and I drank it in one.

Any lingering anger I might have felt about the Cherbourg episode was lost in the euphoric camaraderie one always feels at the end of a hard trip and my gratitude to Sylvie for being such a game crew. We had another brandy and she blew an alcoholic kiss against my mouth, and I felt ridiculously happy again.

We rounded the Kingswear bend in that strange time before the true dawn, when the shadows seem to play tricks, when shapes form and instantly dissolve again. Glancing towards the fishermen's quay beside the station, I saw a large motor launch against the piles, and in my imagination it seemed to me that men were standing on the deck.

As we continued up river, Sylvie kept looking astern and when I asked her if she would go below and find the searchlight she didn't respond. Instead she made a hiss of intense irritation. *Shit! Merde!* she cried angrily. They're coming! Hurry! Hurry!

I looked behind and saw nothing. What the hell do you mean? I demanded.

But she would only growl: Hurry! And when I didn't react she grabbed for the throttle and pushed it as far forward as it would go.

For Christ's sake! I argued, trying not to succumb to the atmosphere of panic. As we charged through the lines of moorings, I kept glancing over my shoulder and finally I saw what Sylvie had seen: some way astern, against the myriad illuminations of the town, the steaming lights of a motor vessel were moving, coming our way and gaining steadily. When I looked ahead again Sylvie had gone below. Controlling my fury with difficulty, I kept shouting at her, asking what the hell was going on.

When she finally reappeared she was almost naked. In the ruby glow of the compass light I saw brief underclothes and a dark band around her waist. Touching the band I felt the smoothness of heavy parcel tape which she appeared to have wound around herself several times. I couldn't work out what the tape was for until she turned to clamber onto the side deck and I saw the bulging packet held to the small of her back. I reached out and prodded the packet: under the plastic it was soft, like flour or sugar.

I kept shouting: What the hell, Sylvie? But it was more of a cry of disbelief than anything else. Even I could no longer ignore an interpretation of events which sickened my stomach and deadened my heart.

I went on yelling at her above the engine noise but she didn't answer. She was too busy working out where we were along the river, how far from Dittisham and where she might be able to climb ashore if she swam for it now, and balancing these factors against the speed of the approaching customs launch.

Above the throb of the engine Sylvie shouted: I wasn't on board, you understand? Not on any of the trip! You went alone! Stick to it or we'll both be in trouble!

Then she clambered over the rails and lunged headfirst into the darkness. Her dive made hardly a ripple. I kept looking back but I didn't see her surface. It was part of her luck, or possibly her judgment, but just a few seconds later the customs boat's powerful searchlight sprang on and bathed *Ellie* in a blaze of blinding light.

I slowed down, I let the launch catch up and come alongside. I answered their challenge. Name of vessel? Where from? Home port? I hesitated over 'How many aboard?' before replying with an uneasy heart: One.

The launch towed *Ellie* to a mooring and two officers came

166

aboard. They went through the ship's papers and my passport. They did not seem surprised that I was alone. They asked me if I had notified them of the boat's departure for France. When I admitted that I had failed to do so they asked me if I realised I had broken the law. I did now, I said. I explained that I had not sailed for some years, that I was out of touch, but all the time I was waiting wretchedly for the moment when they would search the boat and find Sylvie's handbag and passport and all the other signs that there had been someone else on board.

In the end their search was pretty cursory, just a rummage through the lockers and bilges, a hand thrust into the sail bags. They took no notice of the fact that some of the clothes were female. Wherever Sylvie had hidden her handbag she had made a good job of it.

Maybe it was the reference to having lived on the river for many years or the mention of a doctor brother having charge of the boat, but they let me off with no more than a stern caution.

I took *Ellie* up river to her mooring in a state of blank exhaustion. I found Sylvie's handbag in a side pocket of her holdall. It contained hairbrush, lip salve and moisturiser. No passport, no money, no identification. I realised she must have put them in the bundle so artfully strapped to her back. Clever Sylvie. Sly Sylvie. Not missing a trick. Never missing a trick, even with me.

Once ashore I drove straight to the cottage. I told myself that I needed to be sure that Sylvie had survived her swim, but the truth was far uglier and less altruistic. My anger was cold and bleak, I wanted to have it out with her, I wanted to know if my deepest suspicions were correct and she had been using me all along. I wanted to hear it from her mouth.

I walked into the cottage without knocking. There was no one in the lower rooms. Taking the dingy stairs two at a time, I peered into a back bedroom so strewn with clothes and junk that the floor was virtually invisible. Approaching the front room, I heard a slight sound from inside and, heart hammering, hesitated for a second before thrusting it open.

Some dense material must have been fixed over the window because the small room was very dark except for two candles burning either side of a large bed which filled virtually half the available space. Sylvie lay propped up on the pillows, entirely naked and uncovered, like something from a Botticelli. Beside her was the dark hairy figure of Joe, equally naked, like something from a horror film. Sylvie turned her head towards me with immense slowness as though it were very heavy, and creased up her eyes with the effort of focusing. Joe was on another planet altogether, blowing out his lips and chuckling wildly to himself like a bin case.

Sylvie, focusing at last, gave a warm smile and a low laugh. Come and join us, she said.

Joe's manic giggles followed me down to the car and fed my nightmares for weeks to come. In one dream I watched Sylvie dive into the water with a lead weight tied to her back. When I realised she was drowning I did nothing to save her.

EIGHT

I woke beside Ginny in the airy yellow guest room at Furze Lodge and wondered, as I had wondered on each of the previous two mornings, if this would be the day when I would be summoned again. Sometimes I saw the delay as a sign that, despite their investigation of houses, boats and cars, the police had found nothing against me and would soon be forced to admit their mistake. At other less confident moments I saw the delay in more sinister terms. I imagined that somehow or another they had assembled a few miserable scraps of evidence against me and were simply waiting for the right moment to return.

The uncertainty lurked in my gut, I couldn't eat, I slept badly, yet on this morning, as each morning before it, I got into a company car and drove to Hartford as if life were perfectly normal.

I had told George and the others about my arrest, I had made no bones about being under suspicion. I had even managed to make a thin joke about the possibility of being arrested again. They may have noticed how shaken I was, they may even have suspected that so far as my relationship with Sylvie was concerned there was unlikely to be smoke without fire, but on the face of it they refused to take the idea seriously and studiously avoided the subject, as if the outcome of the investigations was so much a foregone conclusion that it required no comment. And so, in the midst of my personal emergency, we continued to work flat out towards the buyout, due for completion in two weeks' time. George was pursuing another fifty thousand, Alan thought he'd identified an investor good for a hundred thousand, we were near agreement with the staff on the wage and productivity agreement, and later in the day the Chartered Bank people were arriving for their crucial tour of the factory.

There was no need to make any sort of announcement about my arrest to the Hartford staff. With forensic people all over Dittisham House and *Ellie* beneath plastic sheeting at the boat yard under a twenty-four-hour police guard, with divers searching the river bed around *Ellie*'s mooring, the news might as well have been broadcast in ten languages on all four channels. The local rag could also have saved itself its rather coy report about an unnamed man being arrested and released on police bail, and printed my name two inches high.

The staff did not mean to make life uncomfortable for me. They smiled to my face and did not stare at me until my back was turned, but their curiosity was so palpable that whenever I went down to the factory floor I felt like an exhibit in a zoo, and it wasn't long before I found excuses to stay away.

Evenings at Furze Lodge had developed their own tensions. While David retreated into his habitual mood of preoccupation, Mary compensated with a bracing show of family solidarity. Her constant flow of chatter gave conversations a certain momentum, it was impossible to distrust her good intentions, yet after a couple of days the verbal onslaught began to wear family affections thin. There was a brittleness in Mary's manner, a determination in her cheerfulness that didn't allow for weakness or doubt, and for me, in my questionable state of confidence, this approach left out too much.

I don't know what I'd expected from Ginny – not a great deal in the way of understanding perhaps – but I had misjudged her. By sheer force of will she managed to impose a rigid dignity on herself, a kind of all-encompassing calm, and, knowing what this must have cost her, knowing how alien it was to her anxious jittery nature, I was doubly grateful. It was as though she had taken a decision to rule herself out of the equation, to suppress her own feelings and concentrate all her efforts on me. When under this new guise she offered small gestures of support, when her thin fingers reached for my hand and grasped it, I was terribly moved.

On the Wednesday evening as we sat in the kitchen after David and Mary had gone to bed I said, 'I wouldn't be able to survive this without you.'

She shot me a look which contained a flash of uncertainty. 'We'll get through it,' she said.

'Once this is over everything'll be different. I promise.'

Her eyelids began to beat. 'Will it?'

'I'll cut down on work, we'll spend more time together.'

'Oh Hugh.' Shaking her head, she said without rancour, 'You'll always work too hard. You won't change.'

'But I want to change. I don't want to go on in the same way. What's it achieved, all this work?'

'It's made you happy.'

'Has it? Once, maybe. But I keep thinking of what it's done to us. It hasn't made *us* happy, has it?' I really wanted to know. 'Has it?'

She said in a wary voice, 'I thought we *were* happy. At least I always felt happy when you were happy.' She stood up abruptly and took the coffee cups to the sink. 'And when you weren't happy any more . . .' She hesitated before saying with sudden anguish, 'Then I didn't know what to do.'

'You should have said something.'

'Should I? But, darling, what would I have said? It seemed to me that everything I did was wrong, that you were determined to . . . move away from me.' She shook her head to deter me from denying it. 'No, it's true, you know it's true.'

'I never blamed you for anything. I just felt – *besieged*.'

She came back to the table. 'I would have done anything to help. Anything. I felt so useless. Worthless. I felt you didn't need me any more.'

'Ginny – it was never a question of not needing you any more. I just . . . lost my way.' But my avowals were beginning to sound contrived even to my own ears, and I fell back on a more certain truth. 'Well, I need you now, that's for sure.'

She smiled ruefully at that, and when we went to bed we held each other for a long time.

Ginny's mood of containment held until Thursday when Tingwall told us that the police wanted her back in Exeter for a

171

further statement. Then, despite her attempts at calm, she showed some of her old nerves.

'It must be the trip to France,' she gasped.

'Why?'

'They didn't ask me very much about it before. Only dates, things like that. They must want more detail.'

We were sitting side by side on the bed in our room at Furze Lodge, the only place where we could be certain of being alone.

'It'll be all right, won't it?' she asked. 'So long as we stick to what we said. That's the important thing, isn't it?'

The desperation of her plea did little to reassure me, not only because it reminded me of how thin our story about France was and how easily the police would see through it, but because it made me suspect that, however much she denied it, Ginny believed I had a lot more than France to hide.

'That's the thing, isn't it?' she repeated, seeking some reassurance of her own. 'To stick to it?'

'I suppose so.'

'You don't sound very sure.'

'Ginny – I'm *not* sure,' I admitted straight away. 'Oh, I know saying we were together seemed like the best thing to do at the time,' I argued cautiously. 'I'm not blaming you, darling, but I can't help thinking how bad it'll look if the truth comes out.'

'How would it come out?'

'I don't know. But it has to be a possibility, doesn't it?'

'You were seen in France?'

'No. Well – not that I'm aware of anyway. Though we had dinner at that restaurant in Cherbourg, the one all the British go to, and you know how it is, there's always someone, isn't there? And then when we set out we rowed out from the pontoon in full view of the village—' I halted, remembering that Ginny herself had seen us, that Ginny had been on the shore somewhere, watching secretly, and an avalanche of unhappy thoughts followed as I wondered how long she had been there and what else she had seen that weekend. I closed my eyes involuntarily at the memory of Sylvie and me on the sofa at Dittisham House, in full view of the uncurtained windows.

'Even if no one saw Sylvie, there's still . . .' I hesitated, weighing up the wisdom of delivering such a belated and unwelcome truth. 'The thing is . . . on the way back from France, coming up the river that night, the customs came and boarded us. Well, not *us*. Sylvie wasn't there. She'd disappeared, swum for it. There was just me. But the point is, I told them I was alone. They could *see* I was alone. And now we've told the police you were on board. If they compare notes with the customs how do we explain you not being there? Why would I have wanted to hide *you?*'

Ginny looked down at her hands and I could hear her breath catching in her lungs. She didn't speak for some time. Finally she raised her eyes towards the window and announced in a tight voice, 'We have to stick to what we said.'

'Yes,' I murmured, though it was more to convince myself than anything else.

Ginny had started to overbreathe and, in an effort to regain control, she tightened her mouth to slow her intake of air before blowing out with a slight hiss, like a smoker exhaling a long plume of smoke.

'Could you take me through it?' she said between breaths. 'What you told them? I want to be sure of getting it right.'

I thought back to the interview room and Henderson and the long stream of questions. 'All I said was that it was you who'd come to France with me, not Sylvie. I didn't give them any details, though. They didn't ask for any.'

'But I must have them, mustn't I?' she pointed out. 'In case they ask.'

So I told her what time we had left the river, and how perfect the weather had been on the way over and how quickly we had reached Cherbourg. I described the market place and the restaurant and the dinner, and the long hard slog back across the Channel. If the police challenged her about the customs raid, I suggested she tell them that she had been in a hurry to get ashore and had asked me to drop her at a jetty in the town where she could find a cab. As an explanation it didn't make a lot of sense, but it was all I could think of.

Ginny absorbed this with a fierce concentration, chewing on her lip, nodding from time to time like an earnest student.

'And the last weekend, when she died, can we go over that

again, just in case?' Her voice faltered and she disowned this display of weakness with a brief grimace.

'I simply told them what happened. How I got down to Dittisham at about seven-fifteen—'

'I meant—' She wheeled a hand. 'What did *we* do? What did you tell them about *us*?'

Here was the focused Ginny, the one who always caught me off-balance. 'Of course . . .' I made another effort of memory. 'I just told them what we did. I said you arrived at about nine, that we had a basic supper.'

'Was I expected?'

'They didn't ask me that. But . . . I certainly didn't say you weren't.' I remembered the sound of the front door opening and the sight of Ginny appearing in the doorway, and how I had stood there in blank surprise.

'Why had we travelled down separately?'

'They didn't ask that either.'

She ventured, 'I could have been held up in London, doing some homework for a committee meeting, couldn't I? What do you think?' she asked anxiously. 'Will that do?'

I laid my hand on hers. 'I'm sure that'll be fine.'

She didn't withdraw her hand exactly, but she didn't welcome the distraction either, and I took my hand away again. I said, 'They didn't ask any of this before?'

'No, it was just times and events, nothing else. Did I say I was arriving at nine or . . . ?' She was thinking the thing through as she went along. 'Or hadn't we said a time?'

'We needn't have said a time.'

'The evening then . . . I'd told you I'd be getting down some time in the evening,' she recited before leading herself resolutely on. 'And after that?'

'Oh, I said we had supper. I didn't give them many details – nothing about what we ate or anything like that – then I said David popped in at about ten and stayed a few minutes. Then we went to bed at about eleven-thirty. It *was* about then, wasn't it? Then they asked about Sunday. I was vague about when we had breakfast – I thought about nine – then I said we spent the rest of the day going through the house and the boat.'

174

'Going through them, that's what you said?'

'Yes . . . Clearing everything out of the house before it was sold. Sorting through the attics, that kind of thing.'

'And the boat?'

'I said we were getting *Ellie* ready to be laid up. They weren't sure what laid up meant,' I added, recalling Henderson's pedantic query. 'I had to explain. They seemed interested in the fact that it was you who'd gone to the boat while I'd stayed in the house.'

'Yes?' she urged.

'I explained that I was busy with Pa's papers, that it was left to you to do the other jobs. I said I didn't tell you to go to the boat, that it just sort of worked out that way.'

'And? What else?'

'That was all.'

'Those were your exact words?'

'I think so. But darling,' I said gently, 'I don't think we have to match our stories word for word. In fact, it'll sound really odd if we do.'

She gave me the look she reserved for my less intelligent statements. 'I do realise that,' she said with a show of patience. 'But I still needed to know.'

'Sorry,' I said, wondering how she put up with me. '*Sorry.*'

'What about the rest of the weekend?'

'I told them we had lunch at about one. That we worked on through the afternoon and left for London at about nine.'

She was waiting expectantly again.

'That was it,' I said.

She looked thoughtful, then, reasserting her new-found composure, said, 'I just wanted to be clear.' Some doubt must have remained on my face because she added, 'I'm frightened of saying the wrong thing, that's all.'

She didn't speak during the drive to Exeter. She looked intently at the road ahead, and I had the feeling that she was going over the story again in her mind.

To avoid any chance encounters with the press we'd arranged to meet Tingwall at a hotel on the outskirts of town before he took Ginny on to the police station.

As Tingwall came across the lobby I searched his face for a hint of developments, but he was too busy giving Ginny a mushy dumbstruck stare to be sending out those sorts of signals.

'What's the news?' I asked, bidding for his attention.

He dragged his gaze towards me. 'News?' he echoed. 'Oh, nothing, I'm afraid. And nothing on the car or the house, either. No saying when they'll be finished with them.'

'What about getting back to London?' I sighed. 'I've had to miss a couple of important meetings.'

'If you can hang on a bit longer. Say, till the weekend.'

'And if something comes up and I have to leave?'

'Let me know. *Please*. Just let me know.'

Before I could say more, Ginny touched my arm, as if to remind me of why we were here.

'All right?' I murmured to her profile as we walked out to the car park but, keyed up for the ordeal ahead, she didn't reply. Tingwall sped ahead and opened the door of his car for her and waited solicitously while she got in. He closed the door like a chauffeur, softly, with only the faintest click. I saw him smile to her as he got in beside her.

I stood and watched them drive off but she didn't look back.

Beginning a potentially long wait, I sat in the car and prepared to make some calls. I hadn't shouted my troubles from the rooftops, I certainly hadn't mentioned them to the people at Zircon or the banks, and Julia had been careful to put the postponed meetings down to general scheduling problems. A small paragraph announcing 'an arrest' had appeared in two of the national dailies that morning, but either the police had been laudably reticent or some legal principle prevented the press from saying too much because neither report had mentioned my name. I had been hoping my anonymity would last but the moment I got through to Pollinger at Zircon I knew my period of grace was over.

The tone of his greeting warned me before he said crisply: 'Hear you've had a spot of bother.'

'This police inquiry, you mean?' I said casually. 'I was interviewed, yes – the victim was someone I'd known years ago – but that was it.'

176

'I heard, *arrested.*'

I didn't try to deny it. 'The police overreacted a bit, to put it mildly. But they let me go straight away without charge.'

'All sorted then, is it?'

'Yes,' I lied.

'Not good for the buyout.'

'I'm aware of that.'

'This sort of rumour needs to be knocked firmly on the head, Wellesley, otherwise it could keep doing the rounds. Get fixed in people's minds.'

I wasn't sure I knew how to go about killing any sort of rumour, let alone one this salacious. 'How did you hear?'

'Me?' Pollinger had gone into the City straight from Winchester; he wasn't used to being asked to reveal his sources. 'Look, all I can tell you is that if the story isn't all over the place by now, it soon will be.'

'What do you think, then? A press release?'

'A bit of a sledgehammer, old chap. A letter to your backers might be a bit more politic.'

Pollinger was right about the news travelling fast. Julia confirmed it as soon as I spoke to her. Most of Cumberland knew, she told me, and at least two of their lawyers, and possibly the Chartered Bank, though she couldn't be absolutely sure about the bank, short of asking them outright. Oh, she added caustically, Howard had called, asking if it was true that I had been charged with murder. She had taken the liberty of telling him that, if his spies couldn't do any better than that, he should think about taking them off his payroll. She hoped that was all right.

It was a strange feeling sitting there in a car park on the outskirts of Exeter, knowing that my life was being picked over in a dozen offices up and down the country. I could imagine how thrilled the banks were at the prospect of loaning their money to someone who looked as though he might be charged with murder at any moment. And I could see Howard hastily diving into his damage limitation mode, rapidly distancing himself from me and the buyout, and casting it about that, in all the years we had worked together, he'd always had his doubts about my stability.

I asked Julia to draft a fax to Zircon and the banks, explaining the situation and setting their minds at rest. I didn't have the heart, or the nerve, to make any more calls after that. I sat listlessly in the car, watching the traffic go by and thinking of Ginny. I pictured her in the stuffy interview room, sitting straight-backed on the worn chair, meeting Henderson's cool gaze as she told him about the cup of coffee she was meant to have had with Sylvie at Dittisham House. I saw Henderson searching her face as she described bumping into Sylvie in the village and inviting her over. I heard him ask her what she and Sylvie had talked about. Then – the tactic was so obvious that I winced at not having thought of it and warned her – I heard him trying to catch her out, asking her what Sylvie was wearing, whether she'd been driving a car, and if so what sort of car it had been. I pictured Ginny pale and tense in the face of this crisis, yet, oddly, I didn't hear her falter. Though I replayed the scene several times, though I built up Henderson into some kind of super-sleuth, Ginny's aura of composure remained unassailable in my mind.

My confidence wavered only when I thought of the places where the police might have found Sylvie's fingerprints – in David's old room, on the bed post – and how hard it would be to explain their presence after a single coffee session. But you could go mad thinking things like that. You could go mad wishing for the hundredth time that you hadn't lied about something so mundane as an extra-marital affair.

I closed my eyes. I must have dozed for quite a time because it was dark when the sound of the passenger door woke me.

'How was it?' I asked Ginny as she climbed in.

She sank into the seat and shook her head. 'I'm so tired,' she sighed. 'I'm so tired. Can we just go back, please?'

As I drove I kept glancing across at her. She had her head pressed against the headrest and her eyes closed. After a minute or two she said, 'I'm not sure. How it went.' And there was something in her voice that sounded a small warning in my mind.

'The weekend in France?'

'He didn't ask about that.' Each word seemed an enormous effort for her.

'Nothing at all?'

'No.' Her voice was so faint I could barely pick it up.

'And having Sylvie in for coffee?'

'No.'

'What – *nothing?*'

'Oh, I told him,' she murmured. 'I told him, but he didn't want that.'

'What did he want then?'

She didn't speak for so long that I began to think she hadn't heard. 'He wanted to know how often I'd been at Dittisham.'

I tried to read her profile in the reflection of the lights. 'What did you say?'

'I said . . . I said I hadn't been down very often. Just three times. He . . .' Another pause. 'He wanted dates. I told him I'd need my diary, that I'd have to let him know. But it wasn't that he really wanted . . .'

'What was it then?'

She dropped her head forward and her hair fell across her cheek. 'That last weekend,' she whispered. 'He wanted to know all about that last weekend.'

'What, the times or . . . ?'

With great weariness she lifted her head again and looked ahead. 'Sunday. Mainly the Sunday.'

'What about the Sunday?' I had to force my attention back to the road.

'Everything.' She echoed bitterly: 'Everything.'

'But what about it?' I repeated doggedly.

She didn't reply.

'*Ginny* . . .'

'The boat. It was the boat.'

I had a bad feeling then, a sick foreboding. When I next glanced across, Ginny had half turned her face towards me, her expression hidden in the darkness.

'They know she was killed on the boat.'

My stomach lurched, I had a strong sense of unreality. I looked for a place to stop and there was nowhere. Finally I saw a farm gateway and lurched to a halt across it. '*They said that?* They said she was killed on *Ellie*?'

'They didn't have to say. It was obvious.'

'What do you mean?' I cried.

'Everything they asked . . . Everything.' Her voice was harsh, close to desperation or tears. 'Wanted to know who'd been on board . . . Why I'd gone out there on the Sunday . . . Whose idea it was . . . Why I'd scrubbed the floor . . . Had I noticed any marks or' – she could hardly say it – 'stains. *Stains*. They didn't have to say, did they? They *know*. They know she was killed on the boat.'

'That's ridiculous!' I argued. 'You must have got it wrong! You must have!'

She shook her head, and kept shaking it.

'But Ginny, that's crazy! How can they . . . How can they . . . Christ! It's ridiculous! You *must* have got it wrong!' I babbled on like this for a moment or two until I drifted to a forlorn halt and, leaning my forehead against the wheel, closed my eyes. 'Christ.' And this time it was an expression of dread.

I heard the squirt of Ginny's inhaler. She gave a couple of deep coughs before whispering in a raw voice, 'Let's get home.'

*

The two men from the Chartered Bank were in their mid-forties, wearing almost identical grey suits, and with the untroubled faintly jocular air of employees of large organisations who have never known what it's like to risk their own money or have their careers seriously on the line.

They liked the glass blowers best. They stood back and shook their heads in self-conscious admiration before venturing forward for a closer look. They asked the standard questions. How did the team of blowers manage to produce the correct shape and thickness each and every time, how did they prevent bubbles from getting into the walls of the glass, and how long did they work before taking a break.

They peered dutifully at the cutters manipulating the blanks against the cutting wheels, they inspected the packing room, and then George and I led them back to the front hall to present each of them with a gift set of six wine goblets and a decanter, which they could safely take home without having to mention it on their tax returns.

We smiled as we escorted them out to their car and shook hands. They smiled back. None of this smiling fooled anyone. No final commitment had been made, no date had been fixed for signing the loan agreement. The two executives would only say that they were returning to the bank for 'final consultations' and would let us know within three days. It was inconceivable that these final consultations would not involve discussion of my fax, transmitted the previous day to all our backers. Julia had written the text. While avoiding blatant untruths, she had managed to suggest that rumours of my arrest were little more than pernicious gossip, put about by those with a vested interest in seeing the buyout fail. When she first read it out to me I'd told her that this was incendiary talk, that allegations of conspiracy could easily backfire, but with so many distractions I was no match for Julia at her most persuasive, and the fax went out more or less as she had drafted it.

George and I waved the car off and strolled back. It was a lovely autumn day, bright and clear with a slight bite to the air. The factory looked almost handsome in the afternoon sunlight, its dingy bricks tinged with a rosy hue, the ventilation pipes gleaming like the funnels of a steamship. The main doors had been given a hasty coat of blue paint for the bankers' visit while the flower troughs on either side were newly planted in scarlet and white. The old place looked like a middle-aged girl tarted up for a new lover.

'I'm sorry if I lose it for us,' I said.

'What do you mean?' But he knew exactly what I meant.

'This trouble of mine – it could be more of a liability than we realised.'

'Nonsense.' He gave me a glare that was both a denial and an acknowledgment.

'Look at it from their point of view.' I tipped my head in the direction of our recently departed guests. 'Would you commit two million plus to someone who might be locked away for life?'

'But you're not going to be locked away.'

'They don't know that though, do they?'

'You're beginning to sound like Howard, for God's sake!'

Realising his gaffe, he gave an exaggerated grimace.

'What's Howard been saying?'

'Hugh . . .' He made a gesture as if to suggest we forget the whole thing, then almost as quickly lifted a resigned hand to concede the uselessness of trying. 'Oh, he's been bleating on.'

'Saying?'

'Talking some tripe about assurances. Saying Cumberland requires assurances.'

'Oh, yes?' I laughed grimly. 'What kind of assurances?'

'That we're in a position to continue with the buyout. That sort of stuff.'

'Or else? What was the "or else"?'

'Hugh, he was just making noises. You know him.'

'What was it, George?'

'Oh, he talked some stuff about having to consider the best interests of the shareholders.'

'He wants to break our agreement?'

'He didn't say that.'

'But that was what he meant.'

'You know the way Howard is – it was just talk.'

I didn't believe for a moment that it was just talk. Howard would have seized any excuse to block our bid and prevent me from making a success of Hartford. He couldn't bear the thought of my showing what could be done with the company when he wasn't around to interfere in it.

The era of extended lunches and early weekends might have died with the eighties, but at four on a Friday afternoon it was still hard to find a lawyer at his desk. Moncrieff's assistant told me that he was at a meeting out of town, while the rest of the legal team were tied up elsewhere and weren't due back in the office until Monday. I called Julia and asked her to reach Moncrieff at home that evening and set up a meeting for the next day.

'And if he can't do Saturday?'

'Sunday, then. And I want a meeting with Howard and the Cumberland people on Monday.'

'Something's happened?' Julia asked.

'Not if I can help it.'

With the decision to leave for London hot in my mind, I stuffed my papers into my briefcase and, amid memories of happier departures, unhooked my coat from the ancient coat stand that had stood sentry since my father's day, and hurried out into the passage.

The traffic was slow. I tried to call ahead to Furze Lodge to warn Ginny to start packing, but the line was engaged. I also tried to contact Tingwall, but I wasn't too sorry when the receptionist said he wouldn't be back that day. It gave me the excuse not to tell him what I was doing until later, when it would be too late for him to try and talk me out of it.

Mary appeared at the door as I drew up.

'How were the bankers?' she called brightly.

'Oh, grey suits. Vapid. Banker-ish.'

'What did they come up with?'

We went into the house. 'Not a lot. Nothing so risky as a commitment anyway. Mary – we'll be leaving tonight. I want to thank you for everything. For putting up with us all this time.'

Surprise passed over her face, then doubt, and finally a sudden effusive delight. 'They've said you can go?'

'No, but I'm going anyway.'

Her expression fell away. 'But do you have to go tonight? You couldn't leave it till morning?' She was trying to tell me something. 'It's Ginny,' she admitted at last.

Instinctively I glanced towards the stairs. 'What's the matter with her?'

'Nothing serious. David's given her something.'

'She's ill?'

Mary raised an eyebrow and gave me a look that contained a trace of disapproval. 'She hasn't been eating. She's been spending most of the day in bed. David thinks it's stress.'

Bemused, I cast back over the last few days. I hadn't noticed Ginny failing to eat, not when we'd been together in the evenings anyway. And days in bed – nobody had mentioned anything about that to me, certainly not Ginny. None of this prevented me from feeling an immediate responsibility; where Ginny was concerned my guilt had no end.

'If that's the case, all the more reason to get home,' I told Mary as I made for the stairs.

183

Ginny was lying propped up in bed, her eyes closed, a magazine open on her lap. As I came in she twisted her head on the pillow and, murmuring a hasty greeting, sat up on one elbow.

I came round the bed and said, 'I thought we'd go back to London.'

She asked no questions. She simply said, 'Are we leaving now?'

'If you're up to it.'

She nodded and rubbed her eyes before throwing back the covers and getting up.

'Mary says you haven't been eating.'

She made a dismissive gesture. 'Mary doesn't know everything.' She went into the bathroom and began running some water.

'You are happy to go back tonight?' I called. 'You would tell me if you weren't?'

She reappeared. 'Whatever you want.' But she spoke carelessly, and I wondered what sort of tablets David had given her, whether they were addling her brain.

'We'll have a holiday once this is over,' I said lightly. 'Somewhere wonderful, like Barbados.'

She lifted her head and considered this. 'That would be nice,' she said and went back into the bathroom.

Following uncertainly, I found her in front of the mirror, smoothing the skin beneath her eyes. Still staring at her reflection, she dropped her hands and asked contemplatively, 'Do you love me? I mean, just a little?'

I made a sound that came out all wrong, an exclamation that was almost a snort. 'Of course I do. More than a little, Ginny. A *lot!*'

'I couldn't bear it if you didn't love me at all. If you hated me.'

I came up behind her and put my arms around her. 'Ginny, I love you very much. I couldn't have managed anything without you.'

'I've got things wrong a lot of the time, haven't I?'

'Nonsense!'

'Oh, I have. I know I have. Things haven't worked out the way you'd hoped, have they? Our life has been – *different*. But if I've

184

tried too hard – oh, you don't have to say anything, I know I've tried too hard – it was only because I loved you.'

'Ginny!' The snort again, as though I couldn't think of what to say. 'You mustn't blame yourself for anything! You've been wonderful. Everything I could have asked for.'

'Not everything,' she corrected me gravely, frowning at her hands. 'Not everything . . .' Her eyes found mine again. 'But it hasn't been so terrible either, has it? Not so bad?'

I turned her towards me and hugged her. When I drew back I gave a shaky smile. 'I do love you.'

'I'm just sorry,' she breathed. 'Sorry . . .' And she might have been apologising for the entire world.

'Let's go home,' I said.

We packed steadily. Ginny finished before me and went and stood at the window, looking out into the dusk.

From the front of the house came the distant crunch of wheels on gravel. Something about the sound made me glance up. Ginny had heard it too. She stared at me, her face blanched of colour. For an instant neither of us moved, then I strode out onto the landing and across to a front window that looked down onto the drive.

Two cars, several uniforms, Henderson getting out.

The scene lurched, my stomach jolted, and I had the sensation of losing my balance. I made my way blindly back to the bedroom.

'It's them! It's the police, for Christ's sake!' Fury had me charging rapidly towards the stairs, ready for blood or battle.

'Hugh!'

But I didn't stop and I didn't look back. The doorbell rang through the house. At the bottom of the stairs I met Mary coming from the kitchen.

'Shall I call the solicitors?' she offered in a worried voice.

I shook my head as I went to the front door and wrenched it open.

Henderson stood before me with Phipps and Reith, and in the rearguard four uniformed officers, two of them women.

Henderson gave me a lugubrious nod. 'Mr Wellesley. Perhaps we could come in?'

'Just get on with it, Inspector,' I said, my throat tight with indignation. 'Just say what you've got to say! But I warn you,

185

you'd better be exceedingly sure of your ground.' I could feel myself trembling, and there was a heat in my face.

Henderson hesitated and looked past me into the hall.

'Just get on with it!'

His gaze fastened itself on a point over my left shoulder.

With a half-glance I saw Ginny moving up beside me.

'Mrs Wellesley,' Henderson said, and it sounded more like a statement than a greeting. His eyes still fixed on her, he turned to face her more fully and for some wild unaccountable reason I suddenly realised what was coming, and even as he opened his mouth, I cried, 'No—'

'Mrs Virginia Wellesley, I'm arresting you on suspicion of the murder of Sylvie Mathieson—'

'*No!*'

'You do not have to say anything. But it may harm your defence—'

'Don't be bloody ridiculous!' I protested. 'This is absolutely crazy!' Phipps moved forward and placed his body halfway between mine and Henderson's, forcing me to step back.

'... something which you later rely on in court ...'

I stared at Ginny. She was very still, her eyes lowered.

'... Anything you do say may be given in evidence.'

'This is mad! *Mad!*'

But Henderson's voice was grinding on. Then, reaching the end of his chant, he was asking Ginny if she understood and she was giving the shadow of a nod. Then everyone was in motion. The policewomen were coming forward and beginning to usher Ginny outside, the detectives were moving out towards the cars. Only Henderson remained.

'For Christ's sake!' I cried furiously.

Henderson said to me, 'Perhaps you'd like to pack up a few things for your wife, Mr Wellesley. Or ...' he glanced towards Mary '... whoever.'

But I could only repeat, 'You're mad! She knows nothing! She wasn't anywhere near the river!'

'Mr Wellesley, we'll be leaving shortly. I do recommend you pack a few things for your wife.'

But my brain was bursting, I couldn't hear.

Mary's voice said, 'I'll go.'

Henderson began to turn away but I grabbed his arm. 'Just tell me,' I pleaded. 'Just *tell* me – *why?* What has she done? What could she possibly have done?'

Henderson made a doubtful face, then, taking a quick glance over his shoulder as if to make sure no one was within earshot, said in a low murmur, 'There is a substantial case to answer, Mr Wellesley.'

'Like what?' I gasped.

He spread his hands, gesturing impossibilities. 'I'm sorry.'

'Like *what?*'

But he had turned away. Unable to grasp the full enormity of what was happening, or unwilling to, I followed him numbly to the car where Ginny was already sitting between the two female officers. I was about to call to her when Mary's voice came from behind: 'Which one, Hugh? Which case? *Hugh?*'

Turning, it took me a moment to understand that she was referring to our suitcases which she had brought down from our room. I fetched Ginny's case and handed it to a constable.

Engines were being started. I remembered Ginny's inhaler. I just had time to race up and fetch her handbag and hand it in through the car window before the final door slammed and the cars sped away.

Watching the last car disappear into the lane I felt Mary's arm around me, and realised that the angry gasps I could hear were the sounds of my own despair.

NINE

'What really worries me,' I said, hearing the emotion that was never far from my voice, 'is that she won't survive in that place. It'll make her ill. I mean, worse than she is already. The dirt, the conditions, the filthy sanitary arrangements. No *lavatories*, for God's sake. It'll kill her. Just kill her.'

'I appreciate your concerns, Hugh,' Tingwall ventured gently. 'But I did make full representations. I sent in the doctor's letter. I checked with the medical staff and they're fully aware of her condition. She's under permanent supervision.' He added in a transparent attempt at cheerfulness, 'And she seemed okay when I last saw her. She said her room was all right. She said they were looking after her.'

The fact that Ginny had talked to Tingwall when, on both of my visits, she had hardly spoken a word to me shouldn't have bothered me quite as much as it did, yet I couldn't shake off the feeling that she was excluding me on purpose. 'We have to get her out of there,' I insisted unreasonably.

'We'll do our best, Hugh.'

We had only just begun our meeting yet already I was facing the wall of helplessness that seemed to dominate all my recent discussions with Tingwall. 'I'm sure you'll try your best but, if you don't mind my saying so, it seems to me that precious little progress is actually being made.'

Tingwall frowned at the surface of his desk. 'Hugh, I realise that the whole thing must be very difficult for you. I realise how anxious you are. However, we're faced with these procedures, and we have to follow them, with no guarantee of the outcome.'

I held up a hand. 'Hang on. What are you saying exactly? Are you saying' – and my voice hit a warning note – 'that we might not get bail?'

'I'm not saying that, Hugh, not at all. But bail is very much the exception in a case like this. We'll have to show good cause, we'll have to argue it carefully.'

'So?' I made a gesture of bafflement. 'If anyone has good cause it must be Ginny, surely.'

'We can certainly set out a case—'

'What about getting a QC? Surely we should have a QC on this?'

'We can certainly approach Counsel—'

'Charles – let's just hire the best man there is. Tomorrow. The *best*.' I was steamrollering him, I knew I was, but the law, with its nonchalance and mind-bending complexities, was testing my patience.

We were sitting in Tingwall's office, a tall room at the front of a converted Georgian house on a noisy road near the centre of Exeter. This was my third visit in a week; my third visit since Ginny had been formally charged late on Saturday night; a week in which I had seen her brought to court and remanded in custody, in which I had twice made desperate ineffectual attempts at conversation in the bleak visiting room at the prison near Bristol; a week in which I had gone through every shade of disbelief and despair, during which I had attempted to apply logic and reason and emotion to what had happened and found nothing but incomprehension and dread. My thoughts went round and round and came out nowhere. My nights were riddled with nightmares and sudden panics. Confusion and doubt had wrenched my anchors away; I drifted back and forth on the tide of my uncertainties, ready to believe anything and nothing, to fight on and give in, to challenge everything and question nothing.

'I'm not saying we won't get bail,' Tingwall was saying. 'Not by any means. But I don't want to raise your hopes too far either.'

'But what could be the problem?' I asked, trying to hit a conciliatory note. 'What reason could they have for refusing?'

Tingwall interlaced his bony fingers. 'Obviously there's no

suggestion that Ginny—' He caught my glance. 'You don't mind? She asked me to call her that.'

'No. Of course.'

'There's no suggestion that she's about to abscond or reoffend – that's hardly an issue. But with a murder charge the magistrates are bound to consider other factors, like the medical report.'

'Well, that'll be devastating, surely. She's already had two bad attacks. What more do they want? Her asthma's triggered by stress and dirt and damp.'

Tingwall gave a slow nod, like a bow. 'We'll certainly cite that, yes. I've already written to Ginny's specialist asking for a letter. But the court will also have the psychiatric assessment to consider—'

'Psychiatric assessment?' I was instantly defensive. Every time I thought I was getting to grips with the procedures something like this turned up, another bolt from the blue.

'I did mention it,' Tingwall pointed out delicately. He waited for some sign from me before continuing, 'In serious cases they always ask for a psychiatric assessment, partly to establish whether the accused is mentally capable of facing charges—'

'Sane, you mean?'

'Yes.'

I couldn't bear the euphemisms that crept in, the fine obfuscating language. 'If you could keep it simple . . . ?'

Tingwall took this reprimand on the chin, with a quick frown of contrition. 'Also,' he continued, 'to assess whether the accused is likely to be a danger to him or herself.'

'Suicide?' I laughed dismissively. 'Ginny wouldn't do that. Not unless she's forced to stay in that place at any rate.'

'Maybe not.' Tingwall felt his way carefully forward. 'But, Hugh, I have to tell you that our man Robertson—' He peered at me. 'You remember, I said it was important to get our own assessment?'

'He's a psychiatrist?' In my shock I could remember none of this.

'Yes. He saw Ginny on Wednesday, and' – he made a regretful face – 'I'm afraid his findings aren't as unequivocal as I would have wished.'

Suddenly I was full of pain. 'He's saying she's unbalanced?'

'What he says is, he feels he cannot vouch entirely for Ginny's state of mind. Not at the moment, anyway.'

'But who is this Robertson?' I demanded, looking for an escape. 'Is he the best person? Do we want a second opinion?'

'He was recommended. But we could consider getting someone else in, yes. But before making a final decision I think we should be guided by Counsel.'

We had completed another circle. 'What are we waiting for then?' I asked. 'Why haven't we got a QC?'

'The best QCs are very busy, Hugh. I'm making enquiries, I'm trying to find out which of the top names are available. It's not always easy to get the person you want.'

I pushed myself to my feet and took my frustration to the window. 'Okay,' I said, descending into sudden weariness. 'So how long is all this going to take?'

'The bail application? I think we should hold it for another week. It'll give us time to prepare really thoroughly, to get this second medical opinion, if that's what we decide.'

Outside, the good burghers of Exeter meandered along the pavements, going about their errands, wearing their own troubles on their faces. I wondered how many had read about Ginny's appearance in court and what they had made of it, whether they had skimmed the item or picked over it with avid curiosity. Whether they, too, had decided she must be slightly off her head. Picturing Ginny's life being raked over in this way was almost more than I could bear. Yet I knew full well that the news coverage so far was as nothing to what would come if the case went to trial.

I turned back. 'This psychiatric assessment – it's standard, is it?'

Tingwall gave me an odd indecipherable look. 'We *could* have refused it.'

I was incredulous. 'Then why the hell didn't we? Why didn't we—' A notion lodged in my head; it seemed so obvious that I couldn't think why it hadn't come to me before. 'How many murder cases have you handled before this, Charles?'

Tingwall inclined his head to acknowledge the fairness of the question. 'Perhaps I could answer that by mentioning that, contrary to what many people think, murder's a fairly rare crime, and this region must have one of the lowest murder rates in the country. And most of the murders that do occur are domestic or fairly straightforward or both, by which I mean there's usually very little doubt as to who was responsible. It's more a question of why, and whether it was self-defence, and so on. There are very few – extremely few – cases in which the facts are . . .' he chose his words '. . . rather more open to interpretation. So, to answer your question, this firm has handled three murders in the last eighteen months, which is a lot by local standards, in fact two more than any other firm in Exeter. Now if Ginny feels she would like to go to people with more expertise, then I would understand completely, and I would do my best to hand the case on to another firm in good order, if that was what she so wished. As for the psychiatric assessment . . . I can only say that I thought it was for the best.'

I dropped back into my chair and regarded Tingwall's thin intense face. 'What's your opinion?' I asked drily. 'Do you think Ginny would do better elsewhere?'

Tingwall pondered this with his habitual diligence. 'Some of the big London firms would certainly have greater experience in this type of case. Against that, a local firm has the advantage of local knowledge, and of being on the spot, with experience of the local courts. A big city firm might have more immediate access to the right experts, to specialist knowledge, but a small country firm, if it does its homework properly, wouldn't let that be a problem. If at first you can't find the right expert,' he recited with a forefinger in the air, 'then you keep looking until you track him down.' He grew solemn again before cocking me a half-smile. 'Being a small outfit, we might also try harder.'

Despite his youth and relative inexperience, despite the gaffe over the psychiatric assessment, my first instinct was to stay with Tingwall. Yet this was Ginny's future we were talking about. Getting this decision right was probably the most important thing I could ever do for her. Before putting the matter to Ginny I decided to check it out with some lawyer friends in London. I said, 'I'll have to speak to my wife.'

'Of course. It's for her to decide.' He gave a diffident smile. 'Perhaps I should say . . . if she decided to entrust me with the case I would give it my very best shot. Everything I had.'

'I'll tell her that.'

A slight softening had come over Tingwall's face, a shadow of his fascination for Ginny, grown distant now, and sadder.

'You're visiting her tomorrow morning?' he asked, resuming a suitable briskness. 'Give her my best regards, would you? And tell her I'll see her before court on Monday.' Behind him the calf-bound legal tomes marched brashly along the shelves, at his elbow a stack of files teetered precariously, and I wondered how many other cases he had on the go.

'What'll happen on Monday exactly?'

'Not a lot. The Crown Prosecution Service will ask for a further remand, and I will ask that it be set for a week, and the magistrates will agree. And that's it.'

'We don't question anything?'

'The evidence, you mean? Not at this stage, no.'

'When, then?'

Tingwall's narrow eyes flicked away briefly, he pursed his lips. 'It's highly unlikely we would want to challenge anything before the trial. Though that can't be decided, finally, until we see the prosecution's evidence.'

I said with disgust, 'And the trial's eight months away.'

'It could be six.'

'And there's no chance of getting the case stopped before then?'

Tingwall was looking uneasy, as he always did when I talked in this way. 'I think we have to face the fact that it's very unlikely.'

My frustration resurfaced. 'It all sounds so *negative*.'

Tingwall considered this with detachment. 'I would hope – realistic.'

I pulled my hands down my face and let my anger go. I knew I shouldn't take my disappointment out on Tingwall, yet a part of me needed to challenge the frightening mood of inevitability which seemed to have attached itself to Ginny's case.

'You think the evidence is that strong?' I hadn't meant to ask this; I wasn't sure that I was ready to hear the answer.

'As laid out by the police,' Tingwall stated cautiously, 'as

193

specified by them, the evidence would seem sufficient to take the case to trial.'

So far I had avoided discussion of the evidence. There are things that aren't that easy to face. But now, finally, I braced myself to confront the facts, partly to test Tingwall's knowledge against my own, but also – there was no denying it – to feed my own hunger for understanding, to embellish the reel of film that kept running through my head with images and colour.

'Tell me what they have,' I asked calmly. 'As you understand it. The evidence so far.'

Tingwall shot me a questioning glance, then stood up. 'Of course. Coffee?' He went to a side table and, pouring two cups from a Thermos jug, brought them over. He pulled up a chair and, setting it at an angle to mine, sat on the edge of the seat, hunched forward with his arms resting on his knees, and began to speak in the gentle measured tones of a storyteller.

'I asked the police for a summary of their main evidence immediately after Ginny was charged. And it was the same as the evidence listed in court on Monday. Now it's possible they may be holding something back on the principle that you don't give away any more than you have to at this stage of the proceedings, but I doubt it. In a case like this I think they'd produce everything they had, just to be sure. So . . .' He clasped his hands together. 'The first thing they stated was that several traces of the victim's blood had been found on the floor of the *Ellie Miller*, thus establishing the boat as the scene of the crime. Now this was a categorical statement, based on forensic evidence, so we can assume that they have run DNA tests and so on. Then . . .' He paused to take a sip of coffee and gather his thoughts. 'Then they said that Ginny's fingerprint had been found in a bloodstain on the boat, and that the blood was also the victim's.'

I had meant to keep quiet, but I said, 'This forensic stuff, it's cut and dried, is it?'

'Usually, yes. In the case of DNA, particularly so.' He was like a cat on a precarious ledge, choosing the safest place to step. 'With other forensic evidence, it can sometimes be . . . open to interpretation. Often it's a matter of the individual expert's opinion – and opinions can differ. Very occasionally they differ considerably. What we can do, of course, is hire our own expert to examine whatever evidence it is and run his own tests. If his findings give us a chance of challenging the prosecution's expert, then – well, obviously we'd pursue that avenue rigorously, get a third opinion and so on. The first step – and I think I mentioned this to you the other day – is to get a pathologist to carry out a post-mortem for us. I've made enquiries and Dr James Bagnall could do it next week. He's the best man, quite famous now. If the police pathologist has missed anything, he'll find it. And his opinion would count for a great deal. He's done a lot of murders – all the ones you read about.'

And now this one: another to be read about.

'I'll go ahead then, shall I?' Tingwall asked. 'With Dr Bagnall?'

'Yes,' I said, trying not to think of Sylvie's body and what would happen to it under Bagnall's knife. 'I interrupted you. On the evidence.'

Tingwall's disconcerting gaze flicked up to me, before fixing itself on the floor some five or six feet in front of him. 'Next ... The police are saying that they have a witness who saw Ginny rowing out to the boat on the *Saturday* afternoon, when she says she was only just starting out from London. Now identification evidence is always soft evidence, and if this was the only thing the prosecution had to go on we'd certainly consider challenging it at an early stage.'

But it was not the only evidence, and he moved quickly on. 'Finally, they cited Ginny's own statement, that she went to *Ellie Miller* the next day, the Sunday, and scrubbed the boat clean. The inference being that she was removing blood and so on.'

In the silence that followed I replayed that Sunday morning in my mind, as I had replayed it so many times in the last week. I saw Ginny in jeans and a loose top, packing a plastic bucket with cleaning materials to take out to the boat. I held her face close to my mind's eye and searched her expression for signs of trauma and despair, I recalled snippets of our dialogue and scanned the casually uttered words for intimations of disaster, yet I found nothing, no hint at all. Casting Ginny in an innocent role, I saw someone keen to participate in the boat-orientated life at Dittisham from which I had excluded her for so long that summer, eager to muck in and show me what she could contribute, and, in so doing, make a go of our marriage again: Ginny the peacemaker, fraught with nothing more sinister than anxiety. Then I cast her as someone frighteningly different, a person I scarcely recognised, someone calculating and vindictive, cold and methodical, someone who was capable not only of committing such a terrible act, but of behaving as if it had never happened, and in this incarnation her mild agitation that morning finally took on a guilty significance.

Tingwall murmured, 'Of course we must wait for the prosecution to serve their statements on us before we can be absolutely sure of what we're up against, and that won't be for some weeks yet.'

'But at the moment it looks pretty bad?' I said, staring straight into his crooked eyes.

'I wouldn't use a word like bad, Hugh. But there's certainly a serious case to answer.'

This judgment, though I had been expecting it, was like a band tightening around my heart.

I braced myself to ask, 'What's the worst that can happen?'

'The worst?' He jerked his head back slightly, as though recoiling from an unpleasant task. 'I really . . . That's something for the QC to advise.'

I persevered, 'If she was found guilty?'

He said with great reluctance, 'For murder, it's a mandatory life sentence. But Hugh, there are bound to be mitigating circumstances, the chance of a lesser charge—'

'Bound to be?'

'Of course! Ginny's case is never going to fall into the same category as a cold-blooded gang murderer. There are so many ways to play this, Hugh. She could plead guilty to manslaughter on the grounds of diminished responsibility, for example. She could say she was under such intolerable strain that she lost her head. She could say she was severely provoked and reacted in an instant of madness. Or she might have been suffering severe clinical depression. There are so many ways to approach this, Hugh. So many ways to win a jury's understanding.'

'And for manslaughter?'

He was not enjoying this game. He blew out his lips. 'It varies so much, I couldn't give you a figure. It all depends on the circumstances and the judge. Anything from a few years to fifteen, eighteen, with half off for good behaviour. It's such a wide range.'

Significantly less than life, at any rate. For some reason I fastened on to the idea of seven years as a time which seemed survivable, a time which, long though it was, had a foreseeable end. I imagined visiting Ginny in prison year after year, the two of us getting older, nearing fifty before we could start our lives again, in France perhaps, or Italy. Survivable.

A lorry shuddered past in the street outside, filling the room with a low rumble.

'So manslaughter might be the best bet?' I said, groping for reassurance.

'We'll have to wait for Counsel's recommendations, and he won't be able to put anything to Ginny until he has everything in front of him, until he has her story.'

Ginny's story. The great unknown. Part of me longed to hear it, the other part lived in dread of what it might contain. 'She hasn't said anything to you?'

'No. And I haven't pressed her. The only thing I would like to know fairly soon, though, is whether anyone can vouch for her whereabouts on that Saturday afternoon. In my experience alibi witnesses are best caught early, before their memories fade. But she hasn't really been in any state to consider that, so I'll ask her again on Monday.'

'An alibi witness?' I said doubtfully. 'You think that's likely?'

He looked rather disappointed in me, as if I had failed to grasp an essential point. 'What I think is neither here nor there,' he stated. 'At this stage we must rule out nothing at all. It would be a terrible mistake to overlook the smallest thing that might help the defence. A case must never be lost for lack of trying.'

He did not remove his energetic gaze from my face until he was sure I had understood the importance of what he was saying, and in that moment I felt an upsurge of confidence in him, and, with this, a small easing of the burden.

'No stone unturned,' I said.

We got to our feet.

'Not a pebble either.' He endorsed this with a diffident smile. 'You mustn't believe there's nothing that can be done, Hugh. It's very rare that nothing can be done.'

But just then it seemed to me that Ginny's situation was almost hopeless.

*

A horn tooted and I looked round to see my car move off a yellow line and sweep in to the kerb beside me. Julia lowered the window and one glimpse of her expression told me that there had been no call from Cumberland.

'Want to drive?' she asked.

I shook my head and went round to the passenger side.

'So, no reprieve?' I asked, getting in.

She cast me a scathing glance. 'Was there ever likely to be? All this talk of asking the board to reconsider at the eleventh hour was just Howard playing off both sides against the middle. There was never a chance!'

It was over then. At some point that morning the Cumberland board had formally accepted a bid from another company, a glass manufacturer called Donington. In their explanatory fax to the Hartford team, sent at six last evening after rumours had been circulating all day, the board had cited their responsibility to serve the best interests of the shareholders, a duty they felt would be best fulfilled by accepting the Donington bid.

So it was over, for me at least. Late last night George had talked about fighting the Cumberland board, about writing to every Cumberland shareholder to put the facts before them, to call an extraordinary general meeting and persuade them to oppose the Donington bid and back our own; he had talked about unleashing every trick in the book, using the media, the politicians, all the spoiling tactics we could think of. He talked fiercely, he made a lot of sense, but in my heart I knew my own fight was over. I was ready to let Hartford go, I was no longer bothered by the idea of Howard beating me. In the shadow of

Ginny's catastrophe my own battles seemed rather insignificant. The only thing that still had the power to upset me was the thought of Hartford closing, of the people who would never work there again, and the death of the furnaces.

Julia drove along the one-way system, muttering at the lack of road signs, until I pointed her towards the Totnes road.

'George has told everyone, has he?' I asked.

'He will have by now. He warned them yesterday, so they'd be ready for it. And while we're on the subject of staff,' Julia added firmly, 'I'll stay on for as long as you want me, a day or a month, and no redundancy required, thank you very much. I've got another job lined up for when I leave.'

'I wish I could keep you on.'

'That's all right.'

'Won't be able to afford you.'

'That's what my boyfriends say.'

I hadn't faced the money situation yet. Now that the buyout had failed I would have to meet the expenses of the bid, for which I had made myself personally liable – the fees of the venture capitalists, accountants and lawyers – a sum I didn't care to add up quite yet but which would certainly run a long way into six figures. And then, most important of all, I would need to put plenty aside for Ginny's defence, on which no expense was to be spared.

'When did it finally come back?' I said, indicating the car.

'Wednesday.'

I looked for traces of the police examination. Fingerprint powder or whatever they used, but the dashboard was clean and there was nothing to be seen on the doors.

'Mary told me they've finished with Dittisham House as well,' Julia added, 'though it's too late to save the sale, apparently. The people got fed up with waiting.'

Or they didn't like the notoriety that was fast attaching itself to the house, though neither of us remarked on that.

'Mary wanted to know if you were intending to stay the night with them.'

I hadn't got that far. All week I had been choosing a place to sleep almost at random, sometimes driving miles back to London after seeing Tingwall, sometimes travelling the forty minutes to Melton after seeing Ginny at the prison, or one day – it must have been Wednesday – just shutting myself away in Glebe Place, drinking and sleeping, occasionally crying my eyes out, until, waking at two in the morning, I had driven through the night to Dittisham and, going down to the quay, sat on a wall watching the dawn come up. When it was light I had gone to the boat yard and through the fence looked at the draped outline of *Ellie* on the hard standing, and briefly wept again.

I hadn't stayed with Mary and David since the weekend. I hadn't been avoiding them exactly, but at the same time I wasn't ready to discuss the details of Ginny's case with anyone but Tingwall. Julia understood this intuitively, as did David, who, though he had called several times, had been careful to restrict himself to practical matters. Mary was unlikely to be so easily rebuffed, however. When we'd spoken on the phone she'd kept asking the sort of questions that I wasn't ready to answer. While I still valued our friendship, while it had seemed natural to confide in her on the subject of Sylvie, Ginny was an entirely different matter, and, for the moment at least, Mary's curiosity had caused me to pull up my drawbridge.

'I'll decide later,' I said.

'Mary said she could leave supper out for you if you were late. That reminds me.' Julia reached behind her seat and handed me a sandwich. 'It's compulsory,' she said.

I didn't argue. I'd been eating spasmodically, if at all, and I knew that if I was to be any good to Ginny I had to start pulling myself together.

We reached Hartford under a darkening sky and spitting rain, which cast a gloom over the factory windows and leached the colour from the flowers around the entrance.

Heather, the receptionist, raised puffy eyes and dabbed at them with a handkerchief. 'Oh, Mr Wellesley, I'm so sorry,' she cried, pulling a tragic face.

'I'm very sorry too, Heather.' And for a confusing instant I wondered if we were talking about Hartford or Ginny.

George, Alan and John were waiting in Pa's old office. We

shook hands with more than usual energy, the closest we could safely get to emotion.

George declared with a defiant upward thrust of one fist: 'We may have lost the battle, Hugh, but we haven't lost the war! They had the nerve to tell us Donington's bid was worth more than ours? Well, it's not! They're taking some of it in Donington shares – aiming for another merger or whatever – and the market value of the shares is ten pence down on the paper value. I've been on to the lawyers. They say it's good enough for an extraordinary general meeting. We can still get 'em, Hugh! We can still win!' And he gave an excited cry that seemed to intensify the flush of his florid cheeks.

Because I couldn't think of what else to say, I murmured, 'You've been busy then.'

We clustered around the table, ready to sit down. There was a pause while Alan and John looked towards George, waiting for him to make some sort of announcement.

'Yes, uhh . . .' George frowned. 'All of us would like to express our sadness at what has happened to your wife, Hugh. And we'd like you to know that if there's anything we can do you only have to call on us. Anything at all.'

'Thank you.'

'I'd like to second that,' said Alan.

John added a brisk, 'Me too.'

'Thank you. I can only say that . . .' It was hard to compose even these few words. 'I appreciate your thoughts. And if my family problems tipped Cumberland's decision against us, then I regret that very much. For you and for everyone else at Hartford.'

George made an exclamation of denial and Alan followed fast with: 'Listen – Cumberland were out to make our lives difficult from the start, weren't they?'

'Howard was, you mean,' George chipped in. 'One way or another.'

Alan urged, 'Don't blame yourself, Hugh. It was always going to be a battle.'

They were saying what they thought I wanted to hear, but I knew, as they must have known, that the publicity over Ginny, the terrible nature of the crime, and the knowledge that, with all

201

my problems and preoccupations, I couldn't possibly sustain any practical involvement in Hartford, must have counted heavily against us.

There was a slight pause, a moment of mutual sympathy and unease, before we left the subject behind.

Even as we were settling in our seats, George launched his plan of attack. 'The first step,' he said blithely, 'is to get this EGM off the ground. All we need is the backing of ten per cent of the equity. What with your holding, Hugh, and your brother's—'

'George—'

Perhaps he knew what was coming, because he frowned at my interruption.

'Are you sure you still have Zircon and the banks behind you?'

I had used 'you' not 'we' and 'us', but if he realised I was excluding myself from this process he didn't comment on it.

'I was coming round to that,' he said rapidly. 'I realise only too well that we'll have to sell them the idea of hanging on. But if we're going to get this EGM off the ground at all, we have to move fast.'

'I think you might have to move fast on the banks too,' I said in my most diplomatic tone. 'I think they'll already have gone cold on you, and the news of the Donington bid will finish them off. I think there's no time to lose.'

This was met by an exchange of glances between George and Alan.

George said, 'In fact, we were hoping you might tackle the banks. We thought it would come best from you.'

'Don't be ridiculous. It would come worst from me. They won't want to know about me.'

'Why not?'

Was this a mistaken show of loyalty or could he really not see the problem? 'George, quite apart from my personal credibility, they'll know I can't possibly have my eye on the ball any more. They'll know I can't possibly give it a hundred per cent, and they'll be dead right.'

'We realise it won't be easy for you, Hugh. We realise your time will be limited. But we've discussed it – and, Hugh, we don't think we can do it without you.'

'I think you could do it without me very well.'

George ignored this. 'You talk the banks' language.'

How to make him realise it was all over? 'I'm out, George.'

'We'll do the rest, all the legwork, all the nitty-gritty. We'll take everything off your back. Just the banks, Hugh,' George pleaded. 'Please – just give it a try.'

I had forgotten how stubborn George could be, and how this quality, so valuable in a production director, could seem less attractive from the receiving end. 'My heart simply wouldn't be in it,' I said, trying to spell it out for him.

'That's the way you feel now, Hugh. And we all understand that. But give it a while. Give it a few days, give it a week.'

'No time,' I argued again. 'I wouldn't have the time.'

'Maybe not just at the moment. But in the future, maybe you'll have more time than you think. Maybe you'll be glad of a project.'

Unexpectedly, this hit a chord. In the months ahead I had been planning to spend my time supporting Ginny, meeting lawyers, doing everything I could. But now that some of the shock had worn off I could see that I had perhaps been idealising my role, or at least oversimplifying it. Once Ginny got bail she might not want me under her feet the whole time, and I might be glad of some distraction; both of us might be desperate for a semblance of normal life.

Seeing the chink in my armour, George played his last card. 'We owe it to our people, Hugh,' he said in a blatant appeal to my conscience. 'Otherwise they'll be on the scrapheap, claiming benefits, having their skills go to waste. Surely we owe them one last go.'

'I might do more damage than good. With the banks.'

'We'll risk it.'

'Don't say I didn't warn you.'

They were waiting.

'I'll *think* about it,' I sighed, realising that this was as good as a promise and that, somehow or another, I had managed to manoeuvre myself into a corner.

*

203

I dropped Julia at the station and drove on to Dartmouth to see David. His surgery, a utilitarian single-storey building which he shared with his two partners, was set on a precipitous slope above the harbour with views across to Kingswear and the marina. Among the sea of yacht masts I found myself looking for the sleek outlines of the customs launch and wondering if the customs men had known of Sylvie's activities before our trip to France. In the next moment I pushed the thought impatiently aside. What did it matter now? It was finished. Sylvie would never be coming back. Except, it seemed, to destroy my life.

The surgery had been refurbished since my last visit. The waiting area had acquired pale wooden chairs with padded seats, potted plants and framed prints, and, on one wall, an electronic announcement board telling patients when their doctor was ready for them.

There were five people waiting, but after ten minutes the receptionist caught my eye and waved me through.

The passage leading to David's room was decorated with photographs and posters of racing cars, pictures which he had accumulated in his early twenties when he'd harboured a passion to become an amateur racing driver. Like most of David's more extravagant ambitions at that time – there had been schemes to fly hot-air balloons and buy into a yacht charter business in the Caribbean – it had fallen victim to the tight financial rein that Pa had kept us on. David had taken this restriction badly, as an unjust denial of his inheritance, yet Pa had always gone out of his way to explain how our trust funds were set up, telling us from a young age that there would be no capital until we were thirty. I could never work out whether David simply hadn't accepted this or had thought he could get round the old man; either way he had been regularly, and to his mind unfairly, disappointed.

David came round his desk and gripped me awkwardly by both shoulders. I thought for a moment that he was about to embrace me, something that would have startled us both, but he gave me a small shake instead, a sort of rallying jolt. He stepped back, looking slightly cross with himself. 'What a bloody awful business,' he exclaimed finally.

I could only nod.

'Now how's Tingwall shaping up?' he asked, waving me to a seat like a patient. 'He's definitely the best lawyer you'll get locally – I've checked up on him again, asked around.' He pulled up another chair and sat next to me on the patients' side of the desk. 'But being the best around here may not be saying too much.' He rolled a despairing eye at the limitations of the provinces. 'You *are* considering people in London?'

'I'm getting advice on that.'

'Make sure you get the best,' he urged. 'And what about a QC? Tingwall's getting you a QC?'

We had already discussed these things on the phone at least once, maybe twice. Whether David had forgotten or was simply anxious to press his advice home I couldn't tell.

'And the medical side?' he continued systematically, like a chairman working his way through an agenda. 'That's under control, is it?'

'We're getting a letter from her asthma specialist, saying she's got to have bail for health reasons.'

'Anything else you need in that department?' he asked almost fiercely.

'That's what I came about, actually. We need a good psychiatrist. Someone who's prepared to say Ginny's not a suicide risk. Otherwise they might block bail.'

David's expression brightened at the challenge. He tapped his fingertips together while he pondered. 'There's a bloke called Jones. Based in Bristol.'

'He'll be all right, will he?'

'Oh, he'll do the necessary, if that's what you mean.' From the confidence of his tone, Jones and he might have been fellow mafiosi who traded favours in the form of foregone conclusions. 'I'll speak to him this afternoon.' He reached for a pad and made a note.

'Tingwall found a guy called Robertson, but' – it still disturbed me to say it – 'he seemed to think that Ginny might be a risk to herself.' Seeking reassurance, I lifted my brows and turned this into a question.

'Well, anyone would be a bit desperate in her situation, wouldn't they? *Christ!* Facing all *that*.' He grimaced at the thought, and gave a sudden shiver. 'But if she's a bit depressed the right drugs will soon sort her out.'

'You really think so?' I longed for Ginny to be released, but sometimes the prospect of looking after her on my own worried me.

'Oh yes. Jones will know what to prescribe.'

A pause, during which we exchanged a quick glance.

'Nothing else I can do?' he asked.

I shook my head.

Another pause as David prepared himself to say awkwardly, 'Look, it's none of my business, and the last thing I want to do is – *interfere* . . .' He contorted his face, waiting for objections, before continuing gruffly, 'But what have they got in the way of evidence, for Christ's sake? What *can* they have? They must have got something drastically wrong, it's crazy to think that Ginny— ' He shut his mouth abruptly as if he'd already said enough.

I would never have foreseen David as an open champion of Ginny's cause, just as I could never have predicted the extent of his concern. I was touched. David had such a long history of detachment, he had always been so wary of gratuitous confidences that he usually steered clear of what he called 'situations'.

'They know Sylvie was killed on the boat,' I told him haltingly. 'And then they have a fingerprint of Ginny's, found on board. And some witness who saw her rowing out to the boat, on the Saturday afternoon.'

David frowned. 'A fingerprint? But what does that mean, for heaven's sake? Ginny's been on the boat often enough.'

'No. No . . . You see, it was in blood. Sylvie's blood.'

'Ah.' He absorbed this grudgingly. '*Ah*.' He stared beyond me in further consideration, then shook his head. 'But couldn't there be some other explanation? Couldn't she have – I don't know . . .' He threw a hand in the air. 'Come into contact with the blood some other way. After the event, or . . .' He ran out of ideas, just as I did whenever I put myself through the same exercise. Catching sight of my face, seeing with alarm that I was close to the edge of my emotions, he added briskly, 'The thing is, there's going to be a way of getting her off, Hugh. There always is. Some fact they haven't checked, some witness who hasn't come forward, some deal to be made with the lawyers. That's why you need the best defence team money can buy. Eh?'

But I wasn't in any mood to be cheered up. 'Ginny's simply not capable of this thing, David. She just couldn't have done it.'

He shifted in his seat. 'No.'

I held on to my voice with difficulty. 'She just couldn't.'

He nodded grimly.

'She . . .' But I couldn't speak, I was clenching my lips too tightly.

Leaning forward, David moved a tentative hand as if to comfort me before thinking better of it and sweeping his hand up towards his chin.

I pulled in my breath with a gasp. 'She has no violence in her. None at all. She couldn't hurt a fly. She just couldn't . . .'

'No.' Swinging to his feet, David fetched water and Kleenex, and, thrusting them at me, waited while I blew my nose and generally pulled myself together.

'I'm keeping your patients waiting,' I said at last.

'Oh, they're used to it,' he declared airily. 'Now what about you? Need anything to make you sleep? Anything to cheer you up?'

'Oh, I'm all right.' I rearranged my expression into something a little less morbid.

'Shall I give you something anyway, just in case?'

I stood up and gave my nose a final blow. 'David, they don't make pills for what I need.'

'You'd be amazed what Prozac can do.' He lifted a satanic eyebrow.

'I'd rather not find out just at the moment.'

'My patients live on the stuff,' he announced, poker-faced. 'High doses – keeps 'em nice and quiet.'

As so often, I wasn't quite sure whether David was spinning one of his darker jokes.

He walked me to the waiting room door then, resuming some

of his old manner, gave an evasive almost irritated smile before turning quickly away.

I was unlocking my car when a horn tooted and I looked up to see Mary's car swooping in through the entrance. Parking untidily, she came striding over.

'I caught you! David told me you were popping in. I'm so *glad* I caught you!' She gave me a firm kiss on the cheek and, gripping my arm, surveyed me with fond concern. 'How are you?'

I pulled a so-so expression.

'Now you *are* staying tonight, aren't you?'

'Wish I could, but . . .' I gestured difficulties.

'Oh, come on. Come and stay!'

'I really can't.'

She made a face. 'Why on earth not? Where will you go, for goodness sake?'

'Oh, Melton. I have to go and see to the place.'

She shook her head at me. 'Well, come back for a quick coffee then!'

'Mary, I wish I could, but I have to rush.'

'But I so want to talk to you!' She gave a rapid smile to soften the rebuke in her voice. 'I've got important things to tell you.'

'What sort of important things?'

'I'll explain, but come and have a coffee. It'll be easier over a coffee.'

I couldn't hide my exasperation as I said: 'But what's it about, Mary?'

She sighed at me. 'Why, the case, of course!'

A flutter of hope. 'You've heard something? What is it?'

'It's hard to explain just like that.'

'Mary, just tell me! Tell me, please!'

She gave me a look of mock anger that wasn't entirely light-hearted. 'I can't see what's so difficult about coming home for a minute!' Her good humour had developed a sharp edge to it, and it occurred to me that she too must have been feeling the strain of our family's instant notoriety. 'All right! All right!' she declared suddenly, as though giving in to the whim of a child. 'Let's get out of the wind at any rate.'

We got into my car. Mary pushed her hair back from her face

and I dimly noticed that she'd done something new and not entirely successful with the style. She had eye makeup on, too, a shade of blue that contrasted strongly with her pink cheeks and dark eyebrows.

'Right!' she declared forcefully. '*What* I wanted to tell you was that I've been doing some research. I went through my old legal tomes – the ones I still have, at any rate – *and* I went and looked through a friend's legal library which is more up-to-date. *And* I spoke to a friend of a friend in London who's a real ace on case law and precedent. Now it seems there have been some very significant cases in recent years.' She spoke fast and emphatically. 'There was one case where a wife killed her husband's lover and pleaded manslaughter on the grounds of diminished responsibility and only got *eight* years. Which means she served four. And *that* was a case where there were definite overtones of premeditation – the wife went round to the other woman's house with a hammer. *Said* she only intended to break the windows, *but* . . .' She made a knowing face before racing on. '*Then* there was another case. A wife discovered her husband in bed with another woman. She rushed down to the kitchen and got a knife and went up and stabbed him. Said it was PMT that drove her to it, temporary insanity. She virtually walked free—'

'Mary, what are you trying to tell me exactly?' I interrupted in a calm voice.

I had broken her flow. 'What I was *trying* to say was that in these types of cases the jury can often overlook the odd bit of premeditation—'

'I meant, your point. What is your point?'

'If you'd let me explain—'

'Mary . . .' I held up both hands. 'I'm grateful, but I don't think I'm quite ready for this.'

She gave a rapid empty smile. '*All* I'm trying to tell you is that if there's diminished responsibility and not too much premeditation then the sentence could be almost nothing! A few years!'

'I see,' I said tightly. 'I see. Well, thank you for going to the trouble.' Not trusting myself to say any more, I scrambled out of the car and stood looking down at the harbour.

I heard Mary's door slam. 'Hugh,' she cried, coming up behind me. 'Hugh! I just wanted you to realise that it needn't be that bad. I mean – a few years! It's not so much, is it?'

It was suddenly a great deal to me, much more than it had seemed in Tingwall's office. And I was terribly hurt by Mary's presumption of Ginny's guilt, the way she seemed to be offering a few years' prison as some sort of consolation prize. In my mood of desolation it struck me that under David's show of concern he might also believe that Ginny was guilty. Perhaps everyone thought she was guilty.

But then perhaps I was reacting so strongly because, deep down, against all my wishes, it was what I believed too.

*

Ginny appeared at last, and, seeing me, cast her eyes down and wove her way slowly between the crowded tables. She was wearing something nice, I noticed, a flowing ankle-length skirt and matching top, and her hair was newly washed and combed so that it gleamed ochre and amber in the light.

We embraced briefly and sat facing each other across the formica table.

I searched her face. 'How are you?'

'Oh . . .' She pondered this. 'They gave me something. Tranquillisers, I think. They seem to even things out a bit.'

This was more than she had said to me during both of my previous visits put together, and I smiled, 'You look better.' This wasn't true: she looked thinner, her eyes appeared larger in her face and the skin of her cheeks seemed to cling more tightly to the bones. But the empty look that had disturbed me so much on my last visit had faded, and I recognised something of the old Ginny in her eyes.

'How's the room? Did they move you?'

She gave the faintest nod. 'I'm on my own. Not everyone's on their own.'

'Well, that's something!'

'It has sun.'

'That's nice!' I replied rather too brightly. 'Health all right? You've got enough inhalers? You've seen a doctor?'

She was slow to concentrate. 'More than one,' she said. 'Two . . . three. Psychiatrists, mainly.'

'I'm afraid that you might have to see another,' I ventured gently. 'A man called Jones. Did Tingwall tell you? It's to make sure we get this bail application through.'

She looked uncertain, as though her memory were playing tricks.

'We need someone to say that you're fit and well to come home. Tingwall should have told you.'

'I didn't know what to say,' she murmured. 'He kept asking me how I felt about the future.'

'Who? Robertson?'

'What was I meant to say?' She cast me a baffled look. 'I didn't know what to say.'

I reached for her hand. 'Darling, don't worry about it. Just leave it to Jones when he comes. He'll make sure it's all right.'

There was a commotion at the next table as a child started to scream.

When the child had quietened down a little Ginny asked dully, 'Will I get bail?'

I hesitated. 'Tingwall thinks there's an excellent chance.' I explained about the QC, and how Tingwall was aiming to pre-empt any objections the police or prosecution might have. But she had seen my hesitation and understood it; she realised it would be a mistake to count too firmly on her freedom.

'But listen,' I said, pushing optimism into my voice, 'I had a long session with Tingwall. We started mapping things out. We've got six months, maybe more, before the trial. That gives him plenty of time to prepare the best possible defence. Now I want you to be quite clear, darling – we're going to have the very best team, the best lawyers, the best experts and doctors – whatever it takes. There won't be a single thing that won't be covered. Not a thing!'

She thought about this but did not seem to draw much comfort from it.

I ploughed on. 'And as for tactics – approaches – there are all sorts of options. Tingwall went through them with me . . . Ginny?'

She had sucked in her lips, she was blinking rapidly: the signs.

211

'Darling,' I pleaded helplessly.

Pulling her hand away, she stared down at the table and shook her head. It was both an appeal and a warning. She did not want to discuss it.

Retreating, I cast around for safer ground. After a long pause I offered half-heartedly, 'Things at Hartford are still frantic. Everyone racing around . . .'

She nodded to show she was listening.

'But I've backed off for a while. Left them to it. Quite nice, being out of it.' I added for light relief: 'Might try it on a permanent basis.'

There was no flicker of an answering smile. 'And the buyout?'

'Oh, more off than on at the moment.' I shrugged: 'There was always a risk.'

'Sorry.'

'One of those things.' Another pause during which I became increasingly lost. 'Oh . . . The estate agent says there might be some people interested in Melton.'

'That would be good,' she said with visible effort. 'Before they next go over the place get Mrs Hoskins to put plenty of flowers everywhere, won't you? It makes such a difference.'

A couple of young children roared past. We lapsed into silence again.

I said, 'Nothing from the agents in France, though.'

She gave a long jagged sigh. 'I'm sorry,' she gasped, and I realised we weren't talking about houses any more. 'I know you were only trying to help.'

'Doesn't matter.'

'I find it so hard . . . You see' – she raised her eyes at last – 'whenever I think about it, I can't see any way out, and it frightens me to death.'

A spark of dread passed between us.

'Ginny, there *will* be a way out. Wait until you talk it through with Tingwall. He'll explain all the options. I promise – there *will* be a way out! Just tell him what he needs to know. I promise!'

She swung her head slowly from side to side. 'But what can I tell him?'

Aware that she might be on the brink of some irreversible

revelation, feeling a terrifying blend of fear and curiosity, I led her slowly forward. 'You must tell him anything that could help. Like where you were on that Saturday afternoon, at exactly what time, and who might have seen you ... Someone *must* have seen you, darling. At Glebe Place, or on the motorway, or ...'

'But I was there.' This comment slipped into the pool of silence, a small ripple which grew and grew. 'I can't say I wasn't there. That's why they're never going to believe me.' She gave a ragged laugh, near tears. 'Never.'

My breath was tight in my chest. 'When you say *there*, you mean ... you mean in Dittisham?'

She nodded bitterly.

'You ...' I could hardly ask it. 'You weren't near the boat, though?'

'I thought you were on board, I went to find you.'

A cold horror settled in my stomach. I felt sick. 'And then?' I whispered.

I thought for a moment that she wasn't going to answer. Her eyes glistened with unshed tears. 'I found her.'

I could hardly speak. 'Found her?'

She put a hand to her head, as though it was causing her pain.

'Ginny, Ginny ...' I tried to keep the shock out of my voice. 'What are you saying? Are you saying she was dead?'

She was silent.

'*Ginny?*' I pleaded. 'What are you saying?'

She rubbed her temples. 'It doesn't matter.'

'But is that what you're saying? For God's sake, *tell me.*'

She looked me straight in the eye then, and it was a look which contained resignation and defeat, and finally, a small but unmistakable flicker of confirmation.

My mind went racing off in several directions, most of them startling, all of them confusing. 'But, Ginny ... why didn't you tell anyone this? Why didn't you report it?'

She shook her head slowly, and kept shaking it for a long time.

I leant across the table, I seized her hands roughly in mine. 'But you must tell them now! You must!'

'It wouldn't do any good.'

'Why not, for God's sake?'

'Oh Hugh . . .' And she gave me a pitying look.

'I don't understand.'

But she closed herself off from me then. Her face emptied, she dropped her eyes.

I struggled to make sense of it, I tried to grasp what she was telling me, but I was hurt and confused by her lack of faith in me, it was all a jumble, and for a while I felt as though I too were going mad.

TEN

In English courts there are two kinds of magistrate, Tingwall enlightened me. There are the stipendiaries, known colloquially as 'stipes', trained lawyers who sit alone on the bench as full-time professionals, and there are the lay magistrates, part-time justices of the peace who sit for a few days a month in a triumvirate with two fellow JPs.

Exeter had no stipendiaries, only JPs. I wouldn't have given this any thought, I certainly wouldn't have seen it as any kind of disadvantage if Grainger, our QC, hadn't commented to Tingwall within my hearing, 'Oh for a stipe.' Seeing I had picked up on this, Grainger elaborated derisively in his affected drawl, 'JPs can be dreadful old women. Paralysed by the fear of doing the wrong thing. And, as a consequence, of course, frequently doing precisely that.'

I did not fret about this for too long. Partly because I saw Grainger's concern as a way of covering his back. Partly because, by the time we had waited in the hall outside the court for an hour, I was beginning to think that Grainger himself might be a far greater liability. His arrogant overbearing London style seemed destined to rub the JPs up the wrong way, as it had so thoroughly irritated me. I tried to talk myself out of disliking the man, but the way he strutted about, his bombastic voice and imperious manner made me so angry that I had to take myself for a walk around the block. Tingwall reassured me that Grainger was one of the top criminal barristers in the country and that he hadn't won this reputation by chance, but by the time we filed into court I had convinced myself that Grainger was in every respect a terrible mistake.

I recognised one of the male JPs from a previous remand, but the second man and the woman were new. Both men were sixtyish, one a successful business type, the other, the chairman, a tweedy countryman, a landowner or professional man. The woman was younger, about forty, and stylish. They were the sort of people Ginny and I had occasionally met on Wiltshire weekends, though I couldn't decide whether to take encouragement from that.

Stairs led straight up into the dock from the cells below, and to the accompaniment of clanging subterranean doors and shuffling feet, Ginny appeared with officers ahead and behind. This sight disturbed me, it seemed grotesque, as though Ginny were the victim of some hideous identity switch.

She did not glance in my direction as she went to the front of the dock and sat down. The business quickly began. Grainger announced that he represented Ginny and made the application for bail.

The prosecution objected to bail due to the seriousness of the crime and the prison psychiatrist's report, which indicated that Ginny was in a frail state of mind and might be a danger to herself.

Rising, Grainger began his plea. I had to strain to hear him. At first I thought he was simply getting into his stride, working his voice up to a theatrical pitch, but then it dawned on me that this quiet unassuming tone was the one he had deliberately selected for the occasion. The actor-lawyer, appearing for this performance only as the sincere advocate without pretensions. As he pleaded Ginny's previous good character, her exemplary life, her charitable work, her poor health which, the doctors agreed, would suffer dramatically unless she were allowed home, I was forced to hand it to him, grudgingly at first, then with increasing admiration. It was a masterly show of moderation and restraint, with just the right dash of humility. If I hadn't met him beforehand, I would have thought he was an extremely nice man.

Without giving the slightest hint as to the way Ginny intended to plead, he managed to suggest that she was incapable of hurting a fly, and suddenly the idea of her innocence was floating gently and inoffensively on the air. He emphasised that Ginny would be returning to the bosom of her family, that she had the full support of her husband, family and close friends.

Calmly Grainger referred the bench to the report of the eminent psychiatrist Dr Jones, which granted that Ginny had been in a state of shock and depression for the first week after she had been charged, but declared that, with the commencement of treatment, she was now in a robust and sensible frame of mind, and constituted no danger to herself. Mrs Wellesley's mental health would continue to be closely monitored by Dr Jones, whom she would be seeing at least once a week. No good would be served by keeping Ginny in custody, he summarised, and no harm could possibly be done by allowing her out on bail. He offered the surrender of Ginny's passport, residence at Melton, and surety at the court's discretion.

Tingwall had warned me that the JPs would withdraw to consider their decision, so I was taken off-guard when, after a short discussion between themselves, and a brief consultation with the clerk, the chairman promptly announced that bail was granted, subject to residence at Melton, surrender of passport and surety of fifty thousand pounds.

Tingwall had the papers ready, the surety was approved, and with that the court rose for lunch.

I pushed my way out of the public gallery, past the usher and into the court. Ginny turned and met my clumsy all-enveloping embrace with impassivity. 'We're going home,' I said with considerable emotion, 'I'm taking you home.'

'You'll be there?' she said.

I wasn't sure what she meant. 'Of course. Where else would I be?'

Grainger came up and I shook his hand.

'Thank you. You were superb.'

He gave a faint smile, as though he was aware of what I had thought of him and took amusement from having proved me wrong. 'You might want to leave by the back way,' he commented, turning his eyes towards some reporters in a gaggle by the door. 'They can't bother you inside the building, but they'll try for a photograph outside. I wouldn't recommend draping anything over the head, it makes a very unfortunate impression.

Dark glasses are not ideal, either. But the head averted, the hair hiding the features? Family on either side and in front?'

I had not been prepared for this. Automatically I looked to Tingwall. 'I'll go and find out,' he said doubtfully, and I realised that he hadn't been prepared for this either.

David's voice came from behind. 'Put me in the vanguard. I'm good barging material.'

'I didn't know you were here,' I laughed.

'Crept in late. Sat at the back.' He kissed Ginny fleetingly on the cheek. 'Why don't I go and get my car and bring it round to the side or wherever it is?'

Tingwall arranged for us to leave through the court office. David, with great seriousness, synchronised his watch with mine and went off to do a recce. Tingwall then took Ginny and me to the court office, as though to do more paperwork. Two sharp-faced reporters followed us across the hall and hung around the office door, making no attempt to conceal their purpose. Someone fetched Ginny's bag from the cells, we found reasons to open the door regularly so the reporters could see we were still in there, then, on the appointed minute, we ran for the side exit and jumped into David's Mercedes.

We would probably have escaped the worst of the press if the automatic barrier hadn't been slow in lifting. Forced to pause in full view of the front of the building, we were soon surrounded by photographers. As they lifted their cameras I called a warning to Ginny and raised my hand to shield her face. And so it was that the photograph that featured regularly in the newspapers over the days and months that followed showed Ginny's head largely obscured by my splayed hand, and, in the foreground, made prominent by the flashlights, my face wearing an ugly aggressive expression, teeth bared, eyes popping, like a dangerous maniac on licence from Broadmoor.

After seeing this photograph for the first time I stopped reading the newspapers.

*

From superstition or lack of forethought or a mixture of both, I had made no preparations for our arrival at Melton. I hadn't phoned Mrs Hoskins to ask her to turn up the heating, and I hadn't bought any food. So it was that we arrived to a cold dark house with nothing in the fridge but a few eggs, a half-empty carton of milk and some tinned pâté which had been open a dangerously long time.

Leaving Ginny in the kitchen with a cup of tea, I went through the place turning up thermostats, lighting fires, drawing curtains. Returning, I found Ginny sitting in the same position at the kitchen table, staring out of the window into the dusk.

'There's hot water,' I told her.

'I'll go and unpack.'

I carried her bag upstairs. In my pleasure and anxiety at having her home, I talked nervously about anything that came into my head: the food I would buy in the morning, the book I wanted her to read, the latest developments at Hartford, much of which I had already told her during the journey from Exeter. I joked that unemployment was making me lazy, that I was enjoying not having to get up in the mornings, none of which was true, but which seemed to form a necessary part of the charade of normality.

One by one she took her clothes from the bag and dropped them into the laundry basket, except for two sweaters which she laid on the bed and folded neatly, following the inviolable pattern she always used. Placing the sweaters symmetrically on the shelf she regarded them for a moment before changing her mind and relegating them to the laundry basket with the rest. 'So dirty,' she murmured. 'I felt so dirty in there. I don't think I'll ever feel clean again.'

'Have a long bath,' I cried rousingly, like some ghastly team leader. 'I'll run it for you.'

She seemed to focus on me for the first time since we had got back. 'You're very good to me,' she said.

'Don't be silly,' I laughed awkwardly.

'I can't tell you how much it means, that you . . . that you're here.'

'Of course I'm here. Where else would I be?' I said lightly.

There was a pause. We both looked away.

'Would you like a drink while you're in the bath?' I asked in the same jovial tone. 'A glass of wine?'

It occurred to me that she had wanted to talk and that, in my present state of inadequacy, I had missed the opportunity, or avoided it.

Attempting to be useful, I took the laundry basket down to the utility room and, not sure what else to do with the clothes, emptied them onto the top of the washing machine.

Staring at the pile, unwanted thoughts rushed into my mind, thoughts of what Ginny had been wearing on the weekend that Sylvie had died. I dreaded these invasions, but I couldn't stop them, I couldn't stop trawling my memory for clues – denials or confirmations.

I tried to picture her in the doorway when she'd made her unexpected appearance at Dittisham that Saturday night. She'd been wearing trousers of some sort, not jeans exactly, more like tight slacks, off-white or cream, a pale shirt, and her favourite raspberry-coloured jacket. A long scarf had been jammed untidily into one pocket. But what I was really trying to see, of course, was the blood. Could I have missed it? Even at my least observant could I have failed to notice stains or spatterings of blood?

I threw the laundry basket down and, calling to Ginny to tell her where I was going, drove to the local pub and ordered chicken and chips to take away. The woman behind the bar, whom I recognised from my occasional visits, told me that strictly speaking they didn't do takeaway, but, casting me a collusive smile, said she would manage something if I didn't mind having it wrapped in newspaper. Waiting in a corner of the bar, I felt the scrutiny of the other occupants, and it struck me with renewed force that whatever happened, even if Ginny walked free, we would never be able to live our lives in the same way again. This realisation, though harsh, no longer intimidated me: there were worse things, for Ginny at least.

Returning with my hot newspaper bundle, I found Ginny curled up on the bed, sleeping the deathly sleep of the exhausted. I put the quilt over her and, though I checked her regularly and kept the meal hot in the oven, she didn't wake again, and at midnight I turned off the oven and crept in beside her. When I put my arm around her waist, she gave a small fearful cry like someone caught in a night terror, then, still without waking, gripped my arm and pulled me close against her back and did not let me move away until morning. It was strange to be together in our bed again, in the serenity of our large comfortable house, to possess the security we had always taken for granted, yet to have lost all certainty of the future. It was like an illusion, a giant exercise in double-thinking whereby nothing was what it seemed.

Listening to Ginny's soft breathing, an image stole around the edges of my mind, the one scene which I had until then managed to block from my thoughts: the vision of Ginny in confrontation with Sylvie. I could see fierce pride in Ginny's face, I could see jealousy and anger, even fury, but the deed itself – that eluded me completely. I could not picture the knife, nor the hand that drove it into Sylvie's flesh; I could not envisage the person who, having committed this cataclysmic act, coolly wrapped the body and bound it and slipped it over the side into the black water. I tried to give the scene substance and action and dialogue, but while it contained Ginny it remained dark and unformed. Maybe I simply lacked the courage for it.

During the first days after Ginny's arrest I had latched on to the idea of her innocence as an essential survival mechanism which would enable us to get through the long months ahead. But since her declaration in the prison I had been forced to confront the fact that, though I longed to believe her, persistent doubts had settled painfully in my mind.

As I breathed the scent of Ginny's hair, and felt in the touch of our bodies the history of our long years together, one thing was certain. We would stay together in this, we would stick it out through thick and thin. I couldn't abandon her, and I certainly couldn't judge her. It seemed to me that my guilt was inseparable from hers, that, in terms of blame, my selfishness was indivisible from her desperation.

I woke early and made a shopping list: what Ginny would have called a man's list, heavy on luxuries, short on essentials.

221

But then Ginny had always organised the food, the cooking, the staff, the maintenance. From the earliest days of our marriage she had actively discouraged me from involvement in anything remotely domestic. She had not wanted a liberated man, and she had not got one.

In town it took time to discover the best shops. Eventually I found olive oil, sun-dried tomatoes and endives to go with the wild salmon and fresh pasta. I bought a few bottles of Ginny's favourite Pouilly-Fumé, I remembered herbs and flowers, and it was only as I arrived home that I realised I had forgotten butter and fruit juice.

I found the house silent, the bedroom and bathroom empty. Suppressing a dart of panic, I hurried through the ground floor calling Ginny's name before emerging breathlessly onto the terrace.

She was standing looking out over the garden, wearing a Japanese wrap with a woollen coat thrown over the top. She said absently, 'I'm here.'

My relief was so conspicuous that she must have guessed what had been going through my mind.

'The roses haven't been dead-headed,' she commented in the same flat voice. 'Oh, and the agent called. The people want to have another look round the house this afternoon at three. They're going to make an offer, he says.'

'That's good.'

'If they do decide to buy, I was going to ask you . . .' She turned towards me, and I noticed how puffy her eyes looked, and how her skin, always so luminous, had lost its clarity and transparence. 'Could we move straight away?'

'Well . . . If that's what you want.'

'If you wouldn't mind.' Her politeness was almost formal.

'The upheaval . . .'

'It won't be so bad. And it'd give me something to do.'

Though she spoke dully, I was encouraged by the normality of our conversation and the re-emergence of her interest in practical matters, which had always been so important to her. As for moving, I didn't need to be persuaded of the benefits of living full-time in London. Quite apart from the cost of running more than one home, I was forever leaving clothes in the wrong place, not to mention documents and, once, an airline ticket.

'And would you mind . . .' The odd formality again. 'Could we rent something? A cottage?'

Hiding my surprise, I said levelly, 'You don't want to live in London?'

'I'd rather not,' she said. 'If you don't mind.'

'Well—'

'Just a cottage, something really small. Near London if you want. Or . . . near Hartford. It doesn't matter.'

Looking out over the long lawns and spiralling leaves, I began to warm to the idea of a cosy cottage without gardeners and housekeepers, a place where we could live anonymously, in every sense of the word. 'Yes, why not?'

'Wish we could get rid of Provence as well,' she said with a glimmer of her old agitation.

'Well, there's no hurry about that. We don't need to decide for the moment. Not until—' I was going to say, *until things are clearer*, but tried to make a small joke of it instead. 'Until I know whether I'm going to be gainfully employed or not.'

'But all that bother. You won't want the bother of running it.'

I noticed the 'you', the assumption that she wasn't going to be around to organise things any more.

'Let's cross that bridge if and when . . . Anyway, we might want to retire there. I was thinking about it – before all this, I mean. It might be something to plan for, don't you think?'

'Retire?' She looked at me as if I were talking gibberish.

'I mean, when the time comes. In ten years. Who knows? Lots of people retire at fifty. It might be rather nice down there,' I rambled on. 'No rat-race. Uncluttered days. Good people. Food and drink. Friends to stay.'

'Ten years.' She was blinking rapidly. 'Is that what Charles thinks I'll get?'

'*What?* No, *no.*'

'What does he say then?'

'Ginny, when I said ten years it was nothing to do with you and the – *case.*'

'But he must have some idea what I might get.'

223

'He can't make *any* predictions, Ginny. None at all! Anyway, we're going to get you off! Good Lord, Charles and I haven't even discussed anything else!'

Ignoring this, or accepting it, she looked away and said, 'I'm sorry if it's a nuisance, renting a cottage.'

'Don't be ridiculous!'

'The thing is, I feel that . . . if we can have a few months in a quiet place – just us – I think I'll be able to stand it, the idea of not coming back.'

'Ginny, you mustn't—'

'Otherwise I'm not absolutely sure I'll be able to cope,' she said gravely. 'Dr Jones has given me all these pills. He says I must be sure to take them, otherwise – well, he doesn't give me an otherwise. I think he thinks I'm half gone already. Sometimes I think I am too.' She gave an unhappy laugh. 'There've been times when it's been so hard just to keep going. It's as though . . . as though I can't take it all in. As though everything's too much for my head. And then I get frightened . . .' She was struggling to express it. 'Because if it's going to be like that, then I'm not sure I'll be able to hold on.'

I put an arm round her and pulled her against me. 'Darling, if you're feeling bad, you must talk to me. Promise you'll talk to me?' I kissed the top of her head, but my heart was plummeting at the realisation of how close to the edge she was, and how fearsome was the responsibility I faced in taking care of her. I wondered if it would ever be safe to leave her alone.

As if reading my mind, Ginny said, 'Oh, I'll be all right while I'm here. Honestly. It's after . . . It's the idea of being put away in that awful place.'

'You talk as though it were inevitable. It's not! Once Charles begins on your defence, once he gets your story—'

She moved away. 'My story? There is no story.'

'Ginny, you've got to tell Charles what happened.'

'There is no story,' she repeated with emotion.

I stepped cautiously. 'What about what you told me – about finding Sylvie dead.'

I always forgot how acute she was, how finely attuned to nuance and omission. She heard the doubt lurking at the back of my words and said ironically, 'But if you don't believe me, why should Charles?'

'I do believe you,' I said. 'I do! I just don't understand why you won't talk about it. I can't see why you have to make a secret of it. What possible point can there be?'

'It was a mistake. I made a mistake.'

Inside the house the phone began to ring.

'A *mistake?*' I exclaimed, as mystified as I was exasperated. 'What do you mean?'

Her lids drooped. 'I feel so tired. The drugs probably . . .' She turned and walked into the house.

I called angrily, 'Ginny!' but she didn't stop.

Crossing the hall, she seemed to hear the phone for the first time and, altering direction to pick it up, lifted the receiver almost to her mouth before changing her mind and holding it out to me.

It was George. Watching Ginny climb the stairs, I didn't at first gather what he was saying.

'. . . in the post. Should be with you today.'

'What's that, George?'

'Something from everyone here at Hartford, something that will speak for itself,' he said enigmatically. 'They feel very strongly, Hugh. Also – and I hardly like to mention it, I know how busy you are – there's a meeting with the Chartered Bank tomorrow. I don't want to press you, but it would make all the difference if you could make it.'

It was hard to focus on Hartford matters again. I had already spent a lot of the previous week persuading Zircon and the banks to hold their loans, and George had somehow talked me into attending several strategy meetings.

'Ten o'clock, in Cheapside,' George urged. 'Just an hour. Hugh – I know it's out of your way, I realise you'll have to come up specially, but it's critical.'

'What's happened?'

'They're threatening to turn us down. This will be our one chance to change their minds.'

'But they were okay last week.'

'Something's made them think again. It's really critical, Hugh.'

225

With George every meeting was critical, every plea for help the very last he would make. While part of me resented the relentlessness of this pressure, I knew that in his position I would do exactly the same thing, that if it weren't for my personal crisis I would be right there beside him, fighting from the front.

'I'm not sure I'll be able to get away,' I told him, already feeling torn. 'Can I let you know?'

'Of course. But Hugh – it would make all the difference.'

I went into the study where I could be more certain of not being overheard before calling Jones. His secretary said he was doing his hospital rounds but should be able to phone me back later.

Even as I rang off I realised I could have saved myself the call. Whatever the psychiatrist might say, however safe he might rate Ginny's mental health, I wouldn't be able to leave her on her own. It wasn't simply a question of watching over her, though that would be a factor for as long as she continued to talk in such disturbing terms; it was also a matter of trust. I had not forgotten the promise I had made to her on the night when we'd searched for the petrol receipt. I had promised that I would never leave her alone again, and though at the time neither of us would have interpreted this as a round-the-clock commitment, I felt I owed her as much now.

I called Dr Jones's secretary and cancelled the message.

The decision was straightforward, the implementation harder. Who would watch over Ginny when I wasn't around? While she had been away I had been opening her mail, and though there had been cards and messages from two or three of her London girlfriends, there was nothing that amounted to a wild rush of unconditional support. And the people who lived around Melton, the people who had been glad to dine at our table, had, whether from reticence or disapproval, been conspicuously silent.

But then friends might not be such a good idea anyway. The few I had seen in recent weeks had expressed the sort of embarrassed sympathy people normally reserve for those who are bankrupt or caught up in a messy divorce. So anxious were they not to seem in the slightest bit curious that they had been breezily distant, almost offhand. Such encounters were not likely to get any easier.

Our families offered even less choice. Ginny was an only child, her father long dead, her mother living abroad. On my side there were only David and Mary, both of whom had heavy commitments and couldn't get away at short notice.

It occurred to me then that Ginny and I had no one but each other, which was, perhaps, all that we had ever had. Despite the frantic pace of our socialising and travelling, neither of us had ever been deeply gregarious at heart. We had gone about our business, we had been surrounded with people much of the time, but at the end of the day we had been glad to retreat to the safety of our own company. Until things had gone wrong between us and we had lost our one safe haven. Then, it seemed to me now, we had both begun to drift.

I called Julia and asked her if she wouldn't mind coming down to work at Melton the next day. Julia, who was staying on until the buyout was resolved, not only had the benefit of being instantly available, but was loyal and discreet. While she wasn't someone Ginny would be able to talk to, she wouldn't intrude either.

The post brought the mysterious missive that George had hinted at. It was a giant greeting card packed with the signatures of the Hartford staff. Above the printed best wishes message had been written: *We're still backing the buyout all the way.* I was touched. At the same time I couldn't help wondering if this gesture of support and encouragement was entirely spontaneous, or something a little more Machiavellian, engineered by George who, in my absence, seemed to have developed unsuspected tactical skills.

I stood the card on my desk, a reminder, if I needed one, that life roared on in the world outside.

I went upstairs to check on Ginny, but she was asleep again, curled up in bed, her mouth slightly open, a faint frown showing above the mask. I glanced at the bottles of pills on the bedside table, but didn't recognise the names of any of the drugs. Taking the extension off the hook, I stole out and closed the door.

Tingwall was in court all morning, his office told me, and it wasn't until after noon that he returned my call.

'How is she?' he asked.

'Very tired.'

'When do you think she'll be up to seeing me?'

'I don't know. But Charles – she won't talk to me. She won't talk about what happened. And I have the feeling she won't talk to you, either.'

'Well . . . it's early days yet. And, Hugh, sometimes people tell their solicitors things they don't tell their own families. Sometimes it's easier to talk to a stranger, particularly when that person is duty-bound not to tell anyone else.' He didn't say: even the husband, though that was what he meant.

'I hope you're right.'

We arranged for me to bring Ginny down to see him in two days' time.

'Dr Bagnall's preliminary report came through.'

The pathologist. The post-mortem. Sylvie's body cut up on a slab. The stench of formalin, like the lab at school. 'And?'

'Nothing very startling, I'm afraid. He agrees with the cause of death, and there's nothing to suggest that the attack couldn't have been carried out by a woman of average height.'

I saw a flash of it then, an image so violent and graphic that it caught me like a panic. Ginny thrusting a knife up under Sylvie's ribs, forcing it home.

To drive the picture out I said quickly, 'But it doesn't prove anything?'

'It certainly doesn't prove that any particular person did or didn't commit the crime.'

'It could have been a man then?'

'Well . . . yes.' That caution had come into his voice again.

'What about the rest of the forensic stuff?'

'I've tracked down a DNA expert, and there's a top fingerprint lab in Wolverhampton. The DNA man isn't free for a couple of weeks, but the fingerprint people can get onto it straight away.'

'And if they don't find anything?'

'Then I think we have to accept there's nothing to be found.'

'We don't have to say that in court?'

'What? No, no. Our barrister will decide what evidence to use, and he'll only use what will actively *help* our case. What did you think of Grainger, by the way?'

'I thought he was pompous and conceited and overbearing,' I said without hesitation.

'Oh.'

'And surprisingly effective.'

'Well, we don't have to commit ourselves to him yet. When the prosecution serve their evidence we could ask him for an opinion, and take it from there.' A pause. 'While we're on the subject – have you come to any decisions about me?'

'You?' I said, knowing perfectly well what he meant.

'Do you want to retain me?'

'You'd better ask Ginny that.'

'Yes, of course. It's just that the real work's about to start and I thought . . .'

'As far as I'm concerned, you'll do, Charles.'

And he laughed, because it was in his nature to take this as a compliment.

I had put out some feelers about Tingwall among my barrister friends but even before the word came back that he was considered competent I had made up my mind to keep him. As a lawyer Tingwall had a rare advantage: he was prepared to become emotionally involved. Let the QC be the bleak professional; for this stage of the case Ginny needed someone who was prepared to go the extra mile.

'Are you married, Charles?' I asked.

'What? Yes. Six years now. Twin boys of two and a half. A real handful.'

I thought: Then you understand. You understand the need to believe that there is going to be a way out.

'I must tell you,' he said, resuming his lawyer's voice. 'The strangest thing. A witness has come forward to corroborate your story.'

'*My* story?'

'He saw you just outside Totnes, driving south, at about six-forty on the Saturday evening of the murder. He was away on holiday when you were arrested. He only heard about it when he got back. Contacted me through your brother last night. His name is Horrocks. An assistant harbour master, I believe.'

I remembered Horrocks. He was one of the men I had stood a drink in the pub when I was trawling for information about *Samphire*.

'He was absolutely adamant about the identification. Knew your car, recognised you. Even waved to you, he said. And – the dream witness – he was in no doubt about the time, because he was due at his sister's silver wedding party and was already ten minutes late. Anyway . . . there we are. Just thought you might be interested.'

'Does Henderson know?'

'I doubt it. But I wouldn't be in a hurry to tell him. Best not to offer information unless it's needed.'

'Ginny could do with a witness like Horrocks.'

'Yes,' he said, as though considering this afresh. 'It would help a lot.'

I woke Ginny for lunch and came down to prepare pâté and smoked salmon and salad. I hadn't tackled a french dressing in years, but I made a passable effort with a combination of the balsamic vinegar and olive oil that Ginny always used, and a dash of mustard.

Ginny appeared and sat down obediently at the kitchen table, like a guest in someone else's house. She looked no less exhausted than she had done that morning. While I cajoled her into eating, we discussed her health. Or I talked about the importance of taking care of herself while Ginny agreed in a vague placatory way. When this subject lapsed I led us on to the practicalities of selling Melton and we discussed it for the rest of the meal. The disposal of the furniture seemed to be the one topic that roused a spark of interest in Ginny, as though she were eager to rid herself of non-essential possessions.

To avoid meeting the prospective purchasers we arranged for Mrs Hoskins to let them in, and drove up onto the downs for a walk. The wind wasn't cold but it was blustery, and Ginny took my arm as we climbed slowly up the rabbit-tracked hill.

'Do you remember that holiday in Brittany?' I asked, resorting to the comfort of nostalgia. 'When we got caught in that downpour?'

She gave a single nod.

'God – the weather!' It had been overcast and rainy for all but two days of our stay. But then La Baule with its long sands and *belle époque* hotels had not really suited either of us. I'd found myself hankering after the craggy coast of North Brittany which had been the scene of so many childhood holidays on *Ellie Miller*, while Ginny had missed the warmth of the Mediterranean and having friends to dine with.

'Not the most successful holiday in the world,' I smiled.

'You wanted to be sailing.'

'Oh, I don't know,' I said with half a laugh. 'Did I?'

'I think so.' She corrected herself: 'I know so.'

'But I still enjoyed the holiday.'

'No, you didn't,' she said with a directness that was quite new to her. 'The holiday was the worst of both worlds. Trying to please each other and ending up doing what neither of us wanted. You should have said, you know. What you wanted. So should I. Perhaps that's where we went wrong.'

She had never spoken like this before. While I welcomed the opening of these dusty attics, I was faintly apprehensive as to what might emerge next.

'But you didn't like sailing,' I ventured.

'Not the long trips, no. But I could have flown across the Channel and joined you in France. I wouldn't have minded going from harbour to harbour.'

'I felt it was too much to ask.'

'But I would have fitted in, I was desperate to fit in,' she said almost to herself. 'I felt it was a necessary part of loving some-one, to fit in.'

This thought settled over me uneasily as we climbed the last few yards to the ridge of the hill and paused to look out over the prairie of ploughed fields below.

I said, 'But we were happy in Provence, weren't we?'

'Oh yes,' she agreed without hesitation. 'It was the one place where you were free of it all. The business. And your family.'

'My family?'

231

She cast me a glance, gearing herself up to voice something that I wouldn't like. 'Your family,' she confirmed. 'Your father mainly. But David and Mary too.'

'But I didn't need to be *free* of them.' Even as I said it, the idea lodged in my mind as a startling and disturbing possibility, made all the more real by the realisation that I had never allowed myself to consider it before. 'Why do you say that?'

'Because you were the one they expected things from. The business. The tradition. All the rest.'

'But my father never interfered. My father never asked anything of me.'

'No?' Her tone betrayed her doubts. Then, attempting to close this unsatisfactory argument: 'But Provence – yes, we were happy there.'

'Hang on,' I said, not ready to let go. 'Are you saying my family put pressure on me? Because you'd be quite wrong, you know.'

The wind spun her hair across her face and she pushed it back and held it against her head. 'Not pressure like that. Not . . . *open* pressure. But it was still there, wasn't it?' She looked at me with a touch of her old uncertainty. 'You having been groomed to take over. Being your father's favourite. The way he made the business into this great and holy thing. This sacred inheritance. I always felt' – the thought emerged bitterly – 'that you were doing it for him.'

'For him? But it was for us too! Always for us! I don't know how you can think that.'

She gave up the argument with a submissive twist of both hands and walked on. But as we tramped along the undulating ridge her words still rankled.

'How could you think I wasn't doing it for us?' I asked hotly.

She came to a slow halt, as though in her tiredness she could not concentrate and walk at the same time. 'Because you went on and on pushing yourself, spending more and more time away, hardly being at home. Not choosing to be with me. It didn't look to me as though you were doing it for us.'

'It was only because it was all going wrong, Ginny. The business, I mean. I was desperate to save it. I thought if I just kept trying harder . . . And then I seemed to get *overwhelmed*.'

She absorbed this silently and looked away into the wind. 'And all that time I was feeling useless, you see. As though I had nothing to offer you any more.'

'That's ridiculous.'

'No!' she argued, a harsh edge to her voice. 'It's not ridiculous. You always say things like that, you always brush things off as if that'll make the subject go away. But I'm telling you – that was how I *felt*. I felt I had nothing to offer you any more.' She stated this with exasperation, as though I had never made any real effort to understand her. 'Oh, it took me ages to work out that I wasn't getting it right, that you hated the people and the parties and the social scene. It took me ages to realise it wasn't what you wanted. I was as bad as you were, you see – I clung on. When things began to go wrong, I just kept trying harder. Because it was the only thing I was good at, organising things, making things happen. I didn't know any other way.' She gave a small shudder. 'But I got there in the end. That weekend when you rushed off to Dittisham, I finally got the message. But by then ... it was too late.'

'Oh Ginny.' All the accumulated misunderstandings of the years seemed to hang over us like so many missed opportunities. 'What a pair.'

Something in this brought her emotions to the surface and, turning swiftly away, she made a move for home.

'It wasn't too late, you know,' I said after we had walked in silence for a time. 'Not for me.'

But she wouldn't answer that because we were talking about the summer, and the summer was Sylvie.

When we got back she went into the sitting room and dozed off in front of an old film. As I scrubbed the potatoes for supper, her comments rolled round my mind. I accepted that I might not be able to judge my family too objectively – who could? – yet had I really understood so little about myself all these years? Had I really been driven by my obligations to them rather than my own needs, or Ginny's. I had always striven to please my father, certainly, and that had never diminished. And given the choice I had preferred David's approval to his annoyance, which could be fearsome. But had I really been driven by the fear of letting them down? It was a dispiriting thought.

I overcooked the salmon and undercooked the potatoes. Ginny assured me that she wasn't very hungry and wouldn't have eaten much anyway. She drank some Pouilly-Fumé though, two full glasses, and was halfway through a third before she slowed down.

'Tingwall – Charles – needs to see you some time this week,' I told her. 'I have to go down to Hartford on Thursday so I could drop you in Exeter on the way. Will that be all right?'

She took a long troubled breath.

'You have to see him, darling. You have to trust him.'

She nodded stiffly.

'He's really thorough, you know. In fact, I'm pretty impressed with him. I think he's well up to the job.' I added tentatively: 'So long as we give him all the help he needs, of course.'

She was staring out beyond the window, focused on some inner world, and gave no indication of having heard.

Suppressing a creep of frustration, I said, 'You will talk to him, won't you, darling? You can talk to him in confidence, you know. I mean, he won't tell *me* anything you don't want him to.'

I found it impossible to read what was going on in her mind. She gave me nothing back. After the revelations of the walk, the sudden burst of communication, she had put up the shutters again.

'He's been busy,' I said in an effort at conversation. 'Getting hold of experts to check the evidence . . .' Lumbering on, searching for points of interest, I added, 'Oh, and would you believe it, a witness has come forward, confirming my arrival time in Dittisham that day. Ironic, really. Henderson was always so transfixed by that missing journey time. Thought he could catch me out, like some Agatha Christie detective.'

I had her attention at last. 'A witness?'

'A man called Horrocks. An assistant harbour master. Saw me just outside Totnes.'

Her eyes burned brightly, urging me on.

'Saw me at twenty to seven, apparently. Absolutely positive it was me. Knew the car and so on. Even waved at me, though I didn't see him.'

'So ... So ...' She was blinking rapidly. 'Does that mean you're in the clear?'

A long confused pause followed.

'Did you think I wasn't?'

'I was worried in case ... You know, I thought ... They'd think that we'd ... together. That you were involved ...' She dismissed the rest of this thought with an agitated shake of her head before repeating more forcefully, 'Does that mean you're in the clear?'

Conflicting thoughts raced uncomfortably round my brain. 'I would think so, yes.'

'What about afterwards? After you arrived? They won't think you could have got down to the boat then and helped me?'

I was struggling to catch up, to fill the gaps in this startling new scenario. 'No. David saw me in town, remember.'

'And after that?'

'Well, you were there. And David dropped in.'

'That's right, that's right. Yes ... You had no time, did you?' Without warning she began to blink back tears and laugh at the same time. 'I was so worried. I thought ...' Now she was laughing more than she was crying, an odd overwrought sound. 'Thank God.'

I went round the table and sat next to her.

She kept repeating, 'Thank God.' Then, with a flash of doubt, 'But can we be sure? Can we really be sure? That it'll be enough?'

'Charles can find out, I imagine.'

'Can he?' She seized on this. 'If he can ...'

I tried to make light of my next question. 'You thought Henderson might come back for me then?'

'What?' From a state of near-apathy she had become taut as a wire, as though hit by the effects of some fast-working drug, and I wondered if the pills she was taking had interacted with the wine. 'Yes. *Yes*,' she insisted. 'There was always a risk, wasn't there?'

Maintaining my tone, I smiled, 'Was there?'

Caught up in her frantic relief, she was barely listening again. 'Ginny?' I prompted. 'There was a risk that he'd charge me?'

'Yes. *God*. It was my nightmare. My worst nightmare. I thought they'd come back for you. That we'd both end up in prison.' And she half winced, half laughed at the thought.

I was missing something fundamental here, something which both alarmed and electrified me. 'So . . .' I felt my way cautiously, aware of how quickly the shutters might close again. 'If this chap hadn't seen me, if I'd had the time to' – I searched for innocuous words – 'get down to the river . . . then Henderson might have suggested that I'd . . . that I'd . . . ?'

'Oh, that you'd killed Sylvie, of course. And that I helped you to get rid of her afterwards.' She went on: 'You see . . . That's what I thought too. That you'd killed her.'

I was very still now. I was hovering on the brink of understanding, but I still needed to hear it from her mouth.

'But I didn't kill her,' I prompted softly.

'I know that now. But by the time I realised . . . it was too late.' She shook her head again.

'Why was it too late, Ginny?'

Through her tears, she gave me a beautiful lost smile. 'Because by then I'd got rid of her. I'd put her over the side.'

ELEVEN

'Oh, I knew the theory. I knew I should sit tight and let it blow over,' Ginny began in a brittle voice. 'Let you get bored with her, get her out of your system. I knew that's what clever women did. But I wasn't feeling clever, not about that sort of thing anyway. And you see – I wasn't at all sure it *would* blow over. In fact the longer it went on, the more convinced I became that I was losing you for ever, that you'd never come back. And I couldn't quite . . . *deal* with that.'

We had come to the smallest of the three living rooms at Melton, the room we called the sitting room, a low-lit room with book-lined walls, soft sofas and a fireplace which threw out plenty of heat. We sat side by side on the smaller sofa, staring into the fire, wine on the low table in front of us.

'It was one thing to suspect that something was going on. But actually knowing, seeing . . . That was *awful*.' And her voice rose to a gasp. 'When I saw you together that weekend, watched you go off in the boat – well, I thought that was it. I could see she was younger. Prettier. And she knew how to sail. Well . . . I couldn't see what possible reason you could have for staying with me. And I didn't need to ask you how you felt about her. I could read the signs. I could see you were completely smitten.'

I forced myself not to say anything, not to offer the kind of instant denials which Ginny seemed to find so meaningless.

'So there I was,' she declared harshly. 'Another weekend on my own, another weekend knowing you were with her. I simply couldn't sit there any more like some animal to the slaughter. The more I thought about it, the more I felt I had absolutely nothing to lose by following you down and making a fool of myself. I'd have gone mad if I'd stayed at home a moment longer. Literally mad.' She stole a nervous glance at me before reaching for her wine and taking a gulp. 'I went through this great debate as I drove down – trying to decide on confrontation versus the oh-so civilised discussion. You know – do you love her, Hugh? Do you intend to leave me? Oh well, in that case, good luck old thing. I knew I'd never be able to carry that one off. Never have been able to deal with things in that way. *Coolly*. Not when I'm . . .' She wrestled with this thought only to leave it unfinished. 'So it was going to have to be the great confrontation. Burst in, have a scene, give you an ultimatum. I knew I'd probably end up behaving . . . *pathetically*. Crying. Making a fool of myself. I knew you'd probably hate me for it, I knew I risked losing you altogether – the hysterical wife, no humiliation untapped – but I couldn't see any other way. At least the whole thing would be out in the open. At least I wouldn't have this feeling that I wanted to die the whole time.'

Catching my expression, she said, 'Oh, please don't think I'm saying all this just to make you feel bad, Hugh. I'm not. Really. I just wanted you to understand how I was feeling, how desperate I was.'

I nodded rapidly, determined not to speak.

She pushed her head back against the sofa before starting off again in a voice that was increasingly unsteady. 'I thought you'd gone straight down to Dittisham that Saturday. When you said you were going into the office for a few hours I thought you were just saying that – you know, to discourage me from joining you, to keep me away. So as soon as I thought you were well on your way I set off. And all the time I was planning what I'd say when I caught you together. I was going to wait until I did catch you together, you see. Awful, I know. Awful to set out to make a scene. But I was hurt. Angry. Off my head with worry. I felt like *killing* you.' She flung me a fierce look. 'Or myself. More likely myself. Anyway . . . You weren't at the house, of course. I didn't drive up. I parked in the village and took the path through the garden. I crept round the house, looking in through the windows like some awful nutter, and then I saw that your car wasn't there, and immediately thought of the boat. I went to the terrace and looked across, and I saw it – the dinghy. Tied up to *Ellie Miller*. To me that meant only one thing, of course. That you must be there with *her*. That if I was quick I'd catch you in the act. Well – I'm not sure I actually wanted to find you in bed with her – I wasn't that masochistic. But together, anyway. I wanted to have a good look at her, you see. I wanted to know just how pretty she was. And I wanted to confront both of you, to make you feel – I don't know – *bad, guilty. Something.* Stupid, of course.' She gave a scornful sigh. 'Never does any good, that sort of thing, does it? Never makes people change their minds.'

I couldn't let this pass. 'My mind never needed changing. I wanted to finish it. I knew there was no future in it.'

'But I didn't know that, did I?' she argued with a spark of resentment. 'I thought you were mad about her. I thought you were about to leave me. Oh, I tried to tell myself it mightn't be that bad, I tried to be ... *sensible.* But it never did any good. I couldn't think of any reason why you should stay with me, you see. No confidence. Never have had. Hopeless.'

A pause while she dealt with this thought and put it behind her.

'Anyway . . .' Her voice was flagging. 'I couldn't get out to *Ellie* fast enough. I couldn't bear the thought of missing the two of you together. I rushed down to the quay. I hadn't thought about transport, of course. But there were quite a few people about. A load of people were just getting into a rubber dinghy and I was about to ask them for a lift when I saw *Ellie*'s dinghy, sitting there at the pontoon. The name and everything: *Tender to Ellie Miller*. Well, that drew me up short for a second. I wondered if I'd got it all wrong. I wondered if someone else was on the boat – a repair man or whatever. Then I thought: On a Saturday afternoon? They never work on Saturday afternoons, do they? So I got going again. I hadn't forgotten how to row. You taught me too well. In the days when I pretended to love boats.' Her voice softened a little. 'Well, I loved being with you, doing what you enjoyed, so in a way I did love it, while it lasted.'

Reaching for her wine she cradled it in both hands as if it might warm her. 'By the time I reached the boat I was shaking like a jelly. I could barely tie the dinghy up. And of course I was trying not to make any noise. My heart was hammering so hard I

239

could scarcely breathe. And then I remembered that I'd left my inhaler in the car. God!' She rolled her eyes at the memory. 'So I stayed in the dinghy for a while, trying to catch my breath, trying to prevent an attack. Sat there like a dummy doing my breathing exercises, listening, half expecting to be discovered at any second. Nothing happened, of course, no sounds from the boat.' This thought created its own silence. 'When I'd finally calmed down a bit . . . I climbed aboard. I—' The horror was revisited on her face. 'I went into the cockpit. I looked into the cabin. I . . .' She could barely speak. ' . . . *saw her*.'

I waited for a long moment. Finally I murmured, 'And she was dead?'

Her face contorted. 'Yes.' And she turned her gaze onto me, searching my expression, desperate for some sort of reassurance.

I nodded, urging her on.

'She *was* dead.'

'Yes,' I said hastily. 'Yes, of course she was.'

'But they're not going to believe me, are they? They're never going to believe me.' And the despair sounded in her voice.

'Of course they will! Why shouldn't they?'

She was drawing great gulps of air. 'You believe me, though?'

'Of course!'

'Really?'

'*Yes*, Ginny. Really. I wouldn't say so if I didn't!'

But for Ginny no amount of reassurance could ever be enough, and she continued to scrutinise my face before she drew sufficient confidence to go on. Even then she kept casting rapid glances at me, never quite satisfied, never entirely convinced.

'I had a terrible attack, of course,' she sighed, picking up the story again. 'Thought I was going to die. Lay in the cockpit. One of the worst ever. I almost blacked out at one stage. I've no idea how I managed to keep breathing. Thought it would never end. God, I really thought I was going to die! I even said my goodbyes. But then – well, it began to ease. And when it was finally over I lay there for a long time, not daring to move – not wanting to move. Sort of hoping I could put the moment off, hoping I could keep lying there and not have to face up to what was in the boat. Then through it all – the shock and everything – I began to think about what I was going to do. Was I going to row ashore and report it? Was I going to shout and wave from the boat until someone saw me on the bank? Then suddenly . . . *suddenly* . . . it came to me. I mean, like a bolt from the blue. That I couldn't report it. I *mustn't*. Because . . .' She made a statement of this: 'Because.'

'I had killed her.'

Her mouth seesawed, she lifted one hand, the beginning of a plea. 'Don't think too badly of me, don't . . . But I couldn't think what else – *who* else – it could have been.'

'No.'

'The way you'd been behaving. Frantic. Off your head. I couldn't think . . .' Again she put it to me, 'Who else could it have been?'

'No, I can see . . . I would have thought the same thing.'

She grasped at this. 'Would you? Would you really?'

'Definitely.' Again I tried to give her the reassurance she craved. 'Finding her there on the boat. You thinking I'd been aboard . . . I was the obvious person.'

'Yes!' she affirmed fiercely. 'You *were*, you *were!*' She jerked her arm so violently that she spilt her wine. I took her glass and, putting it on the table, went to the cloakroom to find a cloth and dampen it with water.

She dabbed at her sweater, breathing heavily, clenching her lips. I fetched a glass of water which she drank greedily.

When we had been quiet for some time, she repeated reproachfully, 'It had to be you. It had to be.'

Her eyes flicked towards me, and I quickly agreed, 'Yes. It had to be me.'

Gathering some comfort at last, she prepared to go on. 'I fell apart for a while,' she said shakily. 'The whole thing seemed so ghastly, so totally un—' the word eluded her 'so un-*saveable*. You know how something can happen which is so ghastly that there's nothing you can do to make it right again. Once it's happened, it's happened. However much you may wish it different, there's no *un*doing it, ever, *ever*. Except this was twice as ghastly as anything I could ever have imagined. But then I thought—Then I thought—' She straightened up in her seat and some of the life came back into her voice. 'Perhaps I *can* undo

241

some of this. Usually I pretend that difficult things aren't happening, don't I? I just push them out of my mind.' She held up a staying hand as if I were about to disagree. 'Oh, I do, I know I do! All my life . . . always. But this time – well, I *could* make things right again, couldn't I? Oh, not totally, of course. But almost right. For *you* anyway. For us. And Hugh—' She opened her eyes wide. 'It thrilled me. I mean – I felt glad. Glad that I had thought of it. Glad I was going to do it. I was absolutely determined, you see. Determined not to be weak and pathetic. Determined to carry it through to the very end.'

The phone was ringing but neither of us made a move to answer it and eventually it stopped.

Ginny was still lost in her story. 'I imagined you'd rushed off in a state of shock. Rushed back to London. It seemed to me that I had plenty of time – time to do the thing properly. So I planned it! I thought it through! I sat in the bottom of the cockpit where no one could see me, and I thought about every detail. I was determined, you see, not to forget anything.' Her mouth fell. 'It wasn't possible, of course – not to make any mistakes. But I didn't realise that then.' Suddenly her control deserted her and she clamped a hand to her eyes. Just as abruptly she pulled her hand away again and went on, as though any loss of momentum might sabotage her chances of finishing.

'I knew there was blood – I'd seen it,' she began at speed. 'I knew I'd need something to wrap her up in, to stop the blood and keep it from— So I looked in the cockpit lockers and found some plastic sheeting and a rope. Then I braced myself to go below. The strange thing was that it wasn't as bad as I thought it would be. Partly because I'd geared myself up for it. Partly because I'd made up my mind that I wasn't going to *let* it bother me. Mind over matter,' she exclaimed with a hint of pride, 'like doctors and operations.' She paused for breath before racing on. 'I didn't look at her, though. I half shut my eyes. And I kept talking to myself, blabbering away, which seemed to help, God only knows why. The hardest thing was getting the plastic all the way round her. Not getting any blood on the *outside*—' She jerked to a halt and cried in sudden anguish, 'God, you don't want to hear all this, do you! You don't want all the ghastly details!'

Part of me wanted to hear everything, but it was a part of me I didn't trust. 'Don't tell me anything you don't want to,' I said.

'Nothing I don't want to,' she repeated with irony, blinking back the hovering tears. 'The awful thing was – half of me was proud of what I was doing! So methodical. So efficient. Not forgetting a single thing!' And she gave a sad empty laugh. Blowing her nose, she continued with attempted toughness, 'So! I put her in the plastic, I wrapped the rope round several times, I knotted it. Then I cleaned up as best I could. I was already planning to come back the next day and scrub the floor, scrub every inch of the boat. With bleach – I knew bleach was the only thing. But there wasn't anything more I could do that night, not until dark, so I sat in the companionway and waited. That was the worst, waiting. The darkness seemed to take for ever.' The pretended toughness had vanished. Large splashy tears dropped silently onto her sweater and dripped off her nose. She had run out of tissues so I went and fetched some more. She blew her nose and wiped her eyes ferociously, as though this might be enough to stem the flood.

'It was hard. Moving her.' The effort of speaking was very great and between gasps her voice was all over the place. 'I used a rope – a halyard or something – to hoist her up. I tried using a winch but the rope got into a terrible mess. It took me ages to unravel it. So in the end I just put the rope over the boom and hauled that way. God, it was hard – *hard*. But somehow, *somehow* . . . I got her up. I got her onto the deck and . . .' She trailed off and with a low moan leant forward and sank her head into her hands.

I put an arm round her shoulders, I murmured vague words of comfort, but I hardly knew what I was saying, the images that crowded my mind were so overpowering. I saw Ginny pulling the body onto the side deck and forcing it under the guardrails, I saw it hanging out over the edge of the boat before it finally broke free and slid into the blackness, I heard it hit the water with a low splash, I saw it bobbing up and floating away on the tide. I saw all this and began to realise what a massive undertaking it must have been for Ginny. I felt astonished at her strength of mind, at the sheer force of her determination.

Not trusting myself to say anything useful quite yet, I resorted to offering tea. Ginny nodded from the depths of her hands. When I came back with the mugs she was sitting up again, blowing her nose.

'Sometimes in the night I dream that it didn't happen,' she breathed. 'I dream that it was just – well, a dream. And then I wake . . .' She took the tea and her hands were trembling.

'You'll tell Charles the whole story, won't you?'

She gave a tight shake of her head.

'*Ginny* – for God's sake.'

'Oh, I *suppose*,' she surrendered wearily. 'For what it's worth. But it's not going to do any good, is it?'

'Ginny, don't be—' I caught myself on the brink of saying *ridiculous*. 'There must be a way of proving what happened. But we can't expect him to even *begin* to help us until he knows the truth.'

'But everyone's going to think I'm making it up, aren't they? They're going to think I'm lying. I mean, who's going to believe that I did what I did if it wasn't to cover up for you? I mean, why would I bother, if *you* hadn't killed her? Or if *I* hadn't killed her? If neither . . . then why . . .' In her weariness she was confused by her own argument and put a hand to her head. Emerging from her daze, she said simply, 'It's no good – I've thought it through, I've thought it through a million times. And Hugh—' Her gaze was like a baffled animal's. 'I can't see any way out. And it frightens me to death.'

I tried to keep my own fear out of my face as I pulled her against my shoulder and murmured reassurances which sounded empty even to my own ears.

We lapsed into the silence of exhaustion, and when I finally spoke again I realised Ginny was beyond further talk. I took her up to bed and watched her count out her tablets and wash them down. As we lay in the darkness she grasped my arm and whispered apprehensively, 'Thank you for believing me.'

Knowing what she wanted to hear, knowing she wouldn't

244

sleep until she heard it, I said, 'I never doubted you for a moment, darling. Not for a moment.'

Later as I lay awake with no chance of sleep, I found myself believing almost too much of what she had said: I found myself believing that there was no way out.

*

'That's right, isn't it?'

I wasn't sure what George had just said, but I gave an authoritative nod.

We were sitting in one of those conference rooms that looks identical to every other conference room in the City, with vertical slatted blinds at the picture windows, neutral walls and an ostentatious elliptical table that stretched almost the length of the room. Our small band was scattered round one end of the table. There was George and Alan and myself, one of our lawyers, and three Chartered Bank people. Significantly – or otherwise – the Chartered party did not include either of the two grey-suited executives who had smiled their way round Hartford on the conducted tour. Instead we had graduated to two full directors.

Now that I was listening properly I realised that George was labouring a point that he had already made twice that morning. The bankers had not been impressed by his argument the first two times around and, hearing it a third time, were looking distinctly po-faced. George was asking them to knock a point off the interest rate they were demanding. He couldn't see why we should pay over the going business rate. He couldn't see that we were in a poor negotiating position, and that the bankers, having let themselves be talked into granting us the loan virtually against their better judgment, were in no mood to do us any more favours. The meeting had gone on too long, we were losing ground. Risking George's wrath, I interrupted him in mid-stream. 'Suppose we agreed to carry this premium for a period of one year?'

They didn't commit themselves, but they didn't turn it down either. They'd probably offer four years, and we'd settle on three,

245

two if we were lucky, which wouldn't be bad under the circumstances. They said they'd come back to us the next day.

I could feel George looking daggers at me as we went down in the lift. He managed to restrain himself until we reached the street.

'It would be nice not to have the ground cut from under my feet,' he said with barely concealed indignation.

'We were never going to win that one, George.'

'Maybe not, but it would have been nice to discuss it, feel we had a *strategy*.'

'We had to concede something.'

'Why the hell should we pay over the odds?'

'Because we have no choice, that's why.'

'It's another twenty grand a year!'

'We'll have to live with it.'

'I'm not sure we can!'

'In that case we shouldn't be here at all.'

He retorted acidly, 'Well, that's a thought!' Then, sighing hard, he shuffled his unwieldy feet and made an apologetic face. 'It gets me, that's all, the way they squeeze us dry.'

'I know.'

He cast a scornful eye over the glass canyons. 'It's not as if they actually *make* anything, is it? Apart from fat salaries. You know, I'm never bothered by anything the factory throws at me. Employees' problems, suppliers, late deliveries – you name it. No trouble. But this lot! They'd screw their own grandmothers, wouldn't they? And then ask for another meeting to renegotiate the terms. You just never know where you bloody are with the slippery buggers. That's what I can't take!'

'Won't be long now, George.'

'Ha! That's true enough! Death or glory.' He rolled his eyes, then, with a conciliatory expression, asked cautiously, 'Look, Hugh . . . can you spare a couple of hours? I wouldn't bother you, but Cumberland's lawyers are trying to throw a whole new set of spanners in the works. And that's only a half of our problems.'

I hesitated, and in hesitating it came to me that a great deal hung on this small and apparently insignificant decision. A couple of hours would undoubtedly stretch into three, and then

246

the whole afternoon would be gone and I wouldn't get back to Melton until nine or even ten. Tomorrow I was due at Hartford for a late-morning meeting which, given half a chance, would run into the afternoon. Before very long I'd be back on twelve-hour days and fast-evaporating weekends. And Ginny would be on her own with time to think and brood.

'No,' I said. 'I'm sorry.'

George stuck out his chin. 'Tomorrow then, after the meeting?'

'It won't be possible, George. I can't give you any more time at the moment.'

'Just for the next two weeks, until after the EGM? Until we sort out the lawyers?'

'I'm sorry.'

'If I came to Wiltshire?'

I knew I was sounding unreasonable. 'No.'

He exclaimed, 'This is our one chance, Hugh!'

'Don't think I don't know it.' If we didn't win the backing of the Cumberland shareholders at the EGM then the buyout would finally be dead and buried.

George clamped his mouth shut and looked away. Then, with a sigh that seemed to settle in his stomach and swell his considerable girth, he said in an altogether softer tone, 'I didn't mean to be, you know – unsympathetic. You've got your priorities.'

'I'm sorry I can't do more.'

'You *will* put the motion at the EGM though?'

'Oh, I'll put the motion.'

'See you tomorrow then.' He touched my arm as he left.

Walking to the car, I wondered how I would feel if the buyout failed at the eleventh hour through some avoidable error, if I discovered too late that George had missed some obvious move. It would exasperate me, it would hurt me, but it wouldn't kill me. Responsibility had its limits, and I had reached mine. In making the decision to distance myself from Hartford, I was wrenching my life out by the roots and shifting it to new ground. But it was my own choice, made on my own terms. Perhaps, if Ginny were right, the first independent choice I had ever made.

Setting off homeward, I called Melton. Julia told me Ginny was having a short sleep and seemed fine. This news took the edge off my concern, but like an ache temporarily suppressed by an analgesic, the throb of apprehension soon returned. I couldn't entirely rid myself of the idea that the prison psychiatrist might have got it right and Ginny might be close to some act of desperation.

The answering machine at Furze Lodge referred calls for Mary to a mobile number which didn't answer the first few times I tried it.

'I didn't know you had a mobile,' I remarked when I finally got through to her.

'Ah, well, you don't know everything about me,' she teased. 'A girl's got to stay in touch, hasn't she?' She was speaking from some quiet place with no background noise. 'Let me guess,' she said. 'You're on the M4 somewhere. Heading west.'

I laughed, 'How did you know?'

'I cheated. I spoke to Ginny at lunchtime.'

'Mary – thanks for doing that. *Thanks*. How did she sound?'

'Oh . . . fairly shattered. But then, that's not too surprising, is it? She *is* seeing someone good, isn't she, Hugh? The psychiatrist?'

'Yes. Well, David thinks he's good.'

'It's Jones, is it?'

'Yes.'

'He *is* the best. And the drugs – they're really amazing nowadays. Prozac and all that. Ginny tells me you might be looking for a cottage somewhere on the edge of Dartmoor,' Mary continued in some seamless train of thought. 'I could keep an eye out for something, if you'd like me to. I hear of places from time to time.'

'Oh . . . would you? Thanks.'

A pause while we waited for me to come to the point of my call. 'Mary, I want some help.'

'Anything.' Behind the warmth I caught a hint of wariness.

'Blackwell Cottage – do you know who owns it? Or more to the point, who arranged to let it, and who exactly they let it to?'

The silence that followed was aflame with objections. 'Hugh, I don't think that sort of information is going to help anyone.'

'I only want a name, Mary.'

248

'Yes, but *why* do you want it, Hugh? Contacting witnesses can get misunderstood.'

'I only want to talk to someone.'

'I really don't think it's a good idea.'

Sometimes I forgot that Mary was a lawyer by inclination as well as training, and that in situations like this her caution was liable to come bustling to the fore.

'Fine,' I said, giving in without a fuss.

A sharp pause, and she muttered in a mock headmistressy voice, 'I suppose that means you'll go and find out anyway, from somebody else?'

I didn't say anything to that. The connection faded as a lorry overtook in the fast lane and she asked: 'Are you still there?'

'I'm still here, Mary.'

'Who do you want to talk to anyway?' she said, trying to maintain a disapproving tone. 'Don't tell me – the long-haired lout?'

'Yes.'

'You realise he's likely to be a prime prosecution witness?'

'I doubt it. He was always completely stoned.'

She gave an admonitory groan. 'All the more reason to stay away. What are you hoping to find out anyway?'

'I'm not sure,' I said, partly playing her at her own game, but also responding to some instinct for caution, a wish to protect Ginny and her story from perfunctory judgments.

'Whoa,' Mary sang. 'If I were to help you – and I'm not saying I am – then I'd need to know what you were letting yourself – and me – in for.'

Still unwilling to give away too much, I offered a limited version. 'I want to find out about Sylvie's drug-taking, the dealers, the people she mixed with. Joe was around most of the time, he must know.'

'And this is going to help Ginny?' she asked in a voice of concern.

'I think so.'

'How, Hugh?'

I wondered if she meant to sound quite so sceptical. 'By digging out some of the facts the police never considered,' I said doggedly.

'How do you know what they considered?'

'Well – we've got a fair idea,' I bluffed.

'This is something for your solicitor, Hugh. *He's* the person to judge whether something needs investigating, not *you*. And he'll have someone he uses for these things, a retired copper, someone who's used to making these kind of enquiries. Someone,' she added heavily, 'who can speak to witnesses on a professional basis.'

'I don't think Joe's likely to talk to a policeman, retired or otherwise,' I said, for the sake of argument.

'I'm getting signals here,' Mary sighed. 'And the signals are telling me that you're determined to do this your way.'

'Well, I can't leave it, Mary, that's for sure.'

'But where's it going to get you, Hugh? What are you hoping to achieve?'

I felt a swell of resentment at this unrelenting flow of difficulties. 'I'm trying to help Ginny,' I said stiffly.

She didn't speak for so long I began to wonder if she was still there. Finally I heard a long sigh. 'Oh, *Hugh*. The things I do . . . All right, I'll see what I can find out. But on one condition. That if I do find an address for Joe-the-long-haired-loon that you don't go near him yourself. That you pass the address straight on to your solicitor – what's his name – ?'

'Charles Tingwall.'

'Tingwall. And that you leave him to deal with it. Promise me, Hugh?'

I heard myself say, 'Okay.'

'You won't make me regret this, will you?' she murmured as she rang off.

I thought hard before making my next call. I thought of all the objections Mary would make to it if she found out.

David's laconic bark announced that I was interrupting him with a patient.

'Won't keep you,' I promised, 'but could you give me Jean-Paul's address.'

'Jean-who? *Oh,*' he said in the next breath as it came back to him. 'Oh, yes. Hang on . . .' I could imagine him leaning across his desk and flipping open his address book and going down to the

'M's. He gave me an address in the Clifton area of Bristol, and a phone number as well.

'Thanks,' I said. 'And, David, it might be best if you didn't mention this to Mary.'

Whether he simply didn't have time to query this or it would never have occurred to him to discuss it with Mary anyway, he agreed impatiently.

'Anything else?' he asked in a more considerate tone.

'Not at the moment, thanks.'

Then, almost kindly, 'Will we see you soon? On the weekend? I think we should see each other on the weekend. I'll speak to Mary.'

'That would be lovely,' I said automatically, wondering as I rang off how Ginny would feel about the invitation.

*

I let myself into the house and, hearing laughter, paused uncertainly on the threshold. Following the sound, I found Julia and Ginny at the kitchen table. Ginny was still smiling, her head on one side, her hair falling onto her shoulder in a cinnamon curve.

Seeing me, she stretched out a hand. 'You're home early,' she declared, and the laughter had made her lovely again. She gave me a kiss and didn't let go of my hand. 'We're celebrating,' she said, and something in her tone put me on my guard.

'Why?'

'The people have made an offer for the house.'

I felt a wash of relief. 'That's wonderful.'

As she gave me the details I examined her surreptitiously. She seemed more alert, far less tired. But there was something else, something I couldn't put my finger on.

Julia stood up and looked diplomatically at her watch. 'Better be going. Messages in your study.' She sent me a well-practised eye signal, and I followed her into the hall.

'Howard called,' she said. 'Wanted to speak to you *urgently*. I told him you weren't available. But it was like talking to a rhino, all thick skin and pea brain, so be warned. He may call this evening.'

'Thank you for coming.'

'Any time. I mean that. Just let me know.'

'Maybe a couple of days next week?'

'Of course. I look forward to it.'

Ginny was loading the dishwasher when I got back to the kitchen.

'You seem much brighter,' I said.

'I am.'

'Having Julia wasn't too much trouble then?'

She flashed a glance at me. 'Don't be silly. I know why she was here.'

'Ah.' I made a contrite gesture. 'It was just . . . Jones thought it best. Until we could be sure the medicines were the right ones for you.'

'I've stopped taking them. Except one.'

My anxiety lurched to the surface. I stuttered, 'Is that wise?'

'They made me feel like a zombie.' She began to hunt through the fridge.

'But darling . . .' I came round the table. 'Wouldn't it be best to discuss this with Jones first?'

'I won't change my mind,' she said, her voice rising a notch. 'My head's so much clearer, I feel I can cope. They were doing me no good.'

I watched her long fingers pulling at some clingfilm and her movements seemed jerky and uncoordinated.

'If that's what you feel.'

She put the packet of food down and said, 'Nothing's going to stop me feeling desperate, Hugh. Nothing.' And her voice rang nervily. 'But I'd rather feel alive and desperate than half dead all the time. Anyway, I'm still taking a touch of the librium. Well, I think it's librium. It's the other stuff that makes me feel so wretched. Really – I feel so much better.' She must have read the doubt in my face because she said with a touch of indignation, 'I'm not going to kill myself, you know.'

I pulled a stupid smile. 'Promise?'

252

'I'll give you notice, all right?' she said. 'If I start planning anything.'

I nodded, not encouraged by the knowledge that this was the one bargain a dedicated suicide would never keep.

Ginny insisted on making the supper. I opened a bottle of Chablis for her, what we called cook's rations, and when I wandered back into the kitchen half an hour later I noticed that the bottle was nearly half empty.

Ginny caught my glance and said, 'Yes, I'm drinking. Got to have something to make me sleep.'

'Fine,' I said.

She picked up her glass and, keeping her eyes on mine, took a long defiant gulp. 'You might have to carry me to bed,' and there was both humour and gentle entreaty in her face.

We kissed, and there was stored-up passion in her mouth, and urgency too, as though time for her were already running short. She pressed herself against my body in a way that was for her quite unusual and brazen. 'See what drink does to me,' she said in a low excited voice, and I kissed her again, much harder than before. We stumbled hurriedly upstairs like two teenagers, leaving a scattering of clothes across the bedroom floor. She did not close her eyes as we made love, but watched my face with unwavering intensity. At first I thought she was doing this to bring some greater reality to our lovemaking, to banish whatever demons came to her when her eyes were closed, but in the moment before I was lost in my own sensations it seemed to me that she was searching out something in my face, a truth or a confirmation that she was half afraid to find there. She cried out as she came.

As we lay side by side, panting softly, shoulders touching, I whispered, 'I love you,' and prepared myself for the expressions of doubt that this simple statement had often engendered in the recent past. But she only said, 'It's a long time since we made love before dinner.'

'Lack of time rather than lack of ambition,' I said. My memory searched lazily back. 'We used to quite a lot, though, didn't we? In the old days, at your flat.'

'*God.*' The memory didn't please her. 'I hated that time.'

I made a show of taking offence, twisting my head to give her a mock glare, and laughed accusingly, 'I don't quite know how to take that.'

'Oh, I loved the excitement of it all, of course I did. But I hated loving you so much and not knowing if I was going to keep you. I was so desperate to marry you and I began to think you'd never ask me.'

This was one of those situations where it was going to be impossible to say the right thing. I ventured, 'Well, you know how I was. Cautious Charlie. One step at a time. Not really appreciating I was on to a good thing.' The truth was that I had hesitated long and hard over making the final leap. There had been a neediness in Ginny which had unsettled me and which instinct had told me would not easily be satisfied. And while she had never been openly possessive she had still managed to make me feel guilty for spending time away from her. I'd known that no marriage was ever perfect, that many of my friends had compromised and settled for a rough measure of contentment, I'd known that Ginny loved me more than was good for her, and probably for me as well; yet I hadn't been able to decide whether my quota of misgivings was normal, whether it formed a suitable basis for a workaday marriage or reasonable grounds for retreat.

'And once we were married?' I asked lightly.

'Then I was terribly happy.'

'So was I.'

'Were you really?' It was a straight question with no apprehensions attached.

'Oh yes,' I replied. 'I felt much more relaxed. I *liked* being married.'

She said in a distant reminiscent tone, 'Then I went and spoilt it all.'

'That's simply not true, darling.'

'Oh, it is, I know it is. I tried too hard, didn't I? Trying to make up for all the things I couldn't do, like have babies. I was always worrying, wasn't I? Always fussing. And about *things*,' she exclaimed in disgust. 'Really! Such a lot of time wasted on *things*.'

'Really, Ginny, you're being far too hard on yourself. I've had no complaints.'

She turned her head and gazed at me with the same fierce intensity as before. 'I wish we were starting again. I wish it were all different. I wish I could show you how I'd love you now, without all that – *nonsense*.'

Touched by this strange declaration, I said without thinking, 'We've got six months.' Then, in a clumsy attempt to cover my tactlessness: 'I mean, just for a start—'

'No, don't say that!' she interrupted with a shudder. 'Please . . . *don't*. Let's just settle for six months. Don't let's think about anything more.'

And with that she gave me a rough kiss before swinging off the bed and reaching for her clothes. I watched her walk into the bathroom and it struck me that from this crisis Ginny was drawing a measure of, if not confidence, then self-possession. It lent her a strength I had never suspected. I was proud of her for it, and maybe a little in awe of her too.

While Ginny made something exotic with chicken I laid the kitchen table with crystal and candles. As we sat down to eat I thought how far away six months sounded at the moment, and how very quickly it would pass.

Choosing what seemed like a good moment I said gently, 'I won't ask again but . . .' She had already stiffened. 'What happened to the other dinghy? To Sylvie's . . .?'

She looked down at the table, she twisted her knife, she brought herself slowly to the subject. 'I took it back to the pontoon, tied it there.' She gave an ironic smile. 'I'd worked *that* one out all right. I just . . .' she raised her head and looked beyond me, lost in memory '. . . didn't clean enough. *Thought* I had. Scrubbed the floor. And the sides of the bunks. And the seat covers. And the table – the legs, everything. Used a ton of bleach. Didn't want to miss anything, you see. Went over it all again, to be absolutely sure.' She grimaced. 'Wasn't as thorough as I thought, though, was I?' She inhaled sharply as if to put this behind her. 'Then . . . I found her bag. A small shoulder bag. I hadn't noticed it the night before. I couldn't decide what to do with it. I couldn't very well chuck it over the side, in case someone saw me and picked the bag straight up again. So . . . I brought it ashore and put it in a rubbish bin in the village.'

Something about this memory made her wince, and I wondered if she had been seen. 'Then I got rid of the cleaning things in a skip. And then I came back. To you.'

At this, we drifted away on our separate thoughts.

'There was nothing else on the boat?' I asked eventually. 'No signs of anyone else?'

'What do you mean – signs?'

'I don't know really. You didn't see anyone rowing near *Ellie*?'

She shook her head.

'On either day?'

'No.'

'Not on your way out that first time, before you found the body?' I heard myself say 'the body' as though it had never been Sylvie.

'No.'

Hearing the strain in her voice, I said placatingly, 'It was just a thought. That was all.'

She nodded, then, eyelids fluttering nervously, she braced herself to ask, 'Was Sylvie looking for you? Was that why she was there?'

This was the question I had asked myself countless times since her death. 'I don't think so. We hadn't spoken in ages. Two weeks, in fact. We had – broken off communications.' Ginny flinched a little and fiddled with the knife again. 'I can only think . . .' I paused to examine the idea again, to test it against my knowledge of Sylvie. 'I can only think that she'd stashed some drugs on the boat and gone out to pick them up. Or to leave some more. She knew where the key was kept, she knew how to get into the boat.'

'But why would she do that?'

'Because she was dealing in drugs, or running them, or both. I think she and her friends brought them over from France and sold them on. I think she didn't dare keep them at her place. She was incredibly organised where drugs were concerned. She planned her life around them.' I thought of the parcel tape she had used to bind the package to her back, and the waterproof material she had wrapped it in. 'She used every opportunity, every person she met. Including me. Well – *especially* me. That trip to France,' I admitted with an undimmed sense of shame, 'it was all about drugs.'

256

Ginny looked away and, following some logic of her own, said, 'As soon as I got back to the house that night and found you there, saw you so normal, so un- ... un-*bothered*, I *knew!* Deep down somewhere, I knew it couldn't be you! But I couldn't bring myself to face it. I couldn't face up to the ghastly thought that I'd done all that – that I'd done everything I'd done – for nothing. *Nothing!*' Reliving this thought she contorted her face as if in pain. 'But then, of course, I realised! I *realised* . . .'

'Realised?'

'That it made no difference.'

And still I didn't get it.

'They would still *think* it was you. Whatever I said, whatever you might say – they'd never believe it, would they? Why should they, after all? So I realised I'd still done the right thing. The only thing.'

I stared at her.

Locked in her memory, she rushed on, 'I still had to finish the job the next day, didn't I? I still had to go and clean the boat out. The floor – the floor was the worst. Bleach was the only thing. Lots of bleach. And the bunks too. It was a nightmare, trying to find every spot—'

She was still in full spate as I reached across and took her hands. 'It's all over,' I soothed her. 'All over now.'

She came to a halt with a final indignant echo: 'It was still the right thing to do.'

The right thing? I didn't know what to say. She had done all this for me. She had succeeded in protecting me – if protection was the word – but at what cost? Could it be worth all this?

'I think I should go to bed now,' Ginny breathed at last. 'Too much wine.' And she gave a single uncertain laugh.

Clasping her hand, I tucked her arm ceremoniously under mine and, leaving the dinner uncleared, we turned off the lights and headed across the hall. The phone began to ring. We paused and looked at it.

'Might be Tingwall,' I said.

Howard's voice said, 'Hugh! There you are. You're really very difficult to get hold of, you know.' He gave a humourless chuckle to show that he was prepared to forgive me this lapse.

I mouthed 'Howard' to Ginny and cast my eyes heavenward.

'Now listen – this EGM business,' Howard said without pause. 'It's a waste of everyone's time, you know. You should pull your hounds off and save yourself a lot of trouble. Really, Hugh, it's not going to get you *anywhere*.' He was using his this-hurts-me-more-than-it-hurts-you voice. 'We've done a straw poll of the institutional shareholders. And I have to tell you that they're going to back the board all the way. I think you'll find this'll do your little consortium a lot of harm, you know. And the publicity. Well, it's bound to be bad, isn't it' – he hesitated for dramatic effect – 'what with one thing and another . . . '

A mixture of anger and exultation stormed through my veins: for once I knew exactly what I was going to say to Howard.

'Aren't you forgetting something?' I began quietly. 'One small detail? Aren't you forgetting that I don't have to listen to you any more, Howard? That I don't have to take any more of your claptrap? The delights of working with you are now behind me. The Cumberland board now have that pleasure – and good bloody luck to them! You have no rights over me, Howard, and the sooner you realise that, the sooner you might also realise that nothing you say is going to make the blindest difference to what I choose to do. *Since* you mention the EGM, thanks to the terms *you* negotiated for all of us, both David and I have shares in Cumberland, so we have every right to call an EGM if we so wish. And we *do* so wish. Along with all the other shareholders who don't like what's going on.' My heart was pounding with savage excitement. 'I also take exception to your gratuitous and insulting attempt at intimidation. Don't talk to me about publicity or any other of your bully-boy tactics. Your threats don't hold any water with me, Howard. And finally – while we're talking about what I take exception to – I take exception to your calling me at home late in the evening. I have a perfectly good office and daytime phone number, and I don't want my evenings interrupted by you, on the telephone or in any other form—'

The line buzzed in my ear.

'Damn – he's rung off,' I said.

Ginny was laughing gently. 'Well, you told him all right!'

'You think so?'

'Great stuff!'
'There's one thing I wish I'd said.'
'What was that?'
'I wish I'd told him to fuck off.'
But I was pleased all the same.

TWELVE

Tingwall's secretary looked up from her work. 'Are you sure you don't want him to know that you're here?'

'No. I'll wait, thanks.'

Ginny's meeting with Tingwall had overrun by almost half an hour, but I didn't want to interrupt them, I didn't want Ginny to feel I was looking over her shoulder.

Flicking inattentively through *Country Life* I came across a full-page advertisement for Melton. The photograph had been taken in early summer, with the wistaria and lilac in full bloom, a last flush of bluebells under the trees and razor-sharp mowing tracks striping the lawns. The house looked idyllic with its wide bays, mellow brickwork and comforting Georgian symmetry, the sort of place that features in glossy picture-books peddling quintessential dreams of English rural life. Nobody is immune to dreams, and being a workaholic I'd probably been more susceptible than most, beguiled as I was by visions of instant tranquillity. Yet for all the ambitions Ginny and I had attached to Melton, the dream hadn't been impossible, just a little too wearing perhaps, just an inch or two beyond the grasp of our busy lives.

Tingwall put his head round his door and called, 'Come in, Hugh.'

I met Ginny on the threshold, on her way out. 'Back in a moment,' she murmured. I couldn't read anything in her face as she passed.

Tingwall's expression was more transparent, a blend of gravity and apprehension.

'She's told you what happened,' I said when he had closed the door.

'Yes.'

'Well? What do you think?'

He considered for a long moment before saying, 'Not for Ginny's ears, Hugh, but I have to say that as a defence it would worry me a great deal. You mustn't go entirely by what I say, of course, you must take Grainger's advice, but for what it's worth I can't help thinking it'll be an extremely difficult defence to pull off. Far more difficult than – well, the other alternatives.'

'What are you saying then?' I said in alarm. 'You're not suggesting she should plead guilty?'

'No,' he replied carefully, perching himself on the edge of his desk. 'No, I would never do that. But pleading not guilty has certain risks – a harsher verdict, a heavier sentence. And if on top of that you're asking the jury to believe that an unknown third party committed the crime – well, it's going to present some serious problems, Hugh. To plead that sort of defence success-fully one needs hard evidence, you see. Something to back up one's story. Now Ginny might come over well in the witness box – in fact, I've no doubt she'd come over very well indeed. But that in itself – well, it's not likely to be enough. Not when the opposition have what seems like unassailable forensic evidence.' Glancing towards the door, he lowered his voice. 'And then – who is this third party? Are we saying it's someone completely unknown? If so, why didn't Ginny report the murder straight away? What was to stop her? That's what really bothers me,' he declared unhappily. 'If she tells the jury that she thought *you'd* killed Sylvie and was trying to cover up for you – well, that's not going to look too good, is it? To put it mildly. In the eyes of the world you'd be branded guilty without ever standing trial. It's a Catch-22 situation for Ginny.' He didn't attempt to conceal his dismay. 'She'll be damned if she tells the truth, and damned if she doesn't.'

'But if we could show that someone else had been there? The killer.'

Tingwall lifted his hands and raised his eyes heavenward: if only.

'What evidence would it take?'

He blew out his lips. He began to speak, he paused glumly, he folded his arms only to unfold them again. 'I'll have to think about that,' he said finally. 'A witness, I suppose. Someone who saw a third party going to the yacht before Ginny got there. Or . . . some forensic evidence, something to show that this third party was aboard at the time of the murder.' His tone was not abounding with confidence. 'I'll have to think about it.'

Faced by Tingwall's loss of heart, I found myself faltering. 'What about hiring an investigator?' I asked. 'Someone who can find witnesses the police might have missed? Who can search out Sylvie's druggy friends – the ones the police never bothered with?'

Whether he suddenly appreciated my argument or, faced by the inadequacies of Ginny's story, was all too ready to grasp at straws, Tingwall showed his first real interest in the idea of a drug connection. 'We can give it a try,' he agreed, talking himself into it by the moment. 'There's a chap I use occasionally, here in Exeter. And another in Bristol, ex-CID man. In fact he'd probably be a better bet for this sort of thing. Rather more high-powered. His name's Pike. Not cheap, I'm afraid.' Catching my expression, he said, 'I'll get on to him straight away then.' He added, 'Of course, the prosecution might be lining these people up as witnesses against us. You do realise that?'

I made a show of absorbing this.

'Mind you,' he said with some of his old spark, 'even if they're with the other side it'll be no bad thing to sound them out. At least we'll get a better idea of what we're up against, won't we? So . . . Any thoughts on where Pike might start?'

'There's a man called Hayden. He owns the boat Sylvie used to go sailing on. *Samphire*. Moored on the river. According to the local grapevine Hayden's a professional yacht skipper who lives, or used to live, near Totnes.' Tingwall was making notes. 'And then of course there was Joe who shared the cottage with Sylvie. Or just dossed there. Probably known to the police. Well, I'd imagine so, the way he dosed himself with drugs. Out of his mind most of the time. I'm trying to get his surname and an address.' If Tingwall thought I was overstepping the mark with my amateur detective work he didn't say so. And if he was wondering at the number of facts I hadn't previously disclosed to him or the police, he didn't remark on that either.

'There was another girl who sailed on *Samphire*, but I don't know who she is.'

He was waiting for more, so I told him about the drug running. 'I don't know how regularly they brought drugs across the Channel, but Sylvie had a contact in Cherbourg. He supplied her with a large packet containing some sort of powder. Heroin or cocaine, I imagine.' Tingwall shot me a dart of surprise and what might have been disapproval.

'I have no idea what she did with the drugs once she got them to England. But I have a theory – I think she may have kept them on *Ellie Miller*. I think she may have been using *Ellie* as a – what's the word? – a cache. And *that's* why she went to the boat that day. And that's why she was killed. Maybe she fell out with someone further along the line. Maybe she hadn't paid someone. Maybe she'd been bringing in extra drugs that she hadn't been telling them about.'

Tingwall had stopped writing. 'You've no evidence for this?' he asked quietly.

'No. But I can't think of anything else. She was bright, you see. She knew they were sniffing around.'

'They?'

'The customs.'

Tingwall put his notebook down. 'I wish you'd told me some of this before,' he murmured.

'Didn't think it would look too good on my CV,' I replied flippantly. 'You know – aiding and abetting the smuggling of drugs. And if I were to say that I'd got involved unwittingly, that I didn't know what was going on – the innocent abroad – well, do *you* ever believe that old chestnut when you read it? No, neither do I.'

Tingwall was contemplating this with a dispirited expression when Ginny reappeared. He straightened up, shuffled his feet and smiled boyishly. Which seemed to make two of us who were rather in love with her.

*

I drove Ginny straight on to Bristol for one of her twice weekly appointments with Dr Jones. During the journey she fell into a listless uncommunicative mood, and I couldn't make out if it was the bad night she'd had or a sudden bout of depression. As we'd got ready for bed she'd become restless and preoccupied, and several times during the night I'd woken to find her gone from the room. Her absences weren't good for my jittery imagination, and twice I'd set off in search of her. The first time I'd found her in the kitchen, staring out of the window into the darkness while the kettle boiled untended on the Aga. An hour later I'd discovered her scrubbing the kitchen table. 'It hasn't been cleaned properly,' she'd complained matter-of-factly. 'Liquid and bleach. You can never get rid of the grease marks without liquid and bleach.' She'd seemed completely unaware of the echoes in this, there was no glint of comprehension, and a warning had begun to tick away in my mind. Feeling out of my depth, I'd remembered the forthcoming visit to Jones with a rush of relief.

The psychiatrist had his consulting rooms in a semi-detached villa in the Kingsdown area of Bristol, not far from the university and the hospitals. Drawing up outside, I said to Ginny, 'If I'm delayed, you won't mind waiting a bit?'

She shook her head and fumbled with the contents of her handbag. I went round and opened the door for her and helped her out. She kissed me absently on the cheek before climbing the few steps to the door and ringing the bell. Watching her pass into the house, I wondered if she would come clean with Jones about the self-appointed reduction in her drug regime, and whether I would be betraying her trust if I contacted him later to find out.

With a street map of Bristol propped against the wheel, I set off in the direction of Clifton. I got lost almost immediately, going down a hill I had climbed just minutes before, but after stopping to get a new perspective on the map managed to put myself back on the right road, and within ten minutes was crawling along the busy street where Jean-Paul lived, squinting at the street numbers. Number nineteen was a flat-fronted terraced house, three storeys high with grimy windows and peeling white stucco and rubbish spinning around the front steps. There were names against three of the bells, none of them Mathieson, so I pressed the fourth, which was labelled Flat 2.

A dog yapped frantically somewhere near by, a succession of heavy vehicles shuddered past on the road behind. I pushed the bell again. I was wondering whether Jean-Paul had changed his mind when the door swung open and he was there, a tall figure standing well back from the threshold. I was surprised at how little he had changed. He was still a string bean of a man with a pinched faced, a thatch of dark hair and heavy brows drawn into a permanent frown. He still wore his hair long and his jeans tight, though after fifteen years he had less of the hungry student about him and more of the lean cerebral air of the academic. I saw no resemblance to Sylvie until he stepped back to let me in and then something in his profile, the set of his mouth, gave me a shudder of remembrance.

'Good of you to see me,' I said as he pushed the door shut with a slam that shook the house.

Jerking his head towards the stairs he led the way up to the first floor. His flat consisted of one large room spanning the full width of the house with an open-plan kitchen in one corner, a bed in another, and a door leading to what was presumably the bathroom. Overloaded bookshelves sagged along every wall, and more books were stacked in untidy piles in and around the massive Victorian desk which stood before the windows, its surface almost lost in paper. Mozart was playing softly in quadraphonic sound.

Jean-Paul faced me in the middle of the room. 'So?' he said abruptly.

I hadn't planned this in any detail. 'First, may I say how sorry I am—'

He flicked an impatient hand. 'Think we can skip that bit.'

I understood this, perhaps I had half expected it. I began again, no more confidently, 'I assure you that my wife did not do this terrible thing. They've got it all wrong. It's the most appalling mistake.'

'So you said on the phone.' His manner was cold.

'The thing is . . . I'm trying to find some of the people who knew Sylvie, to see if they can think of anyone . . . of any reason . . . I was wondering if you could put me on to some of her friends, people who saw her this summer. I thought they might be able to tell me – I don't know – whether anyone had been bothering her in any way . . . following her . . . That sort of thing.'

He raised a dubious eyebrow and, perching himself on the edge of the desk, said in a voice that was heavy with indifference, 'She didn't tell me much. I didn't see her that often.'

'Anybody you can think of. Anything she told you.'

He exhaled irritably as though he was already regretting having agreed to see me. 'All I knew was that she was living in Dittisham, that she was doing her sculpture or whatever it was.'

'Did she mention Hayden, the person she sailed with?'

'May have. Don't remember.'

'Or Joe, the chap she shared the cottage with?'

'A bit.'

'What was his second name, do you know?'

He gave an exaggerated shrug. 'Wilson. Willis. Wilkins. Something like that.'

'You don't know how I could get in touch with him, do you?'

His eyes glimmered coldly. 'Maybe.'

'You've got a number?'

'He may not want to talk to you.' His tone made it clear he thought this highly likely.

'But could you ask him anyway? Explain how important it is.' Before he could refuse, I pulled out a card and, balancing it on my hand, scribbled my home and mobile numbers on the back. 'I'd be most grateful.'

With the bad grace that seemed to be habitual to him, Jean-Paul dropped the card onto the clutter of papers on the desk behind him, where it sank, a small white rectangle, into a sea of white.

'Did she mention any other people?' I asked. 'Not just in Dittisham, but elsewhere. In London perhaps.'

'Not really. She had friends all over the place.'

'What about business associates?'

'*Business?*' he repeated scornfully. 'What sort of *business?*'

I plunged in. 'Drugs.'

266

He tossed his head angrily. 'Oh, *please!*'

'They say she was involved in hard drugs.'

'Who says!' he retorted. 'That's crap. She was into hash, a bit of speed maybe. Nothing more. Who says?'

'The police.'

'Rubbish. They never told you that. Who told you that?'

'The hash,' I said, avoiding the question, 'where would she have got it from?'

'Where anyone gets their stuff from.' He was talking to me as if I were a complete imbecile. 'Everywhere.'

'I wondered if perhaps she could have fallen out with the dealer.'

He gave a harsh contemptuous laugh. 'You've been watching too many bad films. People don't get killed by their hash suppliers, otherwise half the university would be decimated. What were you thinking – that she owed somebody money and they killed her for it? Listen, hash costs nothing, and everyone pays up front anyway. Or if they do get credit, it's never for very long or for very much, believe me.' He gave his derisive laugh again. 'Christ, what a pathetic idea.'

I hesitated, remembering the feel of the package around Sylvie's waist the night she dived into the water. 'Once she had something else. A powder.'

His eyes flashed with hostility. He was trying to gauge whether I'd sprung this on him on purpose. 'So?' he said tightly.

'I thought she might have got mixed up with the dealing side.'

He buttoned down his mouth and glared at me by way of a reply. The Mozart came to an end, and there was only the faint rumble of traffic and the tick of a central-heating pipe.

'Her friends,' I said, bringing us back to less contentious ground. 'Was there anyone she was particularly close to?'

'I expect so.'

'Who, do you know?'

'I told you – she had friends all over the place.'

'What about boyfriends?' I asked, holding my expression.

'She told me about one, yes.'

Concealing my leap of curiosity, I said, 'Oh? Who was that?'

'You.' He had enjoyed that moment, he had enjoyed catching me out.

I gave a slow nod which he could take as a tribute to his little coup if he wanted to.

'Well, I *assumed* it was you,' Jean-Paul said, milking the moment a little longer. 'Sylvie said she had a lover, and he was in *glass*. I didn't know what a lover in *glass* was. So she told me. She said the family *made* glass. I asked if it was you – I remembered something about the glass.'

'Was there anyone else? Any other lover?'

'Should there be?' he asked with a spark of sarcasm, and I realised that while Jean-Paul might be tolerant of his sister's hash smoking, he wasn't quite so relaxed about her love life.

I looked away through misty windows to threadbare trees and spotting rain. 'Did she say anything else about me?' I asked, not quite sure why I wanted to know.

'No,' he said dismissively. Then, tiring of his own animosity, he gave the question some consideration. 'She said you had a boat. She said she was going on it. What else?' He blew out his lips. 'It was a long time ago. I really don't remember.'

'When was this?'

'Oh, April, I suppose. Early May. Thereabouts. Oh yeah,' he said as something else came back to him, 'she talked about some trip you were going to make.'

'To France?'

He frowned at me. 'Maybe. I can't remember.' For no obvious reason he became cross again. He straightened up and folded his arms meaningfully; the interview was over.

'Well, thanks for your help,' I said. 'If you could speak to Joe?'

He made a gesture that was intentionally ambiguous.

'Perhaps I could call you in a day or so?'

'No thanks,' he said bluntly.

'I meant—'

'If Joe feels like making contact, I'll get him to call you direct.'

At the door I said, 'A while ago my brother told me you wanted to see me.'

'That was then.'

'I just wondered . . .'

268

'I had very little to say to you then,' he declared with a rancour that was all the stronger for having been temporarily forgotten, 'and I've got even less to say to you now.'

The door closed sharply behind me and reaching the ground floor I heard the muffled clamour of strident orchestral music drifting down the stairs behind me. As Jean-Paul's last remarks reverberated caustically in my mind, I had the feeling I would not be hearing from Joe.

*

'I'm glad you were able to come,' Jones smiled, gesturing vaguely towards a chair. He began to search for some errant object, patting his outer pockets several times before swinging open a jacket front and starting on the inner realms, only to return once again to the outer pockets, dipping his hands into the same slots time and again like some bemused rap dancer. He spread a palm and smiled in benign defeat, 'My glasses . . .'

He was a man of indeterminate age, somewhere in his fifties or sixties, short and balding. I couldn't work out if this absent-mindedness was genuine or part of some stratagem for putting patients at their ease.

With an exclamation of victory, Jones scooped up his glasses from under some papers and, settling himself behind his desk, cast me a diffident smile.

'I hope it wasn't inconvenient,' he said with a strong Welsh lilt, 'but I felt a chat would be useful.' He had called me late the previous evening after Ginny's visit, to ask if I might be able to come and 'discuss a few things', a request which had sent profound and irrational fears shivering through my heart.

'You worried me,' I told him now. 'You made it sound serious.'

'Did I? Well, I don't think it's anything to be too concerned about,' he said with a caution that managed to convey precisely the opposite impression. 'I just felt there were certain problems which you should be aware of.'

'I know she's not taking all her drugs.'

'Ah.' His eyebrows flew up.

'She didn't tell you?'

'No,' he said with the lack of surprise of a doctor who is used to his patients following their own ideas about what is good for them.

'She's still taking the tranquilliser, I think, but not the Prozac. She said it made her feel worse.'

'I'll have a word with her next time,' he said, making a quick note. 'See if I can find her something that suits her better.' There was a pause in which he gathered himself to tell me what was on his mind. 'Yes, the thing is . . . We had a useful session yesterday, Virginia and I. On the face of it she seems to be coping. She doesn't appear to be too overwhelmed by her situation. She seems to be able to contemplate the future – even the idea of prison – with some degree of composure. But at the same time I'm not absolutely sure that her view of the future, or indeed of the past, is based on reality. I'm not sure she's able to determine what is real and what is not, or to separate what is true from what she would like to be true. Sometimes people evade the truth as a way of managing their fears – evade it, but deep down never lose sight of it. In Virginia's case, however, I think she *has* lost sight of reality. I think fact and fantasy have become profoundly muddled in her mind.'

This was an alien sea, and I was floundering. 'But she's been perfectly – *clear* with me. She's never been confused about anything.'

'Oh, she expresses herself articulately, certainly,' he agreed with alacrity. 'But she's clear on an interpretation of events that deep down she's really quite confused about – if you appreciate the distinction. She would like certain things to be true, but she's not sure whether they are or not. It's not simply a matter of blotting things out, of suppressing unpleasant events, but of having painted herself an alternative picture of events and being unable to distinguish this version from the real thing.'

I was still struggling. 'Are you saying she's not telling the truth?'

'I'm saying she's telling the truth as she sees it, which, as I'm sure you'll appreciate, is rather a different thing. It may well *be* the truth, there's nothing to say it isn't, but she has no way of

270

determining whether it is or not, no way of sorting it out in her mind, you see. And in the end that's what might disturb her.'

I felt as though I had stumbled into an emotional bog, a murky impenetrable place with no points of reference. 'She's told you, then, about Sylvie's death?' I asked, half afraid of what he might say.

'She's told me something,' he said guardedly.

'She's told you she's innocent?'

He made an apologetic gesture. 'I'm sorry, Mr Wellesley, I would be breaking her confidence if I were to discuss that.'

I suppressed a bubble of frustration. 'But what I'm trying to understand is how you've arrived at this view of her? How do you *know* she's getting things muddled?'

'There are certain procedures one can use to determine a patient's state of mind, to establish his or her grasp of reality. These techniques involve discussions of all sorts of existing situations – relationships, family, work, whatever. Now in the course of these discussions Virginia has consistently revealed a confused grasp of existing realities, even of everyday truths. And if someone loses their grasp on mundane matters in this way it's invariably symptomatic of a general and pervasive loss of reality. The delusions they show in small matters extend *to*, and stem *from*, the original trauma and its attendant delusions.'

Delusions. One of those terms like paranoia or psychosis which belong to other people, to strangers with real problems, not to someone you know and love. Fighting my own sense of confusion, I asked fretfully, 'But what sort of things does she get wrong?'

'Wrong is too strong a word,' he commented in his measured Welsh tones. 'But let me think . . . Well, to give you an example, she told me she was an expert sailor, that she'd sailed a lot with you, gone over the Channel many times. But that's not quite accurate, is it?'

He read the answer in my stricken silence.

'I guessed it wasn't, from something she'd said earlier. Now I never dispute her on these matters – I'm very anxious not to undermine her confidence in any way – but if I should inadvertently question something she gets very disturbed. She cannot deal with the idea of being challenged, even on the smallest things. She becomes quite agitated.'

I looked into his bland benevolent face and felt as Ginny must have been feeling, caught between several baffling truths, each distinct, each so fatally blurred that there was no way of knowing which to believe. A man I had only just met was telling me that my wife was mentally unwell and, in trying to gauge the validity of this, all I had to go on was the fact that he had a clutch of qualifications and seemed reasonably well-intentioned.

'Okay,' I sighed. 'Okay. So Ginny wants to pretend. So what does it matter? What's the harm?'

'There's no harm for the moment,' Jones said kindly. 'But if the situation is allowed to continue she will start to find the strain unbearable. Delusions may seem like an excellent self-defence mechanism, but they carry an enormous burden of guilt and confusion. And the real risk comes when and if she is forced to confront her delusions before she is ready, before she's able to come to terms with them in her own way.'

'Risk? What do you mean?'

Jones said in a voice that was suddenly very professional, 'She could become seriously ill.'

The room seemed to crowd in on me and, clambering to my feet, I went to the window and stared unseeing into the back yard. 'So I mustn't say anything to upset her?'

'That's one thing, certainly.'

I turned back. 'What else?'

The light was in his eyes and he blinked up at me from his desk like a dazzled owl. 'It would help if she could get to see me more often. Three times a week if that's possible.'

'But what can I do?'

'You could look for signs of distress. Obsessive behaviour. Worrying excessively and continuously about insignificant problems, like whether the windows are properly closed or an object is correctly positioned on a shelf. And repetitive behaviour. Going back to the same task time and again. Frequent hand washing, showering, skin scrubbing.'

272

I thought: Or table scrubbing, and wished the idea hadn't flown quite so smoothly into my head.

I thanked him before he could come up with any more unsettling thoughts.

As I was leaving I asked: 'She will get better, won't she?' and saw from his face that this was the one question he could not answer.

*

'Hello, darling.' Ginny planted a kiss somewhere close to my left cheek. 'You're early.'

It was four, precisely the time I'd said I'd get back. 'The meeting went well,' I murmured. Taking on a life of their own, my eyes strayed inexorably to the kitchen table, examining the bare pine surface for signs of recent scouring. I couldn't see anything, no patches of damp, and, though this proved nothing, it seemed to postpone the moment of reckoning.

'Julia had to leave half an hour ago,' Ginny reported as she slid the kettle onto the Aga. 'There were lots of messages. George called at least twice. And several business people – lawyers and accountants, so Julia said. Oh – and *Mary*. She wants us to go down on Sunday to have lunch with them and look at a cottage.' Ginny turned to face me and said in a voice sharp with some emotion I couldn't read, 'You've been plotting behind my back.'

'What – the cottage? Mary offered to keep an eye open, that was all.'

'I'd rather you hadn't asked her,' she said tightly. 'I'd rather you didn't involve Mary in anything to do with us.'

'But she volunteered.'

'She would. She enjoys interfering.' I'd never heard Ginny voice such strong criticism of Mary before. Her eyes narrowed with sudden suspicion. 'You haven't talked to her about *us*, have you?'

'No,' I said unconvincingly.

'My God, if you *have* . . .'

'No, I told her about Sylvie, that was all. Nothing else.'

273

'About *Sylvie*,' she gasped. 'What did you tell her, for God's sake?'

'Ginny, does it matter?'

'*Yes*, it matters!'

I sat wearily on a chair. 'I told her about the summer. I told her what happened.'

Ginny's chest started heaving. 'What – *everything?*'

'More or less.'

Ginny clamped her lips together and, holding on to her self-control with an effort which distorted her face, she shook her head at me. 'How could you!'

I lifted my hands helplessly. 'Mary's a friend. She was *there*. I needed someone to talk to.'

'But— God, you just don't see it, do you?' she cried through the pull of her breathing. 'You think Mary's so *special*. You think she's such a *friend*. Well, let me tell you, she's no friend of ours and she *never* has been!'

'Oh, *Ginny*—'

'No, *no!*' And suddenly she was in a fury. 'I tell you, she gives this great impression of being so— so— *saint*-like, so sympathetic, but it's all a big act. It's all a front! Oh, she seems like the great Lady Bountiful all right, she seems so caring – but only while it suits her! She's not Howard's sister for nothing, oh *no*. It runs in the family – all this getting people where she wants them, all this playing one off against the other.' She gave a gasp of frustration. 'Oh, you can't see it, I know you can't! For you she can do no wrong. For you she's this perfect person. But let me tell you, she *uses* people, she worms her way into people's confidence as a way of keeping a hold over them. It's *all* about control.' She glared at me. 'You look at me as though I'm mad, but it's true! You just can't see it. Good old Mary! Generous kind Mary! All that charity stuff, up on her high horse. But there's only one thing Mary really cares about in the whole world, only one thing she even *thinks* about – and that's her beloved David, and how she's going to hang on to him. Everything after that – well, it's all a front.' She waved a fierce hand at me. 'Oh, I can see what you're thinking. You think I'm just jealous of her or something. You think I just hate her! But it's not that – it's . . .' She seemed to

274

pull the thought out of the air: 'It's that I'm *frightened* of her. I'm frightened of her little schemes. She'll go behind your back without a second thought, she'll use anyone and anything to keep herself up there as the great and good Mrs Wellesley. She'll—' Words and breath failed her simultaneously, and striding to a drawer she opened it with a bang, pulled out an inhaler and drew on it.

After a long pause I said quietly, 'I have to say I don't agree, I think Mary's always been a good friend to us. But if that's the way you feel . . .' I stood up. 'I assume you don't want to see them on Sunday?'

'All I want,' Ginny laboured, 'is for you to stop telling her about *us* and our private life. That's all. I don't *mind* going to see them, I haven't *minded* all these years, have I? I can deal with her so long as she doesn't start interfering. And I certainly don't want to get the blame for stopping *you* from seeing them.'

I rubbed my face ferociously and said nothing.

She came back to the table. 'Perhaps I should have said all that a long time ago.' She gave me a redeeming look, subdued and penitent.

'Perhaps.'

'It's what I feel.'

'Yes, I can see that.'

Her lids began to flutter, she twisted her fingers into a knot. 'It would be nice . . . if you felt you could tell *me* all those things.'

'I would. I do. Really.'

A silence, during which her eyelids continued their feather-dance. 'Will you tell me what Dr Jones said then?' Catching my expression, she said, 'Oh, I guessed that's where you'd gone. He phoned last night, didn't he?'

I didn't attempt to deny it. 'Oh, he didn't say a lot really,' I began. 'He just wants me to keep an eye on you, that's all.'

'He doesn't think I'm going barmy?'

I smiled. 'No.'

'What *does* he think, then?'

'He thinks . . .' I shrugged while I struggled to find something approaching the truth. '. . . that the strain might get to you.'

275

Her expression softened. 'You know one of the things I love about you, Hugh? You always try to protect me, don't you?' She cast me a crooked smile that managed to contain affection and rebuke in equal measure. 'Oh, I know what Dr Jones thinks,' she stated robustly. 'Dr Jones thinks I'm a total case. He thinks I'm making it all up. He thinks that I won't face up to what I've done. He thinks I killed Sylvie but I'm suppressing it all, or whatever you do when you're a basket case. He made up his mind right at the beginning. I *knew* it, I sensed it, and now when I see him it's like talking to a brick wall.' She gave a ragged sigh. 'Nice to have your shrink believe in you.'

'He wants to see you three times a week.'

'Oh, does he?' Her voice wobbled. 'Yes, I bet he does.'

'You don't have to. The bail condition is only for twice.'

'But twice a week is quite enough for what he wants!' she exclaimed darkly. 'That's all he needs to wear me down.'

*

'Can we let you know about Sunday?' I asked Mary when I called her. 'It might be rather last minute.'

'Of *course*,' she cried. 'Don't even think about it. I've booked a restaurant but it can easily be cancelled. But you just *have* to see this house some time! It's absolutely sweet. Beautifully furnished, wonderful view, gorgeous garden, and only a few miles from the motorway.'

'Well, if not Sunday . . .'

'I heard about it through a friend, someone who owes me a favour. The owners want some people who're going to take good care of it while they're abroad. They won't expect much rent.'

'Sounds good.'

She gave a knowing murmur. 'But you're doubtful.'

'Well, it'll be up to Ginny.'

'Of course.' And her tone managed to convey both sympathy and pity.

'Any luck with that address?' I asked.

'Address?' She knew perfectly what I was after. 'Oh, the long-

276

haired creature, you mean? Look, I did try, Hugh. As much as I could without getting into trouble anyway. I found the people who own the cottage. Live in Somerset somewhere. Phoned them, but all they did was put me on to the letting agents and – well, it was *difficult*, Hugh. I mean, I couldn't very well say what it was really about, could I? So I waffled on a bit about the last tenants owing me money and could they let me have an address for the chap, Joe whatever-his-name-was, and they told me they didn't know anything about him, that the place had been let to the lady who was now deceased. That's how they put it – *deceased*. So there we are. Sorry.'

'Thanks for trying.'

'Will you try another way?'

'Tingwall's got a private investigator on it.'

'Ah, that sounds better,' she said approvingly. 'Best to keep your distance, Hugh. Best to keep well clear.' She added brightly, 'What's his name, this chappy?'

'Umm, Pike. Based in Bristol.'

'*Pike.*' She made thinking noises. 'Don't know the name. But keep me posted, won't you? Let me know how he gets on. You never know, I might be able to help somewhere else along the line. You *will* keep me posted, won't you?'

'Yes, Mary.'

'And Hugh? I think you're amazing, you know that? Absolutely totally amazing.'

I said goodbye before she could explain what she meant by that.

*

George sat with his back to the study window. Even allowing for the gloom of the rain-swept day, his complexion had an unhealthy grey cast, the pallor of exhaustion and worry, and watching him talk his way through the latest sales figures it occurred to me that with his straining belly, exercise-free lifestyle and rocketing stress levels he was prime heart attack material. Even now he was wading into the chocolate biscuits, washed down by a second cup of Ginny's powerful French coffee.

I interrupted him in mid-sentence. 'What will you do if we find ourselves out of a job, George?'

'Do?' He tried to look surprised at the question, but I could see he'd given it some thought. 'Well, Dorothy fancies a cruise. The *Oriana*, she's keen on the *Oriana*. And me, I fancy some golf. After that . . .' He made a wry face. 'Fifty-five isn't the sort of age when they beat on your door, is it?'

'Retirement, then?'

'I suppose. But I might do the odd thing. I thought – a small garden ornament business.'

'Ornaments?' I couldn't suppress a smile. 'Not gnomes, George?'

'Yes,' he said with perfect seriousness. 'But mainly birdbaths, larger statuary. They've developed this composite that looks like the finest stone but comes in at half the weight. I think there's a market. At the right price.' And we exchanged a smile. 'At the right price' had been a catchphrase of my father's.

'And you?' George asked.

'Me? Ahh. Well, I used to paint. I wouldn't mind having another go at it. Oh, I don't mean professionally – too late for that – but for my own amusement. Watercolours, I expect. Landscapes, like every other amateur.'

'And work?'

In the garden a rain squall was flailing the leaves from the rose bushes and ripping the petals from the last spindly blooms. Grasping at a half-considered thought, I said, 'Something hands-on. Something *impractical*. A vineyard. A small farm.'

'Abroad?'

'Probably.' I let the thought expand and settle. 'Won't make me rich, of course.'

'You wouldn't want something more challenging?'

'More challenging? You mean, more stressful, more time-consuming? No.' And I was surprised and reassured by my own certainty. 'No, I wouldn't want all that again. I've been on the roller coaster too long, George. I want out for a while. I want time to dawdle a bit. To remember each day. To notice its passing.'

George considered this with slight puzzlement before returning his weary gaze to the sales figures. 'Not off the roller coaster yet.'

I almost said: More's the pity.

As we came to the monthly financial summary the phone buzzed and Ginny said, 'There's someone on the direct line. Joe somebody. You asked him to call you, so he says.'

My stomach clenched. I said with false calm, 'Put him on, would you?' I took the phone across the room to the length of its cord.

'Joe?'

A curt 'Yeah'.

'Thanks for calling. I was wondering if I could come and see you.' Silence. I felt a momentary panic. 'Joe?' I said into the silence.

'Yeah.'

I repeated, 'I need to see you.'

'Gimme one good reason.'

'Jean-Paul must have told you—' Aware of George, I lowered my voice still further. 'They've got it all wrong. My wife is not the person.'

'Yeah, well. You would say that, wouldn't you?'

'Maybe,' I said carefully. 'But that doesn't stop it being true. And I can tell you why.'

'Yeah?' The scorn again. 'And why should I listen?'

I sighed, 'Because we both want the same thing. I assume. We want the person who killed Sylvie.'

He exhaled grudgingly into the phone. 'Yeah, well . . . But if you're windin' me up, I'll fuckin' kill you. Okay?'

*

Heavy rain and Saturday night theatre traffic had reduced the western approach roads to a crawl, and by the time I had battled my way along the Marylebone Road and into the dripping labyrinths of Camden Town I was half an hour late. In the glimmer of the tawdry shop lights the *A to Z* offered obscure advice, and after negotiating the one-way system twice, I worked

279

my way onto the Camden Road and, more by chance than design, found the right street.

Joe's place stood at the end of a terrace of identical Victorian houses with blackened brickwork and sullen windows with unshaded light bulbs and drooping curtains. The porch was unlit and if there were names against the cluster of bells I couldn't see them in the feeble glow of the streetlamps. I began to press each bell in turn and, reaching the third, the door sprang open with a loud buzz.

The hall smelled of old frying and new damp and mouldering carpet. Unclaimed letters and circulars littered the floor and a scribbled message on one wall informed the world that Jake and Janey had moved to another address.

I made my way up to the top of the house but no doors opened. Turning back, I followed loud music to a door on the first floor and knocked. A Rastafarian with a knitted hat gave a wide shrug at the name of Joe and waved me doubtfully up the house again. Climbing the last flight of stairs once more, I looked up and saw Joe standing on the landing above.

Through the crack of the open door behind him I glimpsed shabby wallpaper and a Monet exhibition poster, but he didn't invite me inside. Instead he leant against the doorframe with one arm folded and a cigarette held dart fashion in the other. His hair fell in lank waves over his shoulders while a dark stubble crawled unevenly over a thin jowl and scraggy neck. He didn't give the impression of having washed too recently.

'I wanted to ask you about the people Sylvie knew,' I began haltingly. 'Whether there was anyone who might have had reason to harm her.'

'You goin' to crack the case all on yer own, are yer?' he scoffed with an ugly laugh.

'Maybe not,' I admitted. 'But at least I'll have tried.'

'The fuzz been through all this a thousand times, asked loadsa questions. So why should they be wrong all of a sudden?'

'Well, they damn well are,' I said. 'My wife just . . . Well, she found the body, that was all.'

He pitched me a do-me-a-favour look and, drawing on his

280

cigarette, funnelled the smoke expertly out of the side of his mouth. 'And I suppose you don't know nothing about it either.'

'I'd hardly be here otherwise.'

'You'd hardly be here,' he echoed in a mocking imitation of my accent.

Ignoring this, I said, 'I wondered about the drugs. Who Sylvie dealt with, whether she'd got on the wrong side of anyone. A dealer, perhaps.'

Suddenly he was still, his eyes wary behind the wafting smoke. 'A *dealer?*' He shook his head. 'She never got on the wrong side of any dealer. She hadn't been near a dealer.'

'Who did she get it from then?' I added: 'And who did she pass it on to?'

He searched my face as though he suspected me of laying some elaborate trap. 'Pass it on?'

'She collected some stuff in France. Enough for an army.'

He took a last drag of his cigarette before dropping it onto the pockmarked carpet and grinding it in with his heel. 'That wasn't any big deal.'

'It was a large packet.'

'So she got stuff for everyone. So.'

'Everyone?'

'People. Friends. We all forked out for it. It was like a co-op. She made the collection.'

I took a long breath and tried another tack. 'The man she got it from, the man in Cherbourg, was he a regular – *supplier?*'

'Nah. Friend. Doing us a favour.' Now he was watching me with lazy curiosity, wondering how far I would take this, and perhaps also wondering how far he would let me go.

'What about Hayden?'

'What about him?'

'Do you know where I can find him?'

'Why d'yer wanna know?'

I mustered my patience. 'To ask him the same questions.'

'Yeah?' he shrugged. 'Well, he's abroad some place, isn't 'e? Greece. Turkey. On some fat-cat yacht.' Taking some pity on me he added, 'Listen, he can't tell you anything.' I noticed that Joe's grammar, like his accent, came and went, that occasionally the

281

politically correct yoof mumble slipped to reveal the unmistakable education beneath. Minor public school, I guessed. Home counties upbringing.

I said with a small gesture of defeat, 'So if he can't help me, who can?'

Through bleary eyes he gazed at me appraisingly and, with a long lumbering sigh, seemed to come to some kind of decision. 'Look . . . We got stuff in France, okay. Elk knew this geezer in Cherbourg—'

'Elk?'

'Charlie Hayden – Elk. The stuff came from Paris. But it was only, like, twice. A favour, that was all. No big deal.'

Putting a casual note into my voice, I asked, 'What was it, the stuff?'

He looked away crossly, he wasn't certain he wanted to answer that. 'Coke,' he admitted finally. 'And some junk, too.'

Some instinct told me. 'Sylvie was on heroin.'

He raised his eyebrows slightly in agreement. 'She was clean when she went down to Dittisham, she'd done the treatment, the full bit. NA, therapy sessions. But then . . .' He raised a dismissive shoulder and pulled a battered pack of Lucky Strikes from his shirt pocket. I waited silently while he found a light and coughed over his first pull. He tucked one arm under the other and settled into his bird-like stance. 'Then someone started giving her stuff again.'

'Who?'

'Dunno. I wasn't around then. But whoever it was kept it coming.'

'A *dealer*, then?'

He shook his head. 'Nah. Not a dealer. A friend.'

'What sort of friend?' But perhaps that was a stupid question. 'A lover?'

'Maybe.'

'She had a lover?' And the thought sent a sudden tension into my belly.

'I guess. But like I said, I wasn't around then.'

'When did you get down there?'

He blew out his cheeks with the effort of memory. 'Jeese . . . Umm, June? Yeah, some time then.'

I wasn't sure where this was leading, or how best to pursue it. 'Who would know?' I asked eventually. 'Who was around before you got down there?'

He chased something round his teeth with his tongue while he thought about that. 'Yeah – Elk. Elk might know. Yeah. He was around then.'

'But Elk wasn't the guy?'

'What? Nah. Not Elk. Elk never did junk.'

'Was he her lover, though?'

He guffawed, a coarse braying sound. 'Nah. He and Sylvie, they didn't get on. I mean, like they hung out together but they fought. Nah,' he said adamantly, 'not Elk.'

'What about the woman who worked in the pottery shop? Would she have known about Sylvie's friends?'

'Doubt it.'

'What was her name?'

'Liz.' He waved his cigarette vaguely. 'Never knew 'er second name.'

I was drained of ideas. I murmured, 'And there was no one else you can think of . . .'

'What, that mighta killed her? Nah.' His expression grew sly. 'Only you.'

'Don't be bloody stupid,' I said in sudden anger. 'You know it wasn't me.'

He snorted, 'I dunno that! Why should I know that?'

'Because I hadn't seen her in weeks. Because she wasn't coming to see me that afternoon.'

'She said she was goin' out to the boat.'

So that was what he had told the police. 'Not quite the same thing,' I pointed out.

Suddenly he was in no mood to concede this or anything else. 'Yeah, well, you would say that, wouldn't you?'

*

The place was lovely, a sturdy farmhouse in grey stone with a sheltered garden and views of Dartmoor. It wasn't too large, hardly more than a substantial cottage, and it had a tranquil comforting air, the sort of place where you could imagine yourself hidden from the world.

It seemed promising to me. Mary thought so too because she kept extolling its virtues in ever more extravagant terms, but as David and I followed the women into the garden a certain futility seemed to settled over the expedition. I sensed that Ginny had taken a dislike to the place and that nothing any of us could say was likely to change her mind.

'How do you think she looks?' I asked David quietly.

'Ginny? Oh . . . Surprisingly well, really. Getting on with Jones all right, is she?'

We paused by a weathered sundial. I hesitated, caught between loyalty and a painful need for reassurance. 'He thinks she's suffering from some sort of delusions.'

'Christ, aren't we all?'

'You don't think it's serious then?'

'Look, I'm not the right person to ask,' he protested. 'Doctors know damn-all about psychiatry. We just shove patients towards the men in white coats and breathe a sigh of relief when they're willing to take them on. And then again, most of us are a bit worried about being found lacking in the mental department ourselves.' He gave a dry bark of a laugh. 'You know how the statistics go – doctors sky-high in the suicide league, not to mention the alcohol stakes.'

'It's just that I find it hard to judge how good he is.'

'You and me both. There's not one of them that ever agrees. They argue like crazy between themselves. I can only say that Jones seems to be the best around.'

'He thinks she might find the strain too much.'

'Well, I *would* take notice of that. Psychiatric claptrap aside, it's the one thing he's likely to get right.'

Absorbing this as best I could, we strolled on through an arch into a paved herb garden. The women were a long way ahead, disappearing around the back of the house.

'How's the case coming along?' David asked with sudden awkwardness. 'Anything I can help with?'

'Not really. Everything's on hold until the prosecution present their evidence.' We came to a halt again. 'There was something though . . .' I framed the question with care. 'I know you said that you only saw Sylvie a couple of times, and there was no way of telling she was on drugs, but what about heroin? Can't you tell with that?'

David looked away towards the rise of the moor. 'In women they say the skin gets a luminous look – quite beautiful, apparently – but unless you know the person . . .' A dismissive lift of the shoulders. 'Otherwise needle marks, of course. But you would have to *see* them.'

'So no one would have known?'

'Not by looking at her, no. Why?'

I wasn't terribly sure why I was asking. 'Just wondered, that was all.'

David grunted, 'She was definitely on heroin, was she?'

'Yes.' We both studied the view again. 'Where would she have got her drugs from if it wasn't from a dealer?'

David threw me a sharp quizzical look. '*Not* from a dealer? Well . . .' He did a mental double-take. 'You know it wasn't a dealer?'

'Apparently not.'

He went through the motions of thinking about this. 'Well, it could have been legally, from a doctor. So long as she was a registered addict. But she wasn't registered with me. Though . . .' He frowned. 'She could have been registered with another doctor, I suppose. When she signed on with me her notes were forwarded from some private doctor off Sloane Square, but she could easily have had a second doctor somewhere else. One she'd persuaded to give her a long-term repeat script. There are some doctors who specialise in signing up drug addicts to boost their lists, and then go and hand out scripts like confetti from a gravy train, with no intention of weaning them off anything.'

'If she had prescriptions she must have used them locally then?'

David missed the question. 'Otherwise another registered addict,' he mused. But he didn't sound convinced. 'Someone who was willing to share their quota. I've got four or five addicts on my books, but they're all on methadone.' He gave a sardonic grunt. 'I will persist in this crazy idea that they'll get off drugs one day, you see. I go through the motions.'

'A local chemist would notice a prescription for heroin then?'

'For diamorphine – that's the name – well, he *might*. Normally it's only used for terminal cases – cancer. Largely dispensed through hospitals and homes.' He cast me a sidelong glance. 'You think this could be important?'

I gave a wide shrug. 'Who knows? But yes. Yes, I do.'

'You think . . .' He wore the irritated expression that always overtook him when he was forced to voice something that might make him look foolish. 'You think the drugs are something to do with her death?'

'Well, it has to be as good as anything the police have come up with, doesn't it?'

David eyed me thoughtfully, as if appreciating for the first time that I had not given up on the idea of Ginny's innocence. He pushed out his lips and nodded sagely. 'I'll see what I can find out.'

The offer surprised me. 'Would you?'

'Sure. There aren't that many chemists in the area. They're always calling me up.' He grunted disdainfully, '*Say* they can't read my handwriting.'

'Thanks, David.' Then, as if I needed to justify myself further: 'I feel I have to try.'

'Of course.' And I recognised the tone in his voice that signalled fast-waning interest.

The women reappeared at the far end of the garden. Ginny was hugging her arms to her stomach, looking cold.

'This EGM,' David said in a voice that was so remote and abrupt I could only wonder at his ability to switch mood. 'Is it going to come off?'

'Yes. You should have been notified. Next Friday.'

'Isn't it all a waste of time, Hugh? I mean, wouldn't we do better to just take the money and run? Or rather, *keep* our money and run?'

'We have very little to lose, David, and an awful lot to gain.'

'*Do* we? You could have fooled me. It seems to me that

Cumberland must know what they're doing. They've made their decision and we should accept it.'

From across the flowerbeds Ginny caught my eye as she listened inattentively to something Mary was saying, and it was a plea for rescue.

'They'll close the factory, David. They'll put a lot of people out of work. Isn't that reason enough to give it a try?'

'No.' Warming to his indignation, he protested, 'No, it damn well isn't. That's the way *bad* decisions are made.'

'Look, it's not long to wait now,' I said appeasingly. 'It'll all be settled on Friday.'

He growled uncompromisingly, 'Once a ship's sinking . . .'

Mary and Ginny were moving towards us again.

I touched David's arm. 'One last thing – when did Sylvie join your list?'

'*What?*' He was thoroughly incensed now. 'What's that got to do with anything?'

'I wanted to know when she arrived in Dittisham.'

'Oh.' He allowed himself to be slightly mollified. 'March. Beginning of March.'

Ginny came up and fastened herself to my side.

'You're cold,' I said and, taking off my jacket, put it round her shoulders.

'Well, what do you think?' I asked as we followed David and Mary back to the cars.

She whispered, 'I don't like it.'

'Fine.'

'And it's *not* because Mary's so crazy about it, if that's what you're thinking.'

'No, no – I wasn't. No, don't worry about it. We'll find somewhere else.'

'It's got something spooky about it,' she shivered. 'I feel as though someone died here.'

Suppressing faint alarm, I squeezed her hand. 'In that case . . .'

She stopped suddenly and looked up at me, her eyes burning fiercely, and said for no apparent reason, 'I do love you, you know. Sometimes I don't know what I did to deserve you.'

I kissed her softly on the lips. 'It's me that's the lucky one,' I said.

I glanced up and saw Mary at the corner of the house, looking back at us. Instantly, she gave a broad smile and called, 'David and I both know the way to the restaurant. Why don't we split up in case we get separated?' She put on a comically doubtful expression and laughed, 'If that makes any sense!'

I turned to ask Ginny but she was already shrugging her agreement.

David led the way in his Mercedes, and as I fell in line behind I saw him turn his head to Ginny, asking her something, or replying.

'Ginny didn't like the house,' said Mary, fixing her seat belt.

'I'm afraid not.'

'Oh well. Worth a try.' She didn't seem in the least perturbed. 'How's everything else going?'

'Not a lot of progress at the moment.'

'How's the investigator doing – Mr *Pike*. I must say, it's a rather unfortunate name. Aren't pikes terrible predators, gobbling up everything in sight?'

'No word yet. It's only been a few days.'

'So he hasn't tracked down the dreaded Joe yet?'

I answered the question truthfully. 'No.'

She cast me a sidelong glance. 'Awfully glad you didn't get involved, Hugh. It really wouldn't have done, you know.'

'I can see that.'

We drove on in silence for a time.

'Tell me,' I asked casually, 'do you know the woman who worked in the pottery shop with Sylvie? Liz something? I tried to phone the place but it must have closed down. The number was discontinued anyway.'

'Haven't a clue! Don't even know which shop it was! But *Hugh!*' she exclaimed, attempting to moderate her disbelief and exasperation with a laugh. 'Same warning applies, for God's sake. Could be a prosecution witness!' She sighed at me as if I was beyond redemption. 'Why do you want to know anyway?'

'I thought she might know who Sylvie's lover was. The one before me.'

'The *one?*' she questioned drily. 'I thought she never had less than a *bevy* on the go.'

'There was one in particular.'

'Well – who knows then? Any red-blooded male in the area, presumably.'

'This one supplied her with drugs.'

Mary gave me an abrupt glance. 'Oh really? *Really*. Well, there you are then. She was always on to the main chance, wasn't she? Addicts are all the same. Dragging people down into their own little cesspool. Polluting everything in their path. They commit most crime nowadays – did you know that? Muggings and burglary. The new scum of the earth.'

I had nothing to say to that.

'You think you'll find this *lover?*' Mary asked.

'No idea.'

'If you ask me you should try your Mr Pike. He'll know all about that little world. He'll know all about the rot at the bottom of the muckheap.'

THIRTEEN

Tingwall's office lights blazed in the darkened building. A hastily departing staff member let me in and I made my way down the passage and through the dimmed outer office to Tingwall's door, which was open. Catching sight of me, Tingwall stood up in the act of swallowing a hot drink and promptly choked. Spluttering, he put his cup hastily down and waved a voiceless welcome.

'I'm sorry I couldn't make it earlier,' I said. 'A crisis at Hartford.' It would have been truer to say, another crisis in a succession of emergencies. This time it had been a last-minute panic over the documentation for the EGM.

Still speechless, Tingwall clutched his throat and gestured me to my customary chair. I perched on the edge of my seat and, making no attempt to hide my restlessness, looked straight at the clock. Catching this, Tingwall gestured remorse for the delay and, coughing heartily, went to the side and poured himself a glass of water which he downed rapidly and refilled.

'It's just that Ginny will be waiting,' I explained.

'I wouldn't have bothered you . . .' Tingwall gasped. 'If it hadn't been . . . important.' He drew up a chair and, clearing his throat, sat on the very edge of his seat, arms on knees, hands clasped, eyes grave. 'Look, what I'm about to tell you – well, I think we *must* treat it with caution until everything is confirmed and clarified, until we can get a third opinion and be really sure of our ground, *but* – well, it's possible we may have something on the forensic front.'

'What sort of thing?'

He held up a hand as though to pre-empt some excessive

reaction from me. 'I really do think it would be a mistake to get too excited about this,' he warned. Yet behind his calm veneer I realised it was Tingwall himself who was quietly excited. 'It's the fingerprint expert – chap called Armstrong—'

'Our expert?'

'Oh, yes – *our* man. He's looked at the fingerprint that the police took from the boat and he's found two things. First, that it's a pretty poor print – a fragment from an index finger, and lifted off natural wood with a strong grain, which means the print is fairly broken up. Well, I'm not sure if that's the correct technical term, but you can imagine – wood isn't the smoothest of surfaces. *But* even more importantly, he's found only fourteen points of similarity between this print and Ginny's, which is two short of the number which is needed for a positive identification in an English court of law.' He paused to let me absorb the full significance of this. 'What it all boils down to, Hugh, is that in his opinion this print cannot be positively identified as Ginny's. If he's right – and he *is* a top man – then the implications are absolutely—' Losing the word, he wheeled an impatient hand before settling on: 'Crucial.'

Many different thoughts jostled in my mind as I heard myself ask, 'But these points of similarity – fourteen, was it? Isn't that rather a lot?'

'Sixteen is the absolute minimum required in law for a positive ID,' Tingwall repeated, weighing each word authoritatively as though he were in court. 'Armstrong explained it all to me – we'll have to wait for his report, of course – but his conclusion was unequivocal, Hugh. He says that in his opinion it would be unsafe to say these prints were from the same person.'

At some point in the last few weeks I had lost the capacity for hope or joy, and, while part of me recognised the importance of this news, my emotions failed to respond. 'Where do we go from here then?'

'We get another expert. I've tracked down a chap called Benyon in London. Meant to be the best independent. He can get back to us in a few days, though he said it could be longer if it's a complex job.'

'And what happens if he doesn't agree? What happens if he thinks the print is Ginny's?'

Tingwall wasn't ready to allow such negative thoughts. 'Armstrong seems sure, Hugh. And a man of his experience doesn't offer an opinion like that without very careful consideration.'

But part of me wanted to deflate his optimism, if only to protect myself from disappointment. 'What about the police expert – why should he be wrong and our people right?'

'Ah!' Tingwall declared, flipping open one palm like a flashy magician about to produce his best trick. 'We're dealing in reasonable doubt, Hugh. If we manage to cast reasonable doubt on the reliability of the evidence, if we have two top experts saying that they think a match would be unsafe, then the police evidence will be fatally undermined. Reasonable doubt, Hugh. In a case of murder the judge will bend over backwards to make sure that reasonable doubt is understood and acted on by the jury.'

I said ironically, 'But I'm not to get excited?'

Tingwall, whose excitement had become increasingly apparent, had the grace to smile. 'Perhaps I shouldn't have told you at this stage. I'm sorry if you would have preferred me not to. But Hugh, the thing is that if Armstrong is right, and Benyon agrees with him, it will alter our position significantly. The prosecution will be left with nothing but the eyewitness sighting, and eyewitness evidence is always the weakest part of any case. However impressive this eyewitness may be – and we know nothing about him yet – we're back to reasonable doubt. It only needs one small inconsistency, one small hesitation, and a good defence counsel will expose the flaw and rip the evidence apart. Grainger has a reputation for that, you know – demolishing star witnesses.'

Instinct told me that it couldn't be as simple as that. And by way of endorsement, a troubling thought hovered at the edge of my mind and swooped home. 'She cleaned up the boat, Charles. They'll still have that. Why would she want to clean up the boat? Or,' I suggested heavily, 'are we going back to the idea that she was covering up for me?'

292

'The boat cleaning, that's circumstantial. Not enough in itself, Hugh. And as for Ginny thinking you were the murderer, hopefully we won't have to use that, and certainly not if the case never gets to trial.'

'Don't tell me they're likely to drop it!' I said, by now so thoroughly unsettled that I took a harsh satisfaction in arguing against my own interests.

'No, but . . .' An inner debate flickered over Tingwall's face. Finally he ventured, 'We'd have to take advice, of course – *plenty* of advice – but it's *possible* we might want to go for an old-style committal in front of a stipendiary, and try to get the case thrown out altogether. But, look,' he cautioned hastily, 'don't take it from me. I mean, I may be way off the mark!'

Two things struck me: that while Tingwall might be meeting the challenge of the case, he was also feeling the full responsibility of it, and that, for all his dedication and tenacity, he was not as confident as he made himself out to be.

Tingwall hurried on, 'I thought that as soon as we have Benyon's fingerprint report and the prosecution's statements, which should come through any day now, we should have a conference with Grainger, sound him out, see if he thinks an old-style committal's a starter. What do you think?'

I looked out into the black November night, aware of how long Ginny had been alone and the time it would take me to get back to her. 'Can I phone my wife?'

Tingwall looked dubious. 'Do you think it's wise to tell her?'

'I'm not going to tell her over the phone, Charles, if that's what you mean.' It wasn't what he meant, of course. He meant that it might not be wise or fair to tell her anything at all. But it occurred to me as I went to make the call in the outer office that raising her hopes might be no bad thing, that hope was a fairly harmless commodity when you didn't have much else to hold on to.

I could never speak to Ginny on the phone these days without listening for sounds of strain in her voice, for some sign that her self-control was wearing thin, and hearing her now I knew with a small lurch of alarm that something had happened. 'What is it?' I asked.

'Nothing.'

'You're upset. Was it Jones?'

She exhaled fiercely into the phone. 'He *refuses* to believe me. He just won't *listen*. He's treating me like an idiot!'

I cursed my weakness for staying at the Hartford meeting for longer than I had meant to. 'Okay,' I said soothingly, 'we'll sort it out. Somehow we'll sort it out, I promise.'

'He's trying to wear me down, just like I said he would. He undermines everything I say – *everything*. Even you and me – he tries to make me say that I'm angry with you, that I was out for some sort of revenge, that I was really trying to get my own back at you and – oh, I don't know – lunatic things!'

'I'll tell him to lay off.'

'Will you?'

'Of course. I'll tell him to lay off or we'll take our business elsewhere.'

'Oh, will you? Will you really? He makes me feel so dreadful. He makes me want to crawl under a stone.'

'Ginny – rise above it, ignore it. Believe in yourself.'

'But I'm so angry, Hugh, I'm so *angry*.'

I searched for words that might have some meaning for her but could only plead impotently: 'I promise I'll sort it out, darling. Just hold on. Please – don't get upset. *Please*.'

'I'm all right,' she said in a calmer voice. 'I'm always better after I've talked to you.'

Tingwall walked me out to my car. 'It must be a hard time for Ginny,' he said as though he had divined something of my conversation. 'It's always so much harder for innocent people. They feel they're battling against the assumption of guilt. I had one chap up on a rape charge and even when he got off he never stopped feeling hounded. It's an awful lot easier being guilty.'

'I'll take your word for it.'

Climbing into the car, I remembered what I had meant to tell him and opened the door again. 'I forgot – your man Pike needn't bother with Sylvie's friend Joe. I found him.'

'Don't we want to talk to him?' Tingwall asked.

'No.'

'No?' Catching some hint of what had been going on behind his back, he shot me a look in which curiosity, disapproval and the sense to ask no more were neatly fused.

'Has Pike made any progress with Hayden?' I asked.

'Nothing yet.'

'Could you let me know the moment he finds anything?'

'Sure.'

He was still giving me a speculative narrow-eyed look as I drove away.

I had a picture of what I would find on my arrival home. Rooms in semi-darkness, Ginny by an unlit fire picking the skin at the edges of her nails – she had already made them raw – and an air of anxiety which she would expect me to alleviate; the rest of the evening bolstering her confidence, a tricky chat with Jones and finally to bed, to find peace of a sort for a few hours. Another day survived.

The lights were on in the drive, the floodlights around the front of the house too. As I parked, Ginny came out to meet me. She was dressed in a simple black dress with a heavy gold necklace and matching earrings. When I kissed her I caught a waft of *Je Reviens*.

'Did I forget something? Are we having a party?'

'Absolutely,' she smiled, taking me into the house.

'Who's coming?'

'Just you and me.'

'Sounds all right to me.'

Passing the kitchen I caught the smell of wonderful things cooking and saw that she had laid the small circular breakfast table with a white cloth and candles and flowers. She led the way into the sitting room and poured me a glass of champagne.

'You look uncertain,' she said.

'No,' I said rather too quickly. 'No, just – surprised.'

'I wanted us to have a jolly evening for a change. You must get fed up with all my moaning.' She flung me a bright smile. 'I want you to feel you've got something to look forward to when you get home. To know that you're going to be spoilt a bit.'

'But I do. I am.'

'Liar,' she smiled. There was a glow in her face which I hadn't seen in a long time. Part of it, I realised, was makeup, a clever mix of colour and shading that lifted her features and intensified her eyes, and which she hadn't bothered to put on for weeks; but there was an inner spark, too, some new resolve.

I gave up with a laugh and raised my drink. 'Here's to jolly evenings.'

As we drank she caught me watching her over my glass. Some of the doubt must have shown in my eyes because she said, 'What *did* Jones tell you? Did he say I was going off my head? Is that what you've been thinking all this time?' Her voice managed to be brittle and fluid at the same time. 'Oh, don't worry, I wouldn't blame you if you had. He's very persuasive. God – sometimes he's had *me* wondering if I'm going barmy. *But*' – she gave me a conspiratorial grin – 'I've finally done what I should have done ages ago. I plucked up all my courage and half an hour ago I called him! I told him what I thought of him!'

I had paused in the act of drinking. 'What did you say to him?' I asked nervously.

'Say?' Her eyes gave a dark triumphant flash. 'I told him that he'd been out of line. That he'd been intimidating me – well, *bullying* me, really. That he'd been making assumptions that weren't his to make. *Undermining* me. That I didn't deserve that. That no one did.' Reliving her own temerity, she gave a strange high-pitched laugh. 'I can be so much braver on the phone – no eye contact, none of those awful silences that he uses to make me feel guilty!'

I was still immobile, the glass just short of my lips. 'And what did he say to that?'

'Well, he didn't want to admit he was wrong, did he? He said he'd never disbelieved anything I'd said, never made up his mind about anything. But he had – he knew he had. He didn't want to admit he'd been . . . *pressurising* me. I made him promise that in future he'd listen without *deciding*, that he'd listen and accept what I had to say. Just *accept*.' And her jaw hardened, she spoke with a sudden vehemence that made her shudder visibly.

I sat down and said, 'Gosh.'

Finding her mood again, she tipped up her chin. 'I felt so much better afterwards, I can't tell you! I felt as though I'd got a little bit of my life back. Oh, I know you would have waded in for me,' she remarked affectionately. 'You always do. But for once I needed to say it for myself, I needed to feel I was fighting my own battles. And I'm glad I did, *glad*. It's done me so much good!' And she sparkled at me, all shaky confidence and new determination.

'There's something else.' She came and knelt on the floor at my feet and rested her arm on my knee. 'I've been thinking that I really must be much more positive! Things are far more likely to go right if one thinks positive, aren't they? And misery's such a bore. So wearing. I should be remembering all the good things and making the most of what I have!' She gave an excited laugh and – a pang of disloyalty – I couldn't help wondering what she'd been taking. 'I want us to plan like mad,' she declared. 'Everything, all the way through to our old age. Every house and holiday and job and – oh, I don't know! But as though I'm going to be around. I need that, I need to believe it's all going to happen.'

'Ginny . . .' I put my drink down. 'Something came up today.' And I told her about the fingerprint expert, how nothing was definite yet, but if all went well and the two experts agreed then her chances would significantly improve.

She listened attentively, she asked a couple of questions then shrugged carelessly, 'There you are. See what a bit of positive thinking can do!' In her sparky optimism I saw the Ginny of years gone by, the Ginny I had fallen in love with, and in apparent awareness of this, she looked up and we exchanged a glance of shared memory.

I was leaning forward to kiss her when the phone rang.

David's voice said, 'Not interrupting dinner?' Without waiting for a reply, he reported, 'The chemists look as though they're going to be a dead loss, I'm afraid. I got four or five to look back through their registers but nothing out of the ordinary in the way of diamorphine scripts. Without asking them for chapter and verse there's not a lot more I can do, I'm afraid.'

'Oh well.'

'Anyway, I was thinking – she's far more likely to have got her stuff on the open market, isn't she? Bristol's seething with drugs. Buy them on every corner. It's not far, after all.'

Bristol made me think of Jean-Paul. Time had not lent him credibility, and I found myself wondering if he had told me

297

anything approaching the truth. 'No, it's not far,' I agreed. 'Thanks anyway.' I hesitated. 'There was one other thing. The woman who worked in the pottery shop with Sylvie. Liz something. Fiftyish, ethnic clothes, beads. You wouldn't have any idea who she was?'

He made a doubtful sound. 'I know who you might mean. Seen her once or twice. Retired hippy type. Long gypsy skirts. But no – not a patient of mine, not someone I know. Useless again, I'm afraid.'

'Thanks anyway. And thanks for lunch yesterday.'

'Oh, for heaven's sake.' David regarded social niceties as superfluous at the best of times and positively ridiculous within the family. He rang off with a sharp admonitory grunt.

I took the champagne bottle into the kitchen and found Ginny at the table, doing last minute things to some beef that smelled of wine and garlic and herbs. She nodded enthusiastically when I offered to refill her glass. 'Heaven.' And she smiled in such a way that I wasn't quite sure what she was referring to. I was trying another kiss when the phone rang.

'Doomed by the bell,' I muttered.

'Caressus interruptus.'

I snatched the receiver off the hook and was met by the howl of a child. 'Sorry to bother you, Hugh,' Tingwall said over the din, 'but it's Pike. He's found this chap Hayden.'

'Where?'

The screaming reached a terrifying pitch. 'Nothing I can do about this, I'm afraid,' he shouted, sounding harassed. 'In sole charge. Wife at a girls' night. Well, that's what she tells me.' He laughed to show it was a joke. 'No, when I say *found*, it's not quite as good as that. Apparently Hayden's on his way to Heathrow at this moment, heading for the Far East. Pike just missed him in London.'

'Damn. Can he catch him at the airport?' I shouted back.

'He's going to try. He's on his way there now.' Tingwall made some cooing noises off-stage and for a moment the screaming subsided to a succession of wails and sobs. 'At best he might only get a few minutes with Hayden. I've given him some questions to

298

ask, but I wanted to check with you to make sure I hadn't missed anything obvious.'

'Can I speak to Pike direct?'

'What? Sure. He's got a mobile.'

I took down the number and repeated it back to him through the renewed caterwauling.

'Won't be a minute,' I called to Ginny as I rang off and disappeared in the direction of the study.

The number didn't answer first time. When I tried again two minutes later an expressionless voice announced itself as Pike. I explained who I was and Pike told me he was on the motorway, just minutes from the airport.

'If you do manage to find him,' I said, 'try to stop him leaving, will you? Any way you can.'

'I'm not sure I understand you.'

'Offer him whatever it takes to delay his flight.'

'What's your limit?'

'I don't know – five hundred? Two thousand? Whatever it takes.'

'Some people won't be bought at any price.'

'This one will,' I said, though I couldn't have said what gave me such confidence.

'Right. I'll keep in touch.'

I gave Pike my number and went through to dinner. I tried to enter into the spirit of Ginny's evening but I must have been a poor actor because Ginny's intuition soon caught me out.

'The phone. Something's happened,' she said.

'I may have to go out later. If I do, will you be all right?'

'Of course.' But she didn't sound at all convinced.

'I may be late. Well – very late.'

That unnerved her. She didn't like being alone in the house at night. The animation fell from her face. 'How late?'

'I don't know. I might have to go to the airport to talk to someone. I could try to get Mrs Hoskins to come over if you like.'

'It can't wait, this thing?'

I shook my head. 'It's someone who might have information, you see. About Sylvie.'

She gave me a searching, almost hostile look. 'I thought Charles was dealing with all that.'

'He's tied up, and this man's about to fly off somewhere. It's the only chance.'

She was very still. 'Where's all this leading, Hugh?'

'Leading?'

'What's the point of it all?'

I stared at her, baffled by her attitude. 'The *point?*' I heard the impatience in my voice and argued more reasonably, 'Well, someone killed Sylvie, didn't they? So someone has to know *something* about it. The people she mixed with, the dealers . . . If we don't make an effort to find out, then, then—' But mystification blocked my words.

'I think . . .' She hesitated for a long moment. 'I think it would be a mistake to hope for too much.'

'I'm not hoping for *too much*—'

The phone rang and, pushing my chair back roughly, I got up to answer it.

'Bingo,' said Pike's voice. 'But you'll need to bring some cash.' Five minutes later, armed with a batch of traveller's cheques and credit cards, still smarting a little from my discussion with Ginny, I was heading for the motorway.

*

Pike had booked Hayden into one of the smarter hotels on the airport periphery, a newish place with a lobby designed in what Ginny had disdainfully dubbed the mid-Atlantic country-house style, with garish chintzes and hunting scenes and dimpled leather sofas. Pike hadn't stinted on the room either. He let me into a suite with a lobby, three doors leading off it, and a large display of fresh flowers.

Pike was a nondescript man, dead-eyed and stoop-shouldered, with an unhealthy complexion and lugubrious expression. Closing the door behind me, he murmured in the professional undertone of a copper, 'He's friendly enough, but greedy, I'd say. He finally agreed to a grand, cash in hand, plus a replacement air ticket at seven hundred, plus overnight expenses, but I reckon he'll be after more. Shall I sit in?'

'Please.'

Pike led the way into a sitting room with a mirrored bar complete with counter and stools. Hayden was lying back on a sofa watching television, his feet on a low table, drink in hand and a bowl of nuts balanced precariously on his stomach. Removing his eyes unhurriedly from the screen, he disentangled himself from the sofa and rose to a hefty six foot three or four.

'Hi.' His steely handshake was accompanied by a broad lazy smile that was all the more startling for the contrast between his teeth, which were numerous, even and exceptionally white, and the depth of his golden tan. With his springy sun-bleached hair, athletic shoulders and model-boy looks, he might have come straight from a Californian lifestyle commercial. He was the same man I had watched through the binoculars on *Samphire*, but coloured more vividly.

While Pike made the drinks, Hayden grinned some more before sauntering back to the sofa and sinking into the cushions with his eyes fixed on the television again, as though the business session hadn't yet opened and he was still at leisure. When I sat on the chair opposite he didn't hurry to tear himself away from the blaring comedy but waited for some raucous punch line at which he laughed in a loud contrived way before finally operating the remote control.

He turned his smile on me again, and it was a facile smile without warmth. 'Good trip?' he asked as though we were small-talking at a party.

'Fine, thanks.'

'Great.' He nodded a lot, though not as much as he smiled. 'Going straight back?'

'I expect so.'

'Great. I'll be needing cash, did, ah, he tell you?' He indicated Pike with a movement of his head.

'He told me.'

Pike brought the drinks.

Hayden was watching me indolently, like a man with all the

301

time in the world, and I realised he was waiting for the cash to appear on the table.

I produced the traveller's cheques.

He gave an exaggerated theatrical wince, all regretful head-shaking and raised shoulders. 'Ah – *sorry*.' And behind the knowing eyes I recognised someone who was used to getting his own way. I remembered the scene I had witnessed on *Samphire*, the way Sylvie had stood her ground against him.

Pike caught my eye. 'I'll go and see if the management can oblige.' I passed him the cheques and my Amex Gold Card.

'You won't mind if we start?' I asked when Pike had gone.

'Sure.' His tone told me what I already knew, that he wouldn't be telling me anything of real importance until the money arrived.

'I assume Pike's told you what this is about?'

He started picking at the nuts again and popping them expertly into his mouth. 'Sure.'

'Have you spoken to the police at all?'

'I've been away,' he said in a conversational tone. 'Gib, Turkey, Italy, delivering boats. They couldn't've found me if they'd tried.'

'But you were in Devon until – what, August?'

'I was coming and going. I got this dinky little cottage up near Totnes. For my, ah, old age, you know.' And the idea amused him in the way some equally distant prospect like going grey or bald might amuse him. 'Bit of a ruin still. Done the roof. No heating, no light.' He shrugged. 'Next year, I'm hoping.'

'And *Samphire* – you got to do quite a bit of cruising?'

'Sure. Always take the old girl out when I can. Otherwise she rots – you know?' And he smiled his empty affable smile.

Rather than risk questions that he was unlikely to answer, I threw it open. 'Tell me about Sylvie.'

'Sylvie?' He laughed as if I had said something unexpected. '*Yeah* . . . Well, we went back quite a way, Sylvie and me. South of France, Ibiza . . .' He waved a hand, indicating other times, other places. 'Hung out in the same crowd. So when she came around she, ah, got in touch. You know.'

'What brought her to Devon?'

He spread an open palm. 'New start? I guess.'

'She was happy?'

But this question obviously had its price, and his face took on an impenetrable look.

'I saw Joe the other day,' I said, watching for a reaction which I didn't get. 'He told me all about Sylvie's drug—' I almost said 'problems', but amended this to: 'habits. And he told me about the trips to France on *Samphire*, to the dealer there.' Hayden's bland expression did not alter. 'What I need to know – when our business is done' – I offered my own version of a hollow smile – 'is who else she got her stuff from.'

He showed no surprise at the question. Taking a swig of his drink, he creased up his eyes with the effort of some mental calculation and asked, 'When did you come on the scene with Sylvie? I was trying to work it out.'

'Me? What's that got to do with anything?'

'After Easter, was it?'

'June,' I answered reluctantly.

He began his slow nodding again, and did not stop for a long time. 'Yeah,' he said at last, as though he had finally solved the puzzle. 'Yeah.'

Pike reappeared at last with the hotel night manager in tow, and after signing a batch of traveller's cheques and credit card vouchers I took delivery of a thousand pounds in cash.

I plopped the notes onto the table in front of Hayden.

Unhurriedly he leant forward and scooped them up.

'Well?' I demanded.

'Well?' Hayden repeated in the lazy amused manner that appeared to be his stock in trade. 'Where d'you wanna start?'

'The stuff. Where did she get it?'

And still Hayden took his time. 'Can't tell you where she got *everything*. Sylvie had a lot of contacts – you know? But some of the time, back last winter anyway, she had prescriptions. Nicked, I guess. But she never had any trouble with them. Never got thrown out of any chemist or anything. But she was clever about that sort of thing – you know? Used to ring the changes. Sometimes Dartmouth, sometimes Exeter, sometimes Bristol when she was up that way.'

303

'They were made out to her, the prescriptions?'

'Nah,' he said without hesitation. 'She used to fill in the names herself. She had three of her own to choose from, you know. Mathieson and a couple of married names.' He chuckled, 'Or do I mean divorced names?' Enjoying his own joke for a moment, he finally sauntered on, 'She had two passports anyway, one French, one British, in different names. That way she could always produce ID.' While I was absorbing this he added, 'The prescriptions, she had plenty last winter. Must have had a whole pad of the things. Cost her, I bet. Well, that's what I thought—'

'Cost her?'

'Sure. Junk isn't my scene, you understand. But – yeah, she'd have bought them.'

I was being slow, but I had to understand this. 'You mean, pads get stolen and sold on?'

Deferring to the expert, Hayden tipped an amused glance at Pike.

'They get stolen all the time,' Pike confirmed in his bleak voice. 'Doctors' cars, surgeries. Though the thieves don't get much joy a lot of the time because the chemists are on the lookout. Lists of stolen pads get circulated. The chemists check up on anything suspect.'

Hayden drained his drink and wiggled his glass hopefully. Pike got grudgingly to his feet and took the glass for a refill.

Hayden yawned.

'So?' I urged.

'Yeah, well . . . the prescriptions, they seemed to run out in . . . I guess it must have been Easter time, and then she, ah, started on at me to go to France all the time, to pick up stuff there. But listen, that wasn't my scene. I mean, the occasional little trip, a bit of hash, that's okay, you know what I mean? But regularly, for junk?' He blew disapprovingly through his lips. 'Well, that's asking for it, isn't it? And I've got my reputation to consider.' He angled his head a little, as if to show his best profile. 'One run-in with the customs and I'd never work again. Like, *never*. So I just told her to jump. I told her that wasn't my game. Then . . . I can't be sure, you know? But I think she got her stuff from Bristol. Well . . . Let's put it this way, she never came back from Bristol without

304

quite a stash. That's all I can tell you, really. That's all I ever knew. Sylvie – she was, like, quite tight about those things. Protecting her sources, you might say.'

I groped back in search of a loose end. 'You were going to say something just now,' I reminded him. 'Something about the prescriptions . . . ?'

But the thought had gone, and neither Pike nor I managed to prompt his memory.

'What about boyfriends, lovers?' I asked. 'Who was she seeing in the early spring?'

Hayden's face took on an odd gloating look. 'There was some bloke, yeah. She saw him all the way through last winter. That's what our deal was, she used my cottage at weekends, like as a retreat, in exchange for, you know, keeping an eye. She came down from Bristol every weekend, hacked wood, built fires, put buckets out to catch the leaks.'

'She was living in Bristol?'

'Sure. Her brother was there.'

'And the lover, who was he?'

'She never told me. No names, no pack drill,' he smirked. '*But* . . .' He paused for dramatic effect. 'I did see him once. He bowled up at the cottage when I was there. Made off smartish when he realised his mistake. Good dresser, smart car – spanking new Mercedes. Money, definitely.'

It wasn't what I had expected.

'Was he local?'

He said with heavy irony, 'That would have been difficult to say, wouldn't it, seeing him like that.'

'What did he look like?'

He made a face. 'Affluent. Oldish. Your average Mercedes owner.' It was hard to tell if he was being deliberately evasive, but in the silence that followed I began to think I had wasted my time and money.

Hayden let me fret a little longer before announcing lightly, 'Saw him again, though.'

I didn't like being strung along, especially by the likes of Hayden. 'Oh yes?' I said harshly.

'Might even be able to place him for you.' He spread his hands like a market trader producing the best goods from the back of the barrow.

'Place him then.'

A look of sly calculation came over Hayden's face, I spotted the light of avarice in his eyes, and with a stab of cold anger I barked, 'Don't even think about it.'

With an expression of injury, Hayden looked around as if to plead his innocence to a wider audience, but behind this extravagant show he was using the time to gauge his position. 'I wasn't thinking about a *thing*,' he protested, laughing to cover his retreat. 'I'm just trying to tell you, that's all.'

'Tell me then.'

'The guy had a boat on the river. I saw him launching a dinghy from the pontoon.'

A small warning sounded in my brain.

Hayden was watching me closely now. 'The dinghy was the tender to a boat called *Ellie Miller*.'

My heart gave a single beat, a thump against my chest. I held on to my expression, I showed nothing in my face, but Hayden, with all the perception of a habitual dissembler had picked something up. 'Someone you know?' he enquired.

'You're sure it was the same man?' I asked, revealing some of my turmoil.

'*Yeah*. It was him all right. And then I went and asked someone at the yacht charter place who he was, and they said he was the local doctor. Seemed pretty sure. Like I said, you should be able to place him, right?'

The blood seemed to burst in my veins, I was filled with a terrible heat. I held tight to my drink to stop it from spilling. Then a miraculous liberating thought struck me, and it was so obvious that I almost laughed. 'Sylvie was his patient. He was probably making a call when he came to the cottage!' And the relief was already rushing through me.

'His patient. Yeah, that would make sense, wouldn't it?' he said knowingly. 'With the prescriptions, I mean. That was what I was going to say before – right at the end something she said made me think she was getting those prescriptions on tap. Like, on request.'

306

'You're not hearing what I'm saying,' I said, holding on to my temper with difficulty. 'I'm saying he must have gone to the cottage to see Sylvie as a patient. She must have been ill.'

He reflected on this. 'Could be,' he conceded. 'Just one problem.' And he grinned abruptly; he was enjoying himself. 'The doctor had a key.'

*

I didn't attempt to sleep when I got back to Melton. After going up to check on Ginny I shut myself in the study to sit out the remains of the night in silence and darkness, with a brandy at my elbow and misery in my heart.

The more I tried to make sense of the thoughts that bumped and veered around my mind, the more the few remaining certainties of my uncertain life seemed to trickle away, and I had the sensation of slipping headlong towards more appalling upheavals and calamities. On leaving Hayden I had been dazed by disbelief and a smarting sense of betrayal, as though on the subject of duplicity I had anything to be proud of. But now in the long quiet hours of the night the incredulity had begun to fade and, coming to terms with Hayden's revelations, I was left with the most terrifying uncertainty of all: What had I really stumbled across? David had been Sylvie's lover, David had deceived me and, it would appear, everyone else: this much seemed inescapable. But what did it mean? It might mean nothing; it might mean everything. It could be nothing more than an extra-marital affair, or something so frightening that I couldn't begin to imagine where it might lead without pulling up in an agony of doubt.

Out of long habit part of me rose to David's defence. David, who had suffered my father's disapproval for so much of his life, who had increasingly felt the bitter dissatisfaction of his own failures; David, the eldest but second son, who had somehow never quite managed to pull his life together. Pa had always judged him harshly, and I did not want to do the same. I told myself that nothing terrible had happened, that, like me, he had simply snatched at temptation; that, like me, he had been used and discarded by Sylvie. These were not heinous crimes, yet for David with his thorny pride, they would be enough to account for his silence. I told myself that this was all there was to it. Now and again I even managed to convince myself. But I couldn't entirely rid myself of hideous black thoughts which came screeching at me out of the darkness, like birds out of the night, and then I was seized by such a combination of misery and dread that it was all I could do not to pick up the phone and call David there and then.

At about six I showered and changed and, leaving a note for Ginny, set off into the gloomy dawn.

The road was clear, I was through Totnes just before eight. I did not stop at Furze Lodge but went straight on to Dartmouth. David's car was not in its place outside the surgery, but the receptionist told me he was due in at nine and had a steady stream of appointments until eleven. I left him a curt note, saying I needed to see him urgently, and drove slowly to Dittisham to wait.

Drawing up outside the house I sat in the car, absorbing the silence, wishing it would last. At nine my mobile began to ring: George on his first call of the day. As soon as he had given up I phoned Julia and told her to keep everyone at bay for the morning.

'Do you want me down at Melton?' she asked.

'I think Ginny's all right.'

'Shall I check?'

'No, I'll call her myself.'

'If you're sure.'

Ginny didn't answer the first time I tried, nor the second, and then the line was engaged for a while, and then it didn't answer again. Reading more into this than was good for me, I called Julia back and asked her if she wouldn't mind going down after all.

For a time I sat in the quiet again, then, breaking free of my trance, got out of the car and, taking the key from its ledge in the porch, let myself into the musty hall. I made my way slowly through the house, examining each room with a new and jaundiced eye, as though it might contain traces of the past which I had not previously had the wit to see.

If David had brought Sylvie here, then it must have been soon after Pa's death. No qualms about that then.

Pausing outside the kitchen I remembered how Sylvie had made her way here unhesitatingly, how she had known where to find everything. Had they drunk coffee here together, kissed, made love? I saw them making love everywhere, on floors, on sofas, upright, naked, clothed.

And the study: I remembered the way she had appeared at the french windows, as though she were used to coming through the garden and arriving unannounced.

These fragments of proof gave me great bursts of misery but also a kind of masochistic satisfaction and, unable to stop myself, I trudged up the stairs and stood on the landing, taking mental measurements of the distances to the various doors. Had Sylvie pulled me into David's room because it was fractionally the closest, or out of some perverse desire to take a second brother to the same bed?

I glanced over the shelves by the bed, I opened the drawers of the bedside table and angrily closed them again, not even wanting to think of what I had expected to find there. I stood at the window and looked down the river to where *Samphire* lay at her mooring, and felt an unexpected gratitude to Hayden. At the end of the day, knowledge, however bitter, gives you some sort of grip on the future.

Returning to the study, I remembered the night when Sylvie and I had made love with the curtains undrawn, and the sound I had heard from the terrace, a memory which until last night I had pushed from my mind. Trying to give the sound substance now, it seemed to me that it was a garden chair being accidentally bumped across stone. In a trick of the imagination I saw not Ginny but David stumbling across the chair in the dark.

Hearing a car in the drive, I opened the front door and watched David get out and walk towards me. Looking up, his face darkened and he paused in front of me as if to demand what was going on before changing his mind and passing silently into the house. Automatically he made for the study, the room which he, more than anyone, associated with inquisitions and retribution.

I sat at Pa's desk while David pulled a chair away from the

wall and, placing it by the french windows, settled himself warily. 'What's up then?'

Now that the moment had come I could only say, 'You and Sylvie.'

In the pause that followed his mouth twitched but his eyes were steady. 'Yes,' he exhaled abruptly. 'So.'

'You don't think you should tell me about it?'

'What do you want to know?'

'Everything.'

'I don't think you mean that.'

'Don't bloody tell me what I mean!' I blazed with sudden anger. 'Don't bloody talk *down* to me, David. For once, for *once*' – I splayed a furious hand at him – 'just tell me the bloody truth!'

If my anger had taken me by surprise, David met it impassively. Looking away towards the river, he began in a dispassionate voice, 'I met her about a year ago, down on the quay. Pa wasn't too well, I'd been out to look at *Ellie*. I was stacking the dinghy when Sylvie walked up and said, "You're David." That was it, really. We went for a drink. It started from there. We met at weekends. She was living in Bristol. She'd borrowed this cottage near Totnes – Hayden's cottage. Then in March she moved down to Dittisham, rented a place—' He glanced towards me, 'Well, you know about that. Then she broke it off in, oh ... about May, I suppose. We got together again briefly, but ...' His shrug indicated that it hadn't worked out. 'I didn't know about you, I promise. Well, not for a long time. Not until I saw you together on *Ellie*. Can't remember when that was – August some time? But until then I had no idea. Really.' He gave a caustic smile. 'Otherwise I would have warned you.'

Another pause, like darkness. David lifted a shoulder as if to say: Well, that's it.

'Haven't you left rather a lot out?' I said.

He examined my face in the sombre light, searching for my meaning. 'Ahh,' he said heavily. 'You mean, our arrangement?'

'The prescriptions.'

He nodded stoically. 'This was Hayden, was it?' Immediately he dismissed the question as of no importance. 'Yes,' he said with

310

a long sigh, 'it's amazing what one does when one's – how shall I put it? – not thinking too cleverly. Enough to get me struck off ten times over, and then some. At first it was just to *help* her, you understand. One last fix, and then she was going to take the cure. She'd been on a cure just that summer, but it hadn't lasted long. She thought she could control it, you see. Take a hit now and again. You can't, of course – control it. Also she had no real will to stop. She never believed it was doing her any harm. They never do. She didn't think about the future. She thought she could just go on—' He broke off suddenly and his mouth turned down. 'Anyway . . . one thing led to another. She kept asking for more. And I kept handing out. The risk was ludicrous. I got calls from chemists a couple of times, thought there'd be trouble, but somehow nothing ever came of it. Sheer luck. I knew it was madness.'

'So why didn't you stop?'

He raised an eyebrow, and his expression seemed to say: Are you sure you really want to hear this? Reading my determination, he announced bluntly, 'Because I wanted her. It wasn't that I couldn't stop – it was that I didn't want to.' His eyes glittered at the memory. Catching an echo of some powerful and voracious emotion, I felt a tremor of jealousy.

I said sharply, 'And Mary?'

'What about Mary?'

'For God's sake – did she know?'

'If she did, she never mentioned it to me.' He added casually, 'She's never said anything to you?'

'No.' And now I had the feeling he was trying to deflect me. 'You got together again, you said, Sylvie and you?'

'What? Oh yes . . . June. July. She wanted some more scripts. But by then it was what you might call a business arrangement.'

'Business?' And suddenly I was having trouble with my patience again. 'Spell it out for me, David.'

Once more he gave me the do-you-really-want-this look, the raised eyebrow and the down-turned mouth. 'She wanted some drugs, I wanted a good lay. I think that more or less sums it up.'

I couldn't work out if this harsh judgment was designed to

punish me or himself. Whatever, there was something in his manner that rang false, and I thought I caught a hint of bitterness.

I asked, 'And this was all the way through June and July?'

'No, no,' he exclaimed, irritated at my dull-wittedness. 'We managed without each other very well, believe me. Sometimes I didn't see her for weeks.' He retorted, 'Really.'

I recognised this display. He was using the blend of intimidation and defiance that he had always employed as a child to try to bluff his way out of trouble. I suspected him then. I suspected that he was lying.

I said tersely, 'You were still seeing her when she died.'

There was a pause while we stared at each other across the expanse of the window. 'No, Hugh,' he said very deliberately. 'And I didn't kill her either.'

'Come on,' I argued with a semblance of control. 'She was going to the boat to meet someone. It wasn't me, so it seems fairly obvious that it must have been you. Because when you think about it, there wasn't anyone else it could have been. You couldn't use the house any more, could you, because I was always turning up there. You couldn't go to her cottage – too many people to see your car outside and Joe hanging about all the time. Too far to Hayden's place. So it had to be the boat, didn't it?'

He watched me gravely without attempting a reply.

'Well? Have I got this wrong?' I demanded stiffly. 'I mean, where did you meet? *Tell* me.'

He looked away again, and still he was silent.

'The boat. *The boat*,' I chanted back at him. And for a moment my throat seized, I couldn't speak. And still he said nothing 'Christ . . .' My eyes had misted up, my lips were trembling. 'What happened – did Sylvie try to blackmail you or something? Did she get nasty? Did she go mad? Did *you* go mad? Tell me!'

He was looking out at the river, his eyes screwed up against the light. 'It wasn't like that,' he murmured.

'*Well?* Tell me what it *was* like, for Christ's sake. Tell me something – *anything*.'

He made a mildly dismissive movement of his head, as though any comment would be a waste of time.

I shot to my feet and stood over him, and now I was shaking

312

with rage. 'Tell me why the hell I shouldn't go to the police! Give me one good reason! Just *one*, you bastard.'

He considered this with an air of great weariness. 'For one thing it would be a mistake, because I didn't kill her. For another, it would destroy my career.' He added ironically, 'For what that's worth.'

'I don't give a stuff about your career,' I exploded again. 'What's your goddamned career compared to *Ginny!*'

He looked up at me. 'I'm sorry it's got this far with Ginny, I really am.'

I gave an ugly shout. 'Well, I tell you something – Ginny's not going to prison to save your miserable neck.'

He stood up with an air of infinite dejection. 'I didn't kill her, Hugh.'

'And I'm meant to believe you?'

He gave a distracted nod. 'Yes.'

'Jesus.' I sank back on my seat.

'But listen, Hugh – I'm not sure yet, but I think there's something I might be able to do to help Ginny.'

'Excuse me,' I jeered, '*something you can do?*'

'Yes. But I'll need a bit more time.'

I was momentarily incapable of speech. In his more imperious moments David had always had this ability to reduce me to a state of mute frustration.

'Just give me a bit more time,' he repeated solemnly.

'More time – for *what?*' I burst out at last. 'The only *help* she needs is to get off, for Christ's sake.'

'That's what I meant.'

'Oh, for God's sake get out of here!' I cried, overtaken by a new wave of anger. 'Just bloody get out of my sight.'

FOURTEEN

To judge by the seating arrangements, the Cumberland board were not expecting a massive turnout. No more than two hundred chairs had been set out in short rows at the far end of one of the hotel's larger conference rooms, giving the effect of emptiness and insignificance, while stacks of spare seats stood idly at the periphery, in the unlikely event of a sudden rush.

George, aided by Julia, was setting up shop outside the door, with piles of Hartford brochures and information sheets for any shareholders who for some reason had not received them through the post. There were also copies of the resolution that I had drafted and formally tabled for the meeting, requiring the Cumberland board to explain why they had not accepted the highest bid.

George looked harassed and downcast, and I guessed that our final tally of proxies hadn't exceeded the discouraging eighteen per cent we had logged last night.

'Press coverage.' George passed me a folder of cuttings.

Most of it was small stuff, paragraphs tucked away on business pages, but one of the tabloids had run a longer piece just that morning, an emotional David and Goliath story in which Cumberland was portrayed as a heartless monolith, needlessly and cruelly consigning a skilled workforce to the scrapheap.

George commented gruffly, 'Every little helps – so they say.'

But we both knew that publicity wouldn't be enough to win us our resolution, let alone the vote of confidence. Nor would the support of the private shareholders who were beginning to trickle in through the doors. The real control lay in the hands of the institutional shareholders, the pension funds and unit trusts whose vast blocks of equity gave them dominant voting power. Knowing George and Alan had spent the whole of the previous day phoning around some of the institutions, I asked, 'Any luck yesterday?'

'A lot said they'd given their proxies to Cumberland.' He shrugged.

'But some might still be uncommitted?'

George gave me a look that said: If only.

Julia handed me an envelope and began to tell us about a pension fund manager she had been in touch with, but recognising the handwriting on the letter I moved to one side and opened it. *Dearest Hugh, I've got all my fingers and toes crossed for you!* Mary had written. *But look – if it's simply a question of more money, please count me in! Probably too late for all that, but if you do need any more, then I'd really like to help. Went to my trustees – yes, I've still got trustees – and found I have bags more to spare than I thought. Up to half a million. I really mean it, Hugh. If it'll make any difference to winning, it would be the proudest moment of my life. Really! With tons and tons of love, Mary.*

My first reaction was profound gratitude; my next sharp suspicion, made all the more mortifying by the affection that had come before. Where had Mary suddenly found such an enormous sum of money? Why had she left the offer so late? In fact what had prompted her to offer it at all? Giving my darkest thoughts full rein, it seemed to me that this could only have come from David, that only David could possibly have this sort of money lying around. Following on from this came a further rush of unwelcome thoughts: that David was trying to buy me off in some way, and that, being him, he was confident of succeeding; alternatively, that in his proud inarticulate way he was simply trying to help and did not like to do it in person. I wasn't sure which idea made me most uncomfortable. Either way, it was shabby to use Mary.

And then again, perhaps the demons in this were all of my own making. Perhaps this offer was exactly what it seemed. Perhaps Mary in her generosity was simply trying to help and had told David nothing. Perhaps I was simply becoming paranoid, like

Ginny. Two frightened people, reacting badly. It was an oddly heartening thought.

Thrusting the note into my pocket, I headed back towards the doors to be intercepted by Julia, brandishing her mobile phone. She hissed under her breath, '*Howard.*'

I moved out of earshot.

'Hugh?' came the smooth tones. 'Listen, can you spare a few minutes?'

'Is this business or social, Howard?'

'Something we might want to discuss. Something that might be helpful to both of us.'

'You're sure about that?'

'Would I bother you otherwise? I'm upstairs. Suite 223.'

'I'll need to bring George with me.'

'Fine.' Ever the orchestrator, he was already sounding pleased with himself.

George pulled an astonished face when I told him. 'What, *now?* We've only got twenty minutes.'

'That's probably the whole point.'

As we headed for the stairs, George said, 'But what can he want?'

'It'll be an offer of some sort, I imagine.'

'God,' he chuckled nervously. 'A *deal?*'

'A softener, more like. A consolation prize, Howard-style. Which means,' I said caustically, 'that there won't be much in it for us.'

Howard was waiting at the door of the suite. 'Welcome,' he smiled, at his most gracious. He appeared to harbour no animosity towards me over my telephone tirade, but then Howard had always regarded people who got angry with him as having a personality defect.

He waved us to a seat. 'Coffee? No? Are you sure?'

As he went and poured himself a cup at a pace that was deliberately unhurried I could see George beginning to fret over the time, but I knew that Howard would have calculated it down to the last minute and there was no point in rushing him.

Sinking elegantly into a chair, Howard smiled, 'Well, I must say, you've mounted a most impressive campaign. Very

316

thorough. The shareholders, the press and so on. Excellent stuff.'

George, taking this at face value, said, 'Thanks.'

'Pity it had no hope of success. From your point of view, I mean. But, well – it was hardly to be expected, was it?'

'You've got your fifty per cent, have you?' I asked: the proxies he needed to carry the day.

'Of course,' Howard smiled as though it had always been a foregone conclusion.

I wanted to say: Then why are we here? But I knew better than to ask such an obvious question.

'However...' Howard sipped at his coffee and gave us a beneficent gaze. 'The situation has changed somewhat. New considerations have come to light. And, without wanting to go into detail – without being *free* to – suffice it to say that events have shifted to the extent that the board might be prepared to review your bid in a more favourable light.'

Startled, I tried to imagine what could possibly have changed. Donington's share value? As far as I knew it hadn't dropped significantly. Or maybe Cumberland's lawyers had uncovered something they didn't like, some fancy footwork in the small print of Donington's offer.

I could see George sparking with excitement but, deliberately failing to catch his eye, I asked Howard, 'What are the terms?'

'Terms?' Howard echoed with the air of cool surprise he assumed when someone spoiled his timing. 'Oh . . . as before,' he stated as though this should have been obvious. 'As before. With an adjustment for the differential between the two bids, of course. To make good our shortfall. You know how it is,' he beamed. 'Duty to the shareholders.'

I had known there would be a catch. 'But our bid was as good as Donington's,' I pointed out. 'If not better.'

'Ah, but you have to allow for the appreciation of the Donington shares. A steady-growth company. We were banking on an annual stock appreciation of at least seven per cent.'

This was rubbish. No one could bank on steady growth at the moment, particularly in china and glass, which had always been a volatile performer in times of economic uncertainty. It was a load of nonsense, but then Howard knew this as well as I did.

'This *notional* differential,' I said. 'What did you have in mind, *allowing* for the fact that our offer is already pitched at, and maybe even beyond, the maximum value of the company? *Allowing* for the fact that we couldn't justify going to our backers and asking them to invest a penny more? *Allowing* for the fact that we have precisely ten minutes to sort this out? *Allowing* for the fact that brinkmanship goes both ways?'

Howard grinned quietly. He liked nothing better than a good fight. 'Well, we're prepared to compromise, to forgo some of this *notional* gain, as you put it. We're prepared to settle for half a million.'

I felt a pull in my stomach, a chill of disbelief. I told myself that it was a coincidence. I told myself that stranger things had happened. I tried to keep calm, to conceal the resentment and suspicion that had rushed into my face.

'Can't be done,' I said.

'Oh?' Howard affected surprise. 'We'd give you two weeks to arrange the funding.'

'Not at that price.'

Howard looked pained. 'Couldn't square any less with the board. Or indeed the shareholders. The figure's been agreed, you see, as the most generous we could possibly offer. It's not open to negotiation.'

'There's no more money.' And the violence in my tone made them stare at me.

George ventured at last, 'Perhaps we could have a few minutes?'

'Surely.' Howard finished his coffee and pulled himself lazily to his feet. 'I'll be next door.' Scooping up his mobile, he disappeared through a connecting door.

'It's extortion,' I protested before George could say a word. 'Blackmail. And we're not going to pay a single penny.'

George began to make hasty calculations on his notepad. 'But all this publicity might make it easier to raise the money—'

'It's not the money, George, it's the principle!'

George threw me a baffled look, then another, as if he really

318

couldn't work out what I was talking about. 'Maybe they'll come down a bit.'

'But we'd still be paying over the odds, damn it!'

'Yes, but not much. And this is going to be the end of it, isn't it? They won't be able to go back on their word a second time, will they? We'll be home and dry.'

He was right, but I wasn't in any mood to hear the truth, and while he continued to play with numbers I paced up and down the room, nursing a sense of betrayal and impotence, made all the worse for knowing that my feelings were irrelevant.

'The additional interest wouldn't kill us,' George announced. 'But look, we should grab Alan and get him to go through this—'

'No time. That's the whole point, for heaven's sake. We have no time.' I stopped by the window and stared out into the featureless London street, and in that moment the last of my resentment trickled away like so much useless energy, and I gave in to the inevitable. Yet if I had been outmanoeuvred somewhere along the line, if I had been set up, I told myself that I had not yet been bought, and if anyone thought otherwise they would quickly discover the difference.

'We've got the money,' I admitted.

'What?'

'We have the promise of the money. A private investor.'

'Good God! You mean— Then—'

As if on cue a soft knock announced Howard's return. 'Don't mean to hurry you,' he said in his most honeyed tones.

'Just supposing we were able to reach an agreement now,' I said immediately, 'what would happen downstairs?'

'Ah... The board would announce that we were reconsidering your bid in every expectation of reaching a favourable outcome.'

'And Donington?'

'By implication, that bid would have run into difficulties, wouldn't it?'

'And our resolution?'

'You'd want to withdraw it, I imagine.'

I turned on my heel and headed for the door. I waited at the top of the stairs for Howard to catch up. 'Half a million is a ludicrous sum,' I said as we started down.

319

He gave a small laugh. 'That was our valuation, Hugh.'

'Don't give me that crap, Howard. It's just a face-saver, isn't it? A way for your board to go back to the shareholders and say they're getting them a better deal. Anything less than half a million would make you look stupid, wouldn't it? Isn't that more like it? So what's happened to Donington, Howard? Have they pulled out altogether? Have they discovered they can't do business with you?'

'Nothing like that,' he asserted confidently. 'They still have their hat very much in the ring.' Howard was such an excellent liar that it was impossible to tell if this statement bore any relation to the truth.

We halted short of the conference room, and still I was bothered by the fact that I didn't understand what the hell was really going on.

Howard lifted both palms questioningly. 'Are we agreed?'

'No going back,' I warned.

'*Hardly*,' he exclaimed with a look of injury.

I held out my hand. 'You take my hand at your peril, you shit.'

Grasping it, he smiled with something like affection. 'I knew we could do business, Hugh.'

Watching him walk away, I had the sensation of having travelled a long way only to return to the same point. Howard's deviousness did at least have a comforting familiarity.

Julia caught me on the way into the meeting. 'Two unit trust managers have turned up!' she whispered excitedly. 'One I've been talking to all week. He introduced himself just now and pointed out another one. If two have actually bothered to turn up, they can't have given their proxies! And there might be more. Maybe some pension fund managers. I contacted all the unions, you know, every single one. There might be a whole *slab* of votes going begging.'

Maybe that was it. Maybe Howard had lied to me. Maybe the Cumberland board hadn't got the vote in the bag. Maybe we could have won the day on the no-confidence vote and saved ourselves half a million pounds.

'Maybe a lot of things,' I murmured to Julia.

Going into the meeting, I touched the note in my pocket and

320

Ginny's words floated reproachfully into my mind. *Mary isn't Howard's sister for nothing.*

*

Grainger's chambers were situated in a dark building overlooking a secretive courtyard of the Inner Temple, just beyond the soot-stained buttresses of the church. The recessed doorway with its ladder of names reminded me of my old staircase at Trinity, but once inside all resemblance to college was dispelled by the lavish carpets and speckling of spotlights, the rag-rolled walls and confident glow of the reproduction furniture.

Grainger's room had extravagantly draped curtains over matching roman blinds, large Impressionist prints, a scattering of bulbous table lamps with pale silk shades, and a large gas log fire. The effect was of a drawing room seconded for office use, and only the wall of legal tomes behind us and the oversize desk ahead of us with its stacks of papers and box-files gave the lie to the mood of elegant inactivity.

Tingwall was already there and kissed Ginny warmly on both cheeks.

'Mrs Wellesley.' Grainger bowed over Ginny's hand and showed her to a chair at a narrow table which abutted the giant desk in a T-shape. Tingwall and I found seats opposite her, while Grainger ostentatiously took his place behind the desk, like a lecturer facing his students.

As soon as the coffee had been poured Grainger fastened his eyes on Ginny and said without preamble, 'We're faced with a difficult decision, Mrs Wellesley. I expect Mr Tingwall has explained something of it to you?'

'Yes,' Ginny replied in a voice so low it was barely audible. She had been looking tired for some days, despite – or possibly because of – the sleeping pills she had been taking with increasing regularity.

'Well, I would like to explain it to you again, if that meets with your approval.' The formality of Grainger's address, the charcoal pinstripe three-piece with the gold watch chain, the calmly intertwined hands, the neat greying hair and patrician features, all served to create an air of effortless authority which was entirely intentional, and, according to Tingwall, entirely appropriated. Apparently Grainger's grand style and Eton drawl obscured a childhood of poverty and deprivation as the son of an unemployed Yorkshire coal-miner. I didn't care for his chosen persona, but I couldn't blame him for it either. He depended for his living on impressing his clients and intimidating his opponents, although I suspected that he didn't always achieve them in that order.

'Mrs Wellesley,' he began fluidly, 'the decision is a difficult one because it involves risk, and however clear-sighted we try to be, however critically we approach the facts, it will be impossible to assess those risks with any degree of accuracy. All I can do is set out the situation as I see it, explain what is involved in the two principal strategies which are open to you, and give you my opinion as to your best course. After that, the decision must be yours. I cannot make it for you.' In the seclusion of his chambers Grainger's voice, while maintaining the affectation which had so annoyed me at the bail hearing, had lost its hunting-field stridency and taken on an intimate almost melodic tone.

Ginny nodded, 'I understand.'

Grainger assumed an expression of exaggerated concentration. 'Now, our *first* option is to offer *no* defence at the committal stage and let the case go unopposed to crown court. This means a wait of perhaps six months and a full hearing before a judge and jury. Of course, in those six months circumstances could change and cause the prosecution to alter its stance, or indeed for us to alter our position in some way, but let's assume for the moment that we will be pleading not guilty to the charge as it stands – that is, to a charge of murder. The first thing to understand is that this is an extremely serious charge and that if you are found guilty you will go to prison for a long time.' His face took on a suitably grave aspect, his voice resonated sympathetically, and I couldn't help thinking what a performer he was, how he relished every moment.

'The second thing to know is that a jury is a thoroughly unpredictable body, and there is no determining in advance how they may or may not be swayed by any particular piece or body of evidence. The only sure thing about a jury is their ability to surprise.' A pause to allow us to absorb what he intended to be a daunting truth. 'Now, for us the *advantage* of letting the case go unchallenged to crown court is that the prosecution will not have the chance to test our defence in advance, nor indeed to appreciate and shore up the weaknesses in their own case. We will, so to speak, have kept our cards close to our chest. That way we can hope to spring a few surprises on the opposition' – his eyes glinted at the thought – 'to discredit a witness or two, to work away at the flaws in their case, without giving them too much warning of our strategy. For the defence advocate this is an important weapon and one he is loath to give away without good reason.'

Ginny broke the short silence that followed. 'I was wondering . . .'

When she failed to continue Grainger prompted briskly, 'Yes, Mrs Wellesley?'

'Would I give evidence?'

'That is something we would not decide until much nearer the time. It is something which would require very careful consideration. Though it is possible, just possible, that we might decide against it.'

'Against . . .' Ginny echoed with what might have been a touch of relief. Blinking rapidly, she said, 'Sorry – I interrupted.'

Grainger smiled faintly and rearranged his hands into an elegant display of interlaced fingertips. 'Now, for the *second* option,' he drawled. 'The second option is to defend the case at committal stage with the object of getting the case thrown out before it ever gets to crown court. This means going for what is termed an old-style committal. Here all the evidence is brought before, usually, a stipendiary magistrate sitting alone, the important witnesses appear in person, the evidence is open to challenge under cross-examination. Clearly the *only* reason for choosing this option is if you think you have a good chance of persuading the magistrate that there is no case to answer – *no case at all*. He must be persuaded that the prosecution's evidence is so insubstantial or unreliable that at crown court no reasonable jury, properly directed, would be likely to return a verdict of guilty. Lack of reliable evidence is *sufficient* in itself for the case to be stopped, *but'* – he raised a finger – 'if the bench can also be persuaded that we have a valid defence then clearly our chances become that much stronger.'

He raised his eyebrows at Tingwall. 'Now, what we have, do we not, are some promising developments.'

Taking his cue eagerly, Tingwall's eyes darted back and forth. 'I took a bit of a gamble. Armstrong – our fingerprint expert – asked if he could talk to the prosecution's expert. Apparently it's quite common when experts of this calibre disagree for them to what they quaintly call "compare notes". Armstrong said it's done to avoid wasting court time, but – well, perhaps they prefer to avoid looking incompetent as well. Anyway, I told him to go ahead, and the upshot of it was that Armstrong gave the prosecution's man chapter and verse on where he thought he'd gone wrong, and the chap went back and had another look at his opinion' – he paused for effect – 'and he's *conceded* on one of the points of similarity.' He tightened his lips as though he didn't trust himself not to break into a grin and give too much away. 'Which means that the prosecution won't be able to use him as a witness because fifteen points of similarity between two prints are not enough!'

Grainger said smoothly, 'We can't of course rule out the possibility that the prosecution will find another expert or two to back them up.'

Tingwall allowed this reluctantly. 'It's *possible.*'

'But let us assume for the *moment* that the Crown is unable to present any fingerprint evidence whatsoever.' Grainger lifted his head to the thought. 'Then we have a situation where the prosecution would be left without any forensic evidence to link us to the scene of the crime. None at all. I need hardly say that this would improve our situation considerably. *However* . . .' He slid his elbows onto the desk and clasped his hands under his chin: his cautionary look. 'Cases can and do get sent up to the crown court on non-forensic evidence alone. That's the first point. Second, the prosecution will still have this eyewitness of theirs.' He picked up a batch of stapled papers and, hooking some half-moon glasses onto his nose, leafed through them. 'It is impossible to tell from a witness statement how a witness will perform in court, how convincing he will be, but if we are to take this statement at face value it would seem that the witness is confident in his identification of Mrs Wellesley. He is saying' – Grainger skimmed the lines – 'that he was by the river on the Saturday afternoon of the weekend in question, at about five, and that he saw this woman get into a dinghy and set off across the water, and that he recognised that woman as Virginia Wellesley. He recognised her because apparently . . .' His eyes darted over the pages again. 'Apparently he had worked at Dittisham House as a gardener some years ago and knows all the family by sight.'

Astonished, I tried to think who it could be. 'Old Gordon?'

Grainger flipped back to the first page. 'His name is . . . Gordon Latimer.'

'Old Gordon,' I affirmed. 'He must be seventy-five, eighty, if he's a day.'

'Age is not yet a barrier to providing evidence,' Grainger commented drily.

'But surely his eyesight can't be too good—'

'It would be pointless to conject on that until we have the opportunity for cross-examination,' Grainger argued firmly. 'For the moment we must look at this statement as it stands, and I have to say that in my *opinion*, unless the witness is manifestly unreliable, it is likely that his evidence will be sufficient to send the case to trial. You see—' He removed his spectacles in a deft movement that was so reminiscent of David that for an instant I had the strange sensation of facing my brother. 'In your statement to the police, Mrs Wellesley, you said that you went to the boat only once during the weekend – on the *Sunday*. There is no mention of going on the Saturday. So we are left with two options. Either we deny the eyewitness's version of events, which will leave us in a his-word-against-ours situation. Or we accept his evidence and offer an explanation as to *why* we went to the boat on the *Saturday* and *why* we failed to tell the police about it.' He made a neat gesture, a small overturning of the hand. 'You appreciate the problem?'

'I explained,' Ginny said. 'I told . . .' And she indicated Tingwall.

'Indeed,' Grainger said smoothly. 'I have read your account of

325

events, Mrs Wellesley. I have read it very carefully indeed. However, if we are going to say that we went out to the boat on the day of the murder and found the body and disposed of it into the water then we face great difficulties. *One,*' he began remorselessly, 'why didn't we report the finding of the body at the time? Two: if we are going to admit to the disposing of the body, then this is going to cast us in an extremely unfortunate light which will undoubtedly do us very great damage. After all, what motive could we have for committing this deliberate and dangerous act if it wasn't to protect ourself or someone extremely close to us?' He left this thought in the air for a second. 'Three: if we say we were trying to protect our husband, only to discover that he was miles away at the time and couldn't have done it, then what suspects are the jury left with? Who are they meant to cast as the murderer?' This, too, hung in the silence for a moment. 'Four: not to put too fine a point on it, Mrs Wellesley, are we likely to be believed?'

Ginny flinched slightly and looked down at her hands before nodding readily. 'Yes, I see the problem . . .'

'If there was a reasonable explanation for your presence on the river on the Saturday,' Grainger reflected, 'and a reasonable explanation for your having failed to mention it to the police, then we *might* think about putting that forward. But I fear that to put forward your account of events as it stands without any evidence to back it up is . . .' He inhaled delicately. 'Well, it is not likely to be the most rewarding approach. You understand what I'm saying, Mrs Wellesley? You see the difficulties?'

If I had been harbouring any hopes of a way out for Ginny they evaporated then. With a stab of alarm I realised that her situation was bleak, that, even without the fingerprint, the evidence was still stacked against her.

I asked Grainger, 'What *is* our defence then?'

The eyes dropped languidly but when they came up again they were very sharp. 'From what we have so far it would seem to me that our most effective defence would be character-led. The impossibility of someone as respectable, virtuous and fragile as Mrs Wellesley committing such a heinous crime; how her life has been exemplary, etcetera etcetera; how it would have been

326

completely out of character for her to hurt a fly; how she, a chronic asthmatic, was seen to suffer no anxiety or nerves or other ill-effects at the time of the crime, and indeed appeared perfectly normal in every respect. Your brother, Mr Wellesley, will be an excellent witness in that regard, having seen both of you that Saturday evening. Then, on the practical side, if Mrs Wellesley had committed this terrible crime, why was she not covered in blood? Indeed, how could she have appeared later that evening without so much as a bloodstain on her? You will attest, Mr Wellesley, as to how normal and indeed immaculate she looked. And so on, and so on. In this way we would hope to appeal to both the hearts and the minds of the jury, we would hope to cast some doubt on the evidence of the eyewitness. We would *chip* away. We would be going for the reasonable doubt. And don't forget – that's all we need: reasonable doubt.'

Tingwall piped up, 'The old-style committal, are you ruling that out then?'

'We have to balance the likely benefits against the more certain costs,' Grainger ventured with an air of great sagacity. 'It all hinges on this eyewitness. If we want to gamble on his unreliability – and I use the word "gamble" advisedly – then we should go for the old-style committal. The stakes would be high. If he turned out to be an uncertain witness, we stand to gain everything – the total collapse of the Crown's case. But if he turned out to be an unassailable witness then we would gain very little – at the great expense of having revealed much of our defence. A risky business indeed. The *alternative* is to play safe. To keep our cards close to our chest, to hope to catch the prosecution off-guard, and to go for the hearts and minds of a jury in the way I described – in which case we should wait.'

'So what's your advice?' I asked.

He tapped his fingers together while he thought about it. 'It's hard to give such a thing as *advice* when one is dealing with a key eyewitness who is by definition an unknown quantity. However, going by the witness statement . . .' He looked upwards as though searching for a last drop of inspiration. '. . . my instinct – and that's another word I use advisedly – my *instinct* would be to let it go to trial. Trust to the twelve good men and women, and maintain our element of surprise.'

I asked, 'When do we have to make up our minds?'

Grainger addressed Tingwall. 'Perhaps you would like to discuss the matter further with Mrs Wellesley, come back to me with any questions, and perhaps we can make a decision in the next week or so?'

We all stood up and Grainger moved fluidly to open the door. Ginny paused beside Grainger and said in an undertone, 'I have one question.' She frowned over the thought. 'If Old Gordon is a good witness, if he's going to be absolutely certain that he saw me, then . . . wouldn't I do better to plead guilty?'

'Absolutely not,' I protested over the taut silence which followed.

Grainger observed Ginny for a long moment. 'In some cases a guilty plea to a lesser charge can prove the best course. But, Mrs Wellesley' – he fixed her with cold eyes – 'only *you* can decide if this option is open to us.'

*

'Why on earth did you say that?' I demanded, taking an aggressive weave through the traffic.

Ginny looked ahead, her profile unreadable. 'Because in the end it might be best.'

'But you can't plead guilty to something you didn't do. It's ridiculous.'

'It could be the least bad thing to do. You heard what he said.' And there was a nervy finality in her voice, an attempt to shut me out.

'The least bad thing. For Christ's sake, Ginny – how can you even *think* of it?' I kept glancing across at her but she didn't reply. 'Promise me you won't even think of it.'

'But Old Gordon was there,' she argued finally. 'He saw me all right. He even nodded to me. We were just feet apart. He's not going to be mistaken in court.'

'Ginny, *for heaven's sake* – it's still early days yet. Anything could happen. All sorts of things might turn up. I don't know –

328

witnesses, somebody who ... somebody who ...' I broke off in sudden misery, knowing I couldn't put the problem of David off any longer. I had spent most of the last two days persuading myself that there was no point in dragging him into our nightmare, that he had nothing to contribute to Ginny's case. Yet his story had left out too much, the gaps and evasions left me with the wretched suspicion that he had given me something less than the truth.

Grasping some of my turmoil, Ginny had turned to look at me. I hadn't told her about David, partly because I'd been coming to terms with it, partly because the implications of what he'd told me had frightened me too much. 'Listen, something's come up,' I began unhappily. 'I didn't have the chance to tell you before. Well – I *did*,' I admitted, 'but I couldn't, I was feeling too bloody sick about it, too ... The thing is' – and my throat tightened, I could hardly say it – 'I wasn't the only one having an affair with Sylvie.' I felt a fresh surge of incredulity. '*David* was. David was having a great big affair with Sylvie. All the way through last winter and most of the summer too. They used to meet on the boat – some of the time, anyway. And I think—' I had to force the words out: 'I think he was on the boat that day. At least he didn't deny it, for Christ's sake! I think he was there, and I think – oh *shit!*' And suddenly all my emotions shot to the surface and I couldn't see the road, it had become so blurred.

'Stop,' Ginny begged, casting nervous glances at the speeding traffic. 'Stop, *please.*'

I drew into the kerb amid a storm of protesting horns. I pulled out a handkerchief and rubbed it furiously across my eyes.

'*David?*' Ginny echoed as though she'd only just understood what I was saying. 'All through the winter?'

'The summer too.'

She digested this. 'It was serious then.'

'Serious? Well,' I scoffed, 'I don't think it was *love* exactly. From what he told me, more like lust. Lust and drugs. He used to supply her with drugs.' I had made it sound sordid, but then maybe I had intended to. 'He swears there was no more to it, he swears it was just an affair, he says it fizzled out. All I bloody know is that they met on the boat regularly and he didn't bloody deny he was there that day. He didn't – *Christ*, I don't know!' I suppressed a fresh burst of emotion. 'If he's lied to me I'll bloody kill him.' And even as I said it I felt the old ache of responsibility, the old instinct to defend him.

Ginny was looking blankly ahead. 'Tell me,' she murmured in a reminiscent tone, 'what was so special about her? What was it that made you both forget everything – everybody – else?'

I blew my nose savagely, I took my time but in the end I could only say, 'I don't know.' I added, 'But perhaps that was it, perhaps it was the very fact that she was impossible to know, that she was anything you wanted her to be. She gave this great impression of freedom, of anything being possible.'

Ginny gave an ironic murmur as if to say: And I didn't, I suppose; I was the one who held you back.

'And the sex?' she asked calmly. 'Was that especially terrific?'

There are some truths that must never be told. Bracing myself for the lie, I replied, 'I think it was like they say – it's the secretiveness of these things that gives them an edge, the danger of discovery. So, in that way – yes, it was exciting, I suppose.'

'She didn't do anything amazing that I didn't do?'

'No,' I said, trying to push pictures of Sylvie at her most adventurous and uninhibited from my mind. 'Nothing like that.'

'*David.*' Turning the idea over in her mind again, she shook her head. 'He always seemed so – immune. So unemotional. Well – she must have had something.'

I thought: What she had was allure without conscience.

Ginny took a puff on her inhaler and coughed a few times. A new phalanx of traffic roared past and the noise seemed to invade the car. I restarted the engine and pulled out.

Ginny asked unsteadily, 'So you think that . . . ?'

'I don't know what to think!'

She kept looking at me. 'What will you do?'

Making up my mind, I said, 'I'll go and see him.'

'And then?'

'And then I have no idea!' I answered sharply, not wanting to imagine what would happen to David's life if he were interviewed by the police.

She was quiet for a time, then: 'Don't assume too much, will you?'

Jerking my head round, I almost jumped a red light. 'What do you mean?'

'Don't think the worst.'

'I'm not thinking anything!' I exclaimed, feeling a dart of indignation because she had touched on the truth.

*

As we came up the drive in the twilight the figure of Julia appeared at the front door with three brilliantly coloured helium balloons in one hand and a bottle of champagne in the other. She waved them energetically and called out to us, 'The deal's been done!' Then with upstretched arms, in loud theatrical tones as if announcing it to the whole county: 'Hartford is yours!'

'Good God,' I laughed uncertainly.

'The most deserved event of the year!' And she hugged me enthusiastically, champagne, balloons and all. 'George just called. It's in the bag!' She went to embrace Ginny. *'And . . .'* She made another grandiose gesture, a flourish of both arms. 'You have exchanged contracts on the house. It was sold at three this afternoon. I tell you – it's all happening!'

I smiled because everyone else was smiling, and because deep down I did feel glad: glad for George and everyone else at Hartford, glad for Ginny because she could finally get to grips with the move, and, if I thought about it, glad for myself, though, in the shadow of everything else that was going on, the pleasure emerged as a rather pale and inconsequential emotion.

David's surgery said he was out on a call, so I left a message on his pager, and then, with some hesitation, tried Furze Lodge.

Mary answered. 'I gather hearty congratulations are in order!' she cried. 'I'm *so* delighted, Hugh! What a triumph! You must be thrilled!'

'I am. All thanks to you, Mary.'

'Well . . . I'm proud to be part of it all, Hugh. *Proud.* And I know you'll make a success of it. I never had any doubts.'

'I'll do my best.'

331

'You must be over the moon!'

'Yes.'

Her tone shifted. 'You don't *sound* very happy.'

'I'm just incredibly tired, that's all. Hasn't sunk in yet.' I tried to relax my voice as I said, 'Is David around tonight?'

'Tonight? Hang on ... The diary, the diary.' She made searching noises. 'Here we are ... He's in after seven-thirty. In theory anyway.'

'If you speak to him, can you tell him I need to see him?'

'What – tonight?'

'I should be with you about eight.'

A short pause. 'Can I say what it's about?' And her voice was taut with curiosity.

'Oh – just—' I said the first thing that came into my head. 'A legal thing.'

'To do with the buyout?'

Feeling cornered, I said, 'Pa's estate, actually.'

'Pa's *estate?*' She didn't try to hide her surprise. 'And it's urgent?'

'I want to get it out of the way.'

'But you sound so grim, Hugh. Is there something the matter? Not Ginny, I hope?'

'No. No, really.'

'Well, if you don't want to tell me ...'

'Nothing to tell,' I said stubbornly.

Her reproach hung in the air. 'You'll have some supper at least?' she said.

'No, Mary.'

'I'll tell David you're coming then.' And when she rang off her tone contained a note of faint injury.

I stayed long enough to make a quick congratulatory call to George, who from the sound of it was holding a party for the entire Hartford staff, and to glance through the mail and messages, which Julia had laid out in order of importance. I skimmed the letters until I came to an unopened envelope marked Strictly Private. It was from Jones. I sat down and read it quickly, then again more carefully. '... *nothing has happened to change my original opinion ... she has developed severe paranoid delusions with marked persecutory tendencies . . . increasingly retreating into unreality . . . convincing herself of plots, including the notion that I am opposed to her and scheming to give evidence against her. I am concerned that if she continues to refuse medication she may suffer a major crisis . . .'*

With a chill in my heart, I read the letter a third time before locking it away in a drawer.

Charged with a new sense of urgency, I went through to the sitting room to find Ginny.

She looked up from her conversation with Julia. 'You're going now? It wouldn't be better to wait until tomorrow?'

'No. No, I must go now.'

She tilted her head to be kissed.

I asked, 'You'll be all right?' Feeling traitorous, I examined her expression for signs of impending crisis.

Sensing this or something close to it, Ginny frowned, 'I'll be fine.'

'I'll bag a bed for the night, if that's all right,' Julia announced from the far side of the room. 'Not safe on the roads.' She raised her glass and cast me a meaningful look.

Ginny got up suddenly and followed me into the hall. 'You won't forget,' she breathed nervously.

'What about?'

'About keeping an open mind.'

'You make me feel that I'm being unreasonable,' I said accusingly. 'For Christ's sake, Ginny, somebody killed Sylvie!'

She dropped her eyes. 'Yes.' She kissed me again and her lips were cold against my cheek.

*

'He's been delayed. Some emergency.' Mary closed the door behind me. 'Come and have a large drink. You must be exhausted.'

She led the way into the drawing room and threw open the drinks cupboard.

'Whisky,' I said. 'Please.'

She poured a glass and, bringing it over, came up very close and smiled up into my face. 'Now what on earth's this about?' she asked. 'What's the matter?'

'The matter?'

'Why you're here.'

'I told you.'

'Come on.' She cast me a reproving smile that suggested I could do better than that.

I exhaled unhappily. 'It's rather complicated, Mary.'

'You can tell me, surely,' she said coaxingly. 'David and I have no secrets.'

I felt like saying: Everyone has secrets. Instead I murmured, 'In that case he can tell you himself, can't he?' I hadn't meant to sound dismissive, I raised my hand as if to take it back, but a purposeful expression had already settled over Mary's face. Taking my hand, she led me to a chair by the fireside and, pulling up a stool, sat facing me, knee to knee, as she had done all those weeks ago at Dittisham House. Recalling my uninhibited outpourings about Sylvie, I felt an abrupt and belated vulnerability, a sense of having disclosed too much.

'Hugh . . .' She flashed me one of her warmest smiles. 'You're very dear to me, you know. After David and the children . . . well, you're probably the most *precious* person in the whole world to me. I want you to be all right, I want you to be happy, I want you and Ginny to be over this whole ghastly business.' The smile again, which somehow failed to illuminate her heavy features. 'But Hugh darling' – a dipping of the voice – 'it would be quite wrong of you to think that David has the answer to your problems.' Her avid eyes searched my face to see if I had grasped her message.

She had caught me totally off-balance. 'My problems? I don't understand,' I stammered, having a suspicion that I might understand rather too well.

She gave me an appraising look and began again. 'Hugh darling – I believe you have ideas about David that are quite mistaken.'

'Do I?'

'*Indeed* you do,' she said firmly. Then, disdainfully: 'Oh, he got waylaid by that woman' – she gave a scornful laugh – 'if that's the right expression. He had his head turned – but then I don't need to tell *you* about that. But that's *all*, Hugh.' She shook her head emphatically. 'That's *all*.'

I stared at her. 'You knew?'

'Of course,' she declared with a touch of pride. 'All that stuff about a wife being the last to know? Well, I knew immediately. I may be many things, but I'm not stupid. There were a thousand things.' She gave a tiny snort. 'I knew.'

'You never said anything?'

'Oh *no*. The thing was bound to burn itself out quickly enough. She was such a user, wasn't she? Off to the next man, off to the next meal ticket. I knew she'd disappear sooner or later.' She gave a dismissive shrug. 'And I was right. She ditched him, didn't she? Oh, he was upset for a while, went around looking like a whipped dog, but it was just his pride, wasn't it? Feeling his age, needing to know he could still *pull the chicks*' – she used the expression derisively, with a roll of the eyes – 'all that stuff. He was over it in no time. I knew he would be. But Hugh –' she leant forward, arms on knees, eyes locked on mine '– that's all it was. He doesn't deserve to have his career ruined, his life wrecked. He doesn't.'

I felt a terrible tension, a warring of instincts and loyalties. I screwed up my face and managed to say, 'But *someone* was on the boat that day.'

She gave me a soft pitying look. 'Not David, Hugh. Couldn't have been. He was seeing patients all morning, and then he had lunch with me, and then he went to a partners' meeting which lasted most of the afternoon.' She was very gentle with me now. 'There wasn't a moment of his day which wasn't accounted for.'

Part of me tried to accept this, but another confused part of me wanted to shout: But you're bound to say that, aren't you?

'I know the way it must look to you,' Mary conceded with the same patient note of understanding, 'but I *promise* you – he wasn't there. He couldn't have been there.'

I can't have looked terribly convinced because a spark of exasperation passed over her face and she argued with more determination, 'You would be ruining his life, Hugh! And for what? For an *affair*. With someone like *that*. It's too ghastly. Too – unfair. Don't repay me this way, Hugh – *please*.'

I felt a sudden coldness. 'Repay you?'

She dropped her eyes and fanned her fingers as if to withdraw the remark. 'Just promise me,' she said, returning her gaze to mine. 'Promise me you won't ruin his life – *our* lives – for *nothing*.'

I thought of Ginny, I thought of everything we had been through, and I hardened my heart. 'I can't promise that, Mary. I just can't.'

A succession of violent emotions passed over Mary's face, her features seemed to swell. Finally she said in a voice that trembled with feeling, 'I've gone out on a limb for you, Hugh. I've protected you, supported you, *lied* for you. Don't do this to me. Don't repay me this way.'

'If it's a question of repayment,' I said tightly. 'You can keep the money. I don't care about the money.'

She threw me a furious look. 'It's not the *money*, for God's sake.'

We glared at each other, separated by the depth of our misunderstanding.

'*Lied*,' I echoed as her words came back to me. 'I'm sorry you feel you had to *lie* for me as well.'

'Not for *you*.'

'Who for then?'

She shook her head, as though she had already said too much. 'Leave it. Please. Let's just leave it.'

But something in her manner drew me forward, a suggestion of momentous revelations, and I was filled with a strange beating fear. 'You can't say something like that and expect me to ignore it.'

She kept shaking her head. 'If only you could understand that David wasn't involved. If only you could *believe* me, then—' Her eyes sparkled with unshed tears. I had never seen her upset before.

'Mary, don't.'

'I'm sorry,' she said, pulling herself together with an effort. 'I didn't mean to . . .' She fumbled in her sleeve for a handkerchief. 'But Hugh – promise me, please.'

'I can't do that, Mary. I can't promise something like that.'

She gave a shudder that shook her whole body. 'How I wish I didn't have to do this!' she cried. 'I never wanted to have to *say* anything – ever! Ever! I wanted to *save* you that at least. Oh Hugh, how I wish—' She sniffed hard and wiped her eyes, and when she looked up again her makeup had run, a streak of blue that leached down one cheek. 'And, believe me, you *must* believe me, it's *not* an either-or thing – I would *hate* you to think that! It's not as if I'd *ever* go to the police! I'd rather die! I'd rather die than tell them! But Hugh – you *have* to understand that it wasn't David! You *have* to realise!'

As she made her circuitous way towards the point, my sense of foreboding grew.

Mary said again, 'I'd never tell! Never!' Calming herself visibly, she dabbed her eyes again. 'In fact, I'd lie to them again. I'd lie to them every time.' She took a sharp breath. 'I did lie, you see. I lied to them straight away. When David and I gave our fingerprints to the police, they asked me about the day the woman died, whether I knew anything, whether I'd seen anything. And I said I hadn't. But – it wasn't true.' She paused and looked at me in anguish, as if we might yet escape this moment of truth. 'I saw Ginny, you see. I was at Dittisham House with Mrs Perry, and I saw Ginny.'

I kept staring at her.

'I was up in David's old room,' she began slowly. 'I looked out at the river and I saw a dinghy tied up to *Ellie*. I knew it couldn't be David – he was at the partners' meeting. I thought maybe it was someone from the yard. There were some binoculars there by the window. I was looking through them when I saw someone come up on deck.' She gave a tiny shudder. 'It was the woman. There was no mistaking her – the long hair, the tight clothes. It was definitely her. I thought – well, you can imagine. I thought she was hanging around in the hope of seeing David. I thought she was trying to get him back or something. I was ready to get hopping mad. But then – *then* – oh, *Hugh*.' Mary's face crumpled, she clenched her lips together, when she finally spoke her tone rose in despair. 'Ginny . . . came. In a dinghy. She . . . rowed up to the boat. She rowed up to the boat and . . . they talked, she and . . . *her*. For a minute or so. Then—' Her mouth moved but no words came.

'Then?'

She forced herself on. 'Then . . . Ginny climbed on board. And . . . they talked some more. I think they were— No,' she

337

suppressed some unspoken thought, 'no, I couldn't tell from that distance. No – they *talked*. And then . . .' Each word was dragged from her with terrible effort. 'Then . . . they both . . . went down below. Into the cabin.'

My mind was cold and clear, but my imagination was blurry. I saw the two figures climbing down the companionway, but they remained a long way off, I couldn't bring them into focus. I said, 'You're sure it was Ginny?'

Mary nodded sadly.

'From so far away?'

'Hugh, believe me, she was the *last* person I was expecting to see. I couldn't believe it at first, I kept looking. But that hair – no one else has hair like Ginny's, no one. And she was wearing that jacket of hers, the dark pink one – sort of raspberry-coloured. I'd remembered it, it was such a lovely jacket. And she had the same long floaty scarf she'd worn with it before, sort of cream and raspberry mixed. She wasn't really dressed for the water. So smart. And then she turned towards me.' She exhaled sharply. 'It was her.'

I didn't say anything for a while. 'Go on,' I murmured at last.

She continued in a flat voice, 'Oh . . . I waited a while, but Mrs Perry needed to get home and I had to get on. It was after five. I kept going back to the window, looking, but there was no sign of anybody. I thought – well, I didn't know what to think. Maybe that Ginny knew her, that they had arranged to . . .' Suddenly dissatisfied with this idea, she abandoned it with a small movement of her head. 'I had a last look before I left, but I couldn't see anything.' Her final words emerged as a murmur: 'Just the two dinghies.'

The silence that followed was broken only by the sound of Mary's sighs. 'Oh, Hugh,' she said at last, 'I'm so sorry you had to know.'

I pictured Ginny as she had appeared at Dittisham House that night, I saw the raspberry jacket and the long floaty scarf jammed halfway into one pocket, and a strange calm spread through me, and it was the calm that comes at the end of a long and troubled journey.

FIFTEEN

Like an icy hand the cold had stolen in off the blackness of the moor. Climbing out of bed I caught the glint of frost on the window panes. The freeze had begun two weeks after Christmas and, ten bitter days later, was showing no sign of a thaw. I felt my way to the bathroom and, turning on a light, peered blindly at my watch. Not yet seven. Pulling on a robe I went down the narrow cottage stairs to the boiler to see if I could entice it into action. I twisted the thermostat to and fro, checked the setting on the time controller and gave the pump a solid whack. With a shudder of complaint, the ancient furnace roared capriciously back into life.

The boiler wasn't the only primitive contraption in the rented cottage – the cooker was slow, the fridge antique – and in this weather the steep track leading up from the road was icy and treacherous, but Ginny liked the place, she felt safe here, and it was only twenty minutes from Hartford, so, all said, it still had a lot to recommend it. We wouldn't be here for very much longer anyway. With Melton gone and Glebe Place virtually sold and the various loans and mortgages almost settled, we could think about buying a new place in the spring. I spent a lot of my time on such practicalities nowadays, I positively overwhelmed myself with details of every kind. That way I maintained an illusion of usefulness.

Making myself some coffee in the still-unfamiliar kitchen, I heard creaking floorboards above and set out a tea tray for Ginny, with some fruit and a couple of Ryvita, which was about all she ate these days. I found her running a bath. Her nakedness alarmed me, she had grown so very thin, and I had to make an effort not to say anything. She greeted me with a pale smile.

'Would you like your tea here?' I asked.

'Please.'

The morning tea tray was one of our little rituals, along with Ginny's pretence at eating. Normally I was first in the bathroom so as to be ready to leave the house by eight, but since the committal proceedings had begun we had altered our timetable and now Ginny bathed first while I drank my coffee in front of the breakfast news.

'I'm out,' she announced ten minutes later, going past me to the wardrobe. 'I'm not sure what to wear. What do you think?'

We stood before the rail of clothes. We had already decided against anything too bright, and she had worn grey for the first day and navy blue for the second.

'The black?' I suggested.

'Mmm. But it needs something to soften it up a bit.' She pulled out a scarf in muted blues. 'What do you think?'

'Perfect.' But then Ginny always looked perfect. I thought of the stipendiary magistrate who had been sent down from London to hear the case, and, while he was doubtless the most scrupulous of men, I couldn't believe that he would be immune to appearances and that Ginny, with her frail understated femininity, wouldn't make a favourable impression.

When we had dressed we got ready to leave for Exeter. After two days these departures had also developed a certain ritual. I asked Ginny to check that she had two full inhalers with her; she asked me if I had my briefcase. I was certain she wouldn't be warm enough; she told me I worried too much. By such solicitous concern did we conduct our relationship, by such scrupulous consideration did we maintain a veneer of composure.

The track had been gritted but a fresh sprinkling of snow had formed an ice sheet in the night, and, though I took the slope very gingerly, I felt the wheels slip at the last turn. The next instant the back of the car thumped into the earth wall and we began to slither crabwise towards the road. At the last moment the brakes gripped and the car slid to a halt a couple of feet into the road. I reversed back onto the track just as a car sped past, blowing its horn.

'I'll get it gritted again,' I said when my nerves had quietened down a little.

Ginny had her head pressed against the back of the seat, eyes screwed up, breathing sharply.

'Are you all right?'

'Yup,' she rasped.

'Breathe,' I said. 'Keep it slow. Calm thoughts. Plenty of time. No hurry.' I made her unclench her fisted hands, I pressed her shoulders gently down, I lifted her coat collar higher around her neck.

She gave a small gasping laugh. 'What would I do without you?' Taking long steady draughts of air, she opened her eyes and turned her head towards me. 'I really don't know, you know – what I'd do without you. I certainly couldn't have gone ahead with the court thing. Not if you hadn't believed in me.' She lifted my hand and pressed it against her cheek. 'Sometimes I get the feeling that Grainger doesn't. Believe in me, I mean. Oh, he doesn't actually say anything of course, but ever since I asked him if I'd do better pleading guilty he's never quite looked me in the eye again. I think he thinks I *did it!*' She vamped the words and gave an ironic little laugh that didn't quite come off. 'And Charles,' she added with sudden bewilderment, 'sometimes I think he has his doubts as well.'

'That's just not true,' I argued, 'Charles has no doubts at all. Honestly.'

She frowned, not entirely sure whether she could take this protestation of honesty at face value. 'Anyway,' she said with forced brightness, 'you're the only person who matters. So long as you believe in me, then the rest of the world can—' She dismissed the rest of the world with a shake of her head.

I maintained my gaze as best I could. I couldn't think of anything to say.

She brought her face close to mine. 'Thank you, darling. Thank you for giving me the most important thing of all.'

I saw the need in her eyes, and the vulnerability, and my mouth jerked into a smile, I gave an indeterminate shrug. 'Dear heart,' I murmured, gripped by emotions so disturbing that it was all I could do to keep them out of my face.

'Love you,' she said fiercely.

'Love you too.'

Her eyes didn't leave my face but took on a glint of faint puzzlement, as though she had caught something in my expression which confused her.

I said quickly, 'It'll be all right, darling. I have a feeling about it.'

Her lids fluttered, she nodded jerkily, then, hugging her arms against her body, settled back in her seat.

I fumbled with the heating controls and we set off again. Worried about ice, I concentrated hard on my driving, but the road had been salted, it seemed safe enough, and when we had been silent for some time I offered, 'I'm sure you're wrong about Grainger, you know. I think he's right with you.'

She thought about this. 'Oh, he may be with me. But that's not quite the same as believing in me, is it?'

'Well, he seems optimistic enough. I think he's glad you decided on the committal.'

'Oh he just likes the gamble, whatever he may say,' Ginny remarked, loosing one of her perceptive darts. 'He enjoys the risk.'

I had been careful to take a back seat in the decision over the full committal. I had left Ginny to talk the whole thing through with Tingwall and said almost nothing during a second conference with Grainger. I had listened to Ginny's agonised deliberations, I had commiserated with her dilemma, but I had managed to offer no firm opinion. I felt the loneliness of the priest who has heard too much and must now remain silent.

Once the decision to go for the full committal had been taken and the date set, Ginny had started to show signs of strain, as if she had only just appreciated what lay ahead. She had spent the intervening weeks fighting asthma and other obscure nervous attacks which frequently sent her to bed for hours at a time. The weight had continued to drop off her, and the fluttering of her eyelids had become more pronounced. Often she cried out during the night, sudden shouts that had me waking with a racing heart.

Yet as we walked into Tingwall's office none of this was apparent. She assumed her public mask, a look of serenity and

342

quiet acceptance, and I could only wonder at her extraordinary self-control.

Tingwall was also showing his nerves. As we sat down for our daily recap, he didn't so much smile as expose his teeth, and his eyes danced excitedly. 'So, all the police evidence is out of the way now. I thought Grainger made some good points off Inspector Henderson yesterday. Getting him to admit that you had been totally consistent in everything you'd said, Ginny. That you'd never made a single admission in all those hours of questioning. And asking him how he thought a woman of your build might have lifted a body up a steep ladder – well, it all adds up.' He bared his teeth again in the semblance of a smile. 'But the main thing, of course, is the lack of forensic evidence. That will hardly have gone unnoticed. So!' He clasped his hands together, a troop leader boosting morale. 'It's just the eyewitness now.'

The *just* lingered uncomfortably in the air, and Tingwall quickly corrected himself. 'It's Gordon Latimer now.'

I asked, 'Will his evidence take long?'

'Impossible to say. And then there'll be Grainger's cross-examination. Really impossible to say. But I can try to get the occasional message out to you.'

I made my usual face. 'Thanks.' As a defence witness I was not permitted to sit in court, so rather than hang around the door in a state of anxiety I had spent much of the last two days at a nearby hotel, doing business on the phone and waiting for occasional calls from Tingwall's assistant.

At twenty to ten Tingwall drove us to the court. As the building came into sight Ginny delved into her bag and took a puff of her inhalant. She had not forgotten the mass of press who had greeted our first appearance on Monday morning, thrusting their lenses against the car windows and jostling us as we entered the building. Ginny hadn't attempted to hide her face. We had decided that, as someone with nothing to hide, she should hold her head high. But the aggressiveness of their behaviour had shaken her and once inside she'd suffered a massive asthma attack.

There was only one photographer today, a down-at-heel man in a faded anorak who waited until we had got out of the car before taking a few desultory pictures. Inside the building we were left alone: for this hearing reporting restrictions were in place, and no word of the proceedings nor comment of any sort was permitted to be published.

In the hall was a motley gathering: defendants and their supporters destined for other courts – according to Tingwall mainly traffic offenders and TV licence evaders, with a sprinkling of shoplifters and drunks; and then, to one side, Henderson and his henchmen in their best suits, watching us with their unblinking policemen's eyes; and, far to the other side, visible in an adjacent lobby, Grainger, holding court with his junior and Tingwall's assistant.

Grainger greeted us with his usual air of melancholic authority. 'The Crown present their Mr *Latimer* today. Now, Mrs Wellesley, my cross-examination could be long and detailed, but don't be surprised if it is rather less comprehensive, covering only a few major points. Much will depend on how the witness appears, and the strength of his evidence. You appreciate?' He cast a peremptory glance over us all, looking for questions but expecting none. 'All must be decided as the situation reveals itself . . .'

My attention was diverted by the sight of a figure making his way perilously across the hall, a man who was both familiar and strange, someone I knew but couldn't place. It was another moment before I realised with a slight shock that the emaciated bow-backed figure was Old Gordon. His tweeds may have fitted him in younger sturdier days, but now they hung on him like sacking. He walked unsteadily, with a marked shuffle, and leant heavily on his companion, a middle-aged woman whom I dimly recognised as his daughter. It was hard to believe it was the same man I had last seen a year ago at my father's funeral. He seemed to have aged twenty years. His narrow skull was exceptionally bony and his sparse lifeless hair floated above it like down. The skin hung heavily on his cadaverous face and his pouchy eyes had the watery look of advanced sickness.

Grainger must have caught some of my astonishment because when I looked back at him he raised a mildly inquisitive eyebrow.

I said in an undertone, 'Gordon Latimer.'

He followed my gaze. 'The one leaning on the woman?'

'Yes.'

He watched while Old Gordon took a seat, and when he turned back to me a closed uncommunicative expression had settled over his face. 'You're sure?'

'Yes. Though he looks absolutely terrible, poor chap. I can't believe it.'

Grainger murmured as though to himself but pitched for my hearing too, 'Nothing is certain in this life but uncertainty.'

Without explaining this, he summoned his team and moved towards the court. Ginny and I embraced briefly. Watching Tingwall lead her away I couldn't rid myself of a creeping unease, an irrational sense of approaching doom.

A familiar voice said, 'Hi there,' and Julia swooped up to peck my cheek.

'What are you doing here? I thought you had a decent job to go to.'

'Decent jobs – curse of the upwardly mobile. No, I thought I'd come and see if I could be useful.'

'Not a lot to be done,' I said flatly. Then: 'Have you been fired or something?' She'd only started her new job two months before.

'Not that I know of,' she said airily. 'No – I'm on sick leave. I've got flu.'

I peered at her. 'I'm sorry.'

She touched my arm. 'Hugh – not really.'

'Oh. *Oh.* Sorry, I'm a bit slow today.'

'Come and have a coffee.'

There was a trolley selling drinks and snacks, and we carried two cups of watery coffee to a corner.

'How are things at Hartford?' Julia asked.

'Umm . . .' It was an effort to think of Hartford. 'Pretty good. No – *more* than good. Orders up twenty per cent. Packenhams have re-listed us – did I tell you?' She nodded. 'They even gave us a window display at Christmas. And . . . well, the staff have been wonderful. Productivity up. Costs down . . .' I trailed off, easily distracted.

'So ya-boo to Howard!' Julia crowed.

But I was hardly listening. I was watching Old Gordon, and my disquiet returned, a niggling worry that I couldn't quite name.

'Would you do something for me, Julia? Would you go and sit in the court when it starts and come and tell me what's happening?'

'You'll be here?'

In saying yes I realised I had taken the decision not to go and work from the hotel.

'Do you want full notes or—'

'No – just the gist of it.'

She gestured towards the people accumulating around the entrance to the court. 'Never mind about later,' she growled. 'I'd better go now if I'm to get a seat.' She hurried away and, sweeping past the queue, spoke to the usher and, without seeming to incur any objections, stationed herself at the head of the line.

I was about to go and find a quiet corner when I glanced back and paused. Julia had turned to talk to another woman just behind her, and the woman was Mary. I kept looking, I waited until the woman turned her head again, but there was no doubt about it. For an instant I felt put out, even a little indignant, that she should have turned up without telling us. In the next instant I was ashamed of such uncharitable thoughts. Mary would be here out of the best of motives, to support us, and as if to confirm it she turned and, catching sight of me, clasped her hands together in a gesture of encouragement and solidarity. I waved back.

When the hall was almost deserted I chose a seat not far from Old Gordon. The old man was hunched in his chair, staring vacantly at the floor. When his daughter spoke to him he lifted his rheumy eyes and peered vacantly about him. His gaze passed over me without focus or recognition.

An usher called his name. His daughter roused him and helped him to his feet. Watching him walk arthritically into the court, my disquiet took new shape, bringing regular beats of alarm that had me on my feet, then sitting again, then pacing restlessly up and down until Julia finally emerged twenty minutes later.

'He's very doddery,' she whispered, 'and a bit vague. I wouldn't say he was doing too well.'

'Where are you sitting?'

She gave me a sharp look. 'Me? At this end, in the back row, by the door. Why?'

'Who's next to you?'

'No one special.' Reading my mind only too well, she hissed, 'Look, is this a good idea?'

'Choose a moment when there's something going on. Some distraction.'

'I really don't think this is a good idea,' she muttered as she went back into the court. Two minutes later she reappeared and waved me hastily past her and through a second door, which led into the public gallery.

My arrival went unnoticed amid some general movement in the court. Only one head turned as I sat down. Some sixth sense had made Mary glance round from her place in the front row of the gallery. Her eyes widened slightly at the sight of me, then with a quick bright smile she looked away again.

I slid down in my seat and shaded my eyes with one hand. In the witness box to one side of the room Old Gordon was settling himself on a chair and being offered a glass of water. Ginny was sitting in the dock with her back to me. Ahead of her were the lawyers, also with their backs to me. Only the magistrate was facing the gallery.

The magistrate leant forward. 'Are you well enough to continue, Mr Latimer?'

The old man's eyes swivelled nervously. 'Aye.'

The magistrate, an owl-faced man with pebble glasses and thick grey hair, nodded to the prosecuting counsel, who rose to his feet.

'Mr Latimer, could you once again cast your mind back to the thirtieth of September last year?' the prosecutor began. 'You were telling us where you were in the afternoon at approximately five o'clock. You said you were down by the ferry, is that right?'

Old Gordon appeared to concentrate hard. 'By the ferry, aye.' His voice was thin and reedy and breathless.

'When you say the ferry, Mr Latimer, you mean the ferry that crosses the River Dart from Dittisham village?'

The old man's mouth moved several times before murmuring: 'Aye.'

'Mr Latimer, what were you doing there by the ferry that day?'

Gordon's hooded lids blinked heavily and his jaw slackened,

and it seemed to me that he was having difficulty in comprehending even the most basic question.

'Sitting,' he muttered at last.

'You were sitting where exactly?'

Gordon's eyes wandered anxiously. 'By the pub.' Then after another pause: 'Always sit by the pub.'

'This is the pub called the Ferry Boat Inn?'

Another pause. 'Aye.'

'You were sitting on a bench, were you?'

He nodded distractedly.

'If you could say yes or no, Mr Latimer,' the prosecutor reminded him gently.

Gordon hesitated for a long moment, as though he had forgotten the question. 'Aye,' he said finally.

'Thank you. And this bench overlooks the ferry pontoon?'

The old man seemed beset by a growing air of apprehension, as if each question were leading him further on to perilous ground. 'Aye.'

'While you were sitting on the bench that day, could you please tell us what you saw?'

'Saw ... Mrs Wellesley,' he whispered, and his eyes were agitated.

'You mean Mrs Virginia Wellesley?'

The pause stretched out.

'Mr Latimer? This person was Mrs Virginia Wellesley?'

'Mrs Hugh,' Gordon said at last.

'By that you mean Mrs Hugh Wellesley? Virginia Wellesley?'

This seemed to confuse him for a moment. 'Mrs Hugh,' he repeated in a voice that was increasingly quavery and fearful.

'Quite. Mrs Hugh Wellesley. Do you see her in court, Mr Latimer?'

The rheumy eyes registered something like bafflement, the mouth began a gasping fish-like motion.

'Mr Latimer, do you see Mrs Wellesley in court?'

A measure of understanding dawned. He began to cast about uncertainly. His glance came past the gallery, stopped momentarily before drifting away and roaming the room. Screwing up his eyes, leaning forward slightly as if to focus better, his gaze finally settled on the dock. 'Aye.'

'You can see Mrs Wellesley? Could you point her out to us, please, Mr Latimer?'

Gordon raised a hooked finger at Ginny.

'Let it be shown that Mr Latimer was indicating the defendant. Now, Mr Latimer, could you tell us what Mrs Wellesley was doing when you saw her that day?'

The jaw sagged again. The effort of memory seemed almost beyond him. 'A boat. Took a boat.'

'Did you see her go to this boat?'

Pause. 'Aye.'

'Where was she when you first saw her?'

His brows pulled down, he seemed to glower.

The prosecutor tried again. 'Did she pass close by you?'

Gordon gave a slight nod. With the bent shoulders and gaping mouth, with the bony head hanging forward on the scrawny neck, he had the look of an ancient bird.

'Was that a yes, Mr Latimer? If you wouldn't mind speaking out . . .' Getting no response, the prosecutor urged, 'Did she pass close to you, Mr Latimer? If you could say yes or no?'

'Yes.'

'How close would you say?'

This question troubled him. 'Close,' he offered tentatively.

'As far as she is from you now, in this courtroom? Further? Nearer?'

'Same.'

'So, two yards at the most. And did you get a good look at her?'

'Aye – Mrs Hugh.'

'You were sure it was her?'

The eyes were fearful again. 'Aye.'

'Now this boat she went to, what kind of a boat was it?'

He thought for a long moment. 'Small boat.'

'A rowing boat perhaps?'

He nodded vaguely.

'Was it a rowing boat? If you could just say yes or no, Mr Latimer?'

'Aye . . . yes.'

'And Mrs Wellesley went off in it, you said?'

Another pause: 'Aye.' The old man reached out for the glass of water. The prosecutor waited while he grasped it with clawed hands and brought the rim unsteadily to his lips. As he drank, water spilled down his chin and fell onto his jacket. An usher came forward and took the glass from him and placed it back on one side. Old Gordon made no attempt to mop up the spilt water and it formed a darkening stain on his lapel.

The prosecutor continued, 'So she rowed off, did she, Mr Latimer?'

Old Gordon's concentration seemed to have drifted again, and the question had to be put to him a second time. 'Aye,' he said at last.

The magistrate, who had been making notes much of the time, was now watching Gordon intently.

'Which direction did she row off in?' asked the prosecutor.

Silence.

'Was it up river, or down river, or across river?'

Gordon frowned a great deal before breathing, 'Up.'

'Up. She rowed off *up* river.' The prosecutor glanced down at his papers and, coming to what looked like an abrupt decision, said, 'Thank you, Mr Latimer,' and, nodding to the bench, sat down.

Grainger rose to his feet. 'Mr Latimer,' he began in a kind unhurried tone, 'you are fond of sitting there by the pub, are you?'

Pause. 'Aye.'

'You like to watch the world go by?'

The empty colourless eyes seemed to focus momentarily. 'Aye.'

'And there's quite a bit to see, is there? The ferry, the pleasure boats coming and going, and so on?'

A whisper. 'Aye.'

'You go there regularly?'

Grimacing, Gordon sucked in his thin lips. 'Not so much.'

'Not so much now. What about last autumn, Mr Latimer, in September at the time you say you saw Mrs Wellesley on the pontoon – did you go there regularly then?'

Much thought again. 'Some.'

'How often did you go in a week, Mr Latimer?'

350

The troubled look again, the groping for words. 'Sundays. Other times. When it were fine.'

'You would invariably go on a Sunday?'

'When it were fine.'

'So last autumn, if it was fine, you would go on a Sunday. And other days too, if it was fine?'

The old boy was flagging. His shoulders bowed further, his chin descended almost to his chest. 'Aye.' And it was little more than a gasp.

'I'm so sorry – did you say yes, Mr Latimer?'

'Aye – yes.'

'So how often might you go and sit by the pub then, Mr Latimer? As often as three times a week? Four? If it was fine.'

He had to think about that for a long time. 'Sundays. Tuesdays sometimes. An' Fridays.'

'As many as three days a week then? What about Saturdays?'

Gordon seemed uncertain about that.

'Did you go there on Saturdays at all?'

'At my daughter Saturdays.'

'Ah. So you generally visited your daughter on Saturdays?' A pause. 'Have I got that right?'

Gordon's mouth began to work in increasing agitation. 'Aye, to my daughter.'

'Where does your daughter live, Mr Latimer?'

Another long pause. 'Primrose Cottage.'

'That's in Dittisham village, is it?' When he had his reply Grainger said in a pleasant almost reminiscent tone, 'So on a day when you went to visit her, you would stay until what time?'

'Teatime. Leave after tea.'

'*After* tea? And what time did tea finish?'

This was the one answer which came without hesitation. 'Half past six.'

'So on the days you visited your daughter you wouldn't leave until after six-thirty?'

'Aye.'

'Now on a day you went to see your daughter, would you also find the time to go and sit by the pub?'

The old man looked thoroughly bemused at this. His pale eyes cast anxiously about, his mouth drooped at the corners and his lower jaw reverted to its strange gasping motion.

Grainger repeated the question carefully.

No one moved. The court seemed to hold its collective breath.

Finally the thin voice rasped, 'At my daughter Saturdays.'

'Forgive me,' Grainger said, selecting a compassionate tone, 'I just need to be clear. Last September you were in the habit of visiting your daughter every Saturday until seven. So are we to understand that you never went and sat by the pub on a Saturday?'

The old man's face crumpled further, he seemed thoroughly confused. Eventually he gave an odd movement of his head.

'Can I take that as a yes, Mr Latimer?'

Another indeterminate movement.

Grainger turned towards the bench, as though for assistance. The magistrate leant forward and said in the ringing tones that people usually reserve for the deaf, 'Mr Latimer, do you understand the question?'

Old Gordon's mouth went through its frantic motions.

'I'll ask Mr Grainger to put it to you one more time, shall I? Mr Grainger, if you please.'

Grainger repeated, 'Last September you were in the habit of visiting your daughter every Saturday until seven. Can we take it, then, that you never went and sat by the Ferry Boat Inn on a Saturday?'

Old Gordon closed his mouth and nodded distinctly. 'Aye.'

'Thank you.' And Grainger's tone left no doubt that he had made his point. 'Now, Mr Latimer, if I may I'd like to take you back to the occasion when you saw Mrs Wellesley setting off in the boat. Which day of the week was that?'

It was as though the old man suddenly appreciated his predicament. He became increasingly distressed, his face contorted into a grimace of woe and confusion, his mouth wobbled. Finally he shook his head.

The tension was like an electric charge. My mind told me that it was all over, logic insisted that we had won, but the consequences of this thought were so overwhelming that for the moment my emotions refused to follow.

Grainger was driving his advantage home. 'You can't say?' he repeated. 'So it could have been a Sunday?'

The old man lifted a bent hand to his chest as if his breathing were giving him trouble.

'So it might have been a Sunday?' Grainger pressed with the urgency of a man who senses he is running out of time. 'Mr Latimer?'

'Can't say.'

The magistrate leant forward. 'Mr Latimer, are you feeling unwell?'

'Can't say,' Gordon echoed miserably.

'Mr Latimer.' The magistrate raised his voice again. 'Are you feeling all right?'

'Can't remember like I used to,' Gordon cried plaintively.

'Is it your memory that's troubling you, Mr Latimer, or are you feeling unwell?'

'Memory . . . bad.'

'So apart from your memory you're feeling all right?'

Old Gordon nodded despairingly, and he seemed close to tears.

'In order that the court can be absolutely clear,' the magistrate continued with great deliberation, 'you are saying, Mr Latimer, that you cannot be sure which day of the week it was when you saw Mrs Wellesley go off in the boat?'

The old man's mouth turned down almost to his chin, he blinked rapidly and shook his head. 'Memory . . . it's terrible.'

The magistrate took his time writing his notes before looking towards Grainger. 'Any more questions, Mr Grainger?'

'No, sir.'

There was a pause as the usher helped Gordon from the witness box. The old man's corrugated cheeks were streaked with tears, and his eyes held the terrors of bewilderment.

The prosecutor stood up briefly and said disconsolately, 'Sir, that completes the case for the prosecution.'

The magistrate looked expectantly at Grainger, who rose and announced in a firm voice, 'Sir, I would like to move that there is absolutely no case to answer. The Crown has offered no forensic evidence *whatsoever* that links my client to the scene of the crime. Nor has it produced a *single* piece of forensic evidence to link her to the victim. Indeed, its case relies solely on Mr Latimer's eyewitness evidence, and Mr Latimer *cannot remember* which day it was that he saw my client rowing off "up river". Now we do not dispute the fact that my client took a dinghy from the pontoon and rowed out to the yacht *Ellie Miller* on the day *after* the murder, on the *Sunday*. My client herself volunteered this information to the police at her first interview, and was happy to repeat it in her subsequent statement. What we dispute utterly is that she was anywhere near the water on the day before, on the *Saturday*, and indeed the prosecution have entirely failed to prove that she was *anywhere* in the vicinity on that day. Thus, sir, I submit that there is simply no case to answer and that it would be unsafe in every respect to allow this case to proceed any further.'

Grainger sat down. The magistrate studied his notes before bending forward to have a word with the clerk. Looking out over the court, he said with a long sigh of exasperation, 'I agree with you entirely, Mr Grainger, for all the reasons you have stated—'

There was a startled cry, and a banging of doors as some people hurried from the gallery.

'The prosecution have failed to produce any reliable evidence to connect Mrs Wellesley to this crime—'

I buried my head in my hands.

'. . . In my view it would be unsafe in the extreme to allow this case to proceed to the crown court. I find that there is no case to answer, and the defendant is therefore discharged.'

He addressed Ginny then – something about being free to go – but I couldn't hear his words for the violence of my own emotions. Julia's voice sounded in my ear and her arm came round my shoulders, and she may have been crying too.

Even before the magistrate had left the court, the place erupted into noise and movement. Someone close by began shouting, a man pushed roughly past me. Julia led me out of the gallery and into the well of the court. In the midst of the people congratulating her, Ginny looked small and dazed. Reaching her, we embraced uncertainly as if neither of us could quite absorb what had happened, and then her arms tightened around my waist and she was gasping, and laughing a little too.

Tingwall was hovering, grinning all over his squinty-eyed face.

'Not too late to fire me,' he chuckled.

'I always said you were too young for the job.' And I embraced him.

I heard Mary's voice. 'Ginny!' she cried, and, sweeping past me, enveloped Ginny in a large hug. 'I'm so, *so* glad!' she declared. 'I'm so pleased! Oh, Ginny! I'm going to phone David this minute! We're so thrilled!' Throwing up her arms as though lost for further words, she laughed in an odd overexcited way and enveloped Ginny again.

I went over to Grainger who was packing his papers away. 'Thank you,' I said simply, and shook his hand.

'It would have been hard to lose,' he said with a sigh of disappointment, like a prize fighter cheated of a good bout. 'That old man . . . In the circumstances it was a lucky thing that your wife is something of a gambler.'

'You still handled it brilliantly.'

His eyes narrowed. 'Did I? You were in court?'

I smiled at how easily I had been caught out. 'Just at the end,' I admitted.

'Oh, Mr Wellesley.' He shook his head with an ironic show of disapproval. 'If we had gone to trial, that little escapade could have made our lives very difficult.'

'Perhaps I'm a gambler too.'

He thought about that. 'Yes,' he drawled in his unfathomable accent, 'I think you probably are.'

Before I could ask him what he meant by that Tingwall came bustling up with something he wanted me to read.

'I prepared this for the press last night. A statement.' Waving the paper in the air, he giggled like a child. 'I knew, you see. I knew!' Waiting for my grin of acknowledgment, accepting it with a small swagger, he read from the handwritten sheet. 'Mrs Wellesley has protested her innocence most vigorously ever since she was charged, and with the throwing out of the case her position has been entirely vindicated. There was never the slightest evidence against Mrs Wellesley, yet she has been forced to suffer months of needless distress as a result of a charge that from every point of view should never have been brought. Her

355

family would now ask that she be left in peace.' He looked up. 'I would have liked more time on it, but what do you think?'

'I think it's fine.'

I turned to find Mary at my elbow. She drew me aside and whispered fervently, 'Hugh – you've no idea what this means to me. *No* idea. I've been *praying* for this from the very beginning.' Her eyes with their garish blue lids looked fiercely into mine. '*Praying!*'

'I know.'

'What we need to do now is forget,' she said in a confidential tone. '*Forget* we ever had that talk. *Forget* what I said.'

I stared at her in open astonishment, wondering how she could possibly imagine I could forget something so devastating, something which was going to darken my life for ever. '*Forget?*'

She grasped my arm. 'As far as we can, of course.'

I shook my head.

'All in the past now, Hugh,' she insisted. 'The *past*.' She laughed suddenly, the same odd laugh again. 'Well – I must go and phone David! He'll be so thrilled.' With a jolly wave, she hurried off.

The next few hours were a confusion of downward-floating emotions. Tingwall went to the front of the court building and read his statement to the horde of waiting press who had materialised, as always, out of nowhere. Then when Tingwall's assistant had brought his car round to the front we left the shelter of the building and launched ourselves at the jostling photographers and shouting reporters for what I fervently hoped would be the last time. Ginny ignored their questions until, on reaching the car, a BBC reporter put a microphone under her nose and asked how she felt. 'I feel immensely glad that it's all over,' she replied.

Back at Tingwall's office we drank champagne, made a few calls to spread the news and took the congratulations of the firm's partners before going to lunch at a nearby restaurant. Tingwall and Julia chattered excitedly, but Ginny and I were rather more subdued, too drained of feeling for such straightforward emotions as joy or relief. I drank too much wine and compounded the error with two brandies, so that when we set off for home it was Ginny who had to drive through the gathering dusk.

356

The cottage was icy. I thumped the boiler to no avail while Ginny answered a steady stream of calls from friends and well-wishers. Finally, at nine, we took the phone off the hook and huddled side by side in front of the fire with a sandwich and a glass of wine.

'I think back to last winter,' Ginny murmured reminiscently. 'I think of everything we had then and how unhappy we were. And then I think of what we have now, and – well, I wouldn't change all this for anything, not for *anything*. I wouldn't be anywhere else but in this freezing little dump of a cottage with you. I feel so lucky, Hugh. The luckiest person in the world. Most of all' – and her voice was rough and low – 'I feel so terribly lucky to have you.'

'Darling.'

She pulled back a little and looked into my face. She asked softly, 'I do have you, don't I?'

'Of course.' I added a smile. 'Of course you do.' And something in my heart felt infinitely weary.

'It's all I've ever wanted, you see. You and me. For us to be happy.'

I put my wine down, then hers, and we wrapped our arms around each other. I saw the future stretching out before us, and it seemed to go on for ever. I saw Hartford growing steadily, I saw us in a pretty house near by, I saw summers in France and, when Hartford didn't need me any more, I saw us going to live there amid the vineyards: I saw all these things, and none of them could assuage my loneliness.

Ginny moved against me, her lips travelled across my cheek, she opened her soft mouth to mine. Soon we went upstairs to the warmth of our bed and, as Ginny's passionate body pressed itself against mine, I felt a surge of love, and a chasm of emptiness.

SIXTEEN

Entering the silent house, breathing the musty blend of furniture polish and wood smoke that took me lurching back to my childhood, I thought: This is the last time I will stand here, this is the last time I will feel so close to my past.

The remains of the furniture had been removed during the week, organised, like everything else to do with the sale, by Mary. Two geometric patches of deeper colour marked the spot on the study carpet where Pa's desk had stood, and ancient scorchmarks long hidden by a well-placed rug fanned out from the grate, from the days when Pa had favoured blazing open fires. The shadowy outlines of pictures lined the stairs, and in my old room the dusty curtains framed unwashed windows clouded with the grime of the long winter.

The bed had gone, the side table too, but, as Mary had forewarned me, everything that neither she nor Ginny had claimed and which was otherwise destined for jumble sales had been stored here, an accumulation of old lamps, rickety chairs and cardboard boxes stacked high with kitchen utensils, chipped china and battered paperbacks: the family detritus of fifty years.

I found my old paintings in a cardboard box half crushed by a pile of *Eagles* dating back to the sixties. The Winsor & Newton watercolours, the set of sable brushes which at fourteen I had saved up for so carefully were not with them however, and, though I hunted desultorily through a few of the neighbouring boxes, I soon realised the search was hopeless. My old lamp with its parchment shade lay on a chair but when I picked it up the top lurched over and I saw that the shade had acquired a second split.

Shutting the door, I carried the paintings down to the car and, after one last look around the hall, locked up the house. Touched by a last bout of nostalgia, I took a wander round the side of the house to the terrace. Dark shadows dotted the flagstones where the flower urns had stood, and one of the flowerbeds showed signs of fresh digging where a plant had been removed. That would be Mary, who was always on the lookout for additions to her garden.

The river was grey under a cold March sky, and an exceptionally high tide had lifted the water almost to the branches of the trees overhanging the opposite bank. Another boat lay at *Ellie Miller*'s mooring, a modern tub with its name displayed garishly down the side. *Ellie* had been taken to Plymouth to be refitted, renamed and, in due course, we hoped, sold. There would be no buyers for her here.

I went down the steps to the middle terrace and on to the lower garden. Under the bare trees the last of the crocuses lay flat like fallen warriors, and in the rough grass the daffodil shoots stood stiff and tall, awaiting their moment.

I glanced up and saw beyond the summerhouse a bowed figure standing among the apple trees, head canted upward in contemplation of something above his head. He had his back to me but as I made my way towards him I recognised the bony head and the bent shoulders under the baggy tweed jacket.

'Hello there,' I called.

Old Gordon turned. 'Mr Hugh!' he exclaimed amiably. ' 'Day to you.' He raised a gnarled hand in salute and gestured on upwards at the trees. 'Need a good prune. Won't get much fruit without a good prune.'

'Aha.' I inspected the branches dutifully. 'I'm afraid everything's been rather neglected.'

'Not too late, if it's done quick.' He nodded and hummed a little. 'Mrs Bennett – she's keen on her fruit. Likes makin' apple pies, she does. Does 'em for the fête.' He chortled, 'Dozens o' the blessed things.'

'Ahh.' The Bennetts, who had lived on the other side of the village for some years, were the new owners of Dittisham House. 'You'll be working here then? I thought you were retired, Gordon.'

'Ah, yes and no, yes and no. Still do bits and pieces. Can't risk the prunin' meself, o' course. I'd be no sooner up a ladder than sailin' off it again.' He cackled at the thought, showing a fine set of false teeth. 'But I don' mind a bit o' diggin' and weedin'. Keeps me goin'.'

'You're feeling pretty fit then?'

'Can' complain, Mr Hugh. Can' complain at all. Good to be back on me feet again, I can tell yer.'

'I, er ... I'd heard you hadn't been too well.'

He made an exaggerated grimace. 'Bad winter. Bad. Rheumatics. Heart. *Angina*. Felt somethin' terrible. *Terrible*.' He blew out his sunken cheeks at the memory, before brightening suddenly. 'But I'm all set now.'

'I'm so glad.'

The old man's face puckered again, and he cast me a troubled glance. 'Sorry about the court business, Mr Hugh.'

'It doesn't matter, Gordon. Really.'

'They kept askin', the police. Never stopped askin'. Dates, times. Dates, times. On and on. What a palaver.' He rolled his drooping eyes and jerked a clawed hand in a gesture of disbelief. 'Then they got me makin' this statement. Puttin' me name to it. And all the time I thought maybe I was helpin' out, yer see. Thought I was doin' good. An' then, next thing I know, they says they want me in court, and, I tell you, Mr Hugh, if I'd 'a' realised ...'

'I understand, Gordon, really.'

'I didn' know I was sayin' things against Mrs Hugh. They never told me that.'

'No, I'm sure they didn't.'

'If I'd 'a' known, well ... I'd 'a' kept me mouth shut.'

'But you couldn't have known. Honestly – we didn't blame you, Gordon. Not for a moment.'

He was lost in his reminiscences again. 'They kept sayin' ter me – just say it like you said it before, in the statement. But comes to it, comes to the day, an' I couldn' get a darn' thing straight in me head. I was feelin' so bad with me heart. Been bad for weeks. Between you and me, Mr Hugh, thought I was on the way out. Thought me number was well and truly up.'

'Gordon, don't worry about it. After all, everything worked out fine in the end.'

He grunted, 'Gets so you can't be sure of anythin'.'

Nodding solemnly, I contemplated the truth of that remark. I looked up at the trees. 'Hope you get a good harvest.'

'Better, hadn' I? All those pies to fill!' The cadaverous face split into a quiet grin.

'Take care, Gordon.'

He laughed, 'That's one thing you may be sure of, Mr Hugh.'

I drove away at a crawl while my thoughts circled restlessly, stirring up long-suppressed ideas that I had almost persuaded myself to forget, converging on a single unhappy notion which proceeded to worry at me like a cracked tooth. Absorbing the idea, allowing it houseroom, it seemed to me that truth was a terribly overrated objective, that in going after it you ended up not with the hoped-for sense of resolution but with yet another bout of turmoil and unhappiness.

But there was one thing more unsettling than an unhappy truth, and that was the kind of uncertainty which was eating away at me now. Accelerating to the next junction, I took the turning for Furze Lodge.

The house was open. No one answered my calls and I wandered from room to room until, coming into the kitchen, I spotted David through the window, digging a hole in the lawn.

Coming closer, I saw it was a long shallow trench.

'Drainage?' I asked.

He spun round, looking startled, and flashed me a reproachful look. Calming down just as rapidly, he offered, 'Electricity cable.'

'Floodlighting?'

'Mary wants a summerhouse in the far corner there, and maybe one day a swimming pool, though I think they're a total waste of time myself.' In a movement that was almost violent, he plunged the spade into the ground and shovelled some earth. 'How's Ginny?'

'She's fine.'

'And the new house?'

'Oh, dust and mess. We're camping at the builders' convenience – you know.'

361

'And Hartford?'

'Fingers crossed, going better than I ever dared hope.'

David said drily, 'That must please Howard no end.'

He shifted a few more feet of earth before resting on his spade. 'I should have hired a digger.'

'I'd help if . . .' I gestured as though for a second spade.

David swung his gaze on me and I could see that he was in a prickly mood. 'So what brings you here after all this time? I was beginning to think the Cold War had set in.'

'I was just picking up some stuff from Dittisham. I thought I'd pop in.'

He raised a sceptical eyebrow and waited for me to tell him something nearer the truth.

'I wanted to ask you something,' I confessed. 'I wanted to ask if Old Gordon was a patient of yours.'

'Of course.' He gave small snort. 'How else do you think I fixed him? And to answer your next question, it was a mixture of codeine, antihistamine and a tranquilliser called thioridazine. Guaranteed to addle the brain in the right doses.' He snapped irritably, 'And you don't need to look so bloody disapproving. It wasn't going to kill him. He's perfectly all right now.'

There is an instant after a truth is confirmed when, though you've known what was coming, the facts still seem bald and shocking.

David growled, 'Besides, his memory had been dodgy for years. He'd probably got the whole thing wrong anyway. The wrong day, the wrong person – who knows? So it wasn't as if I was perpetrating a great miscarriage of justice, was it?'

I didn't say anything.

David cast me a scathing look. 'You didn't realise?' he asked, working himself up into some kind of fury.

'I half guessed. When I saw him at the court . . .'

'Come on, you must have known! I'd promised, hadn't I?'

'Promised?'

'I said I'd help.' He repeated almost crossly: '*I said I'd help*. You must have realised!'

'I suppose I didn't want to think about it. I didn't want to . . .' I shrugged, 'deal with it. But now . . . well, I can only say thank you.

God – that's totally inadequate, isn't it? What I mean is – I'll never be able to thank you enough, David. Never.'

'Stuff your gratitude, Hugh,' David said with sudden vehemence. 'I may be an adulterer and a liar and a few other things besides, but I wasn't going to let Ginny go to prison for something she didn't do. Even *I* thought that was a bit much. You know – something I might *just* have difficulty in living with for the rest of my life. I may be a shit, but not *that* much of a shit.'

'It's all right,' I said quietly. 'I know what really happened. Mary told me.'

I had caught him by surprise. He stared at me in dismay or alarm or both. 'What did Mary tell you?'

'Oh . . .' I still found it hard to say. 'That she saw Ginny go out to the boat and talk to Sylvie and go aboard and—' I cut myself short with a sharp gesture.

'She said *that*? My God.' He shook his head incredulously. 'God.' He gave an unsteady laugh that was suddenly quite devoid of assurance. 'You should know better than to believe anything that Mary tells you.'

I felt a momentary disconnection from the conversation, as though it were happening at some other time in my own past or future. 'She'd seen Ginny,' I argued hoarsely. 'She must have. She described what she was wearing. She . . .' But I was silenced by the look on David's face.

'You poor sod,' he murmured pityingly. 'You thought . . . all this time . . .'

Doubts roared through my mind. I felt a tug in my chest, a sudden heat, followed by the first stirrings of a fearsome anger. 'What the hell are you saying?'

'Hugh – I'm saying that Mary was lying.'

'She never saw Ginny?'

'She never saw Ginny,' he sighed. 'Not then anyway. Ginny arrived a lot later. I'm sorry. I'm really sorry.' He sounded genuinely shaken. 'When was this? When did Mary tell you this? Were you about to go to the police? Was that what it was? She'd have done anything, I'm afraid, to stop you doing that. Was it the police?'

I didn't trust myself to speak.

'I'm really sorry, Hugh.' He raised both shoulders in an exaggerated appeal for understanding.

'*You bastard!* She was protecting *you!*' I exploded at last.

He flinched, he was halfway to making a contrite face when my anger burst over me in a hot wave and I lunged for him. Grabbing him by his shirt, I twisted it tight under his chin. 'You bastard! *You bastard!*' My rage was huge and ugly and inconsolable, I was overcome by the lust for revenge. I wanted to inflict the most terrible pain and suffering on him, as he had done on me, and at that moment no punishment could possibly have been too terrible. I pushed my fists higher and higher under his chin, driving his head back until he was forced to twist away. As he straightened up, I aimed a punch at his face but my swing was wild and hopelessly wide and, seeing it coming, he lashed out with an arm and deflected my blow. I came in with a weak left hook but he ducked under that and my fist swished uselessly through the air. In my rage and frustration, I became more cunning. I dropped my arms to my sides as if in surrender and the moment he relaxed I sent a sharp little jab into his stomach which doubled him over. As his head came up for air I splayed my feet, dug in my heels, and put all my weight into a low upward swing that whistled up under his chin. Even before my knuckles made contact I knew it was going to be a powerful blow. There was a loud crack, the impact sent a sharp jabbing pain into my hand, David cried out and jerked back before falling slowly onto one knee. Clasping a hand to his chin, panting hard, he looked up at me with what might have been a plea for truce, but if he thought I was finished he had another think coming.

He staggered to his feet and we faced each other warily. He tried to say something but I wasn't listening and I went for him again with a tight swing of my left fist, a feint which I intended to follow with another solid blow from the right. But he caught my first arm and held onto it and tried to twist me off-balance. I shoved my shoulder under his arm in a half-remembered wrestling manoeuvre, but he hooked his foot behind my ankle and the next moment we fell untidily to the ground. For a few seconds we grappled ineffectually. I became aware of a frenzied barking and growling from one of David's dogs. Perhaps it was the fear of being bitten that gave me new strength but I managed to push David over onto his back and land a quick knuckle on his face. I didn't think I'd hit him very hard until I saw his nose spout a stream of blood. While I stared at the blood spreading down his face, his fist came out of nowhere and caught me high on the cheek, just under one eye. I felt my head snap back, I saw stars and, falling sideways, rolled slowly onto my back.

There was a silence broken only by the sound of our panting. After a second or two I heard a different sort of panting and felt a wet nose snuffling at my face. I pushed the dog away and it went to inspect David, who murmured, 'Piss off, Bodger,' so I knew he couldn't be too badly hurt.

My face was throbbing painfully, and my hand too. I touched them gingerly, but as far as I could tell nothing was broken. I'd only ever got into one serious fight, at school, and that had ended in defeat after one blow. I was rather surprised that I had managed to land any sort of a punch on David, let alone a couple which had found their target. But I felt no sense of satisfaction, far less triumph, only a depressing futility.

Pressing a hand to my burning cheek, I sat up cautiously and looked across at David. He was still lying flat on his back. Opening one eye a crack he peered blearily at me before closing it again. The dog stood nearby, wagging its tail sporadically.

'Couldn't let her go,' David said without warning.

My breath caught high in my chest. I kept very still, as if by ignoring him he might leave the subject alone.

'Just couldn't do without her.'

'For Christ's sake shut up!' I retorted furiously. 'I don't bloody want to hear.'

'Please,' he asked simply. When I didn't reply he continued with a gasp, 'Never thought anyone would ever get such a hold on me. I'd never . . . in all my life . . . Never been so – *taken*. So – *mesmerised*. Or perhaps I mean obsessed,' he said in the bemused tone of someone who still hasn't quite worked things out. 'Hardly knew what to do with myself. Got so I couldn't even *think* when I was away from her. Couldn't function. She was so – *different*. So – *crazy*. Made me laugh. Made me feel— *Okay*,' he conceded as though I'd put up some sort of argument, 'Okay, it was sex to begin with. I mean, I hadn't strayed for a long time, I'd forgotten how ... well, how bloody fantastic it could be.' His voice shuddered at the memory. 'But then ... then it was more than that. Much more. I always felt so good when I was with her. For the first time in my life – good, *good*. I thought, so *this* is what it's all about, this is what people go on about. She made me feel alive, Hugh. That was the thing – ' the gasp again ' – *alive*.' His tone dropped. 'I thought we had a future. I thought I could cure her, you see. I thought I could get her off the drugs. I thought she would do it for *me*. That's the worst thing, thinking that someone's going to change because you want them to. But I really believed—'

He broke off suddenly. I looked across at him and his blood-smeared face was so contorted with grief that I quickly looked away again.

'I believed she'd do it for me,' he whispered at last in a raw voice. 'But I was wrong. She was never going to change. I didn't give up trying though. I never gave up trying. I had this plan. I was going to take her away. We were going to make a new start, somewhere completely different. America. Italy. Somewhere were she wouldn't know people in the drug world. Somewhere she could do a sculpting course and study her New Age stuff. We made plans. Lots of plans.' He made a harsh sound, a sigh that was also an expression of despair. 'Right up until the end, until the last day. More plans.'

The dog, who had been sitting down, got up and, whining softly, tried to lick David's face. Holding it at bay with one hand, he went on, 'I stopped her drugs when I realised she was making no effort to cut down on them. Well, that was the reason I gave for stopping them – because she wouldn't cut down – but really I was trying to force her into coming away with me. I couldn't think of any other way. She'd never agree on a date, she was always wriggling out of it for some reason or another. It had got so she wouldn't even talk about it any more. I began to imagine the worst – imagine that she was going to finish the whole thing. I was terrified she'd just up and off one day and I'd never see her again. I thought that if I cut off the drugs she'd come crawling back.' He grunted at the idea. 'Of course, crawling back wasn't Sylvie's style. She just found other ways of getting what she wanted. Her brother in Bristol. That chap Hayden and the excursions to France.'

And me, I thought. Don't forget me.

As if reading my thoughts, David said matter-of-factly, 'I didn't cotton on to you for a long time, honestly. Amazing what you miss when you're not looking. I thought you were simply having troubles with Ginny. When you kept coming down to the boat I thought you were just trying to get away from it all. I didn't realise until the very end, really. Until just before . . .'

Cautiously, patting his nose gingerly, he pushed himself up onto one elbow. Then, just as slowly, he sat up and, pulling his feet towards him, rested his forearms on his knees and stared out across the garden. Our breath formed puffs of vapour in the cold, the ground was very damp, but neither of us thought of moving.

'She was furious with me,' David went on. 'When I stopped the drugs. I saw the wild side of her then, and how. But it didn't change anything. It didn't stop me wanting her,' he said gruffly. 'Nothing could do that. She was my drug, you see. I could never get enough of her, even after all those months. Could never *imagine* getting enough of her.' His voice cracked, he shook his head as though he himself scarcely believed the power she had exerted over him. 'Part of me knew what she was like, knew she wasn't too good at commitment, that she'd never stayed with anything for very long. But I thought it would all be different once we got away, once she was off that bloody poison.'

He raised a weary hand and rubbed his eyelids. 'She always came back,' he said dully. 'Always. Oh, sometimes it was to wrangle a script out of me, sure. *Sure.* But most of the time she came back because she needed to see me, just like I needed to see her. Because we couldn't stay away from each other. Underneath it all we had something, you see. Something *strong*. We were two of a kind. She always said so. Two of a kind.' His voice rose and he stalled momentarily. 'I think we could have made it together, you know. I think we could have been happy. I think – I think—' He could hardly say it. 'I think I loved her. I think I really loved her.' He dropped his head into his hands and snatched at his breath.

I looked away and watched a magpie prowling through the trees. After a while I said, 'What about Mary?'

He brought his head up heavily, dragging his hands down his face as he did so. 'Mary,' he sighed. '*Mary*. At the beginning – well, what she didn't know wouldn't hurt her and all that. But then – yes, I would have left her, I would have left her like a shot if Sylvie had ever got her act together, if she'd ever committed herself.' A slight shrug. 'I can't say our marriage was bad exactly, but it was pretty mechanical. It had never been much else, really. In those days I thought you just settled for a nice efficient person who shared some of your interests and who'd do a good job with the children. That sounds pretty unfeeling, I suppose, but that was what I thought it was all about. I never minded the fact that Mary wasn't a great beauty – I never thought that mattered. I wanted someone who'd be a good wife, who'd fit in with my life, back me up.'

When he showed no sign of continuing, I said, 'She found out.' It was half a statement, half a question.

'I guess so,' he breathed distractedly. 'I guess so.'

He turned away, and we sat in silence for a time. Only the dog stirred, cocking its ears to some far-off sound and lifting its nose to the air.

My anger had evaporated; only the sour aftertaste of violence remained. I had no feelings left for David, except perhaps pity. And, for the moment at least, gratitude for having told me his story and set me free. I almost left then, I almost got up and walked away to start the miraculous new existence which unexpectedly stretched before me, the new life with a Ginny whose only crime was to have tried to save her worthless husband. I almost got up and walked away, but something made me hesitate.

'I had no idea. No idea at all,' David murmured at last, giving voice to some thought of his own. When he next spoke, it was with new emotion. 'I'd arranged to meet Sylvie on the boat that day. Most of the summer we'd been meeting at someone's house, a chap who'd gone away for a few months. But that day we decided to meet on the boat.' He paused, and it was only with a visible effort that he forced himself on. 'I got delayed – a stupid meeting – then they paged me – a heart attack. By the time I got down to the river I was almost an hour late. But I knew she'd wait. When she'd called she'd sounded really happy, really keen to see me. I knew she'd wait.' He rubbed his head, close to misery again. 'But when I got down there I couldn't find the dinghy oars. Then I couldn't find the *dinghy*. Thought someone must have pinched it. I was about to borrow someone else's when' – he inhaled sharply – 'when I looked up and saw someone rowing the dinghy towards me. I thought it must be Sylvie, that for some reason she'd taken my dinghy instead of *Samphire*'s. I almost called out to her. It took me ages to realise that it was Mary. She was wearing this baggy old oilskin, one of Pa's relics, with the hood up. As soon as I realised it was her, I knew she could only have been to *Ellie* – I mean, there was nowhere else she could have been. At first I persuaded myself that Sylvie would have made herself scarce in some way, that she would have seen Mary coming. That's what I wanted to believe anyway, that's what I told myself . . .' He screwed up his eyes, his mouth turned down, he said bleakly, 'Although deep down . . . deep down I had an awful feeling, even then.'

I had been avoiding the moment of confrontation, I had been shutting it out, but there was no escaping it now. Feeling emotionally sick, I gave the thought life. *Mary*.

'Mary never went out to *Ellie* normally,' David was saying, 'she could hardly row a dinghy. There had to be a *reason*, and the only reason . . .' But he couldn't cope with this thought and pushed it aside. 'So there I was . . . I couldn't face a scene there on the river, so I went up the road and round a corner where Mary wouldn't see me. As soon as she'd landed, she rushed off, went straight past me. I couldn't decide what to do then. I looked for Sylvie, of course. I'd bought her a mobile phone but she never remembered to take it with her, she was always leaving it in the wrong place, so I wasn't surprised when it didn't answer. And then I looked for her dinghy. I couldn't see it at *Ellie*. I couldn't see it at *Samphire*.' Quite suddenly he began to cry, awkwardly, with great contortions of his face. A trickle of tears mixed with the drying blood and dripped in a pink stream off the end of his chin. 'It must have been

369

there, of course, at *Ellie* – I just didn't see it. I can't stop thinking that if only I'd gone out there, *if only I'd gone and had a look* then maybe I could have saved her.' And he gave a loud sob, a howl of irretrievable loss that made the dog recoil and whimper uneasily.

I stared at him, this brother I hardly knew. I reached out and gripped his arm. 'You mustn't think about that—'

'I can't help it!' he cried helplessly. 'It's all I ever think about! If only I hadn't been late, if only I hadn't been called out, if only— Oh God, oh *God*,' he wailed, 'it's all I ever think about!'

I shifted closer and put an arm round his shoulders. In my mind's eye I pictured the shadowy figure spying on Sylvie and me from the terrace at Dittisham House, and I saw Mary there in the darkness, I saw Mary creeping up to the window and bumping the metal chair across the stone flags, and I wondered how often she had crept up on David and Sylvie, how often she had seen them together.

'Afterwards I couldn't get rid of this – this *feeling*,' David said despairingly. 'I knew . . . I just *knew* something was wrong. I drove around most of the evening. I went to her cottage, I went to Dittisham House and found you and Ginny. And I couldn't find her, I couldn't find her anywhere. And then, next day when they found her . . . When they found her . . . *Christ* . . .' Weeping again, he shook his head and kept shaking it. 'But I needed to know, you see. I needed to know for sure, so before Mary went out I went and looked at her car. And the oilskin was there in the boot, in a plastic bag. With some clothes. And the clothes, they were . . . covered, absolutely covered . . .'

A wind had sprung up, intensifying the cold. My hands were frozen and I thought I felt David shiver. 'Come inside,' I said.

'I wouldn't have let Ginny go to prison,' David said as I helped him to his feet. 'I swear it.' He faced me for the first time since I had hit him, and I saw that one eye was swelling badly. 'I swear it,' he repeated.

'I know that.'

He nodded emotionally.

We walked towards the house.

'Does Mary realise?' I asked.

'That I know? That I saw her? No. We've never spoken of it, or

370

anything to do with it. I don't think she has any idea. But I'll be leaving quite soon,' he said firmly. 'I thought it wouldn't be safe to leave before, in case the police thought – well, whatever they might think. But I'll leave quite soon now. In a week or so. I'll miss the children, of course . . .' He made a hopeless gesture.

We went into the kitchen and David reached a hand into the serving hatch and pulled out a bottle of cognac. He poured two measures and we knocked them back.

'You'd better go and clean yourself up,' I told him as he refilled our glasses.

He ran exploratory fingers over his face, and raised a critical eyebrow. 'You too. You're going to have a real shiner, I'm afraid.'

I drained the last of my drink. 'I'll wash on the way out.'

We faced each other.

'Don't think too badly of her,' David said with a bitter ring to his voice. 'She worked very hard on Howard, you know, to get him to bring the Cumberland board round. In fact, I'm pretty sure she swung it for you.'

'Swung it? But how?'

'Oh, I think she knew things about Howard that he didn't want the world to know.'

Ginny's words came to me again: *She's not Howard's sister for nothing*, and the sick feeling crept back into my stomach.

We heard the car at the same time.

I touched his arm and hurried towards the downstairs cloak-room to splash water over my face. Glancing back, I saw David pouring himself another drink. Looking up, he raised his glass in an ironic salute and his battle-scarred face took on its habitual mask of sardonic indifference.

I emerged from the cloakroom as the children burst noisily into the house. They gave me a happy unsurprised wave before roaring on towards the kitchen.

'Hugh! How lovely!' Mary advanced rapidly on me. 'Good God!' she laughed. 'What *have* you done to yourself!'

'I walked into something,' I said.

And mustering a smile, fixing an expression of pleasure on my face, I bent down to kiss her.

*

Living up to their reputation for maximum disruption, the builders had left a pile of gravel just inside the gates. Forced to abandon the car, I loaded the box of pictures under my arm and strode up the drive. Fumbling with the door handle, I sent the half-painted door against its stop with a bang.

'Is that you?' Ginny called, appearing round the kitchen door.

I dropped the box on a chair and faced her.

'Oh!' she cried, clamping a hand to her mouth. 'Good God! Whatever happened to you?' She came and raised gentle fingertips to my face.

'I've been stupid.'

'*Have* you?' She had a wonderful way of making it sound the most unlikely thing in the world.

'I can't believe how stupid I've been.'

Looking alarmed, she took a fearful breath. 'Not the car? You haven't had an accident?'

'No. Nothing like that.'

Her worst fears allayed, she pressed a hand to her chest, she took a series of sharp breaths. 'What then?'

'I walked into something.'

'Into *something*?'

'A large man in a pub?'

But her anxiety wasn't going to be bought off by thin jokes. 'Oh yes?' she said sternly.

'Okay,' I laughed, preparing to parade my stupidity. 'It *was* the car – but not while it was going anywhere. I opened the door to put something inside and I turned round too quickly – I just wasn't looking – and the door swung back in my face and the corner got me right here.' Pointing at the swelling, I put on a gormless expression: the complete idiot.

She frowned, not entirely satisfied with this, I could see the questions hovering, then with an obvious effort she put her doubts behind her, and a smile bubbled to her lips. 'A large man in a pub is going to get you far more sympathy.'

'In that case, the large man has it.'

She raised herself on tiptoe and kissed my bruised cheek.

'Was that the sympathy?' I asked.

She slipped an arm round me. 'You might get a raw steak for the eye if you're lucky.'

I would have said I loved her then, but just at that moment my heart was too full.